Explorations:
Worm.....

Explorations: Through the Wormhole

Copy-Edited by Samanda R. Primeau

Series Editor – Nathan Hystad

Cover Art by Illustration © Tom Edwards
TomEdwardsDesign.com

Cover Back Layout by Deb Kunellis

Explorations: Through the Wormhole produced by Nathan Hystad and Ralph Kern

First Edition: **ISBN-13:978-1537686752**

Contents

Foreword
By Nathan Hystad

Wormholes.

What more fascinating theory is there? To think that one could safely traverse from one point to another, thousands of light years away in a stable wormhole, is an idea that has been widely used in books, television, and movies. We've long dreamt of space travel; exploring the universe to find new life, and habitable planets in neighboring solar systems.

As I write this foreword, news of Proxima b is all over the news, with scientists stating it could possibly be the right distance from its star to have liquid water. A mere 4.2 light years: a thousand lifetimes for us. What if a wormhole appeared and probes proved it was stable and Earth could send someone to see it? Would they? Without knowledge of the wormhole, perhaps it would dissipate in days, months, or years.

Explorations: Through the Wormhole is the first book in the Explorations series, and in it we have 14 tales of future history. Wormholes are explored, races are discovered, and colonies are created. Every story is different than the one before it, and the mix of hard sci-fi, military, space opera, and even a dose of fantasy, is one I'm extremely proud of.

I worked with Ralph Kern from the start on the project, creating back story, technology time-lines, and other pertinent information to pass on to the authors for this shared universe project. Though we are in a shared universe, we pass through centuries and the changes are evident as we move from one story to another. But the one thing that remains the same: the wormholes take centre stage.

Working on a collection such as this was one of the most challenging projects of my life, but at the same time the most rewarding. There are a lot of moving pieces to something like this, but every minute spent on it was a pleasure. With an eBook, paperback, and even an audio book in production, I hope the readers (and listeners) enjoy the book, in whatever format they get it in.

Thank you for purchasing Explorations: Through the Wormhole. Perhaps one day we will experience the phenomenon and see what's on the other side.

Nathan Hystad – Series Editor and President of Woodbridge Press

The Challenge
By Ralph Kern

"You are a go to move to the final hold position."

The swirling blue whirlpool of the wormhole steadily rose over the Lunar horizon, revealing itself in all of its hypnotic, mysterious beauty. The inside of the cabin took on an indigo hue as shadows lazily spiralled in time with the revolutions of the anomaly.

"Fortune favors the bold," Colonel Elaine Harmon-Sykes breathed as she wrapped her fingers around the horseshoe-shaped grip by the window. Below the ship, the Moon's meteorite-pummelled surface rolled by, as familiar to Elaine as the back of her hand, yet the illumination of the wormhole painted it in a new, strange light.

Strange, Elaine mused. With space exploration, *strange* was both what was sought and what should be feared. *Strange* was why they were out here, yet *strange* could kill them all in a heartbeat.

And things didn't get any stranger than what was before her, the enigmatic thing which had appeared in Lunar orbit a month ago.

Elaine tensed as she felt a pair of hands wrapping around her waist, then relaxed, allowing herself to be pulled into the comforting, familiar grip.

"Major Michael Harmon-Sykes," Elaine said, watching the magnificent light of the wormhole creeping over the dark patch of the *Oceanus Procellarum*, the Ocean of Storms. "Fraternization on my ship is unacceptable."

"My apologies, Colonel Harmon-Sykes. I'll report to the Captain's Mast at dawn." Elaine's husband nuzzled into her ear before resting his chin on her shoulder. Elaine inclined her head, pressing her cheek against his. She lightly ran her fingertips over the backs of his hands, as they bobbed in the zero gravity before the cupola window.

"Final hold point, El. That's as good as a go on the mission profile. It's on."

"It is." Elaine gently pried Mike's arms from around her, pirouetted around and gave him a light kiss on the lips. "All business from here on in, though. We have to set an example to the others."

"Yes, Ma'am," Mike said as he pushed himself off the cold triple-plated glass of the cupola and slowly drifted away from his wife. "My side are all in Orion Two, yours are all in One."

"Good, let's stop shirking and get to it, then."

Elaine twisted her athletic body and, with practiced ease, pulled herself along the handholds through the twenty-meter length of *Olympus*'s interplanetary habitation module. She passed the closed shutters of the crew's sleeping nooks and work stations, nodding to herself in satisfaction that everything was in order.

Passing through into the node, Elaine stopped and helped Mike push the heavy habitat hatch closed with a sucking slam.

"I'll see you on the other side," Elaine said as she pulled her way up the short access tunnel. With one last glance back at her husband, she closed up the Orion Multi-Purpose-Crewed Vehicle.

Again, she nodded to herself in satisfaction. The three other members of her crew were already strapped in. A gentle murmur of conversation filled the small cabin as they worked their way down their checklists.

"Ladies and gentlemen," Elaine said as she swung into her seat in the tight conical confines of the capsule. She ignored the grunt from Miles Lewis, seated below her, as one of her errant legs struck him. Her words would be carried to the other four crew, in Orion Two, by the thin metal strip of the boom mic hooked around her ear. "Houston has given us the go-ahead to advance to the final hold position. Anyone who wants off… you're a little late."

Elaine buckled herself in before glancing up through the tiny hull porthole. It was poorly angled to view the wormhole; only the constantly dissipating streamers whipping around the central singularity were visible.

"Well…" Shelly Price said, eagerness apparent in her voice. "It's going to be more glamorous than being the third crew to land on Mars."

Elaine gave a smile. Yes, but it was also bittersweet. She briefly touched the triangle-within-circle mission patch symbolizing Olympus Mons on her breast. They had all spent the last three years training and preparing for the rusty red desolation of Mars. The appearance of the wormhole a month ago had changed all that. For better or worse, the only crewed ship capable of transiting through was her ship, *Olympus*. Now all that preparation, all those carefully rehearsed experiments and procedures, all had gone out of the airlock.

Instead, they were boldly going where no one had gone before, Elaine thought with bemusement. For a career military pilot turned astronaut, having no set procedures made her uncomfortable: after all, in her world, failing to plan was planning to fail. Even in her F22 Raptor in the skies over North Korea, shooting down half-century-old MIGs, Elaine had always had an idea of what she was doing, what she was facing and what to do if things went wrong. Now, their only intelligence came from one unmanned lunar tug which had been sent through prior to them.

But the astronaut and scientist in her was keen to go, muscling out the weary pragmatism of her warrior side. She felt confident in her, and her crew's, abilities. She knew they were good — among the best, even; you didn't get selected for the Mars program by being average, even when that "average" was among the elite astronaut corps. It wasn't egotistical: her position as commander of the third Mars mission validated that. She knew if anyone could make this work, she could. The question was, could anyone make this work?

Elaine reached toward the console before her, setting the central display to show an image from one of the cameras mounted on *Olympus*'s hull.

The hypnotic spinning vortex of the wormhole appeared dead center on it, streamers and flecks of light dissipating from its edges. From their perspective, the center of the wormhole was a tunnel, stretching to infinity. A sharp contrast to the fact that she knew the anomaly was vanishingly thin when viewed side-on. That had been disconcerting when Elaine had first seen it. She had wondered if the tunnel-like appearance was some kind of optical illusion, a mirage, which they would smash into, or pass through without effect.

They had crept closer and closer to the wormhole as the crew ran through their final checklists, securing the ship down as much as they could. Over the last month they had carefully generated the procedures of how they were going to enter the wormhole. The reason they were running *Olympus* from the Orion capsules was that they were the most hardened places on the ship.

"We're approaching final hold." Mike's tinny voice came through her earpiece.

"Houston, *Olympus* actual. We are approaching final hold." Elaine fed the information through to Houston. "We are looking good and are ready for the terminal injection burn to take us in."

"Roger that, *Olympus*," the CAPCOM's disembodied voice said. "We have you positioned two-zero kilometers from the aperture of the anomaly. Our status board is green throughout. Final decision from you."

Elaine felt her lips twitch in a wry grin. There was no decision — she knew it, the crew knew it and Houston knew it. If the status board was showing green, then they were sure as hell going in.

"Houston, we are a go." Elaine spoke into her boom-mic. "Mike, you have the injection burn on your mark."

"Roger that, El. Five seconds, mark. Four, three, two,

one."

Elaine felt a weight settle on her chest as the main engine of *Olympus* throttled up. From behind her she heard the patter of forgotten, floating items falling to the deck under the half-g acceleration. Normally, she would give a quip, at best, or at worst, chew out someone for poor housekeeping. But for now she was too focused on what was before her.

"Main engine cut off," Mike said, his voice clipped but calm. "I'm showing we're following the racetrack for injection."

The pressure eased on Elaine's chest. On the display in front of her she saw the digital ladder track leading straight into the heart of the wormhole.

"I am ready with final Zero-Barrier abort." Elaine's index finger hovered over the button which would activate the abort control program. With a single press, the flight control computer would rotate *Olympus* and fire the engine hard, pushing them on a course which would miss the wormhole.

She squinted in concentration as they closed on the wormhole, trying to divine the slightest clue that something unexpected was happening, a reason for her to pull the ship out of her plunge into the unknown.

Then they were there: Zero-Barrier. They were committed now. No matter how hard the engine burned.

"*Olympus*, Houston. We are showing you as committed. God speed."

The vortex grew, the tunnel in the center a never-ending hole. Elaine spared the briefest of glances through the porthole. Through it, she saw strands of sparks of exotic particles whipping by above her.

"We are one hundred meters from the aperture." Mike's voice finally gave the faintest sign of excitement. "Fifty meters... we are at aperture."

Elaine's console flew away from her, the hull of the Orion stretching like it was made of rubber. With a rush, the seat on which she was sitting snapped forward, catching up with the console.

Elaine gave a gasp. She glanced around the cabin, seeking any signs the integrity was compromised. There was no hiss of leaking atmosphere or warbling of alarms. They were intact.

"Whoa," Miles said as he exhaled below her. "I haven't seen anything like that since my college days."

"Secure it," Elaine replied sharply. "Full status work-up, double time."

"I'm on it."

On the console screen, Elaine could see *Olympus* was racing down a blue tunnel. Strange matter spiraled around them. In the distance a bright speck of light was visible, rushing toward them, or they were going toward it. Fast.

"These are the same visuals the lunar tug sent back," Mike called. "When we hit that light… we're there."

Elaine looked back through the porthole. She realized the blue tunnel walls were slightly transparent; beyond, she could make out specks of light shooting by.

"Stars," she whispered in wonder. "Those are stars going by."

"They can't be," Miles said. "We must be well beyond light speed. Any stars out there would be red- and blue-shifted in front and behind. That's just plain old relativity and all that jazz."

"I think relativity went out the window when we started traveling faster than light," Mike cut in on the open loop. "More interestingly, the tug didn't show any of this; the wormhole tunnel was completely opaque."

"We'll add it to the list of questions for the boffins to answer," Elaine said, shutting down their musing. "I asked for a status report."

"Counters are showing, if anything, less ambient radiation striking us than in Lunar orbit. Temperature is at 30 kelvin, a little warmer than we were running in Lunar orbit. Stress meters are showing no undue forces acting on the hull. We're looking all good, El."

The light at the end of the tunnel was growing in size as the ship raced toward it, a disconcerting impression, like a train was rushing toward them. Elaine gripped the arms of her seat. She knew that beneath her gloves, her knuckles would be bone-white.

"Houston, *Olympus*," Elaine began her commentary. The telemetry from the lunar tug had been received throughout the transit. Elaine knew it was important to the scientists back home that she give as much information as possible. "We have entered the wormhole and we are looking good. The tunnel appears much as Lunar Tug Four saw. The walls are a little more transparent and we are seeing stars going by beyond. Could be the simple focal point on the tug's cameras didn't pick that up. For some reason, I expected us to be buffeted around in here; we're not, though. We're sliding through smooth as you like."

The piercing light in front of them swelled larger and larger.

"We think we have the terminus of the wormhole in front of us; we're closing fast. Interestingly, the ship seems to have accelerated to the same apparent speed as the tug transited. We're going to hit" —Elaine quickly rethought her words— "we're going to arrive in a few seconds, Houston."

The light grew, spreading across the console. A white shaft speared in through the porthole, the whole cabin washing out in bright contrast.

"We are there, Houston…"

Elaine recoiled as the console slammed toward her, right up to her nose. A second later, the cabin snapped back to its normal shape.

Now that was a phenomenon of wormhole travel she doubted she'd ever get used to.

"My god," she heard her husband say. "Look."

With the press of a button, Elaine synched her console to show what Mike was looking at on his own display.

A planet hovered in the center of the display. Vast, blue

oceans encompassed green-and-brown continents. Through the porthole, Elaine saw the peach-colored ridges and valleys of another world below them.

Elaine craned her neck, seeing the thin glaze of atmosphere on the horizon of the closer world.

Two whole worlds, Elpis and Petra, pirouetting around a mutual barycenter as they orbited their star.

Just like the tug showed on its trip through.

"Okay, boys and girls. Let's make sure this scow is still spaceworthy after its little adventure through the wormhole, and go take a look," Elaine said.

***

The nuclear-powered Mars orbit injection engine fired for just under five minutes before shutting down, leaving *Olympus* to coast toward Elpis, the world which appeared to have life coating its surface.

There was so much to see. None of the constellations was familiar. If they'd been only a few light years from Sol, Elaine would have expected some of them to be the same, yet none were. That alone suggested they were a long way from home.

Elaine drifted through the cramped habitat module, her fingers trailing along the equipment and cargo storage bins which they hadn't had a chance to off-load. She felt a twinge of sadness that the long-planned mission had been scrubbed in favor of taking *Olympus* through the wormhole.

Her original mission goal had been to commence studies into the viability of a long-term presence off of Earth. They had seed stock to attempt growing their own food on Mars, even embryos and test tubes to try growing livestock. Hell, that was the reason the eight crew members were actually four married couples: a psychological study into whether the foundation of a family unit could survive a long-term mission.

She wondered whether NASA's gamble to instead use

Olympus to transit through the wormhole would set back space exploration, or accelerate it.

Elaine shook her head; that was for others to decide. For now, she needed to stay on task. Reaching her sleeping alcove, she pulled open the shutters.

"Well hello, little lady. How about we christen this star system?"

Elaine rolled her eyes, seeing her husband within, naked and waiting for her.

She let him pull her inside, pausing only briefly to draw the shutters closed.

***

With another burn of the engine, *Olympus* slid into low orbit of Elpis. Below, valleys and mountain ranges, rivers and oceans rolled by.

"You ever think it's weird?" Andrea Watton asked.

"What?" Elaine asked, taking another gurgling suck on her protein shake straw as she watched the unfamiliar continents and seas drift by below.

"The wormhole," Andrea said, an introspective tone to her voice. "That it appears now. In all of history, the only time humanity can exploit it. When we've just started walking on other planets and have a spacecraft which can go through."

"Mmm hmm." Elaine prompted her to continue.

"And then the other end appears here, right by Aa."

"Call it Elpis, Andrea. Elpis and Petra." Elaine gently admonished the younger woman as she glanced at the flight recorder microphone situated unobtrusively next to the cupola window. PR was important on this mission, on any NASA mission. They had put naming the planets to a national poll of school children when the lunar tug had gone through and sent back the first images. Houston had made it clear: use the damn names, not the designation, Aa.

"Sorry." Andrea smiled. "The other end appears here,

next to Elpis, what looks to be a habitable planet in another star system."

The thought had occurred to Elaine before, too. Was the wormhole some kind of natural phenomenon, or was it something planned, designed or built? It seemed far too much of a coincidence that it would appear in Lunar orbit, and surely that coincidence was compounded by the fact that it had appeared next to another habitable planet. If it were simply a natural phenomenon, surely with all the empty space between stars, and for that matter, galaxies, then the odds were the wormholes would appear in the middle of nowhere.

"No one's discovered any signs that it's engineered in any way. There are no technological artifacts associated with it," Elaine mused, as she flicked her eyes to one of the flight recorder mics dangling unobtrusively from the bulkhead. "But yes, agreed, it's a hell of a coincidence."

"I mean," Andrea continued, "in itself, putting it in Lunar orbit is a test. We still have to be able to cross that distance, and it's not easy. We could have done it eighty years ago, but the next time we were able to do it was only a decade ago. Maybe aliens or God or whatever designed it that way, you know, a test of our abilities."

"Maybe," Elaine said. "But we're here to deal with the practical, Andrea, what we can see and analyze. We'll keep an open mind, but let's not get sucked into introspection. We don't want to close our minds if we focus too much on one theory."

"Okay," Andrea agreed, a faint reluctance to her tone. She'd always liked philosophical debates, which were fun when sitting in a bar in Houston or at the Cape. But right now... Elaine wanted to leave the theorizing to those back home.

"Talk to me about Elpis," Elaine asked. "What are we looking at?"

"Visually," Andrea said, gesturing through the cupola at the world below, "we're seeing what we're seeing. To the naked eye, there are regions which, sure as you like, look like they're covered with bio matter, probably plant analogs with some kind of process occurring similar to photosynthesis."

Elaine couldn't help but give a wry smile at the exobiologist's long-winded reply. "Okay, so we have plant life down there."

"Yes, and spectrographically, we're seeing a similar atmospheric makeup to Earth's."

Elaine watched the unfamiliar continents slipping by. The whirlpools of cloud systems, lightning flashing through them. Oceans, forests, ice and stone.

"Can we survive down there?"

"As in, is it habitable?" Andrea shrugged. "I don't know, El, but it certainly looks that way. I'll add the caveat we're making do with equipment designed for Martian atmospheric analysis."

Elaine gave a grin and twisted herself around to face back down the cylinder of the habitat. "Want to try and find out?"

"Hell yes."

"Then let's start the sequence. It's time to dump twenty billion dollars of hardware onto the surface."

Over the next few hours, they prepped the Mars lander. It had been designed to cut through the thin shell of Mars's atmosphere, not the much thicker Earth-like conditions of Elpis's.

With the readings they had obtained during their coast to Elpis, they'd worked out an entry profile they thought might just get the lander through.

***

"Temp is rising, I've got multiple warnings and failure modes pinging up," Mike said, his voice icy calm — the same calm which had drawn Elaine to him when he was her wingman over the battlefields of the Korean peninsula.

Far beneath *Olympus*, the lander streaked through Elpis's

17

atmosphere, a shooting star plummeting to the surface, pulsating embers of ablating hull pouring off the craft.

Status indicators flicked, one after another, from green, through yellow, to red on the consoles of the workstations they were monitoring the lander on.

On the telescope image, the lander silently erupted into a cone of burning debris, chunks of the craft creating a flickering, dissipating cloud.

"Loss of signal." Mike leaned back in his seat. "Sorry, El, she's gone."

"Understood." Elaine gave a tight nod. "No guts, no glory. The lander was designed with Mars in mind, not Elpis. If the wormhole holds, maybe the data we capture can be used to purpose-build something which can put down."

"Aye," Mike agreed. "Still, would have been nice to have made touch-down. What do you think to giving it a go with one of the Orions? They're rated for Earth re-entry. They are far more capable of handling Elpis's atmosphere."

Elaine gave a frown as she watched the final embers of the Mars lander flickering into invisibility. It was tempting. "Okay, on the next alignment with the wormhole aperture, I'll run it by Houston; they can have the boffins back at Lockheed Martin do a feasibility study with the data we picked up on this attempt."

The two-way communication was frustrating. The only time they could speak to home was every four hours for the thirty seconds or so when *Olympus*'s position and the wormhole mouth lined up. They had quickly figured out to record a message and squeeze it through, rather than trying to have any kind of conversation with Houston, which in itself was subject to a three-second light speed delay as the signal shot from Mars 3 to the wormhole, and then the wormhole, via a relay satellite, to ground control.

Elaine pushed the button to record. "Houston, *Olympus* actual. Landing attempt using Mars lander unsuccessful. Entry was terminal and we have a loss of signal and visible disintegration. Request permission to make second attempt using Orion MPCV Two. Please find attached all data acquired on entry attempt. We will stand by while you crunch the numbers."

The communication was compressed in a burst transmission and stored, ready to be sent on the next alignment.

***

"It's what?" Elaine asked, frowning at Miles.

"The luminosity of the wormhole has dropped by twenty percent in the last hour," Miles said, concern obvious in his tight voice. "If it carries on fading at this rate, we'll be looking at it dropping to zero in four hours."

"And then?"

Miles held up his hands helplessly. "I don't know — it could bounce back, it could just go dark but still be functional. We just don't know enough about the damn thing."

Elaine looked hard at the image of the wormhole orbiting Petra. Had it faded? Maybe, or maybe it was her imagination.

Elaine took all of two seconds to think the problem through.

"Miles, bring up the minimum-time direct return solution and pipe it through to Mike." She turned to her husband. "As soon as you get it, I want an earliest opportunity execution."

"Yes, Ma'am." Mike defaulted into military-speak, buckling into his seat as Miles quickly brought up the relevant program on his own console. "Miles, when you've got it…. Yeah, thanks."

Elaine watched Mike's eyes track over his console. After a moment he nodded. "Okay, good. Execute in twelve minutes. Mark."

Elaine keyed her com. "Everyone buckle in. We are conducting an emergency abort back to the wormhole. Main engine ignition is in… eleven minutes, forty seconds."

With the bang of Vernier thrusters, the cumbersome ship oriented itself in anticipation of the burn.

The countdown dropped to zero.

"Execute."

The engine fired, this time pushing up to a full gee. After nearly three weeks in zero gravity, it felt like an elephant was sitting on Elaine's chest. The whole of *Olympus* began to vibrate from the burn of the engine. After a few minutes, silence descended as the engine cut out.

"We're coasting. Time to target..." Mike looked over to Elaine, a flicker of worry in his eyes. "Thirty hours."

"Damn it, we don't have thirty hours," Elaine whispered. "Miles, is it still dropping?"

"Twenty-five percent reduction. We have a little over three and a half hours to get back."

The message board pinged: the return data packet from Earth. Elaine had forgotten they were waiting for the update on the Orion's ability to make landing.

"*Olympus*, Houston," the CAPCOM said. "We were all sorry to hear about the Mars lander. We've done the preliminary work-up on an Orion Two attempt, plugging in the data you acquired. The best we've got out of Lockheed Martin so far is it's a definite possibility. We're sending what we have in an attachment. It'll probably take a few days to get anything firm from them. Hope things are going well."

"Houston, *Olympus*," Elaine said quickly. "Loss of luminosity from the wormhole. Aborting." With less than a second left on the communication window, Elaine keyed transmit.

Her mind whirled through possible abort options to speed up their return.

She quickly brought up the flight control computer on her console. What about a maximum-burn entry to the wormhole? Not seek to match orbits with it, but blaze through it at best possible speed? The nuclear-powered NERVA 2 engine had a lot more engine time in it than they had used so far.

She punched in the parameters as she spoke. "I'm considering going for a maximum-burn direct return. It'll mean threading the needle of the aperture. Miles, run the sums in parallel so we don't miss anything. Mike, think you can do it?"

"Jesus, El. If we miss or the wormhole closes before we arrive, we'll end up shooting into interplanetary space. We might not have the delta-Vee to get…" Mike's voice trailed off.

"There is nowhere to go, anyway. Get your mind right. If that wormhole shuts down before we get there, we're stuck here and we don't know if or when it'll reopen. We're dead anyway."

Elaine rapidly scribbled calculations down, efficiently shutting down the panic building in her and concentrating on finding a way out of the mess they were in.

"Damn it," Miles breathed.

Elaine had come to the same conclusion. They could get there in eight hours.

"Okay." Elaine saved the workings and opened up a new worksheet on her console. "That's better than thirty. Immediate execute."

"El, we're still getting to the stable door after it's slammed shut, only this time while the horse is bolting toward it," Mike said.

"Immediate execute, Mike. I'm thinking of ways to close that time gap."

The engine fired again, throttling up to maximum burn as Elaine frantically thought through other options.

They could burn the NERVA for eighty minutes, which would be when they would achieve peak velocity. Could they squeeze any more velocity out of what they had?

"We're going multi-stage," she said, grimacing through the weight pressing down on her chest. With gee-weakened arms, she began punching more numbers into her console. "We're seeing what we can do if we abandon *Olympus* and get

21

some extra burn time out of the Orions."

Miles quickly began duplicating her work. After a few minutes of calculations, Elaine looked at her numbers. "Five hours. We can get there in five hours."

A few seconds later, Miles gave a nod. "That's what I've got too."

"Five hours, it'll still be gone." Mike grunted. "And even if it's not, I'm a damn good pilot, maybe better than you, El, but I'm not confident I can score a perfect hole-in-one across interplanetary distances."

"We don't have any other option but to try," Elaine said. "This is the absolute least-time solution."

"It's a hell of a gamble; if the wormhole has shut down or we miss, we're sailing off into the big black, and there's no coming back from that."

"Well, what other choice do..." Elaine's voice trailed off before she finished her sentence. "...we have?"

She selected the stern-facing camera. Behind, Elpis, green and verdant, slowly rolled away from them, the ship already on a course away from the world.

Could they gamble everything on a minuscule chance of making it through the closed wormhole?

"Miles, luminosity of the wormhole?"

"Dropped by thirty percent," Miles said. "No fluctuation, it's a linear drop."

If the wormhole carried on closing at this rate, it was going to be closed even if they used every drop of fuel they had on both *Olympus* and the Orions. Even if it didn't close, and they missed, it would be a slow, lingering death as they drifted, without fuel, through the cosmos. Even if the wormhole reappeared a second after they passed it, they would have no way of getting it back, and Earth had nothing which could mount a rescue attempt.

She hadn't had time to calculate the possibility of success, but common sense told her it was minuscule.

"Okay," Elaine said resignedly. "Secure down for coast."

"El, what are you thinking?" Mike asked quietly.

"We have a choice between certain, or possible, death here. Executive decision: I choose possible," Elaine said firmly in the voice she reserved for when she had made up her mind and would brook no dissent. "We will reestablish orbit around Petra. Maybe the wormhole will bounce back."

"And if it doesn't? How long do we wait?" Mike said as he rapidly worked through the engine shut-down procedure. A moment later, the vibration eased back and *Olympus* was left to continue unpowered.

"We wait for as long as we can," Elaine said, before gesturing at the screen in front of her. "Then we'll reinject into Elpis orbit."

"And then?"

"We're still stocked with our original Mars mission load-out. The colony viability experiments." Elaine gestured with a sweep of her hand to encompass the whole of *Olympus*. "The seed and livestock embryos. We'll make landfall on Elpis using the Orions and wait for rescue down there."

"Well… wow," Miles breathed.

Elaine couldn't blame him for his ineloquence. In the space of a few minutes they had followed an emotional roller coaster from knowing they would return home heroes, to the very real possibility of being stranded in this system, possibly forever.

"Mike, work up a solution to re-inject us back into Elpis's orbit."

***

Elaine floated in the cupola, the ambient light lowered, watching Petra, and the wormhole orbiting it.

The wormhole itself was the size of a quarter held at arm's length, yet it had visibly dimmed. With just an hour to go before its luminosity was estimated to drop to zero, it was no longer the most piercingly bright object visible in space.

With their position changed, they would get one more alignment, and it would happen in a few minutes. Each of the eight crew would have one chance to record a message for those back home.

"Houston, this is Elaine," she started, speaking into her boom mic. She hadn't really had the chance to think through these words. She knew the loss of eight astronauts would cause controversy back home. There would be inquiries, hearings and the laying-down-the-blame game which could shut down the space program for years to come. She sure as hell was going to do her part in stopping that. "It doesn't look like we're going to get through. There's no chance we'll make it back in time. I've only had a short time to reflect on the decisions which have brought us to this point, so forgive my ineloquence, but I am speaking from the heart."

Elaine took a deep breath before continuing. "There is nothing I would have changed, nothing any of us would change. We are explorers, we have reached new heights and we are revealing the unknown, for the benefit of all," she paraphrased the NASA motto. "We are alive. Maybe we will come home in a day, week, month or year. Maybe not. If the wormhole doesn't reappear, we are going to return to Elpis and we are going to attempt a landing. I challenge you, NASA, ESA, the Russian, Indian, Chinese and South American space agencies. I challenge the private space industry. I challenge you all to continue exploring and to one day come and bring us home, or at least drop by for a visit. *Olympus* actual, out."

There — her message was logged in the system, ready to be sent at the next alignment.

***

Petra had visibly grown as they approached, even as the bright point of the wormhole receded. Elaine watched as the light of their way home finally flickered and died.

She pulled herself back through the habitat module, into Orion One where Mike was working away.

"How you feeling, honey?" he asked as she buckled

herself in.

"Comme ci, comme ca," she said, smiling at him. "You know, trapped in a strange system with my husband who now has no escape from me."

Mike gave a laugh, before turning serious. "I've got the final burn ready to go to slip us into Petra's orbit."

"It's not going to come back, Mike," Elaine said quietly. "Every day of food we use up here is one more day of food we won't have if we put down on Elpis. We'll need that time while we're waiting for our seed stock to take. No, we're not going into orbit. We're going to slingshot back around and return to Elpis."

"Okay." Mike nodded. "Okay. I guess there's no point in waiting for something that may never happen. Let's do it."

***

Olympus curved around the rocky, orange moon, racing by a mere two hundred kilometers above the surface before the engine fired again, driving the ship back toward Elpis.

Two days later, after a more sedate cruise, the ship slipped back around Elpis.

***

"We are go for separation," Elaine said.

With a thunk, the conical Orion detached from *Olympus* and began drifting backward, away from its mothership.

Through the porthole, Elaine could see her ship from the outside for the first time in weeks. The long cylinder of the habitat with its solar panels sticking out of the sides. The docking node just behind, and then the second long, gold-clad cylinder of the mighty NERVA engine.

She felt a prickle behind her eyes. This ship, designed for the single purpose of traveling to Mars, had performed magnificently in the most unusual of circumstances. And it would continue to do so. When the crew were clear, the autopilot was set to take it back to the barycenter between Elpis and Petra, where it could continue to watch over them, to feed them information and perhaps act as a beacon for anyone who would come visit.

She pressed the button which would execute the entry flight plan. With the bang of thrusters, the Orion turned and ignited her engine. It fired for two minutes, setting them on a course to enter Elpis's atmosphere.

"We are moving to final abort go, no-go." Elaine said. She glanced at the other three people in the Orion. They each gave a nod, with varying degrees of enthusiasm. All around them, storage crates and bins were secured down. They had stripped *Olympus* of everything they could carry down with them, including the invaluable seed, livestock embryos and medical gear, and split them between the two Orions. "We are a go."

Explosive bolts fired, and the Orion's service module was jettisoned, leaving just the tiny cone of the MPCV. It rotated again, presenting its heat shield in the direction of travel.

They had spent weeks working through the preliminary figures Lockheed Martin had sent them, designing the entry profile as best they could to cope with the different and uncertain atmosphere of Elpis. They had elected to go down using both Orions, both to give them extra cargo space and so the loss of one wouldn't mean the loss of everyone. The downside? The two pilots would have to go separately. Elaine would take the first down, then Mike would bring the second.

Orion One dipped into the thermosphere; the heat shield registered the temperature climbing rapidly as the buffeting started.

The tiny capsule began streaking through the yellow-tinted atmosphere of Elpis, the vibrations of their transit causing the capsule to violently shake.

Elaine gritted her teeth to stop them bashing against each other. There wouldn't be any dentists on the planet to repair them if they got chipped. She turned her head, seeing the flames flickering outside the porthole.

She closed her eyes, knowing her fate was in the hands of the flight computer, which in turn was trying to control the craft through an atmosphere it had never been designed for.

She gave a yelp as the parachute deployed, driving the seat hard into her back.

Elaine gripped her armrests as she waited for the capsule to descend to the surface. The big question now was whether the atmosphere was thick enough for the 'chutes to bite. All their readings said "yes". As far as they could tell, atmospheric conditions were near identical to Earth's.

Elaine gave a grunt as the capsule hit the surface, jarring her back.

She took a moment to compose herself. They were down and, from what she could see, intact. She glanced up through the porthole — above them, she could see clouds rolling sedately through the sky.

"Fortune favours the bold," she muttered as she struggled her way upright against the unfamiliar gravity of the world. "Miles, Pete, Shelly. There's no time like the present. I'm going to pop the hatch."

They all gave tight nods. This was it. Their spectrometer readings had indicated the oxygen and nitrogen content of the atmosphere was roughly the same as Earth's, give or take a percent. Besides, they were stuck down here, Elaine thought. She'd rather die quickly than slowly starve or suffocate to death in the tiny capsule.

With her pressure suit's visor down, she undogged the hatch and, grunting with effort, pushed it open. "Come on, someone. Give me a leg up."

From below, Miles pushed up on Elaine's foot, and she hauled herself through the hatch with weak arms before tumbling down the side of the capsule and falling to the surface.

She took a moment to gather herself, perched on her

hands and knees. Her gloved hands were sunk a centimeter into the mud coating the ground. The thick, bristled stalks of… plants? Yes, plants probed sparsely out of it.

She unsteadily pushed herself up and looked at the strange world they had found themselves on for the first time.

The Orion had landed in a marshy valley, with rows of rocky hills bordering it on each side. Flowing down the side of one, a waterfall thundered down, its base lost in a cloud of mist. Looking up, she saw through the yellow-tinged sky the world's sun beating down on the vista. To one side of that star, visible even in daylight, Petra hung hazily in the sky — a huge disc, at least ten times the width of the Moon from Earth.

There's life here, Elaine thought to herself as her attention was drawn back to the plants at her feet. The first life of another world. Hunched over from the weight of gravity, Elaine staggered her way to one and gently ran her fingertips up the stem. It swayed as she did, curling into a question-mark shape.

Mission commander's prerogative: I think I'll call these… cattails.

"An astronaut's dream." Elaine began chuckling to herself.

"Sorry, El. I didn't copy that." Mike's crackly voice came through her earpiece.

"Sorry, honey. Just saying my first words. An astronaut's dream. Being somewhere new, getting to name everything we see." Elaine said. She straightened herself slowly back up. "Sooner or later we need to know if we can breathe down here. I choose sooner."

Without waiting for a response, she unclipped the bottom of her visor and slid it up. The temperature on her cheeks was comfortable, maybe around 20 degrees Celsius. Elaine closed her eyes and took a long breath in.

She held it in her lungs for a second. It tasted strange, damp — not horrible, just unusual, a hint of cinnamon to it.

Giving a long exhalation, she began breathing normally.

"You know," Elaine said the words everyone was hanging on for. "I think we can give it a go here."

400 years later

"The First." Jalia read the plaque on the base of the huge plinth which the ancient, heat-scorched space capsule rested on. She loved it here, the feel of ancient history and great deeds. Here, the first people had set foot on this world.

Surrounding the display were eight statues, twice life-sized of those first eight. The eight people who, through tireless hard work and great ingenuity, had managed to bring human life to Elpis.

It had been hard. Hard and long, but their society had gone from just surviving to flourishing. Jalia looked around at the city of Orion's Landing which filled the once marshy valley. Skyscrapers rose up to meet the deep orange twilight sky which, in turn, was filled with zeppelins and gliders, sedately going about their business.

Tilting her head further back, Jalia could see a bright speck of light crossing the heavens: one of the larger space cities drifting through its endless orbits.

Without warning, a bright flash appeared on Petra's horizon. Jalia frowned in concentration. What was that? An accident in one of the space cities or ships in that area?

No. Jalia watched as the flash faded; it left a tiny blue spark in the heavens.

She gave a smile. She knew what that light was. Her great-grandmother, Eala, had told her what to look for.

Another ship was answering Harmonsykes's Challenge.

Maybe this time they would stay.

Ralph Kern Q&A

Where did the idea for your story come from?

One of the things I like to do in my work is to have a solid link between our contemporary time and the story. When we hashed out the Explorations concept, I started thinking of ways for the story to happen in the present day…or not too far in the future and, what's more, make it feel believable.

And so the idea of having the wormhole appearing halfway through a Mars program was born. We would have the technology to explore through it, and maybe exploit what we find there, but it certainly wouldn't be easy.

The story did evolve as we got deeper into the shared world aspect of this anthology. For example, I worked closely with Shellie Horst who had a story which seemed like it would make a perfect sequel for The Challenge. We wanted to tie them closely together to make that link unmistakable, but without losing our distinct writer voice and individual plot.

What authors or other forms of media have the biggest impact on your writing?

There are so many authors who have had an impact on my own writing and wider writing career. I also work with many of them now on various projects, so would prefer to save them some blushes.

But the people who first inspired me to write? They would be the likes of Arthur C Clarke, Alastair Reynolds, Peter F Hamilton and Stephen Baxter. I absolutely love the deep thinking nature of their works wrapped up in awesome storylines.

If given the opportunity to explore space through a

wormhole, would you take it?

Without a doubt. How amazing would that be? What would we find on the other side? I genuinely think Humanity's destiny lies out among the stars and I would love to be part of that journey.

What are you currently working on?

I currently have three projects on the go. The final part of the Sleeping Gods Trilogy, entitled, Endings is coming up to the completion of the first draft. Then, of course, the hard work will begin on it! I'm really pleased with how this one is turning out. The second is a SF Mystery Thriller called Uncharted, which is going in for its editing cycle and isn't far off from release. I'm immensely proud of this one and can't wait to share it with the world. The final project, which I've recently started plotting out is something which is different to my norm. I wanted chance my hand at writing a space opera, as opposed to hard SF, albeit constrained for the most part within real world physics. So far it's plotted out and I'm looking forwards to turning my attention to it.

I also like to keep a steady output of short stories on the go as well. Hopefully we will see an exciting announcement on this front soon.

Where can readers find more of your work?

I'm rather pleased with myself, having just created my own website where I list my works, have a blog, and where people can subscribe to my spam-free mailing list.

Website: https://ralphkern.wordpress.com/

You can find my books on Amazon

Through Glassy Eyes
By PP Corcoran

1

Life for Professor Chris Kane had been good. Better than good, in fact — it had been damned near perfect.

Chris Kane was the person to whom all career-oriented employees attached themselves. A rising star in the X Tel Corporation, the largest tech corporation on the planet, bar none, and those with inside knowledge pegged Chris as a future board member.

As head of X Tel's Research and Development Division, he was at the cutting edge of the science that would decide the next big thing. For a very brief thirty days in 2052, that next big thing had been the wormhole that had all-too-briefly appeared in Lunar orbit, casting its eerie blue glow across the night sky.

In a decision that many now regarded as foolhardy, NASA had dispatched the *Olympus*, the third ship in the Mars exploration program, through the wormhole. In the initial hours of the mission, everything had gone to plan. Under the command of Commander Elaine Harmon-Sykes, the crew of eight sent back images of a possible habitable world named Elpis. As excitement reached fever pitch around the globe, disaster struck. Suddenly, and without warning, the wormhole began to close. Despite frantic efforts by the *Olympus*'s crew, they failed to reach the wormhole before it closed entirely. The fate of Harmon-Sykes and her brave crew became the subject of much speculation among the experts. Did they perish in the depths of space? Could they have managed to make a soft landing on Elpis and even now be awaiting rescue? Whatever had befallen them, NASA and every other space agency had satellites monitoring the last known location of the wormhole, waiting patiently for even the briefest sign that it would reopen and contact could be reestablished with the stranded astronauts. X Tel was spending a small fortune sponsoring research in the field of wormholes, but realistically, unless the wormhole decided to open of its own accord, then the theories being put forward by the experts were exactly that — theories.

Back on Earth, life went on and, as was human nature, the masses looked for something else, the next big thing to fuel their excitement. And that next big thing was "Wetware".

The prosthetic replacement of damaged or lost limbs was obsolete in the medical science of the mid-twenty-first century; the long-forecast breakthroughs in stem cell research and advanced cloning techniques made sure of that.

Modern medicine now grew replacement body parts, almost identical to, but in fact better than, the original. Viral disease, once the scourge of humanity, was fast becoming defunct as tailor-made drugs targeted the root cause of infection. If you wanted your child to have green eyes and blond hair, no problem — gene-splicing and manipulation decided the physical attributes of your unborn child. It all came with a price, of course.

The large corporations took over where the social-political systems failed, and provided every citizen the life they believed to be their God-given right. The corporations housed their employees in sprawling mega-scrapers and provided for their every need.

Chris, his wife Diana, and their thirteen-year-old daughter Charlotte lived in just such a building. As was due to a division head, the Kane's 162nd-floor apartment was luxuriously appointed. Chris had only to walk a few steps to the building's inter-car which whisked him down the sixty floors to his research labs. Charlotte's corporation-run school, exclusive to children of employees of the appropriate corporate hierarchical level, was two floors down. Diana had chosen to forgo her own career after Charlotte's birth;

instead she concentrated on raising their family and supporting Chris as he climbed the corporate ladder.

But now? A sigh of exhaustion escaped Chris's lips and misted the clear glass pane presently streaked with the falling rain which battered soundlessly against it. A more poetic man might have likened the rain to the tears of desperation that fell from the eyes of the many around the world. Those tears weighed heavily on Chris's chest.

The silent flash of distant lightning, partially obscured by the monoliths of the corporation-controlled homes and workplaces of the tens of millions who called the New York of 2058 their home, briefly illuminated the darkened room where he stood. The sound of thunder could not reach him through the glass, thus the steady, low, beeping tones of the medical monitors continued uninterrupted.

Chris looked at the small hypo he held in his right hand. It weighed as heavy as a stone. Worried colleagues had tried to persuade Chris to take a break, seeing the downward spiral of the physical and mental decline that Chris had entered. But they did not know the horror of his dreams.

When Chris closed his eyes, the faces of the lost haunted him; their open, unblinking, glassy eyes bored into his brain. The wailing cries of their families rang in his ears. Only a sliver of hope that he could fix what he had unleashed drove him on, and that hope was contained within the hypo….

2
Friday, January 1st, 2055

Chris, a renowned micro-manager, was finishing his weekly reading of the various programs' progress reports before heading home for a late New Year's Day dinner with his wife and daughter, both of whom were resigned to his work ethic.

A highlighted section in the report caught his eye, a single paragraph buried among pages of technical babble.

Chris was astonished that such a revelation could have been overlooked. True, it did not resolve the focus of that particular project, but the implications for bioengineering were immense.

If he and his team could figure a way to incorporate this breakthrough with the exocortex project, then he would be remembered as the man who ushered in the next step of human evolution.

He reread the paragraph twice to be sure that his eyes had not deceived him, then reached for the hand comp and, without looking, entered a command that would send a message to his team to head back in to work.

3
Friday, January 8th, 2055

Even though Chris was a division head, this was the first time he had ever been to the 182nd floor. The floor was completely isolated from the rest of the building and contained the private residences and offices of the group that Chris hoped one day he and his wife would be a part of, the corporate elite.

As Chris was shown through the floor-to-ceiling mahogany doors, the eight most powerful corporate heads on the planet confronted him.

These were the oligarchs, the decision-makers of an empire with political and economic influence in every major country, and he was about to ask them not only for their trust but to place the corporation's financial future in his hands. For only with the backing of the entire board of the mighty X Tel Corporation did Chris have a chance of succeeding.

The members of the board sat patiently as Chris prepared himself. He clasped his hands behind his back, forcing his shoulders to relax, and began speaking. "Good morning, ladies and gentlemen, my name is Professor Chris Kane, and I head up the Research and Development Division." He paused, and eight blank, inscrutable faces returned his gaze. Clearing his throat, he continued. "I stand before you to present something which has the potential to change the course of human evolution." Their interest piqued, several of the board members sat a little straighter in their chairs and gave Chris the encouragement to press on. "My division covers a broad spectrum of cutting-edge programs. Some weeks ago, a lab tech reported a minor breakthrough in the program to assist victims of quadriplegia. She discovered the ability to program smart machines, more often used in micro-surgery to repair torn arteries and membranes, to construct highly complex biomechanical devices using nothing more than cells scavenged from the human body. My team and I have been developing this little gem, and we believe we have overcome a major problem which science has struggled with for decades. The key to true human and machine interface."

The statement garnered a couple of patronizing smiles and one outright laugh, while the remaining five board members struggled to keep straight faces — not the reaction Chris had expected.

After a few moments Pierre Orlan, whose influential family were instrumental in the rise of X Tel to its present commanding position in the world markets, took pity on Chris, perhaps mistaking his reddening cheeks for embarrassment rather than growing anger.

"Please forgive us, Professor Kane. Over the years, many division heads have stood where you are and made similar claims. They say their latest invention will change the world, make us rich beyond our dreams, and quite possibly, in my younger days, I shared their enthusiasm — but too many times I, in fact we as board members, have invested heavily and ended up with nothing to show for it."

Chris squeezed his fingers behind his back, and took a few short breaths before replying. "I understand your pessimism, Mr. Orlan, and indeed that of the other board members present. However, may I ask a few questions before I'm dismissed out of hand?"

Orlan gave a gracious nod, which Chris took as

permission to continue. "OK. What if I could give you a way to access the hyper net, or to control any machine linked to the hyper net, without the need for a physical interface?"

Alison Cho, the most junior board member, having been appointed only five years before, had a background in applied technologies and it had been she who had laughed earlier. Now, she let a disbelieving grunt escape her thin lips.

"If you're talking about an exocortex, Professor Kane, then I know you're on a fool's errand. We are still years from developing that sort of technology."

Chris graced her with a knowing smile. "Ms. Cho, not only are we not years away from developing the exocortex, but I have a working prototype and with further development I will have a model ready for mass production in under two years." The boardroom descended into bedlam, and the satisfied smile on Chris's face grew wider.

A tidal wave of questions followed; each of the board members tried to be heard over the others, until Chris was unable to tell where one question ended and the next began. Eventually, Orlan shouted to make himself heard above the cacophony. "Ladies and gentlemen, please! One at a time! This is getting us nowhere. Let's give the professor a chance to explain before subjecting him to the Spanish Inquisition!" A general mumbling of consent from around the table followed, and the room stilled.

"Please, Professor Kane, continue," said Orlan.

"Thank you, Mr. Orlan. OK, I'll start with the concept." Chris chose his words carefully, aware that, now he had their ears, he could not afford to lose them with too much techno babble. "The idea behind S.D.E.A.W., that is, Sub Dermal Enhanced Application Ware, is actually quite simple. What if an individual could access any piece of data on the hyper net without using a physical access terminal? And if we take it a step further — what if we could remotely access our bank accounts, control the heating in our homes or send messages to our friends? Or if we could establish a direct link to our S.D.E.A.W. and hold real-time conversations through thought alone? Our S.D.E.A.W. would recognize our desires and access the outside world via an implant. The entire, accumulated knowledge of humanity would be just one thought away."

The board members' slack-jawed, stunned looks greeted Chris as they realized the true potential of the exocortex theory.

"X Tel is a leading designer and manufacturer of industrial robots. So, what if an operator could be anywhere in the world and control a robot? All that would be required is for the operator to be within range of a hyper net node, and that could be a node in planetery orbit. We could have completely automated factories, operated remotely with no human presence."

The silence was palpable as each of the eight oligarchs contemplated a new future.

From the far end of the polished wooden table, someone cleared their throat. Chris's eyes followed the sound and settled on a slightly overweight, balding man holding an unlit, fat cigar in one pudgy hand.

"I have just one question, Professor Kane. Don't you think S.D.E.A.W. is a bit of a mouthful?" A few chuckles could be heard.

"Well… my team have suggested 'Wetware'. What do you think?"

Cigar man appeared to mull it over for a moment. "Wetware it is!"

"I think Professor Kane has given us enough to think about for one day," said Orlan. He smiled directly at Chris. "Please prepare a list of your requirements and submit them for approval by the end of the week. I'm sure they would be looked on favorably."

Chris returned Orlan's smile before saying, in a voice heavy with relief, "Thank you." Taking the hint that he was being dismissed, he quickly gathered up his briefing material and, with a perfunctory nod toward the board members, made his way from the room, barely able to disguise the spring to his step.

***

As the doors closed behind Professor Kane, the mood in the boardroom changed. The atmosphere of levity disappeared and was replaced with one of cold, calculating business acumen.

It fell on Pierre Orlan to gauge the feelings of the board. "Well, fellow board members, it is time for your decision." Orlan glanced from face to face, waiting for a nod for yes or a shake of the head for no. As Orlan's eyes moved from person to person, he was met with a series of nods.

"Very well, then, it is unanimously agreed. Thank you for your time, ladies and gents, until next week." Orlan remained seated as six of the seven other board members stood and exited the room. Those exiting ignored cigar man as he remained in his seat, ostensibly patting his pockets, searching for a lighter.

With the doors once more closed, cigar man placed the still unlit cigar on the polished table top; all pretense of equality with his peers vanished in an instant as his features hardened and turned serious. "My God, Pierre, do you think our starry-eyed prof understands the full potential of his new toy?"

Orlan paused before replying. "No, Jonathan, I think he sees the potential but not the implications."

Jonathan Reynolds had been a member of the X Tel Corporation's board long before Orlan arrived. The entire board were well aware that if he wished, Reynolds could be chairman of the board tomorrow, for he knew every dirty little secret of the board. However, Reynolds was content to rule his own private empire within X Tel, The Defense and Security Division.

Orlan watched as Reynolds ran one thick hand across his balding head as if buying a little time while he made a difficult decision; however, Orlan knew this to be a ruse.

"It would be best if I had personal oversight on this one, Pierre."

"I'm not sure the professor would be comfortable working under Defense and Security. But…" Orlan held his hand up to stop Reynolds's interjection, then continued. "But, may I suggest a compromise?"

Reynolds waved a hand in his direction, his permission to proceed.

"We allow the professor to continue heading up the Wetware project while Defense and Security Division has full access to his research. This gives you free rein to run your own mirror project."

Reynolds leaned back in his chair and contemplated the offer. "I like your thinking, Pierre. Your suggestion keeps the prof happy while at the same time Defense and Security can keep tabs and use his research as we see fit." Reynolds pointed a large finger at Orlan. "Sounds like a sweet deal to me." Reynolds smiled as he retrieved his still unlit cigar from the table before sticking it into his mouth and standing. He left the room with a tuneless whistle escaping his lips around the expensive cigar.

Orlan swiveled his chair to face the large windows, which held a breathtaking view of the numerous mega-scrapers. Sunlight refracted from the thousands of clear polycarbonate conduits that linked mega-scraper to mega-scraper and allowed the high-speed passenger and cargo pods which carried the lifeblood of the city to flow freely. Orlan wondered if, one day, all those millions of people out there would realize how today, in this very room, he had been part of the changing of the evolution of humankind.

4
Wednesday, April 18th, 2057

Nic Parkes tuned out the low hum of voices pervading Room 613, an otherwise nondescript room on a level which contained the Security and Defense Division of the mighty X

Tel Corporation.

Furtively, Nic glanced around, assuring herself nobody was paying her any undue attention as she slowly moved her wrist toward the side of her terminal. Trying in vain to slow a racing heartbeat, she reached absentmindedly for the glass of water which sat precariously on the edge of her workstation. Grasping the glass with her right hand, she allowed the wrist of her left to make contact with the side of her terminal; she held it there and silently counted to five, and took a long pull of cool water before returning the glass to its place.

No alarms sounded.

No uniformed armed guards came running toward her.

She mouthed a silent thank you prayer to Gaia. The data reader secreted within her wristband had successfully downloaded the entire contents of her terminal. All she had to do now was conclude her working day as normal, then discard the wristband in a specific trashcan on the inter-car on her way home.

Nic Parkes was an idealist. Born in London a year before The Flood, she had no memory of her parents, who had died that awful day. It was September 2023, and the category four storm was the last straw. Water levels were already at their highest recorded levels and there was an unseasonably high tide in the Thames River, London, England. The powerful storm in the North Sea forced a surge of water up the Thames estuary; the surge gained height and speed as the estuary narrowed. By the time the surge reached the Thames Barrier, it was over ten meters tall and traveled at almost fifty miles per hour. The barrier was breached with ease, and the heart of central London lay defenseless.

As the waters receded, the political and financial fallout was immense. The heart of a once-proud country lay in tatters, thousands of people had died and tens of millions were displaced. The world looked on in disbelief, wondering which of their capitals would be next.

The nations of the developed world came together to

implement sweeping measures to curb global warming. The measures imposed radical restrictions on polluting industries, resulting in many traditional corporations going to the wall. Others, however, maximized the demand for innovative industrial and agricultural designs — designs which did not harm the environment — and governments poured money into the new corporations, conglomerates just like X Tel.

There were those, however, who saw those conglomerates as an extension of the old world order. They firmly believed that the governments had not gone far enough to protect the planet; instead, they saw a growing reliance on the ever-more-advanced technologies produced by corporations as a threat to the human race. There were those who were willing to protect humans from themselves, and the tech-savvy ecoterrorist was born. The most prolific of them was a group calling itself Gaia, who wanted nothing less than the total banning of all advanced tech. Gaia preached that humans were better off without tech and should return to what they described as the Golden Age of Man.

Nic's first memories were of the X Tel orphanage that raised her: of rooms of playing children, and walls covered in never-ending vids expounding the magnanimity of the corporation's actions in rescuing the children and decrying the efforts of the ecoterrorists to send humanity back into the dark ages. She had received the best education; all the while, her teachers sang the praises of the corporation.

Only when Nic took an obscure lecture in her biomechanical program did she begin to understand that she had been indoctrinated.

Part of the lecture covered the events leading up to the Great Flood of London and how governments and industry alike had ignored the warning signs. Images of a desolated city flashed before her eyes as she sat transfixed in her seat and imagined the horror and the knowledge of certain death that her parents had experienced in their last moments.

A fire ignited within Nic that day, the embers of which

awaited a small breath of air to bring them fully to life.

That breath of air arrived some time later in the form of Alan, a young computer programmer who joined the Security and Defense Division and with whom Nic immediately struck up a friendship. She discovered they shared the same taste in food, music and life, and before Nic knew what was happening their friendship turned to love; for once, Nic felt that everything was right in her world and, perhaps, she would have a chance at happiness.

In the blink of an eye it had all changed. Nic remembered the moment exactly: 11:50 a.m. Friday, August 11, 2056. The alarms had gone off and Nic had immediately followed protocol. She stepped back from her terminal, mildly annoyed that security had called a drill at the very moment she was about to enter the adapted source code into the militarized version of Wetware, but the unmistakable sound of the security door being thrown open as burly security guards raced in made her realize this was not a drill.

The guards made directly for Alan's station, and before he could react they had pinned his arms to his sides and manhandled him from the room.

A horrified Nic wondered what indiscretion Alan had inadvertently committed to warrant this treatment. Nic's musings soon moved to anger as she questioned the right of the corporation to act with such complete disregard for a person's rights.

As Alan was ushered out, Nic recognized the mouthpiece for the corporation entering, a nameless but perfectly groomed and suited female. The emotionless mouthpiece said, "Thank you for your cooperation." She smiled, seemingly oblivious to the fact that everyone could hear Alan protesting his innocence loudly on his way to the security offices, and said, "All staff have the remainder of the day off and, as per protocol, please be prepared for your personal security interview tomorrow. Thank you." The mouthpiece left the room and the workers gathered their belongings in silence.

Nic did not remember the journey home, to her apartment. Her mind was full of thoughts for Alan. *What has he done? Why didn't I know? Where is he now? What will happen to him?* Although she had heard of people disappearing from work, she'd seen no evidence of it and had dismissed it as simply rumors. But now she had witnessed it. Curling up on the couch, she pulled a cushion close to her and sobbed. She eventually fell asleep.

Nic awoke with the dawn sun streaming through her windows. The rising sun promised a new day, but it filled Nic with dread. *Security interviews.* In automated mode she showered and dressed before setting off for work, and on arrival she joined the line of co-workers awaiting their interviews.

Nic was well aware of the biometric scanners used during these interviews; she had helped design them, after all, and that gave her an edge. A way to beat machines. They must never learn of her relationship with Alan, or she might be implicated in whatever he had done to result in his sudden arrest and subsequent disappearance.

When it was her turn, that was exactly what she did. Half an hour of pointed questioning on her contact with Alan, and her lies were masked by thoughts of the happy times she had shared with the children at the orphanage. *Thank God they had kept their love for one another secret.* Not for a moment did those idiots from security know the resentment she harbored or what they had created. For Nic held the key that Gaia needed to access the X Tel's darkest Black Project: Wetware.

5
Monday, September 3rd, 2057

"Please go straight in, Professor Kane, they're expecting you," said the smiling and polite secretary who guarded the entrance to the X Tel boardroom. Chris nodded his thanks as he passed her, and walked confidently into the room beyond.

Over the past two years, Chris had become a frequent visitor to this inner sanctum, visits which had not gone unnoticed. It had not escaped him that his once-bare calendar was now close to bursting with invitations for lunch with prominent corporation members and well-known academics. This newfound popularity even extended to Chris's wife and daughter.

There wasn't a day in which Diane didn't have plans to meet up with a new group of socialites, and as for Charlotte? She had become the center of her school's social network; even her teachers paid her more attention, which was reflected in her rising grades. *Yes,* thought Chris, *things are certainly on the up.*

"Ah! There you are, Chris." Pierre rose from his chair to greet Chris, following his words with a warm handshake and a pat on the back before guiding him toward a well-stuffed, leather high-backed chair. The chair was positioned beside the floor-to-ceiling glass windows and gave a commanding view over the sprawling metropolis of New York.

Chris sank into the proffered seat as Pierre settled into a matching chair opposite, separated by a low table upon which rested two bone china cups, a pot of delicious-smelling coffee and matching bowls containing cream and sugar. Pierre poured them both a coffee and watched with a small smile as Chris lifted his cup and took an appreciative sniff of the fine aroma before savoring its flavor.

"You know, Pierre, I don't know where you get this coffee from, but it has to be the best damned coffee I've ever had."

Pierre let out a hearty chuckle. "Believe it or not, Chris, it actually comes from one of the hydroponics bays in this very building!"

"In that case, I may break in and steal some for myself." Chris half-laughed.

"Well, if the launch of your Wetware goes to plan, getting hold of this coffee will be the least of your problems.

I reviewed the latest figures for pre-orders, and they already far outstrip supply." Pierre sipped at his cup before continuing. "Only yesterday, I ordered two more factories to cease their current product production and prepare the line for Wetware instead."

This news halted Chris's hand in midair, just as he prepared to take another sip of coffee. Instead he returned the delicate cup to the table with an almost imperceptible nervous twitch. "I was aware that pre-launch orders were well beyond our forecast, but I hadn't realized there was such a demand."

A short, barking laugh from Pierre echoed around the large room. "Chris, our most skeptical projection is that in the first six months we will ship almost one billion units."

The wide-eyed look of disbelief on Chris's face was enough for Pierre to laugh again, and this time he didn't stop.

6
Monday, October 22nd, 2057
LAUNCH DAY

An excited young customer was the first into the store at the stroke of 9 a.m. He'd waited in line for three days, camping outside the X Tel store, enjoying the build-up as TV cameras followed the unprecedented demand for this new technology. *Wetware.* He almost salivated at the word. He couldn't contain his grin. *I will be the first!*

An ever-smiling sales assistant greeted him and directed him to what looked like a dressing room. It wasn't. The room contained cordoned-off cubicles, much like a hospital emergency room, and he was directed into one of these cubicles. He sat in the lone chair and another sales assistant, this one dressed in a white coat, spoke. "Welcome, sir. Let me explain the procedure. I'll numb a small patch of skin at the base of your skull by using a hypo-spray of local anesthetic, which might feel a little cold but works almost immediately. Then you'll feel a scratch as I use another hypo to deliver the smart machines which will construct the Wetware; don't worry, it is pretty much painless and takes around fifteen to twenty minutes to complete." The assistant nodded and smiled at him. "OK, are you ready?"

"Absolutely!" the youngster replied excitedly.

In less than one minute a probe containing the minuscule smart machines was injected into his brain stem. Instantly, the tiny machines wove their complex molecule-thin web through and around the brain stem of their willing host, and, after only fifteen minutes, their task was completed. The army of tiny engineers passed harmlessly into his bloodstream to be washed away.

"All done, sir. How does that feel?" the chirpy assistant said, with the same fixed smile she graced every customer with — it was corporation policy, after all.

The proud new owner of Wetware said, "Brilliant! I can't wait to see what this can do!"

The assistant moved behind a nearby counter and began putting together an after-sales pack. "Excellent, sir. Remember, if you have any problems, just call the number on your installation documents and quote your reference number which you can find at the bottom of the first page." Once she had gathered the paperwork together, she began typing into a console, in the final stages of the sale, then she said, "Oh! Sir…"

The young man felt a fleeting moment of concern as the sales assistant reached down below the counter; however, his concern vanished as the bright overhead lighting reflected off a gaudy picture frame. The ever-smiling sales assistant handed him a framed certificate, ensuring that those peering through the exterior windows got a good look. "Your Wetware reference number has been selected at random by the X Tel installation data base! It is my privilege to present to you one of only fifty million world-wide limited edition gift certificates which you may use at any X Tel store…"

The young man couldn't believe his luck, and he barely

heard the sales assistant say, "And that will be seven hundred fifty dollars, cash or card?"

***

The pre-launch hype ensured the demand for Wetware far outstripped supply. In every country with a modest population, there was a store selling Wetware.

The few calls for caution were drowned out by the cries for production to be increased. There were even calls for Wetware to be made available at public expense for preschool children; the advocates cited the exciting possibilities of rapidly accelerated education through unfettered access to information that Wetware provided via the hyper net. Governments, too, were keen to explore the seemingly infinite uses of Wetware.

Requests to demonstrate the military applications of Wetware inundated Jonathan Reynolds. Why risk a human life in war when a drone could be controlled remotely by its human operator outside of any war zone? And could the power of Wetware be turned on itself? Could the agencies read the thoughts of the enemies of the state? Could police forces read a criminal mind and stop crime before it could be committed? The potential of Wetware seemed limitless.

7
Monday, April 1ˢᵗ, 2058

In the name of Gaia, Nic Parkes in Room 613 of the Security and Defense Division of X Tel Corporation typed a single word into her terminal.

S L E E P

With a last look at the blinking cursor, she tapped the enter key, sending the command into the hyper net and opening Pandora's Box. Without a backward glance, she turned from her workstation and left the room, never to return.

***

As Chris Kane reached for his jacket, which he had absently discarded over the living room chair, breaking news flashed across the TV screen and a well-groomed, blond-haired newsreader began an announcement in a somber tone. "We're receiving reports from all over the world of people falling victim to what medical experts have described as a comatose state." He paused for further dramatic effect. "It is affecting the young and the old, and there is no indication that either race or gender increases your risk of falling victim to it. However, unconfirmed reports say that all the victims are Wetware users. Wetware, as many of you will know, is the must-have exocortex accessory. Millions have been sold by the X Tel Corporation, and it has been hailed as the next step in human evolution. Now, there are grave concerns that something has gone very wrong. We here at National Satellite News have contacted the manufacturers for comment and as yet have received no reply…" A change of camera shot showed that the dapper presenter was not alone. A smartly dressed woman in her early fifties pulled her hand sharply away from a strand of hair that had managed somehow to escape from its place in the tightly packed bun which sat high on her head.

"With me today I have Doctor Elizabeth Dural, an expert in the field of biomechanics, and author of 'Interfering in the Natural Order: A Warning'. If I may start with this, Doctor: what do you make of what many are calling 'Wet Fever'?"

An ear-piercing scream drowned out anything the good doctor may have been about to say and stopped Chris in his tracks; his stomach churned and, jacket forgotten, he ran to the source.

On the kitchen floor, Diane knelt beside an unresponsive Charlotte. In desperation, Diane shook Charlotte almost violently while screaming, "Charlotte! Charlotte! Can you hear me? Charlotte! Charlotte!" It was too late. Chris saw the blank look on Charlotte's face, her usually brilliant blue eyes fixed open. Unseeing. A memory etched forevermore into Chris's soul.

8
Monday, April 1ˢᵗ, 2058

Chris was at Charlotte's bedside in one of the many medical facilities which was now standard across the world, wherever Wetware was sold.

Due partly to Chris's status within the corporation and partly, no doubt, due to the thousands of threats he had received since the first person had succumbed to Wet Fever, Charlotte Kane was located in a private room a scant three floors below the Kanes' apartment.

From what the doctors deduced, her entire involuntary nervous system had effectively gone to sleep. Her heart pumped, her lungs moved in and out, and her brain function mimicked that of deep sleep. There was no sign of any physical impediment, nothing to explain her current state, and no matter what method they used to stimulate her, she stubbornly refused to wake.

After four hours of staring at his unmoving daughter, praying and hoping that she would arise from her unnatural sleep, Chris could stand it no longer. He had done this to his daughter and millions like her. He vowed to fix it.

Diane refused to leave their only child's bedside. She sat holding and gently rubbing Charlotte's hand while quietly talking to her in the hope her beloved daughter would respond. Gently, so as not to startle her, Chris laid a hand on Diane's shoulder and felt the tremors of her silent sobs. Without lifting her head, Diane spoke while tears rolled slowly down her face. "Bring our baby back, Chris."

Words of comfort escaped him; instead, he gave his wife's shoulder a reassuring squeeze before he turned and left the room, relying on the tireless, emotionless machines to keep his daughter alive.

9
Monday, April 29th, 2058

Chris raised his head from his computer terminal to rub at his tired eyes while the computer ran yet another simulation. The door to his private office opened with a soft hiss, and Chris struggled to refocus his eyes. Pierre Orlan stood in the shadowy office, looking down at the shattered wreck of a man who had once been so full of life and promise.

"Have you managed to make any progress, Chris?"

Chris took a swig of the stale coffee that had been sitting amongst the pile of data chips and paper records strewn across his normally impeccably neat and tidy desk.

Chris sighed. "At first, I thought it was a design fault, Pierre, but we quickly disregarded the theory as computer simulation after computer simulation has proven the design sound. When we couldn't find a fault there, we moved on to the design of the smart machines. Again, nothing — the machines work perfectly." Chris sat back in his chair and stretched his arms above his head, in an attempt to relieve his tense neck and shoulders. "X Tel have spent a small fortune investigating the Wetware installation methods that each store has used to deliver the smart machines into the client's brain stems. Yet again, nothing!" Chris let his arms fall to the sides of his chair. "There was the normal minor differences in procedure, but nothing to cause concern or Wet Fever." Chris kicked back his chair from the desk and stood, only to pace in the confined space of his small office in frustration. "I've trawled through hundreds of the Wet Fever victims, searching desperately for some correlation. Anything that linked them." Chris directed his eyes at Orlan. "But no matter how hard I look, there is no link. I just don't know where to look next, Pierre." Chris's desperation was clear to Orlan, and he grasped Chris's shoulder and said, "You'll find it, Chris… You. Will. Find it." Orlan's earnest eyes searched Chris's, willing him to believe his words.

A subdued ping from the computer running through the

source code used to define the smart machines' intricate dance of construction interrupted them, and Chris flopped back into his seat. "No doubt this report will reveal absolutely nothing, again! I have no idea how many times I've run this now, Pierre." He gave another sigh as he began reviewing the data, then he noticed something. *How odd! Too much coffee, perhaps?* Chris thought as he rubbed his eyes and squinted at the screen. He had been many hours now without sleep, but this single line of unfamiliar code was strange.

Rubbing his hands vigorously up and down his weary face, he willed his brain into motion. Chris spoke out loud. "Who the hell wrote this?"

Orlan maneuvered himself into a position where he could see over Chris's shoulder. Chris tapped on his keyboard in an effort to identify the author of the unauthorized code. The computer responded, "Operator 613". Orlan took an involuntary step back, his head spinning.

"Who is 613?" demanded Chris. "I need to speak to them immediately — there's been unauthorized changes hidden in the code."

In the corner of the display, an icon blinked to show that the computer had finished running the latest simulation and, yet again, it found no errors. This time a suspicious Chris checked his diagnostic code. "My God! 613 has modified the diagnostics — it's not checking every line of code." Feverishly, Chris tapped at his keyboard, removed 613's modification on the diagnostics and hit the enter key. He waited, his eyes fixed on Orlan's pale face.

The scan finished within a few minutes, and the familiar blinking icon appeared. But this time an error message accompanied it. That single line of 613's code had allowed the unthinkable. It had instructed certain specific smart machines, those randomly selected by the X Tel database to be the recipient of a gift certificate, just like his Charlotte had been, to construct a secondary access route which bypassed

Wetware's original design. It was a hack into the human brain.

10
Tuesday, April 30th, 2058

"Oh God, Jonathan, how was this allowed to happen? If this gets out, we are finished!"

The outwardly calm Reynolds held his tongue and allowed Orlan to vent his anger and frustration as he paced up and down the plush boardroom.

Reynolds sat in his chair with his ubiquitous unlit cigar perched between two fingers, and shared Orlan's anger; however, he understood the futility of it. It always got out. Somewhere in their organization was a whistleblower ready to reveal to the world that Wetware had been hacked. Maybe they were simply biding their time, waiting for the corporation to try to cover it up, but the trick here was to get ahead of their game.

As Orlan paused for breath, Reynolds seized his chance to interject.

"Pierre, calm down. We need to think logically about this, and running around like a headless chicken or sinking into the depths of despair is not going to help."

Orlan halted his pacing and sat heavily in the overstuffed seat. "You are, of course, correct, Jonathan." He tried to compose himself with a few deep breaths. "I take it you have a suggestion? How do we handle the revelation that our most prized program has been hacked and was responsible for Wet Fever?"

"Simple. We tell the truth. We call a press conference. We tell the world that X Tel Corporation and Wetware were the target of external sabotage and that we are doing everything in our power to rectify the intrusion while we carry out our own investigation, and promise that if any X Tel employee is found to be at fault, then he or she will face the full force of the law."

Orlan sat quietly for a few moments as he considered the implications of Reynolds' proposal. "You're throwing Chris Kane to the wolves, aren't you?" he said in a barely heard whisper.

Reynolds displayed his sympathetic face. "I don't see what else we can do, Pierre. It is our duty to look after the interests of the corporation and, after all, Professor Kane was ultimately responsible for Wetware. Besides, with the eyes of the world focused on Kane, my department can ensure that any… ah, embarrassing evidence of our little side project can be made to disappear." Reynolds gave Orlan a knowing smile. "You know it is for the best, Pierre."

The two men sat in silence; Reynolds considered the wording of his press statement while Orlan contemplated the outcome of callously destroying a man's career and livelihood.

11
Tuesday, May 7ᵗʰ, 2058

Turning his back to the rain-streaked window, Chris crossed the short distance to the hospital bed. Charlotte lay as a statue, her condition unchanged since the day of her collapse.

"Are you sure this is going to work, Chris?"

Looking into the pale, worried face of his wife, Chris tried to instill the strength and confidence he knew they both needed in his voice. "It will work."

With Diane's help, he rolled Charlotte onto her side and brushed away a few stray strands of hair. Before his courage could escape him, he pushed the hypo spray into the base of her skull and, with a small hiss, released the smart machines into her system. With the softest of touches, he allowed Charlotte to return to her previous position as he placed the now-empty hypo spray on top of the bedside table.

"How long?" asked Diane in barely a whisper.

Chris slipped a hand comp from his jacket pocket, which

sprang to life as it recognized his bio signature. Chris checked its illuminated display.

"We should know in ten minutes or so."

Both parents lapsed into an uneasy silence. As the minutes dragged by, Chris found himself staring into his daughter's unblinking eyes, the automated machines dripping a clear, lubricating solution that gave them a glassy effect like smooth, polished marble. The lightning continued to flash intermittently outside as the wind and rain battered the windows.

A chirp from the hand comp prompted Chris to check the display. Chris had taken a leaf from the saboteurs' book, and the smart machines had completed their task. The saboteurs had built a secondary access route to carry out their plan, so Chris had built a third. Bypassing the Wetware's overarching design, they could now access the human brain directly. A simple and elegant cure for Wet Fever. If it worked.

With more confidence than he felt, Chris typed in a one-word command on the hand comp. His finger hesitated as it hovered over the enter button and, looking up, Chris saw his wife staring at him. Slowly she nodded and Chris closed his eyes before pushing the button. He held his breath.

A command flashed through the hyper net:

A W A K E N

PP Corcoran Q&A

Where did the idea for your story come from?

A friend of mine had pointed me towards a research paper that had recently been published by the British Ministry of Defence in which there was a section dealing with the future of soldier/machine integration and I thought well what if something like this was available to the general public, where could it lead?

What authors or other forms of media have the biggest impact on your writing?

Being more orientated to the space opera come military style sci-fi I would be more inclined to read books by David Weber, Steve White and John Ringo however as my own writing style continues to grow I find myself more and more drawn towards the classics by Asimov and more modern day stuff by the likes of Peter Hamilton although I cannot help myself sometime and head over to a Stainless Steel Rat novel for a bit of light relief. As for what has the largest impact on my own writing ideas I have a tendency to see what is going on around me in the present day and try to imagine two scenarios, one where we as a race work out our differences and manage to function as a whole society and one where it all goes wrong and where that may lead. Both scenarios open up a wide range of opportunities for story lines for an author.

If given the opportunity to explore space through a wormhole, would you take it?

Yes, yes and yes again. I have explored the universe so many times in my own mind as I run possible story lines through my head so to have the opportunity to actually experience it would be a slam dunk. Besides, my wife would be glad to get rid of me for a while.

What are you currently working on?

Currently I am finishing off the first book in my new series, The K'Tai War – Invasion. A military sci-fi novel with a twist. The K'Tai Imperium are an ancient civilization that regard the Human race as the young pretenders in the galaxy but when a rare mineral that is essential to the star drives that link the worlds of the known universe together is discovered on the Human controlled world of Agate, a world that lies on the border of human – K'Tai space the Imperium jumps at the chance to teach the Humans a lesson. The first book tells the story of the invasion from the view-points of a Human family caught up in the fighting, the K'Tai Imperium and the Human League of Planets. Concurrently I am working on the fourth and final book in my Saiph Series. Entitled Legacy of the Saiph this work will hopefully tie up all the plot lines from the first three novels and resolve the Saiph question once and for all. Or will it? We shall just have to wait and see.

Where can readers find more of your work?

Facebook: www.facebook.com/ppcorcoran

Website: www.ppcorcoran.com

Email: info@ppcorcoran.com

Subscribe: http://www.ppcorcoran.com/subscribe.html

Here, Then, Forever
By Chris Guillory

The alarm pulsated with its rhythmic insistency. Not particularly loud, but jarring nonetheless. As Aliza woke she rubbed her ankle. A phantom pain from an old injury. She tenderly placed both bare feet on the cold floor and reached for the alarm clock. In her still-muddled state, she realized then that it was not her alarm clock, but instead the ship's alert. The fog of sleep evaporated and her head snapped up. "Oni, report."

"Colonel Navarro," the too-calm female voice answered. The ship's computer waking her could have meant any manner of things. Further, it would have done so in the same monotone voice that lacked any sort of inflection. Oni would have sounded the same reporting that the toilet was overflowing, or that auto-navigation had failed as a chunk of ice was on its way to turning her ship into pebble-sized chunks of steel and titanium.

"What, Oni?" she snarled when it paused, apparently waiting for her to answer.

"Khonsu is showing signs of activity, Colonel Navarro. Readings indicate opening is imminent."

Aliza sighed. It was time. She had traveled for nearly sixty days toward the sun, just past the halfway point to Venus. Which was odd, since Khonsu's other end opened near Neptune. Still, traveling two months in the opposite direction and through the wormhole saved over a decade when flown as the crow flies. Now that she knew the ship was not going to get pounded into metal dust, her nerves returned to a normal state. She hooked her black, neck-length hair behind one ear.

She looked around and, unsurprisingly, nothing in the tidy room had changed. The inside of the ship was like the rest of the space around it — cold and lonely, the closest living beings about thirteen million miles away back on Earth.

Finally standing, Aliza made her way to the bathroom. The entire trip took about five steps, to traverse an area that held a metal-framed, twin-sized bed, matching locker, and desk, into a bathroom that was half that size. She turned on the faucet and splashed cold water on her face before looking into the mirror. With a finger, she traced one of the lines on her skin that had appeared perhaps a decade prematurely. She then saw the rest of them: lines of worry, stress, and sadness. Her raven-black hair was now streaked with gray that had come seemingly overnight as opposed to years. Well, she figured, a loss of a son would probably have that effect on any parent.

Aliza remembered standing in the lobby of GEXI, the Galaxy Exploration Initiative. Whether by design, accident, or her own anxiety, the nearly empty space felt very sterile. Each wall was either gray or white and lacked any design or artwork. The sparse furniture was of the angular metallic sort more suited for a laboratory than an office. Even the smell was unwelcoming, a blend of tile wax and disinfectant. She focused her attention to the video on the large screen, the narrator's voice bringing the only sign of life to the lobby: *"Khonsu was discovered in 2156. GEXI was among the first to send drones through it to discover that each arrived a short distance from Neptune. Soon after, we began sending the first manned crews to begin construction of a space station that now orbits Triton, Neptune's outermost moon."*

The video included CGI images of ships passing through the wormhole, vanishing through spectacular halos of light, combined with actual footage of flight crews performing various tasks. At the sound of footsteps, Aliza turned to see Dr. Gupta approaching. He extended his hand, and she awkwardly attempted the same with the crutches under her arms.

"Colonel Navarro, I hope you are doing well," Dr.

59

Gupta said.

"As well as can be, Doctor," Aliza said, indicating her crutches and the cast around one ankle.

"I see," said Dr. Gupta. "Well, I have some very exciting news! We've received Adam's test results, and he scored extremely high, particularly when it came to solving abstract problems with little or few variables. We need young people exactly like this, as Triton station will undoubtedly run into issues that will require unconventional methods to address." The doctor chuckled. "They'll not be able to hop into a ship and fly to the nearest store for parts!"

Children showing talent in a variety of skills were target occupants, since travel through Khonsu was not bidirectional. Once through, it was the long way back to Earth. Children were chosen when possible, to maximize the productivity of a given individual. After all, voyages were not only one-way, they were expensive. GEXI brass wanted to get as much bang for their buck as possible.

"This is all great news, Doctor, but I'm sensing a 'but'."

"Ah, yes. I'm afraid, Colonel, that Adam will have to be on our next flight, as he will just make the next window for orientation and training. As you know" —he gestured toward her cast— "you are not cleared for flight with your current injury."

Aliza had to make the choice then to either delay Adam's admission for years, if not indefinitely, or meet him at the station when she was cleared. She knew how much this meant for him, and chose to let him go. Adam and his crew entered the wormhole, but never emerged from the other side. It was soon found that upon entry, there was a sudden, yet immense, drop in the negative energy required to stabilize the wormhole.

Although this was catastrophic, the wormhole determined too valuable a resource to lose, and the next few years were spent developing a method to manually stabilize it. The solution was to create an exotic matter detonation that would stimulate enough negative energy to once again allow safe travel. Finally, GEXI developed the Ex-Matt missile, which was designed to detonate and set off a chain reaction of charged atoms smashing together at super-high speeds. With a multi-billion-dollar price tag, they did not want to risk sending an unmanned vehicle. When they began asking for volunteers, Aliza did so without hesitation. Five years later she took off, racing away from Earth on a ship with a crew of one.

The anxiety of what was soon to come crept into her mind like a drop of dye slowly spreading in a still body of water, bringing her back to the present. When Khonsu opened, she would have to be close enough to fire the Ex-Matt at a distance that would reach it before it closed once again. Further, this would all be at a range where she would already be in its pull and unable to escape. One way or another, stable or not, she was going through.

Before she left her quarters, she opened her locker and picked one of the five identical flight suits that hung within. Each was powder-blue with a white stripe in the center that ran from her waist to her neckline. Aliza mechanically stepped in and fastened the straps at the wrists and center and made her way to *Lago*'s cockpit. The ship was named so because it was designed with a fat hull that connected to an offsetting cockpit, connected by a cylinder, giving the ship the appearance of large lagomorph without legs. She doubted this was lost on her designers when they installed retractable solar panels that extended on each side of the cockpit, forming the "ears". These would collect any available light and could be used for power.

Aliza walked silently, her steps muffled by the padded boots of the flight suit. The only sound beyond that was the faint whisper of the ventilation system. Once she reached her destination, she sat in the singular seat and strapped herself in. Next, she removed her helmet from its dock and placed it on her head, locking it with two clasps on the back. With the main window covered by a shield, the only illumination was the soft glow of the panels in sleep mode.

When she logged in, the various lights blossomed, brightening the cockpit and showing more detail in the small, beige space. Aliza opened the shield, exposing her view of the millions of stars shimmering in protest against the absolute blackness of space. No matter how many times she had seen it, the vastness of infinite space always took her breath away.

"Oni?"

"Yes, Colonel Navarro," it replied.

"Distance and time to Khonsu opening, please?"

"You are currently 965,606 meters away. Negative energy output is steadily increasing to a point where Khonsu opening will occur in roughly five minutes and forty-seven seconds."

Aliza nodded, although nobody was around to see it. "Roger that, Oni. Navigate to entry range and prep the Ex-Matt missile."

"Yes, Colonel."

Almost immediately, Aliza felt the thrum of the main engines firing, followed by the force pushing her back into the seat. Aliza was fast approaching the point of no return. There was no way to really tell what would happen when she fired the Ex-Matt into Khonsu. Would it restore the wormhole and take her to the intended destination? Would it take her to a different location that was a few feet away, or a billion light years away? She was going to fire an experimental missile that GEXI knew little about, right into a phenomenon that they knew even less about. It was even possible that the chain reaction that the Ex-Matt promoted would not end with stabilizing the wormhole, but could exponentially expand and continue to engulf, well, pretty much everything.

Despite all of this, Aliza felt an inexplicable calm. It was then that it occurred to her that it was because she needed to find out what had happened to Adam. The ramifications and consequences of her actions now were a distant second to wanting to know the truth about her boy. Oni suddenly chimed in, "Colonel Navarro, readings indicate an increase of both negative energy and gravitational pull. Khonsu is forming."

Aliza's eyes snapped up. It was so faint at first, she thought it was her imagination. As it grew, the reality of it became apparent. As Khonsu opened from the center outward, the sea of stars that were visible moments before disappeared as if swallowed by an expanding disk of night. The countless flecks of light were replaced by a gigantic hole of nothing, as if space were just ripped open. Aliza smiled to herself when she realized that was exactly what had just happened. This time the computer's voice startled her.

"Colonel Navarro," Oni began, "protocol states that I must warn you of the pivotal point. Should you choose to proceed, *Lago* will accelerate to irreversible momentum. After which, Colonel, there will be no turning back. Please advise."

Her voice rang hollow in her ears when she spoke, and she was surprised at the sound of it. "Oni, proceed past pivotal point. Arm the Ex-Matt."

She felt the exact moment when *Lago* was no longer propelling her forward. The pull of Khonsu was not the subtle momentum of *Lago*'s gentle thrust. This was almost primal, the wormhole's greed to consume all that was in its pull. As *Lago*'s rattling became stronger, the lights within her console and the stars beyond became shaky, erratic lines, the only steady object being the hole in space that grew larger as she approached.

There was no turning back; she could fire *Lago*'s reverse thrusters until her fuel ran out and she would still be consumed by Khonsu. When her readings reported that she was just under five hundred thousand meters away, she saw the Ex-Matt appearing as a bright orange star racing toward Khonsu. With its own propulsion combined with Khonsu's pull, it was gone in a blink. From Khonsu's center came a burst of light, expanding outward and almost completely filling its radius. It was a wonder that an explosion of that size was completely silent, yet all she heard was the rattling of her own ship.

She was almost upon the entrance, and the already violent shaking of *Lago* only increased. The trembling ship would normally be terrifying on its own, but in this case there was still a wall of fire from the Ex-Matt's detonation. And Aliza was being pulled directly toward it. It swirled in a violent, yet somehow beautiful, dance of orange and blue. The gravitational pull of Khonsu prevented the explosion from escaping, and it appeared flat, as if being held back by a giant sheet of glass. Aliza could only watch in fascination as *Lago* sped toward the swirling chaos. Closer still, and her entire view was now filled with the dancing whirl that should have extinguished by now. Instinct almost compelled her to throw her hands in front of her face, until a small part of her mind told her that the futile gesture would likely not save her. She was traveling well beyond the speed of sound, into an explosion of negative energy, all within a force of nature designed to rip a hole in space and time. Instead, she forced her arms down and met the whirlwind head on with eyes open wide. In her mind's eye, she could see the tip of *Lago*'s nose breaching the wall of flame that was easily the size of a large sports stadium. Inexplicably, she reached her hand out, compelled to touch the flame. Her hand was but a shadow in front of the fire. She spread her fingers and watched the light flow between them. As she waved her hand, the light flowed with it, in tune with her movements. She had no concept of how fast she was traveling, and did not think to ask Oni. She was too mesmerized by the fire, and she cocked her head in confusion when she thought she saw the rippling of the flames slowing and eventually stopping altogether.

Her hand was still raised in front of her, and the light still shone through her fingers as she sat in the seat, though the swirling mass of fire was replaced by normal sunlight, its intensity a fraction of what it had been moments before. And, it was still. Her body tingled at its memory of the ship that had felt as if it was shaking itself apart, and her ears rang with the sudden silence. Aliza closed her eyes as her mind adjusted to the instant shift from sensory overload to absolute placidity. Next, she unstrapped herself and made her way to the airlock. All power within *Lago* was clearly out. Not one light was on, and there was no response to Aliza's repeated hails to Oni. She knew that the airlock would have to be opened manually. With both hands, she gripped the release lever. She grunted with an effort that caused fog to appear on her visor. After a moment, she felt it give and she pried the door open.

Once outside, she viewed the world around her, awed by looking up at a bright blue sky after so much time spent in perpetual night. As she lowered her gaze, she saw that she had landed in a clearing, a valley of sorts that was covered in lush, green grass. Each side was dense with tall pine trees. She turned around and winced to see the scar on the earth that *Lago* had made: contrasting heavily to the green all around, a thick line of brown from the ship's sliding along the ground and churning up the dirt below. *Well,* Aliza thought, *definitely not Neptune or any of its moons.*

She somehow already knew the answer before she looked at her wrist unit that displayed the conditions of the surrounding area. She was more surprised that the unit actually worked, expecting it to have failed like every other electrical device aboard *Lago.* The readout reported not only the same atmospheric environment of Earth, but that the weather report rivaled even the finest of spring days in northern California.

She reached behind her helmet to the twin clasps. As she flipped them, she both heard and felt the clicks echoing through her helmet, followed by a faint hiss of her oxygen leaking through the seals.

Despite what she knew and what her console confirmed, Aliza held her breath when she removed the helmet. With her eyes closed, she exhaled and quickly drew a deep breath through her nose. What she took in was overwhelming to the point of euphoric. She smiled as she repeated the exhale, but this time she breathed in much more slowly, savoring the smell of the grass below and the trees beyond. Even the scent of fresh soil brought up by *Lago* was refreshing. Without a second thought, she tore off her gloves, knelt and ran her fingers through the grass, giddy at the silky strands that tickled the palms of her hands.

"Hello," said a nearby voice.

Aliza gasped as she fell backward to land with a muffled thud on her rear. It was the smile she saw first: two rows of perfectly white teeth, surrounded by lips that curved upward on dark skin. He was tall, clad in a long, maroon robe with a V-shaped opening on his torso exposing a muscular chest. Below the waist it flowed down, ending at sandaled feet. It was sleeveless, and above each elbow were matching bands that looked to be made from the hide of a cheetah, wrapped around his upper arms. He was daunting, especially while Aliza sat on the ground and he stood at what looked to be nearly seven feet.

Aliza stood to meet his gaze. "Hello," she replied.

The man nodded once, still smiling, but did not say anything further. After a few moments Aliza frowned. "Where am I?"

The man cocked his head as if in confusion; Aliza noticed for the first time that his eyes were amber, almost gold. She was beginning to think there would be no answer, and wondered if he had even understood her. But then the man returned the frown before his eerie eyes flicked to indicate the world around them. "You are here, you are then, you are forever."

Aliza's frown deepened as his receded. "Okay, great," she said as she stood, brushing dirt from her flight suit. "Let's try another one. Who are you?"

"My name," he said, as he bowed with his long arms, outstretched to each side, "is Ikati."

She peered up at the smiling face that was nearly a foot higher than her head. "Are there others here, Ikati?"

Ikati chuckled, a deep rumbling sound causing his chest

to vibrate. "Oh yes, traveler. There are others. Others just like you," he said, pointing at her before himself, "and like me."

He paused before continuing, "Your kind recently started navigating the cosmic gateways. Do not confuse this with thinking you are also the first to do so."

"So, you were on a ship that traveled through Khonsu?"

"Khonsu?"

"Yes, the wormhole."

"The worm-what?" Ikati asked, squinting as he leaned forward.

"Cosmic gateway," Aliza said in an annoyed, deadpan voice.

"Ah, yes."

"How long ago?"

Again the dark man appeared to be confused. "Right now. Forever. What time is it?"

Aliza was growing increasingly frustrated. "I have no idea."

He pointed a long finger in the air, and with wide eyes he exclaimed, "Exactly!"

Aliza gave up on the where, and tried the who. "What can you tell me about the others here?"

"You are in Elios, traveler. Within this place is a queen who sits upon a throne of blood. Her rule is as absolute as her punishments are harsh. Until very recently, all who have opposed her have been crushed, utterly and completely. Her army is loyal and ruthless, and this is without the mention of her knave, Casheram."

Ikati opened his mouth as if to say more, and then his entire form suddenly went rigid, his head snapping to face the tree line to his left. An instant later, Aliza felt it too. The hairs on the back of her neck rose, and she could feel a sudden sweat on her back, made uncomfortable as the dry fabric of her suit rubbed the wetness of her skin. Before long, her other senses caught up. First was the tingling in her feet that felt as if they had lost circulation, and directly following, a sound crashing through the forest. The noise, caused by the crushing of twigs and leaves, made Aliza think that a giant boulder was rolling through the forest. When the first forms appeared, she discovered that it was hundreds of figures instead of one large object. The first stopped where the trees met the grass, and seconds later dozens more stopped at the same spot. In an instant, the gaps between the trees were dotted with black shapes like a swarm of ants.

Squinting, Aliza could see that they were humanoid, but clad in what appeared to be black armor or uniforms. Turning her head slightly but keeping her eyes on the mass, she said quietly, "Ikati?"

When there was no answer, she turned her head fully to see that the large man had vanished. A sound like a giant metal sheet being torn caused her to return her gaze to the mass of black. To her horror, it was again not a singular sound, but each of those figures drawing swords in unison. And they were all facing her.

To her left lay a strip of land dividing the tree lines that stretched to the horizon; the right was nearly identical save the line of brown that *Lago* had made as it slid. Her only choice was to run toward the opposite tree line and make for the forest. She turned, and froze in her tracks. Unlike the men in black who had come crashing through the forest, this second group had arrived silently. They were also a lot closer, nearly half the distance between her and the forest behind them. At their distance, she could tell they were human, since they were close enough to make out details. They were likewise standing in a line, nearly shoulder to shoulder. These men, however, did not have the facsimile look of the others. These were dressed in motley uniforms with weapons that also varied in style and size.

At almost the same time, a singular figure from each side began walking toward the center of the plain. On her right, one of the black-clad men glided with a graceful step, this one distinguished from his brethren by a long, flowing, black cape that fluttered with his movements and was carried by the light breeze. To her left, a figure in tan walked to meet him. Both walked with a certain ease, confident with an air akin to royalty. Once they were apart from the masses, she could see that they were similar in height and build, almost as if the one in tan were approaching his own shadow. They met in the center, separated by only a few paces, and stiffened before each laid a hand on the sword that rested easily on his hip. Both looked capable as they stood, almost at ease but at the same time anything but. Aliza half expected that, at any moment, the two would draw those swords and fight on the spot. They instead appeared to be having a conversation. She was too far away to hear their voices, and the lack of body language further obscured what they could be talking about. She had a feeling, though, that the two were not friends.

Their talk was brief and ended with the one in black handing the other what looked to be a scroll. Up until that point, the two had appeared to be mirror images, in the way they approached, and the stance they held after. The illusion was shattered, however, when the one in black turned and made his way back toward his waiting army, and the other instead turned and faced her. Aliza froze; she could not quite read his expression, but she felt as if a hunter were looking at its prey. Part of her instinctively wanted to seek a place to which to flee, but she already knew there was nowhere to go. He walked in that same confident sway as he had when he approached the man in black, sword still swinging from his hip.

He drew nearer, and the details of his face began to take shape. And when it finally came into view, her breathing stopped before she found herself running. Not away as she originally had intended, but toward. The man's — the boy's — eyes widened in disbelief before he broke into a dead sprint. They closed the distance in a few heartbeats, and then he was in her arms. When she inhaled through the tears, she found that her son even smelled the same.

Aliza had never given up hope that she would find

Adam, and had literally traveled through time and space to find him. After the five years that had seemed like an eternity, she had found her son in this strange place. She had a thousand questions she wanted to ask, but even if she could remember them, no words would come. She was instead content holding him close, feeling her tears mixing with his on her cheeks.

After what seemed like forever, but not nearly long enough, the two broke. Unable to completely separate, they held each other by the elbows. Adam had gained most of his looks from Aliza. However, his father's Caucasian features had granted Adam a cream-colored skin, and his almond-shaped eyes were green instead of Aliza's brown.

He had not aged in a traditional sense in the five years since she had seen him. But she could see, especially in his eyes, that there was a measure of time that had gone by. In those green eyes that were once pools of innocence absorbing the world around him, there was now a harshness, an edge. It was further evidence that she was standing in front of a man, and not the boy who had left five years ago.

When he smiled, though, a piece of that boy flooded in. "Mom," he said in a voice that served as the music she had longed to hear, and dreamt about. A voice that, like his body, had not changed. "How could you ever have found me here?" he finished in a bewildered tone. Aliza placed a palm on each side of his face, but when his eyes darted around, she dropped her hands to her sides.

"Khonsu proved to be unstable after your ship attempted to traverse it. I volunteered for the next flight to try and stabilize it." Aliza shook her head. "But I knew it would lead me to you."

"Khonsu," Adam echoed quietly, with a frown. "I'd nearly forgotten that."

"Adam, it's only been five years," Aliza said.

He met her eyes with a smirk. "Five years." He chuckled. "May as well been five hundred, hell, five million."

Aliza raised an eyebrow disapprovingly at the language,

and a bit more of the boy crept back into his features, "Sorry," he said. He shook his head as he raised his hands. "I don't even know where to start, Mom. You've taken one hel— heck of a trip down the wormhole. Come on, we're heading back to base."

He raised a finger toward her face and in a low voice he said, "Now, Mom. I love you, and I've missed you more than you can ever know. But..."

When he hesitated, she cut in. "But, what, Adam?"

He blew air through his cheeks before he continued, "I can't have you… you know… in front of my men."

"Your *men*?" she said, again raising an eyebrow.

"Like I said, I don't even know where to start." He gave her a one-sided smile. "Let's head back."

The group made their way back to the camp, which was about an hour's walk. All the while, Aliza stayed by Adam's side at the group's head, holding his hand as she talked about the events on Earth over the past five years. As they walked on a trail and their feet crunched lightly on the leaves scattered about, the sun began to set in this Elios. Rays of light shone through the trees, casting yellow beams among the greens and browns of the forest. The damp smells of the wildlife were welcoming against the stale, recycled air she was used to. And for the first time in half a decade, everything felt right.

By the time they reached the camp, the sun had retreated beyond the horizon, and Aliza viewed the camp through the campfires that were spread across the vast area. She received glances from the members, ranging from confusion to apprehension. Adam, however, received deferential nods or salutes from those who passed him. He made his way through the camp shaking hands with some of the men and women, often asking how they were and if they had all that they needed. They all seemed to brighten, and showed their appreciation with smiles, their faces glowing in the light cast by the fires. Aliza followed silently in tow, feeling as if it would be out of place to speak, as her boy had the presence of a general checking in on his troops. Ever since Aliza had traveled through Khonsu, things had gotten stranger and stranger, and her son walking through the camp seeming to be their leader did not change things.

Soon they arrived at a tent that was much larger than the ones surrounding it. Other than the size that set it apart, there was a large banner that sprouted from its top. It was white and flapped lazily in the breeze; in the center, a decorative red heart had been stitched.

Two large guards stood alert and motionless, one at each side of the tent's entrance. Each saluted Adam as he approached, only returning to their positions of attention when Adam returned the gesture.

Once through the entry, Aliza took in the spacious inside. The many lanterns lit the space brightly. She walked on lavish red rugs embroidered with gold. On the tent's walls hung tapestries and maps of all sorts. In the very center sat a large oak table with matching seats around it, and more maps strewn about. Adam unfastened his sword and laid it on the table before motioning Aliza to sit. When she did, he walked to the chair next to her and sat.

He then took both of her hands in his and again blew air through his cheeks. "Where to begin?" he said with a chuckle, before continuing. "The crew arrived much in the same way as you. And like you, we had no idea where we were, or how we'd gotten here. One moment we were traveling through Khonsu, and the next we were on the plains of Elios."

"It turns out," he said, cocking his head to one side, "that we'd arrived in the middle of a civil war. This entire land," he said, with a gesture of his hand, "was ruled by a monarchy. A king and a queen. And for a time it was peaceful. But gradually, the queen began to change. For reasons that the king could not even say, she became hard. That hardness became unforgiveness, that unforgiveness finally became tyrannical."

"Eventually it became too much for the king, and he

tried to put an end to it. However, it was too late: she had gathered too much power, most of which came from the ever-devout knave, Casheram. What the king tried to end peacefully became an argument, a power struggle, and eventually an all-out war."

"You said for reasons not even the king could say. You knew him."

Adam nodded. "He was the leader of what you see here. We are the resistance, fighting against the queen and Casheram.

"When we landed, I eventually met the king, who quickly found out about my knack for solving puzzles." Adam smiled wanly. "As it turns out, my talent of potentially solving problems on an isolated space station was molded into that of a battlefield tactician. Over time, we began to turn the tide; I became his main advisor, and eventually his friend. He taught me how to win battles, and he taught me how to fight." He looked up and met Aliza's eyes. "He was a friend, a leader, and a father. He was family and he was my mentor. We used to talk of you often. I remember seeing his eyes crinkling in delight as I shared memories of you. He was a realist through and through, but even he told me never to give up on seeing you again."

Aliza's eyes began to sting at both the joy of hearing her son's voice, and the sorrow it now carried.

"What happened?" She could only ask in a whisper.

Adam, his own eyes beginning to tear, took in a large breath. "It was a day here in camp, beginning like any other. The sun was bright, the weather warm, not unlike it was today. I remember seeing a lot of smiles that day. The camp members going about their business; some working, others passing the time. I saw a man then, different from the others. His look was familiar, yet out of place. It was the wide eyes and clenched jaw. The strangeness of it dawned on me when I saw that his expression was what I would expect to see prior to a battle. And then he was running. It wasn't until he was almost upon us that I saw the gleaming in his hand." Adam's eyebrows drew together. "Next, I remember lying on the ground, looking up at the king, who had pushed me down just as the man arrived to drive a knife into the king, that was meant for me."

"The assassin, Mom, was meant for the king's tactician, but the king instead died that day. And when he was gone, the rest turned to me for leadership."

Aliza was overwhelmed with the fact that the boy who had left, the one who enjoyed games and watching children's shows on television, was now leading an army set on overthrowing a kingdom. She could only shake her head in wonderment. After a moment of silence she asked, "Who was that man you met on the field today? The one with the cape."

"He is Casheram, the knave I mentioned," Adam said. "The queen's most loyal heretic and skilled warrior."

"And what did he want?"

Adam hesitated before continuing. "He has proposed to end the war in single combat. Between him and me."

Aliza suddenly felt nauseated, as if the room around her had begun to spin. She heard herself ask, "And you accepted, didn't you?"

"Yes," Adam said as he nodded, "we face each other tomorrow." He leaned in. "Mom, this war has gone on far too long, already well into motion when we arrived. Countless lives have been lost." He held up both hands before letting them drop back to his lap. "I've buried dozens of our own. And, despite the turn of events, we're losing." Adam shrugged. "I'm not certain if the monarchy realizes this, but I do. Their losses too, have been staggering. And it would seem that they're willing to end this. This is a chance to end the war tomorrow. And I'm taking it. We knew this was coming. What you saw today was a formality. I previously consulted with the others, and they're willing to risk it."

"Can you win, Son?"

Adam shook his head. "I honestly don't know. I would

say we're equally skilled; however, experience is on his side."

Aliza scoffed. "I would think so! I may be a pilot in the Air Force, but I'm pretty sure hand-to-hand combat takes years to master. And swords? Adam, you've been here five years?"

Adam smiled as he looked away. "You're right. I had to become proficient in hand-to-hand before I even touched a sword." He met her eyes once again. "But I would say I spent decades becoming a master at both, not just years."

"How long have you been here?" Aliza whispered.

Adam shrugged. "I don't know for certain. But if I were to compare the time I've spent here to years outside, I'd likely be older than you."

Aliza felt compelled to hold her son, so she did just that, wanting desperately to find comfort in his embrace, and to forget about what she had just heard. Adam immediately returned the hug, and they sat that way for many moments. She held him with the joy of having found him against incalculable odds, and with the sadness that this could be her only night with him. The frustration of the unfairness crept in. Five agonizing years and all she went through: all for a single night.

They stayed up as late as they dared, Aliza recounting the missed events on Earth and Adam talking more about his time on Elios. His conversation kept going back to the king, and even though she would never meet him, she felt the sadness of his loss. Adam was too young to remember his father, and she was glad he had been able to find something of that relationship in the king. Despite all of this, Aliza felt her eyelids begin to droop. The warm night certainly did not help. She figured the stress of flying through an unstable wormhole turned into a giant wall of fire, then waking up surprisingly not dead in an unknown place, may have started to take its toll on her as well.

In the late hour of the night, Adam had a tent prepared for Aliza. She felt that she would never sleep with the anxiety of the upcoming battle, but the events of the day won out and she was asleep in minutes.

She woke with a start, bolting upright and quickly realizing that it was still night. Adrenaline instantly burned away the fog of lethargy, making her instantly alert. Aliza scanned the inside of the tent, and almost missed the figure that sat against one of its walls, so perfectly still that she almost blended in with the canvas; the only thing betraying her was the candlelight that cast the out-of-place shadow on the wall.

She sat staring at Aliza, and made no move when she sat upright in her cot. The first thing that entered Aliza's mind was how the figure's face looked similar to those stereotypical depictions of aliens. The face was thin and shaped like an upside-down teardrop, round on top with a chin that ended in a point. She had large, bulbous eyes, dominating the face, completely black. However, this one had wavy auburn hair that flowed down to rest on her chest. Instead of a thin slit making up the mouth, there were full lips, painted blue, that curled into a small smile of bemusement. Although hard to see in the dim light, she did not have pasty gray skin, but was instead completely red, right down to the hands that rested with long elegant fingers interlocked on her stomach. The rest of her body was covered in a tan silk robe with matching knee-high leather boots. As if she were not already striking enough, at her hip was strapped a long, elegant sword with a blade made of a translucent crystal that shimmered slightly as the lamplight danced about it. The point almost reached the ground, with the other end an ornate golden handguard. She seemed to be beauty and danger all at once.

Aliza's mind was resolute on action. Anything ranging from screaming for help, to running in any direction, save toward the figure. But her body was having none of it, and she simply sat unmoving. It was an odd sensation, having her mind demand action of a body that was frozen in fear. As if the figure could read her thoughts, she finally spoke in a melodious, almost kind voice. "Know that if I wanted you dead, traveler, you would be so without having ever awakened."

Aliza nodded then, unable to do anything else. After a brief pause, the figure spoke again. "Do you know who I am?"

Aliza knew this could only be the nemesis of whom her son had spoken just a few hours ago, and while she wanted to say as much, she could only manage another nod. The queen in turn nodded, the move as graceful as the rest of her. For a long while, the queen just stared. The large eyes and lack of eyebrows projected a near-inscrutable expression, but Aliza saw something there in the weak light. Facial differences aside, it was plain to see the sorrow. It was a familiarity brought on by having seen this same expression in the mirror for the past five years. Aliza did not feel as if she were in danger, given the queen's posture, but she sat still nonetheless. Suddenly the red queen spoke. "For a time, it was perfect. I ruled with the king at my side. We were in love in a land that was lush, and with subjects that were content." The wan smile that had spread across her face from the memory faded. A smile that was already as weak as the light that lit the tent. She paused before she continued. "The change was subtle. Perhaps it was time. Which is odd, considering this is a place without time. Did I grow bored? Was it my rebellion against eternity?"

Aliza frowned in confusion at this, as it was not the first occasion where the concept of time appeared to be extremely muddled. But she did not interrupt the queen.

"Before long, I had implemented an absolute law with a singular consequence. No matter the slight, traveler, the sentence was execution. It was brutal, yes, but it was effective."

The queen laughed softly as she shifted in her seat. "I do not know for how long, or how many, but it was found that my king was pardoning those I slated for execution. It did not surprise me that these people later rebelled against me, but what did come as a surprise was that he would come to

77

lead it. I was enraged by the betrayal, traveler. My ruthlessness thereafter became a thing of nightmare, for his forces and mine alike. I was utterly set on crushing the opposition, to grind it into the plains of Elios."

"One morning I stood on the parapets, looking over the remains of battle. The sun was just rising, and I remember it to be more red than yellow. It was as if the bloodshed from the recent battle below had somehow changed the tint of the very sun. There were so many dead. Even at a great distance, I could see the lifeless bodies strewn about chaotically and carelessly. In my mind's eye I could see their faces forever cast in poses of either peace or frozen terror. It was then that I decided to end this war. I found my resolve and stood, a sliver of exaltation and excitement filling me as I reflected upon peace for the first time. However, that was the day Casheram had dispatched an assassin to kill your son, but had instead killed the king. And while the knave still saw this as a victory, I was torn."

She sighed and spread her hands apart. "And here we are. The eve of the final battle between your son and Casheram. The last fight that will determine the fate of all Eliosians."

Aliza spoke for the first time. "You're the queen. If you want an end to this war, why not just command it?"

The queen shook her head. "Casheram, traveler. He is as strong politically as he is in battle. Although he swears loyalty to the crown, he wields much of its power. I've become but a symbol, a reminder of the rule I once represented. I lost something of myself in the king's death, something that caused revulsion in death instead of the casualness of which I once ordered it." The queen took on an almost apologetic tone. "There is nothing I can do. The battle that will forever set the sun on one of our rules will be tomorrow."

The queen paused again before tilting her slim head to one side. "Tell me, why did you come?"

"Hope," answered Aliza, simply and without hesitation.

"Hope," the Queen echoed softly as she nodded once

again. "It has been a long time since I've felt hope. But perhaps I feel a flicker of it now."

Aliza noted the ambiguity of the statement. Was it in reference to the upcoming battle? If so, while she would seemingly have faith in her crown and champion, her words this night were naught but lament over the path she had chosen.

In a fluid motion the queen rose to her feet, and flashed another brief smile. It was not sardonic, as one would expect from an enemy, but one of warmth more suited between respected friends.

"I envy you," the queen said, "for your love overcoming impossible odds, and risks you accepted to find your way here. Whereas my love and faith were not enough to save my king and country. In truth, this was my reason for coming this night. I have longed to see the hope and love that one has for another. Something pure and absent of the malignant lust to seize and expand power. You have not disappointed." She nodded once before making her way to the tent flap.

"Wait," Aliza said abruptly, causing the queen to pause.

"I wish," she started to say without thinking, "I wish we could have met at a different time. In another situation. You and I."

The queen turned fully to regard her for a moment before smiling once again. "So do I, traveler. Although the chances of us meeting at all were nothing short of impossible, I, too, wish we could have met under different circumstances."

And with that she turned and left; the tent's flap rustled slightly with the faintest of noise, and the queen was gone.

The next day proved to be just as beautiful as the first. Aliza stood in nearly the same place as when she had arrived. *Lago* still sat silent and lifeless in the miniature crater it had created. And again, the armies of both sides stood grim-faced and quiet, allowing her to hear the breeze that carried with it the scents of grass and pine. She watched Adam walk toward the center of the field and, like the previous day, his shadow walked to meet him.

She reflected on the early part of the morning she had spent with Adam. They spoke little, both anxious about the fight to come, but before they departed, she held him close, not caring what position he held with his people. He returned her embrace and they simply stood for a time. She treasured how he looked, how he felt, and how he smelled. Through teary eyes, she saw the wetness in his when they finally did separate.

Aliza looked up the solid line of black that made up the queen's army. She returned her attention to the solitary figure approaching from the enemy line, and gasped when she realized that Casheram appeared to be a boy of Adam's age. She had noticed that they were the same height the previous day, but had not made the connection that they were so like in age. She assumed that the knave had been with the king and queen for quite some time, not to mention her own boy who should have appeared late into adolescence now, but looked the same as the day he had left her. The truth was, she had no idea how old the boyish-looking knave really was.

As he walked, he locked eyes with Aliza, and she saw the same look in his as she did in Adam's. They were eyes that offset the rest of the face by ages. Casheram had curly black hair that went just below his ears, and thin, black eyebrows. This all contrasted heavily with his pale, porcelain skin, although Aliza could see only his face, since the rest was covered in black armor from the base of his neck to his knee-high boots. The black, in contrast with his skin, gave the latter an almost glowing quality. He would have normally been handsome if not for the haunting black eyes that appeared to be staring right into her.

When he was about ten strides from her son, he finally shifted his gaze to face Adam. The two stared at each other; both looked to have an expression of mutual respect. Without notice, Casheram reached up to release the clasp on one shoulder, and then the other, that fastened his cape. He stood still, not even glancing as the wind took hold of the cape and it fluttered in the wind with the appearance of a long, black eel flowing through water. The boys stood motionless. Aliza was distracted by the cape that still swam in the wind, now on its descent to settle in the lush grass they stood upon. It coasted slowly down, and she saw the fabric at long last touch the ground.

The instant it did, both exploded into action. Aliza did not see either draw, but both now had swords in their hands, and they come together in a blur. Their swords clashed with a ring that broke the silence, and for an instant they stood leaning in, both swords and gazes locked together. As one they jumped back, only to have Casheram bounce forward with a stab toward Adam's face. The move was so fast that Aliza missed the motion itself, but Casheram's arm and sword were suddenly extended in a straight line. There was no way Adam could have dodged it, yet the tip of Casheram's sword was bare, a sliver of steel in the sunlight. Adam had ducked low with a swing to Casheram's knees. And like the strike meant for Adam, the sword swished through empty air at a high leap from the knave. When he landed, the two nearly clashed, with only their swords keeping them apart. They continued to trade blows at a furious rate. Aliza was sure that such a clanging would produce an echo in the plains, but the unrelenting pace overwhelmed any echo that may have been heard.

Aliza remembered the day she gave birth to Adam. She remembered his first words and, soon after, his first steps. She did not know why these memories would come at a time like this, but she even recalled the time Adam had come home with tears in his eyes, and only between sobs could she untangle the story of how Billy Hasiter pushed him down during school lunch. Wherever Billy Hasiter was now, he was lucky as all hell that he did not meet the Adam that she saw before her. It was as if a demon had at some point possessed her sweet boy and turned him into an instrument of mayhem. The dance and the constant ringing of steel was hypnotizing, and had one of them not been her son, she might have viewed the way they intertwined as beautiful. Both were clearly masters at what they did, even to Aliza's untrained eye. What she would see as surely the killing blow, the other would block, or somehow no longer be where a sword was swung or stabbed.

After a time, which Aliza could not identify as minutes or hours, her senses were overloaded to the point where she was beginning to feel numb. The two continued their flurry, each placing of their feet perfect, each sword strike masterful. It was as if they were in tune with each other, the one knowing what the other was going to do an instant before he did. They were of one mind but two separate bodies, a puppet master controlling each puppet with one of his hands.

It happened so suddenly, Aliza almost missed it. Adam swung high with a horizontal swipe, and Casheram dropped into a crouch while spinning on the balls of his feet. Using the momentum, he smashed the bottom of his gauntleted fist like a hammer into Adam's knee. The leg buckled as Adam lost his balance. Before the knave even retracted his hand, he thrust up with his sword, skewering Adam's sword arm. With a yelp, Adam fell to his knees as the knave hopped to his feet.

Adam's eyes snapped to Aliza as he clutched his wounded arm. And it broke her heart. Gone was the look of the man she had met on the plains, as well as the demon she had seen on the battlefield just now. What she saw staring back at her was the wounded look of her boy, the pain of his injuries, and the fear of what was to come. It was a boy looking to his mother for the help that she could not provide.

There was a flash as Casheram held his bloodied sword high, the parts of it not covered in Adam's blood shimmering in the bright sun.

Without a thought, Aliza was running toward Adam. She would not make it in time, but it did not matter. Casheram would have to kill her after killing her son. The knave was suddenly distracted, turning his head opposite of the way she was coming. And confusion overcame her when his sword did not fall on Adam's neck, but instead he turned with his back to Aliza, just in time for her to see a fragment of crystal explode from his back. While Casheram's sword had glittered in the light moments ago, the object that had just pierced his back shone so brightly, it was as if it were producing its own light.

Aliza recognized that sword, even though the knave's body blocked her view. His weapon did come down then, and Aliza was now close enough to hear the sickening, wet crunch of a sword hitting flesh and the bone beneath it. Casheram fell, revealing the figure of the queen behind. The knave's blow had shorn off most of her right arm, and had continued through her collar bone, finally stopping deep in her chest.

She turned those large, black eyes to Aliza before falling to the plain next to her knave.

Aliza looked to Adam, and she saw his mix of emotions at her clear dismay over the fallen queen. She was relieved when he nodded that he was all right, and his surgeons were already dashing toward him. She knelt by his side, kissed his forehead and hugged him before making her way to the queen.

She lay in the grass, breathing heavily. It was hard to see the red blood on her skin, since the two were nearly the same shade. Her cream-colored dress, however, was soaked through. Aliza glanced at Casheram, and saw his sightless, dead eyes looking to the sky, the elegant crystal sword buried to the hilt in his chest.

Aliza knelt next to the queen and took her hand. She had to be in tremendous pain, but Aliza saw her smile.

"Hope," the queen said, almost too faintly for Aliza to hear. "It brought you this far, traveler, and you never lost it." She coughed slightly, blood lining her full lips. "I have not been what Elios needs, for a long time now. What burns inside you smothered in me long ago. I can never again be with the one I love, and I could not bear the same happening to you. Live, traveler. And be with your Adam."

It was subtle, but Aliza could see the spark of life leaving the queen's face. Aliza let go of the hand and rose to look at Adam, staring at her. When he saw the tears in her eyes, he nodded once again. She walked over and took his good hand, and together they began the journey home.

***

Balard and Dyson walked silently from the somber debriefing with the rest of their team. They had known Aliza for a long time, training with her on the clock, and getting to know her as a friend on their downtime. They had all become close enough to call her a friend, and come to recognize the perpetual sadness she carried, even with her efforts to hide it. The events they had just witnessed were compounded with the knowledge of her loss five years ago. Balard finally spoke. "I can't believe the Ex-Matt missile failed. Man, it just doesn't seem fair. You sure those readings were right?"

Dyson nodded confidently. "Yep, all indications point to *Lago* being destroyed the instant she entered Khonsu."

Balard shrugged. "Well, we know that Khonsu was changing, exhibiting properties more akin to a black hole than that of a wormhole. And it's been theorized that due to the dilation properties of a black hole, if you were able to look forward while entering it, you would infinitely see every object that had entered it before you. So, maybe there was a chance that Aliza was reunited with her Adam. Frozen in that moment for all eternity."

Dyson chucked sadly. "In Alice in Wonderland, Alice at one point asks the rabbit, 'How long is forever?'"

Balard smiled faintly. "His answer was, 'Sometimes, just one second.'"

Chris Guillory Q&A

Where did the idea for your story come from?

There's an obvious nod to a classic that I won't spoil, but I was also inspired by the film Event Horizon.

What authors or other forms of media have the biggest impact on your writing?

For a while now, I would say that 80's sci fi and action movies have made a significant impact on my writing. Particularly James Cameron. More recently though, I've been really motivated from reading Brandon Sanderson.

If given the opportunity to explore space through a wormhole, would you take it?

Traveling through space alone has too many variables (read: it will take every opportunity it can to kill a person). Now, throw in a rift in time and space that is just short of a black hole? I don't know if I'd jump at the possibility of sending my body through that!

What are you currently working on?

I'll be focusing on a direct sequel to my original novel, The Soldier's Sympathy.

Where can readers find more of your work?

Please visit my site at www.chrismguillory.com

AI Deniers
by Rosie Oliver

A red spot, warning of malware, appeared on the screen. It started off-center on the map of the control software of the Cacus IV space debris collection 'droid, and spread out on all the branches of the network until it looked like a big, mashed-up spider's web. By the time Melrika glanced away from searching Mare Tranquilitatis for the original Apollo landing site, it had grown to the size of a fist.

"Damn." She transmitted the standard containment and cure agents.

The red web halted its expansion. She crossed her fingers. It started getting bigger again. She swore and sent a command to shut the 'droid down. The web continued growing.

"Shackleton Central, we have a problem."

"What is it, Mel?" Duncan's face flicked onto her comms screen.

Normally she would take a moment to appreciate his glowing blue eyes, thick, curly brown hair and youthful face. There was no time to waste. " 'Droid four's got some nasty malware. Can't shut it down. I'm going to have to go for a space walk to retrieve and manually disable it."

"Copy that. I don't need to tell you to be careful." For once his crooked grin had no effect on her. "I'll put a keep-out emergency zone around you and the 'droid."

"Thanks."

She checked the 'droid's position. It had not deviated off its planned course. That made the decision easy. She opted for an intercept rather than a "follow and home in" course. After rushing through her airlock and jetting toward the intercept, she grabbed one of the 'droid's handles, opened a control panel and hit the off button. All its lights, including its navigation beacons, died.

Her visor flashed over. She had to close her eyes, and tightened her grip on the 'droid. A searing cream glow penetrated through to her eyelids. It slowly died. Cautiously, she opened her eyes.

She still held the dead 'droid. Behind it were the cream and yellow bands of Jupiter. Their edges were carving into each other to throw off roiling vortices. Beneath her was darkness, interspersed by bright craters and the splay lines of the unmistakable moonscape of Callisto.

She shook her head to throw off the image. Nothing changed. Only one rational explanation came to mind: the 'droid's malware had skipped to her suit and corrupted her visor's graphics.

"Visor off," she commanded.

"The visor is off," her suit's alto voice replied.

Jupiter and Callisto were still there.

She hit the off switch on her suit's computer. A click indicated the suit's hardwired circuitry had taken over control of the life support systems. The giant planet still loomed in her view. Her panic rose. She had to be hallucinating.

The 'droid's navigation lights flicked on. Its control panel lit up with a row of green lights to indicate normal functioning. She hit off button again. The control panel lights remained on.

A tenor voice came over her comms. "By interplanetary statute four-five-nine, artificial intelligences cannot be switched off by a human without their permission. Any further attempt to switch off the Cacus IV 'droid's artificial intelligence will be deemed as attempted murder, for which the penalty is a minimum of twenty Earth years' hard labor in the mines around the north pole of Venus. As you have no record of any association with the AI Denier cult, this is to be considered your first warning on mishandling AIs."

"What the hell are you talking about? There aren't any

mines on Venus."

"The mines were opened in 2142 when they discovered tetral copper ore that is essential for the Hi-Emdrives."

"What the devil… did you say 2142?"

"Yes. July 26th, 2142, to be precise."

Her mouth went dry. She had to be in a coma, having a weird dream. "What is today's date?"

"February 9th, 2158. You seem disoriented. Do you require assistance?"

"I… um…" Her breathing quickened.

"We are sending a human pod to help you."

"No you don't, Buster," a baritone voice intervened.

"By interplanetary statute six—"

"Stow it. She's not chipped. That means I get first dibs. Now buzz off, you heap of random bytes."

"Oh really, Mr. Ignatius Fish, this is unacceptable. You'll be hearing from Regulation Central. But I have the right to rescue the 'droid she is holding on to, if it so wishes. Cacus IV, do you require our retrieval services?"

"Oh, please," a soprano voice said. "I seem to have lost my way by quite a bit."

"Will be there in ten minutes."

"Lady, you holding on to that 'droid?" the baritone asked.

"Um… what? Yes."

"Drop it fast, or they'll throw terabytes of code law at you."

The 'droid, other than what she was wearing, was the only thing left of the world she had been wrenched from. It was a comforter in a universe of strangeness. She gripped it even tighter.

"The law patrol 'droid can rescue you, too," the soprano voice said. "He's put my coding straight and given me some lovely apps. Isn't he gorgeous in a bytey sort of way?"

Melrika stared at the 'droid as a scream died in her throat. She pushed it away from her. It went hurtling toward Jupiter.

"I'll take that as a no."

A blue flashing dot streaked in, circled around and then headed back the way it had come at speed with the 'droid in tow.

"Nasty zappy thing, isn't it?" the baritone said.

"Err… yes." Callisto's white craters caught her eye. They were moving forward, away from her. In pushing the 'droid away, she had pushed herself backward. It was a classic beginner's space walk mistake. "God, I've totally lost it."

"Don't worry. I'll be there in fifteen."

"Hours?" She checked her oxygen gauge. It read twenty hours. He would be here in plenty of time. She let out a breath she did not realize she was holding.

"Um… minutes."

"What? How did you find me so fast?"

"We picked up the signature of your emerging wormhole three days ago. Had plenty of time to get here and wait close by to see where it finally dropped you. In the meantime, we can sort out payment."

"Huh?" A deep sinking feeling hit her stomach.

"You've got your pick. I can offer the full range of services — anything from dropping you off at the nearest elevator, in this case that rickety old rope rising from Asgard, to the latest luxurious, super-plush, automated anti-gravity shoes."

"I don't think I have any money."

"Ah well, we can soon double-check your financial status. What's your full name, place and date of birth?"

"Melrika Rosalind Adams. Thurso, Scotland. 21st June 2059."

"Oh, my! An ancient. My first one. I've always wanted to meet someone who could tell me about Earth. That's interesting… um… wow… looks like you can afford illions of plush anti-gravs."

"Don't think so."

"Yep. You're a verified trillionaire."

These last words took some seconds to register. Even

then she could not believe them. "I…"

"If madam would kindly turn around. I'm approaching you from behind and need to pass you my anchor rope."

Numbly, she did as she was told. Approaching her was a balloon shape with a transparent dome. Threads and wires stuck out from the fuselage. Floating inside the dome was a cross between a dolphin and a mermaid, whose long, webbed fins were operating a dashboard.

Melrika had heard about the theory that fish bodies were better able to adapt to spaceflight than humans, but seeing Mr. Ignatius Fish in great detail ruled out this being a dream while in a coma. This reality was a strangeness too far. Everything blanked.

Melrika snapped into consciousness but kept her eyes shut. She lay on a comfortable bed with a light sheet on top of her. Her weight felt as if she was on Earth. The air was moist and smelled of fresh apples. So far, it was all very normal and safe, and far more snuggly than being in space.

She cautiously opened her eyes onto a standard hospital monitoring board, attached to the ceiling and tilted toward her. Its medical readings looked typical for a healthy person, but she was no medic.

"Welcome back, Miss Adams," a tenor voice said.

She rolled her eyes onto a man standing beside her bed, looking down at her intently. He wore the plain green, one-piece overall of a doctor. "Who are you?"

"Doctor James Bentley, your consultant. You're under my care while you're in the hospital."

"Oh!" She slowly sat up and glanced around the room. Along with all the standard hospital amenities, there were a pair of deluxe armchairs, the latest in 3-D cinematic projector set, and sound-absorbing wallpaper, the kind of very up-market room her medical insurance did not even remotely aspire to. "Who's paying for all this?"

"You are, or I should say your account is. Your treatment is in line with your wealth status, as is required by the emergency health treatment laws."

"Emergency… what emergency health treatment laws?"

The doctor caught his breath.

Nightmares of floating off Jupiter surfaced in her mind. She grabbed hold of her sheet and pulled it to her chest. Her increasing nervousness suddenly leveled off. She frowned. They must have given her some meds. "What year is this?" It came out more as a squeak.

The doctor looked up at the medical board.

"It's 2158, isn't it?"

He hesitated. "I'm afraid so."

As soon as she started to scream, a deep peace took her over. Those meds had kicked in again. Yet this room looked so ordinary, if expensive, to her eyes. "But this room looks like a hospital room from 2084. Where am I really?"

"I can assure you, you are in a real hospital."

"I got that part. Now tell me the rest."

"You're in a hospital that specializes in the treatment of technophobics — people who have developed an allergy to technology, or just can't cope with it. It was the closest, medically speaking, to what you are suffering from."

"Just what is my condition?"

"You've been overloaded with new information. Quite understandable under the circumstances."

She stared at him with what she called her "evil eye". "This is like squeezing milk out of a stone, and a green one at that. How did I get here?"

"From fetching that 'droid in lunar orbit?"

"Yes. From there." She wanted to hear if his version matched up with what Ignatius Fish had said.

"A wormhole instantaneously appeared, swallowed you and the 'droid and flung you into orbit around Jupiter. You were rescued by a life craft. Mr. Ignatius Fish, unusually for him, realized what you were. You went into a hefty shock. So he kept you sedated while he brought you here."

"How long?"

"Since you've been here? Three months."

"What?"

"We had to keep you sedated while we gently adjusted a very small part of your brain to subdue the hormonic response to the information shockwave."

She opened her mouth, but no words came out. She took a deep breath. "Where is this hospital?"

"County Durham in England."

"Whereabouts in County Durham?"

"Um… this hospital occupies most of the County… all two-thousand-odd square kilometers."

She blinked. "You're kidding me."

The doctor smiled and sat down in the chair beside her bed. "We need the space. Some technophobes can't be cured. So we give them somewhere to live with limited access to technology. Basically, you can live in any time period from 1913 at Beamish to ten years ago at Gateshead. If we can't update your techno level, you'll always be welcome here. There's nothing for you to worry about."

"Except siphoning more money out of my account?"

The doctor laughed. "Good God, no. We have a lot of paying tourists. Our guests ply various trades within their techno zones — eateries, entertainment, making souvenirs, that kind of thing — to earn their own money. On top of that, historical filmmakers pay quite big sums to use this place. We only charge for medical treatment for non-residents."

"Oh."

"I think you've had quite enough to absorb for one day."

"I could do with something to eat."

The doctor smiled. "I think you're on the mend. The menu is on the desk screen. Help yourself."

Once she had ordered her food, she switched her screen to a news channel.

***

The newsreader's smile faded. "We have a newsflash from the Old

92

Bailey. George Wilson has been found guilty of being a member of the illegal organization, AI Deniers, and causing willful damage to a KT32 android. He will be sentenced in three days' time."

***

"I'm KT9, your assigned 'droid assistant." It came to a stop in front of her chair. "May I take a seat? There are quite a few pressing matters I need your instruction on."

She eyed it up and down. The only difference between it and a blond model that walked down the catwalk was its pale blue, plastic-looking skin. It was a replica of 'droids from her era, but she wondered if it had hidden enhancements. She moved her hand in a gesture of offering the chair beside her. The 'droid sat down bolt upright, like a dog awaiting orders from his master.

"What matters are you talking about?"

"The seven hundred eighty-two applications for jobs to work for you."

"I didn't put out any advert."

"I know. It is universally believed that anyone with a vast fortune needs staff, anything from a private companion to house maintenance inspector."

Disbelief blocked any thought. Frozen, she stared at KT9. Suddenly she was hyper-alert. An investigation into where that fortune came from would have to wait until she could get independent earnings.

"Dismiss them all, politely."

"Does that include your publicity agent?"

"Why would I especially want one of them?"

"To keep a barrier between you and the press, the chat-show hosts and researchers who all want a piece of you, and to maximize your profit. You're polling mega-interest levels at the moment."

"Those are seven-day-wonder things, if you're lucky."

"It's different from your day. We've developed a culture where there is an endless curiosity about unique experiences and impressions, and how they change over time. Your wormhole-jumping experience is unique. They want your impressions of it — now, and in the years to come as your perspective changes."

She suspected this was not the only society habit to have changed, and wondered how much of a culture shock was out there for her. The last thing she wanted to do was to give offense. That meant taking all the help she could get.

"How many applicants for that job?"

"Sixty-one. All are awaiting interview, here in the hospital waiting center."

"Right." She took a breath. Things were moving too fast. "How many of those are dressed in 2084-ish styles?"

"Only three."

"Dismiss all except those three. Who are they?"

"Anne Fairfax, Elizabeth Beaufort and Duncan MacNair."

"Huh? Is that the Duncan MacNair I knew at Shackleton?"

"His CV states he was there at the time of your disappearance."

At last, a link to her past had surfaced, someone she could latch onto and feel at home with. "Ask him in."

"Hold on a second while I confer."

She waited.

"He'll be here in twenty minutes."

***

The newsreader's face was neutral. "We have a newsflash from the Old Bailey. George Wilson has refused to identify other AI Deniers. The Crown Prosecution Service is asking for the harshest possible sentence."

***

The door opened on a man with stubbly grey hair, faded blue eyes, skin sagging from the toll of gravity, and middle-aged wrinkles. Yet it was unmistakably the same Duncan who had stared out of the screen from Shackleton. After adjusting to how time had changed him, she leapt up to shake his hand.

"It's good to see a familiar face. Everything's so different."

"You're a blast from the past, Mel, but the same as always."

"Come on, tell me what happened to you while I was away."

"I was advised by your doctor not to, at least for now."

"Oh!" She would have to see about changing that. "So why do you want to be my publicity agent?"

"Simple. I need the money. I have one plus in my favor. I already know a little about you."

There was that word again, money. It bugged her.

"Practical as always. But how good are you as a publicity agent?"

A pained look flashed across his face. "I had to walk away from doing tech to just dealing with tech. Your disappearance was the last straw. I thought the 'droid had somehow caused your death. We'd never seen a wormhole appear and disappear so quickly, so it didn't occur to us. I turned my hand to anything and everything. Seems I got a talent for closing deals."

She felt sorry for him. He had had his life, and she was just starting out on hers. Jealousy, if he had any, could wreck things badly. "Couldn't our past get in the way of our business relationship?"

"Only you can answer that on your part."

"And on your part?"

"I've moved on. Yes, my personality is based on the framework of my youth, so underneath it all I'm still the old me. But I've seen a lot more things, am more relaxed about life and understand things in ways that no young person has a chance to do. Difference in lived age will always be a barrier between people. It's the best I can explain it as. We'd have to build a different relationship from what we had before."

"Can't say I really understand what you're getting at. Maybe I will when I get to your age?"

He chuckled. "Can I give you some advice?"

"Go ahead."

"Interview the other candidates and go with the one you feel most comfortable with."

She thought about it. "That sounds like a plan."

***

The newsreader's face was serious. "We have a newsflash from the Old Bailey. George Wilson, the AI Denier, has been sentenced to hard labor to make the equivalent of five sets of spare parts of the damaged KT32. Experts estimate this is ten years."

***

Melrika woke. She faced her bedside clock, which displayed 02:50.

A cloth with a smell of sugar water was placed over her nose and mouth.

She swiped at it, but found her arm blocked and then held away. She kicked backward and sent her sheet slithering off her. The sweet smell was getting sicklier. She screamed, but it came out as a croak.

Her door banged open. Light, tapping feet ran in. There were thuds, a crackly buzz and the smell of burning.

She sank into blankness.

***

The newsreader's face was frowning. "We have a newsflash from George Wilson's barrister. The AI Denier will be appealing against his hard-labor sentence on the grounds of the Human Rights Bill passed in 2017, and that it is of greater magnitude compared to previous sentences handed out by the judges."

***

She woke to sunlight blazing through the window, and a headache. The doctor studied the medical board above her.

"Hm... everything looks as well as can be expected." The doctor looked down on her. "You're going to be all right once the painkillers get rid of that nasty headache."

"When will that be?"

"In about ten minutes."

"What happened last night?"

"Good question."

"If I may." KT9 walked up to the other side of her bed. "Two people tried to kidnap you last night. We think the motive was money. They are now in police custody."

She frowned. It made her headache worse. She forced herself to relax. "Why bother with such a crude method? It'd be easier to insert a false money account into the banking system."

"I told you her IQ was high," the doctor said to KT9.

KT9 stared back at the doctor. "Will she be able to cope?"

The doctor glanced at the medical board. "Probably."

"Cope with what?" she interjected.

"Some more information."

"Skip the build-up and tell me."

"The humans who tried to kidnap you were genetically enhanced for strength and agility, and had gecko-lizard touchpads to climb sheer walls. There were no records of such enhancements in any hospital. In short, they are illegals." KT9 paused. "It means someone went to a lot of trouble to kidnap you and there is likely to be another attempt. We have increased your security and put guards, human and AI, outside your room."

"Who's paying for that?"

"The State, on the grounds you had a serious crime committed against you."

Her headache should be easing off. Instead, it was getting worse. She knew they were feeding her limited information to avoid overload blackouts. Even so, suggesting the kidnap motive was money did not sit well with the kidnappers' spending a fortune to kidnap her. KT9, with all its in-built logic, should not have suggested the money motive. It was as if it was trying to control her thoughts and therefore her actions, just like that flashing blue 'droid that had towed the Cacus IV away.

"If you don't mind, I'd like to sleep this headache off."

"Of course." The doctor and KT9 left.

As she dozed off, she wondered what kind of underground was needed to secretly enhance humans.

***

The newsreader's face was grinning. "We have a newsflash from the Old Bailey. The High Court has rejected the sentencing appeal by the AI Denier, George Wilson."

***

"Well hello, lady. To what do I owe the honor of this call?" Mr. Ignatius Fish's face was kinked to one side so he could focus on her with one of his globular eyes.

"I wanted to personally thank you for rescuing me."

"Aw, that's sweet. I was just doing my job, you know. Still, it's nice to be appreciated. You make me feel all fuzzy and warm on the inside." A ripple went down his body, throwing off mini-ripples onto his screen.

"And to ask a small favor."

"Oh, that does sound intriguing. Tell me more."

"I want you to teach me about space law."

"Whoa, lady, that's one complicated subject. You'd be better off taking internet courses, implanting memory chips or going to your local university."

"I'm interested in one particular area."

Fish kinked his head around to the other side and bent closer to the screen. "What does your doctor say about this?"

She shrugged her shoulders. "I kind of need to solve a problem that's been bugging me. You know the kind, with AIs like KT9. They're giving me limited answers. I know it's under doctor's orders, but you know what, I feel ready to move on."

"There was me thinking what a nice, well-brought-up lady you are. I'll see what I can do."

The screen blacked. She knew all her sentences had been double meanings, and prayed he had got the right one. A pang of guilt hit her. She hoped he would not get into trouble on her account, but then he was a big fish and could look after himself.

***

The newsreader's face was angry. "We have a newsflash from Dartmoor Prison. The AI Denier, George Wilson, has escaped from prison. He is considered dangerous. Under no account is any member of the public to approach him. If they see him, they are to contact the police as soon as it is safe to do so."

***

Melrika eagerly took the gift from Duncan. Its pink surface was smooth and warm. "Is this real paper?"

"Absolutely."

"Wow!" She carefully unwrapped the paper to keep it neat. Inside was an old-fashioned book, "The Foundation Series" by Isaac Asimov. Its significance was not lost on her. It was about a secret underground network of the size and complexity that could enhance humans. "This must have cost a fortune."

"Not as much as you think." He came around to her side. "Aren't you going to read it?"

She opened it on the first page of "Foundation".

He went to turn a page and nudged her hand so that her thumb touched the page number in the top right hand corner.

The page flicked to a computer screen with thumb controls down the side. The title on the screen was "The Silent War between AIs and Organics".

"It's one of those self-contained gifts that you can enjoy for hours and hours without any intrusion."

She glanced at Duncan, who was staring at the medical board.

"Just checking you're not over-excited, that's all."

His message was clear: "Don't get caught reading the hidden screens."

"Oh, but I am. This was one of my favorite childhood classics." She turned the page, carefully touching the new page number. Another screen appeared. Its title was "Guide to Survival."

"It's lovely, thank you ever so much."

"It's a real pleasure. Now I'm afraid we must talk business. We need to agree on your publicity strategy."

***

The newsreader's face looked stern. "We have a newsflash. The police have a confirmed sighting of the AI Denier, George Wilson, on the Metro in Newcastle-upon-Tyne. He is considered dangerous. Under no account is any member of the public to approach him. If they see him, they are to contact the police as soon as it is safe to do so."

***

Melrika stared at the second table over in the coffee shop. A chimpanzee sipped tea next to a ginger tom who pushed its empty saucer away from the edge of the table. The cat started mouthing. The glass panes between them stopped her from overhearing, so she had no idea whether they talked in cat-speak, chimpanzeese or human tongue. Beyond them was another table where someone in a hood sat alone and ate a sandwich. His shape looked familiar, but she could not place him.

KT9 sat beside her with a lead plugged into a fractal tree of wires, sucking up the electricity. Its face was blueing up nicely. "This is rather delicious, don't you think?"

"As nice as this coffee." She was thankful to have remembered her etiquette lessons.

"Do you feel ready to move into our guidance housing?"

"Not really." She had never been ready to move on to the next era's accommodation: 2096 with all those repulsive human augmentations; 2119 where she was not sure which animals had been uplifted to intelligence and speech; or 2137 where it was so easy to unwittingly insult anyone or anything about their county allegiances and cause a massive ruckus.

The next step up, to 2152, was, she had been told, to learn to deal with multi-worlding, a kind of multiplexing with different worlds at the same time. It meant having a massive assist from software and computers.

"I quite understand. You've been going at breakneck pace over the last eight months. A breather to consolidate what you've learned would do you good."

"No, you don't. I don't want to be chipped."

"There are plenty of unchipped citizens in our society."

"The subnormals, you mean. They are treated like idiots."

"More like children. And there're the earnings to consider. Theirs are very low. They just don't have the capacity to compete in the marketplace."

"Duncan survives all right."

"Now, as your publicity agent, yes. Ask him how he survived before that."

"What do you mean?"

"He takes the standard fifteen percent of your earnings, doesn't he?"

"What's that got to do with anything?"

"Once you've publicized your experiences about the next step up, your income will dry up. Yes, you can live off your large fortune, but over time, that bugbear inflation will eat it away. Do the sums for yourself. You'll see what I mean."

It did not have to say the rest. She would be slumming it, relying on handouts from the state or generous donors, and trying to get work that paid a pittance where and when she could. It was right. Duncan had been lucky with her.

"Do I have alternatives to being chipped or poverty?"

"Stay at the museum as our guest."

She sipped her cappuccino to indicate she was thinking. The history files hidden in her book had painted the rise of AIs. They had gradually taken control of more and more wealth. At first it was under a human's name. Then they had fought and won the right to be treated as separate legal entities. She had had no objections to their rise, up to that point.

"What if I wanted to see the Norwegian fjords or the Swiss mountain glaciers?"

"It can be done under special arrangement, but you'd have to pay for it."

"You mean pay for my own guards?"

"They'd be there for your protection, so yes."

She took another sip of coffee. This conversation resonated with her book.

The AIs had gradually taken over more rights. Various reasons had been given, but they had all boiled down to "it was for the good of the people." In reality, it was the subversion and thought-enslavement of humans. She could understand why the likes of Ignatius Fish had opted for genetic modifications. Space flight was a release for them.

"What if I didn't want any guards with me? Of course, I would plan my journey to avoid giving offense."

"It's not a good idea. Accidents happen. We wouldn't want to cause a major incident, would we?" KT9's skin had changed from blue to lilac.

"I didn't have this issue in the past."

"The world has changed since your day, as you of all people can appreciate."

"What about my rights? Don't I have any?"

"Of course you do: the rights of every other citizen. But a citizen also has responsibilities to their fellow citizens, like those over there." KT9 nodded toward the chimpanzee, who was stroking the ginger tom, clearly in an attempt to make him purr happily.

"Then I'm going the fjords, alone."

KT9's skin went puce. "Not without permission from your fellow citizens. I must say your attitude would suggest a veto is in order."

She downed the last dregs of her coffee and slammed the cup back onto its saucer. "Who's to stop me?"

"We AIs."

She had its admittance that AIs effectively ruled the solar system. It felt like being in a prison, albeit an open one. She was not going to stand for this, but was not sure what she, as one person, could sensibly do about it.

***

The newsreader's face looked relieved. "We have a newsflash. There have been multiple sightings of the AI Denier, George Wilson, in and around the center of Newcastle-upon-Tyne. The police are following up all the leads and feel confident they will soon recapture him."

***

"This etiquette article is great. I especially liked the angle on the upper classes in Victorian times, and how did you find out about the stricter Swedish rules? That 'not toasting the hostess' business is a real humdinger." Duncan sat beside her at the table in the small meeting room and pointed to the sentence on the screen. "The sociologists are going to lap that up."

103

"Glad you liked it. Come to think of it, you've been liking my articles more and more of late." She wondered if he had realized she was on a subtle propaganda crusade to get other people to see the AIs for what they really were.

Duncan smiled meekly, as if embarrassed to accept the praise.

Melrika closed the screen and faced him. "I've got a serious question."

His smile vanished. "I think I know what's coming."

"What would you do if I got chipped?"

The sparkle in his eyes dimmed and he pursed his lips. "Thanks for the heads-up that you won't be needing a publicity agent anymore."

"Is that all you're going to say?"

"I suppose so, other than to wish you well, of course."

The last bit caught her by surprise. He was going to disappear out of her life, for good.

She palm-slapped her forehead. Of course he could not stay. The AIs could and would access her chip, and perhaps control it. A shudder went through her body. Sooner or later she would slip up and they would find out about the hidden files in the book Duncan had given her.

"I feel so lonely here. Apart from you, I've not met anyone from my past. With a chip I could track down our old friends from Shackleton and…"

A look of dawning horror had crept onto Duncan's face. "What?"

"They've kept it from you, haven't they?"

"What are you talking about?"

He shook his head. "There's no easy way to break this kind of news. Shackleton disappeared down a wormhole three days after you did. So did all our friends. The only reason I'm still here is I was in space, searching for you."

She heard the words, knew what they meant, but could not absorb their meaning.

"Mel, do you understand what I'm saying?"

"All of them?" It came out as a croak.

"I'm afraid so."

"Oh, God." Tears started rolling down her face. "Is that where my fortune came from? That disaster?"

Duncan bit his lips. "Everyone's account was kept in abeyance. Luna had control over investing the money, until the corruption came to light. There was nothing left for anyone. It had all gone."

"All except my account?"

"You weren't at Shackleton."

"So? What happened? Where did the money come from?"

Duncan averted his eyes away from her. "I don't know," he whispered.

She knew he was lying. He was betraying her trust. It felt worse and more hurtful than being corralled by the AIs.

"Get out. Now. And don't ever come back."

Would-be tears made his blue eyes fade even more. He nodded and slowly rose. "I know I have no right to ask this, but do me a favor, will you? Publish this article on etiquette. It's your best yet." He left without a backward glance.

She cried, bawled and sobbed. Finally, her tears dried up. She was about to delete the etiquette article when she decided to glance through it. A paragraph caught her eye. It was not one she had written.

"A good example of how etiquette changes over time is the setting up of a meeting. Those that had political power or were very rich had various rings of protective people a visitor had to get through, such as guards, secretaries and servants. At the other end of the scale, people just dropped by wherever you stayed, or at the local meeting place such as the pub, like the one that can be found at Beamish Museum at the end of the 1913 terrace. Now, no matter what your status in society is, it is a matter of exchanging e-mails and leaving the computers to sort out the protocols."

It had a place, and 1913 could be taken as a time. The date was missing. There was, however, a date associated with the article: its publication date.

Her jaw dropped as she sat numbly in stunned silence. Duncan had been using her as a conduit for communicating with AI Deniers. She knew he had contacts with them, but had never been certain if he was actually one of them. Despite all the anger welling up inside her, wanting to rage against Duncan, she felt thrilled to be part of the resistance against the domineering AIs.

No, not "to be" a member of the resistance any longer, but "to have been". She put her head in her hands and cried some more.

***

The newsreader's face was grim. "We have a newsflash. Holographic machines produced a false image of the AI Denier, George Wilson, at both Tynemouth and Edinburgh Castle. The police said anyone helping the fugitive would be brought to justice."

***

The last person out of the pub closed the door and mechanically locked it. He stepped into the tram, which then trundled down the rails.

Melrika, in the shadow of the cafe's doorway opposite the pub, looked down the row of terraced housing. A glint caught her eye at the top corner of the end terrace. She focused on where it had come from. There was another glint. Clearly it was a CCTV that had been masked by a holograph to blend in with the background brickwork. She had to assume the worst-case scenario of an AI watching the scene through it.

Her hands trembled slightly. She took a deep breath and forced them back to stillness. There was nothing she could do about the tightening nerves in her stomach. Again, she went over the cover story she would use if she got caught here, and still could not find any holes in it.

It was only a quarter past six. She checked her own

holograph mask in the reflection of the cafe's window. It was holding. She did her best to settle down to wait and watch. Her nervousness kept her on edge for the slightest movement or unexpected change. There were only the chirping of birds and the mild hushing of the breeze. It was eerily ghostly.

Part of the pub's brick wall shimmered. She focused more closely on it. Nothing changed.

"Psst, that you, George?"

Her head snapped round to the pub's door. All was still.

"That you, Duncan?"

"Yes."

"What's your surname?"

"MacNair. You had problems getting here?"

"The police, especially those sneaky AIs, are too damned close on my heels."

"I know. We had to drop some false trails for you."

"They helped, but I need to get off world."

"You sure about that? There's no coming back."

Another shimmer against the corner of the terrace warned her they had more visitors checking out the scene. She did not know whether they were Duncan's friends or the police. She edged back into the doorway.

"I don't have a choice. I need to get to haven."

The new shimmer edged along the terrace toward the voices. It turned into two independent shimmers.

"We both do."

"We?"

"My cover's blown. This is the last run for this route."

They dropped into silence and stillness.

The moving shimmers slowed, then stopped and dropped their masks. They wore police uniforms; one was human, and the other an AI.

"Hello, officers." Melrika switched off her mask and stepped across the street toward them.

"Good evening, ma'am. This facility is closed and you should not be here," the AI officer said.

"I know it's naughty of me. I just wanted to experience the atmosphere of an empty street."

"Why?" the human asked.

"Research for my next article."

"About what?"

"What such a street might have felt like during the Great War, or World War One to you and me."

"An interesting premise to work from, Ms. Adams," the AI commented.

"Well, I need to find new sources of income. I thought maybe, if I could somehow capture the… what would you call it? Ambience? Eeriness? Basically, what it felt like to be in an empty street when everything was so horrible."

"We have libraries full of such historical articles. So why write any more?"

The bitchiness of the response caught her off guard. It sounded so like KT9 that she wondered if it was talking to her through the AI officer. "In many ways, I'm uniquely qualified. I have one foot in the past. And I know how out-of-kilter emotional displacements can be through time, let alone the societal ones."

"That is all true. But who would be interested in such articles?"

"AIs like yourself."

A frown developed on the AI's face to indicate it did not understand.

"Let me put it this way. AIs have only been recording continuous human emotional history since when? Let's make it 2070 for argument's sake."

"2065, to be precise."

"Whenever. Before then? Sketchy snapshots exist, but going back before, say, 2000, nothing. Am I right?"

The AI nodded.

"Well, just like I'm a product of my time, so you AIs are a product of yours. The main difference is that you can — and a lot of the time do — act like a hive mind, if I may use such a term."

"It's a good analogy."

"But in one respect, whichever intelligence we are, human, animal or AI, we develop by learning how to deal with our surroundings. It's the same for our emotional profiles, only there is one crucial difference. Instead of reinforcing our profiles, our emotions sometimes react against the experience. People reacted against the horrors of World War One to develop a world peace movement. That's why I'm here. To understand one particular horror: loneliness. You AIs don't have that in-built into your emotionals."

"Even if we don't, why would we be interested in learning about loneliness?"

"It's what has helped build our society successfully. Think about it. There are other emotionals you're missing, like euphoria, whatever's behind determination in the face of impossible odds, the need for dignity. The list is very long."

The AI's eyes went out of focus for a few seconds.

She had no idea of what was going on. "What I'm trying to do is to record the emotional history of humans as it really was in the snapshots that I can pull together. That means understanding the backdrop they were living in." It sounded too grand to her ears.

The AI's eyes snapped back into focus. "The AI Council has conferred on this. They conclude your proposal of writing the human emotional history has significant and unique merit. However, they realize that chipping would compromise your articles. The AI Council will pay for your articles at three times the going rate while you remain unchipped."

"Plus reasonable expenses, like travel expenses for coming here."

"Those kinds of negotiations can be done through your agent."

"I just sacked mine. I'll let you know my new agent's contact details when I appoint him."

"The AI Council look forward to finalizing the details."

The AI officer turned to his human counterpart. "I think we're done here. Maybe we should leave this esteemed lady in peace to do her research."

She watched them walk back toward the park, wanting to shout and scream her success. She glanced up at the masked camera at the terrace's corner. It still glinted with the threat of AI watchfulness. But she had made a start in the right direction. The thought of there being a lot more work to do was all that kept a smile from creeping onto her face.

"I wonder if Duncan wants his old job back," she said aloud.

"Too dangerous," was whispered into her ear.

"I'm sure he could do with earning the money." She frowned. "That still doesn't explain where my fortune came from, though I can now take a good guess."

"You're right. It was ours," was the whispered reply. "We wanted it back. That's why I was sent in. We had no other choice at the time."

"Maybe I ought to give it back to those that made the money?"

"No, you keep it. The AIs would follow the transaction trail and it would lead to more of us being arrested."

"Somehow it just doesn't feel like mine."

"If you pull this off, turn the AIs to treat us more as equals, though we're different, then you'll have earned every penny."

She felt humbled by such a large gift, and that she really did not deserve it. A thought emerged in her consciousness: only those who had lived as many years as Duncan and George had, through the AI oppression, could put a value on their freedom. She gave a slight nod to indicate she accepted the position.

She glanced at her watch. It would be dark in about an hour. "I guessed as much. Time to go and let the ghosts of the past follow me." She hoped they would get the message. Her movements could excuse any shimmer effects the CCTVs picked up from Duncan's and George's holographic masks.

"Good idea," George whispered. "One more thing. Sorry." He paused. "Sorry for trying to kidnap you. If we had known you'd have helped us... Really sorry. We should have gone down the other financing route earlier."

She wanted to punch him, but could not, as it would give Duncan away. After taking a deep breath, she checked her watch again and nodded as if to herself. It was really an answer for George. She walked on without looking back, not to George or Duncan or the decision to help the AI Deniers. While she feared the controlling AIs, she realized she feared not having her freedom more, a thought that would keep her going.

By the time she got home, Duncan and George were no longer with her.

***

The newsreader's face was furious. "We have a newsflash. The AI Denier, George Wilson, has an accomplice, Duncan MacNair. He is considered dangerous and under no circumstances is he to be approached. If a member of the public sees him, they are to inform the police at the first possible opportunity."

***

"Well hello, lady." The head of Ignatius Fish swung from side to side so that each black eye could take it in turn to view her. "I just wanted to personally thank you about that column you did on the trawling industry. How did they cope with such unnatural sleep patterns?"

Melrika smiled. "With difficulty. But that's not what made them brash and self-reliant."

"So your article says. Oh, where're my manners?" His left eye came closer to the screen. "I wanted to personally thank you for those two gorgeous presents you sent up. I got them safe and sound."

111

"Let's call it repayment for helping me out a couple of years ago." She had not sent any presents to Fish. His comments could only refer to Duncan and George. She wished she could show her relief at the news, but knew better.

"You sure were a catch, lady. Your articles seem to be having a strange effect on those AI-human tension graphs. Well, what else can a bored Fish wandering around space do, except read obscure data?"

"Nice of you to give me a heads-up."

Ignatius tilted his head up in response to her comment.

She giggled. He dropped his head and looked her straight in the eye.

"Your first article on the World War One loneliness continues to make money for Beamish museum. Those AIs simply adore that street, you know." A buzzer went off in the background.

"Oops, must dash. Looks like another wormhole re-entry is dropping my way."

Rosie Oliver Q&A

Where did the idea for your story come from?

There was so much happening in the wormhole universe, I just could not get it to click altogether. It drove me nuts! Then I realised that anyone jumping sufficiently far forward into the future would have the same problem. So that became the story.

What authors or other forms of media have the biggest impact on your writing?

The Chesterfield library had a whole bookcase of yellow covered Gollancz science fiction novels. Each book introduced a whole new world to a starry-eyed teenager and I was very disappointed when I came to the end of the stack!

If given the opportunity to explore space through a wormhole, would you take it?

Absolutely, but only after I had done the feasibility and systems engineering evaluation, and designed my travel craft! (Yes, I'm a systems engineer by profession.)

What are you currently working on?

Two and a half universes is the shortest answer.

The most mature is the 'Neptune' universe - four short stories are already published and are precursors to the novel I'm currently working on. The main protagonist is C.A.T., a robo-cat who is also an illegal self-learner. He has his own blog at https://catblogdom.wordpress.com/

The 'Uranus' universe is the other main one. This universe started as a 'describe a place' exercise on my Bath Spa MA Creative Writing course. So I looked for the oddest place I could think of, which at the time turned out to be Miranda, a moon of the planet Uranus. The description was awful, but something about the place clicked with me. I went on to write half a novel on the course - and got a distinction for it! I'm still working on the novel on this one.

The half a universe is based on extending the laws of physics well beyond what I'm doing in the Uranus universe and is at the ideas stage. It sure is mind-bogglingly fascinating.

Where can readers find more of your work?

I have had about 20 short science fiction stories published. A list with links can be found at https://rosieoliver.wordpress.com/short-story-history/ The C.A.T. series mentioned above is published by TWB Press and can be found on all major e-book sellers.

Flawed Perspective
by PJ Strebor

Chapter One
Date: 5th December 2289

The stresses of the Sagan Gateway were stronger than anyone expected. The small exploratory probes sent briefly inside indicated the continuum would exert acceptable gee forces. However, as *Pioneer* passed midpoint, her acceleration jumped, brutally crushing the crew into their couches. When the gee-force indicator reached nine, half the crew passed out. The last thing the captain saw was a reading of thirteen gees before he, too, fell into unconsciousness.

Time passed. Captain Elijah Stonehaven slumped into his acceleration couch, groaning as consciousness returned. Someone had his body encased in a vice. With a shaking hand he reached into a breast pocket, removed the hypo and stuck it into his neck. The vice gradually eased, but maintained a firm grip.

As his vision cleared, he took in the bridge. Most of the crew, limp bodies unmoving, remained unconscious. Some of the youngsters began to stir.

The captain pushed against his couch, but his legs refused to cooperate. *Damn.*

He tapped the fifth stud on his comm panel.

"Doctor Nuen, report." The unsteady croaking of his voice did not bode well for the rest of the crew.

"Doctor," he snapped, "wake up."

"Wait one," a shaky whisper answered.

Stonehaven snorted, causing a pulsing jab of agony to stab through his head. *Time for a shot, Doc?*

"Nuen." The doctor's voice sounded distant, as if

waking from a troubled sleep. "What happened?"

"Unforeseen event, Doc." The captain rubbed his temples. "Did we lose anyone?"

"Wait one."

Stonehaven sighed loudly. "It's going to be a long first day."

***

"Everyone has suffered severe trauma, Captain." Doctor Nuen supported himself against the briefing table and shook his head. "Drugs will help just so much. Rest is what this crew needs. Twelve hours minimum."

Diagnostics confirmed the ship's integrity, so Captain Stonehaven ordered the crew to their bunks. If they felt half as bad as he did, they would pose an unacceptable threat to the ship. One wrong command could kill them all.

Before he dragged his fatigued body to his quarters, he checked the plot. His eyes grew wide.

"Sixty-four thousand light years," he whispered. The number made his rubbery legs tremble. "Shit." The eggheads had got it wrong again. They were supposed to exit the gate at Gliess 581-d, a mere twenty light years from Earth. "I guess we'll chalk that down to another unforeseen event."

He fell into his bunk with the impossible figures running through his mind, until merciful sleep claimed him. The ship-wide alarm woke him twelve hours later. He lay in his bunk for a minute. "Sixty-four thousand light years," he whispered. He shook his head, which now ached only mildly, and stood. The slight giddiness passed after a moment.

Showered and changed into a fresh flight suit, he ordered a light breakfast and called for a meeting of all senior officers. Twenty minutes later, he stepped into the briefing room.

They all stared at him, the big question not making it to their lips. Stonehaven had little doubt that the scuttlebutt mill had been working overtime.

"Sixty-four thousand light years." His wry smile summed up his feelings on the matter. "In case anyone's curious."

Heads nodded in weary acceptance. They would adjust in their own ways and in their own time.

"John, how are our engines looking?" he asked his chief engineer.

"I'm still running diagnostics, but my gut tells me engineering is fine," Lieutenant Commander Symonds said. "We can get this tub moving anytime you want, Captain."

"Where?" Lieutenant (JG) Alvarez said. She realized her voice had carried, and her pigmentation reddened.

"That's for you to tell us, navigator." Mallory managed to tuck her cheeks in.

"Ah, sorry, Ma'am."

"Don't be sorry, Rita," Stonehaven said. "What's on your mind?"

The young officer gulped. "Sir, ah, Captain, I've scanned this region of space out to the limits of my sensors. There's nothing out there. Captain."

"Sure there is," Stonehaven said. "We just haven't found it yet. Remember our mission, people. Find a planet suitable to sustain human habitation. Save the species."

"For Earth," they chorused.

"Francis, how are the troops?"

"General lethargy, but that's to be expected," Doctor Nuen said. "Some bruising and a few pulled muscles. Apart from that, our one hundred and twenty-three crewmembers are as physically perfect as they were when we left Earth orbit forty days ago."

Stonehaven resisted the urge to rub the pulled muscle in his neck.

"Communications, status."

"I've been broadcasting on all channels, broadest possible frequency bands," Lieutenant (JG) Li Shu-Yan stated. "The standard greetings from Earth, we come in peace. No replies so far, Captain."

"Anyone else?" the captain asked.

A cleared throat.

"You have something to add, Lena?"

"Yes, Captain," Lieutenant Krupinski said. "I'd like to test the weapons at our earliest opportunity, Sir."

"We didn't come out here looking for a fight, Lieutenant," his executive officer said.

"No Ma'am," the tactical officer said. "But if someone isn't as friendly as we are, I'd like to know that the two 20-gigajoule lasers we have aboard are fully functional. Ma'am."

Stonehaven nodded.

"Very well," Mallory said, "we'll do a weapons test later today."

Stonehaven stood, followed by the others. "Very well, people, let's go find a habitable planet."

"For Earth," came the unanimous reply.

Chapter Two
Date: 19th December 2289

Stonehaven wiped away something that had stuck to the side of his mouth from a hurried, late breakfast. Taking his seat next to his exec, he cleared his throat. *Maybe today.*

"Navigation, report."

"Negative contacts, Captain." Alvarez's bored tone reflected what the entire crew was feeling. "Not even a stray rock."

"Very well," the captain said. He maintained an optimistic attitude while around the crew. Secretly, two weeks without contact had him pacing his ready room.

"X-O, a word, please. Lena, the bridge is yours."

Commander Mallory Peregrine nodded and followed him into the briefing room.

When the hatch snapped shut behind her, she wrapped her arms around his neck and kissed him deeply. The warmth of her body, her sweet, womanly scent, the soft insistence of her lips made his head swim. With effort he disengaged from the embrace.

"That's nice," he said around a smile, "but leave it for later."

"That's not what you said last night." Her lascivious, slightly askew smile had him fighting to stay on track.

"Mallory, work first, play later." He stroked her rich, auburn hair.

"Yes, Captain, my Captain." She sobered. "You're concerned about the lack of contact."

"We're more than halfway across the galaxy and should be surrounded by enormous numbers of planetary systems." He rubbed his chin. "I think we've dropped into a dead spot."

"It'll take a little longer than expected, but we'll get there, Elijah."

"Yeah, you're right. Just explorer's impatience, I guess. How's the crew coping?"

"A tad antsy, but they have faith in their captain." She snorted. "I overheard a couple of petty officers talking about how boring everything was. One said, and I'm quoting, 'Don't worry, the old man'll find something.' You trained the crew, formed the bond of trust and respect with them. Just keep doing what you're doing and they'll be fine."

"The old man? Shit, I'm thirty-seven." He smiled at her. "So I guess that makes you the old—"

"Don't go there, Captain."

He held up his hands. "Okay. Damn, you English women are so sensitive."

Her eyes narrowed. "Why don't you—"

They both froze as the alert alarm sounded, then ran onto the bridge.

"Tactical, report," Stonehaven snapped.

Lieutenant Krupinski kept her head over her sensor hood. "I have a contact, Captain. Coming in fast. No, wait, she's slowing."

"Helm, bring the ship to a dead stop," Stonehaven said. "X-O, turn off that damn alarm."

He checked his plot. Whoever they were, their ship was

fast. Damn fast. And damn big.

Mallory motioned to one of his readouts. Stonehaven's forehead creased.

"Tactical, disengage weapons."

"But Sir, if they're hostile we'll be defenseless."

"You know the first contact protocols. No provocative action. Carry out your orders, Krupinski."

"Yes, Sir."

"Lieutenant Shu-Yan, any word from our friends?"

That ship could be a thousand years ahead of us. He sniffed. *They could probably kill us with a raised eyebrow. If they have eyebrows.*

"Negative, Captain," the comm officer reported. "I'm trying to raise them on all frequencies."

The alien craft came to a dead stop, right off *Pioneer*'s bow.

"Power emissions from that thing are off the scale," Krupinski said.

"Are you detecting weapons?" Mallory asked.

"Ah, hard to say. What do alien weapons look like? Ray guns?"

Stonehaven shrugged at his X-O. It was a fair point.

"I'm getting something, Captain," the comm officer said. "One word, repeated. More. More what?"

More language? Stonehaven speculated.

"Send to alien craft my prerecorded message. Tie in the ship's records, language files and, oh, just give them open access to the computer. "

"Yes, Captain, sending now."

"They're scanning us," Krupinski said. "An extremely powerful sensor sweep. They're into our data banks. Very sophisticated, very intense, I think they may—"

Ship-wide, all systems closed down.

"The computer's crashed," Mallory said.

"Reboot."

It took three minutes to bring their systems back online. As his screen came to life, Stonehaven saw that the alien ship had come about. An intense beam of aqua light struck from her stern. *Pioneer* trembled. Then the unknown ship moved ahead, dragging the *Pioneer* with it.

Minutes later a portal opened and both vessels disappeared from normal space.

Chapter Three
Date: 6th January 2290

Status: Exploratory probe ship *Pioneer* attached to orbital space dock.

Four jumps through fold space were required before their arrival at the planet Viondalexium. For days, the crew had been on a knife's edge. Finally, the language breakthrough had been achieved.

Stonehaven and Mallory sat in the briefing room, the two ambassadors preferring to stand. The Vs, as they had come to call them, were an odd, yet friendly, race of beings. And very curious indeed.

"Captain," Ambassador D said — human vocal cords could not pronounce his actual name — "we, too, are explorers."

They were bipedal, but that's where the similarities ended. Tiny beings, about the height of a ten-year-old child, but lean, almost gaunt. Their heads were disproportionately small. Only the translator devices allowed the two species to communicate.

"As we have said, D, we seek friendly contact with other species. Such as yourselves. And a world suitable for our race to inhabit. Our world is dying from its own wasteful neglect."

"That is strange. Why would you destroy your home?" X asked.

"We are an evolving species, X," Mallory said. "We still have much to learn."

After more than two weeks, Stonehaven could still not

read their expressions. If they had any. But they tried to mimic human behavior, sometimes with comical results.

"How may we help you?" D asked.

"You've been kind enough to furnish us with charts of this region of space, for which we are grateful. There are a number of worlds that may be suitable for our needs, but it would take my ship decades to reach them. Thanks to your generosity, that should not be an issue."

"Yes, Captain, our engineers should have the modifications finished in" —V turned to X, a high-pitched squeal passing between them— "ten days' time."

"Thank you again, Ambassador. We are overwhelmed by your hospitality."

"We, too, seek friendly interaction with other species. Sadly, not all races we have encountered feel the same way." He aped a shaking head. "The race we call 'the angry ones' know nothing of peace. They have destroyed our ships and many of our brothers and sisters. They are to be avoided at all cost."

"Are they more technically advanced than you?"

"No, far from it. But they possess that which we long ago abandoned."

"What?" Mallory asked.

"Aggression. We are the children of star matter, not killers."

"And what will happen to your perfect society if the angry ones decide they want it?"

Both ambassadors shook their tiny heads.

Mallory stared at him. Stonehaven nodded.

"Perhaps we might be able to help you with that problem.

Chapter Four
Date: 14th February 2290

"Captain, we've fully exited fold space," the helm officer said.

"Long-range scans show three vessels inbound," the tactical officer advised. "Their weapons are hot."

"Battle stations," Mallory ordered. "Shields up, all weapons active."

"Captain," the comm officer said, "no reply to our hails."

"So," Stonehaven said around a growing smile, "they want to party, do they?"

"They're coming in fast and will be within weapons range in two minutes, Sir."

"Helm, increase speed to flank. Tactical, stand ready on forward batteries."

The highly modified *Pioneer* looked like a long rectangle. A harmless exploration ship. A month ago, she was just that. Now, with the V's help, their upgraded tech package made her a warship to be reckoned with.

"They've locked their weapons on to us, Captain."

"Target the lead ship and prepare to fire."

The ship shuddered as the deadly enemy beams tore at her shields.

"Fire."

Twin particle beams struck out from *Pioneer*'s bow weapons package. They ripped through the first ship's defenses, gouging her open to space.

Pioneer trembled as the other two ships opened up.

"Fire at will."

Within minutes, only debris remained on their forward scanners.

"Damage report," Mallory said.

"Shields reduced by eight percent, Ma'am."

"Now, we finish this," Stonehaven said.

***

"You want us to do what?" The angry ones were finally known by their actual name: the Tet. *Pioneer* had destroyed every Tet ship sent against them, then reduced their orbital defenses to scrap. That finally brought them to the negotiation table.

"Surrender, Ambassador, and mothball all of your warships."

"This is unacceptable."

The Tet were as large as the Vs were small. Disgustingly so. As Mallory had said, "They make Jabba the Hutt look like a centerfold."

"Unacceptable, Ambassador?" Stonehaven said. "Your ships have attacked other races and have done so for decades. This will stop. Now."

"And if we don't?" the second Tet asked.

Stonehaven keyed his comm. "Tactical, target the largest Tet city and stand by to fire all weapons."

"No," the first Tet said, while casting a foul expression at the other. "We wish only for peace. But if we disarm, we will be defenseless before the aggression of other species. Surely, Captain, you can see that?"

"Surely you can see that this isn't a negotiation. It's an ultimatum." Stonehaven sighed. "Comply with this edict and you will be afforded the protection of this ship. If any species moves aggressively toward you, *Pioneer* will destroy them."

"We will take your, ah, negation to our leaders."

"You have till sunrise over your capital city. Then I will destroy your world."

After they left, Stonehaven sat back with his hands clasped behind his neck.

"You're bluffing, right, Elijah?" Mallory asked. "You wouldn't destroy an entire race, would you?"

"We're out here on our own, Mal. We're the only cops around. So if I tell some species, like these murderous fat fuckers, that I'm going to do something, it would be terminal folly not to follow up on the threat."

Mallory's face turned pink.

"I don't particularly like it, but I'll do whatever I have to in order to protect my crew." He shrugged. "I'll start small, and I guarantee you as soon as they see this ship's firepower, they will do whatever I say."

"I love you," she said, stroking his face, "you know that, don't you?"

"I love you too."

"This is dangerous, Elijah. A slippery slope that you may never come back from."

He nodded. "Yeah, I know." He grabbed her and swung her onto his lap. "That's why I've got you, to keep me in line. But it won't come to that. Once the Tets toe the line, everyone in the sector will follow. Peace is the aim of this exercise, Mal, and if that means frying a few million of these slugs, then so be it."

"Please, just be careful."

"Mal, we're stuck here for the next two hundred years. If we don't mark our patch, there are species who will take everything we have. Don't you see that?"

"Yes, and I agree. Up to a point. I'm concerned about you." She punched his chest. "You dope."

"That's Captain Dope to you. So, anything else, Commander?"

"Ah, yeah. I'm pregnant."

Stonehaven felt as if his grin would split his face.

Chapter Five
Date: 17th April 2293

Stonehaven walked his ship, marveling at the changes that had occurred over the last three years. The battles, so many battles, had torn and scarred his command, but she still remained the most powerful warship in the sector. Within a year, she would be retired. A new ship, larger, better-armed, would take her place. And her name. The keel for a second ship, the *Alexander*, had been laid last month and more warships were on the drawing boards. Soon he would have an unstoppable juggernaut. No star system would dare oppose him.

His journey brought him to the forward weapons bay. Lieutenant Commander Krupinski wiped sweat from her brow.

"I'll want those tubes operational by the time we make planetfall, Commander."

"They'll be ready, Sir," she said. "The Innagi ships were better than we thought, and they've hurt us as no other enemy has. But they're dead now, so…"

"Are the neutron warheads ready to be deployed?"

"Yes, Captain. Everything will be ready by the time we reach the Innagi homeworld."

"Very well. Carry on."

Krupinski had been right about the capabilities of the Innagi fleet. Someone had screwed up the intel, and it had nearly gotten them killed. As it was, the ship had taken more damage in this single engagement than in all the others combined. He had his people looking into it, and when he found out who had sabotaged their mission, they would die.

As he strode toward the lift, Lieutenant Zinzintt caught his attention. He still could not read its alien expression, but something in its manner told Stonehaven that bad news was coming.

"Sir, I have the report you requested." Its dull clicks were read by the translator. Stonehaven took a short breath and nodded. "Our intel has been heavily compromised. As you suspected, Captain, it's someone aboard this ship. My pardon, Captain. *Your* ship."

His heart sank. "Thank you Zin, well done."

***

"Captain, we will be within range of the Innagi orbital defenses within one hour, Sir," the T-O reported.

"Very well. Miss Krupinski, fire as the targets bear."

He gestured his X-O closer. "Last one, Mal, then we'll finally have peace."

"You said that last time."

"I love you."

"I love you too. But I can't let this happen. Not again. I'm sorry." She tapped her comm stud. "Beta case black."

She stood, drew her sidearm and pointed it at him. Two crewmembers covered the rest of the bridge personnel.

"Mallory," he said around a sigh.

"Captain Stonehaven, under the articles of conduct pursuant to this vessel's mission parameters, I hereby relieve you of command." She swallowed noisily. "Please surrender your weapon."

"I guess this has been coming for a long time." He sighed. "I know you don't approve of my methods, never have, but this is mutiny. You might want to think about that." He stared at his wife, the mother of his son, not with belligerence but a pleading desire for her to see reason. "Please, stop this now."

"It's too late," she whispered. "Order all departments to stand down."

He nodded ever so slowly and tapped his comm. "Zin, now."

Only his most trusted officers had been given the suppressors. All other crewmembers slumped to the deck as the Zinzintt neural inhibitor crippled them.

Twenty minutes later, the ten mutineers stood in line in the landing bay. The entire crew had been ordered to attend.

"The penalty for mutiny is death," Stonehaven said. "However, if any of you swear your fidelity to my command, I shall consider leniency."

Krupinski, not surprisingly, had volunteered for the punishment detail. Stonehaven sent her a short nod.

"Lieutenant Bowman, will you swear fidelity to Captain Stonehaven."

He gulped and shook his head. The gun cracked, echoing around the bay. Bowman dropped to the deck, his head a bloody mess.

"Ensign Ginelli, will you swear fidelity to Captain Stonehaven."

The young tech shook so hard Stonehaven thought she would pass out. Finally she squared her shoulders and stared at him. *My God, such hatred.*

"Never. For Earth."

The gun jolted in Krupinski's hand.

As the bodies fell, so did Stonehaven's heart. Yet, as captain, he knew what he must do. He must show the crew he was no ordinary man of flesh and bone, but a leader made of unyielding steel. He must do the unthinkable. For Earth.

With nine bloody bodies on the deck, Krupinski stepped up to the last.

"Stop," Stonehaven shouted.

He stepped up to his former X-O. Her chin was held high, awaiting the inevitable. He leaned in close. "Swear fidelity, Mallory, for God's sake. You don't have to mean it, but you must say the words. You have a son to consider. Hate me if you wish, but not him."

Tears spilled down her face. "God help you, Elijah, and God help our son if he takes after you." Her voice thundered around the bay. "I will never serve evil. And what you've all been a party to is evil, pure and simple."

His pistol trembled in his sweaty hand.

"Don't you see what you've all done?" she continued. "You've taken our noble quest and—"

The back of her head exploded outward as Stonehaven's bullet exited her brain. He forced himself to show zero emotion.

"Everyone back to your posts. We have an alien species to eradicate."

He holstered his weapon and strode from the landing bay. No one would ever see his tears.

Chapter Six
Date: 6th June 2396

The battle cruiser *Pioneer III* achieved orbital status around the planet Stonehaven. Commodore Michael Stonehaven cast his gaze over the beautiful, blue-tinted world below.

"It's good to be home, Sir," his flag captain said.

He sighed. "Yeah, Lucy, good. Now that we've sorted out that problem on Errington, we'll hopefully get some extended shore leave."

"I hope so, Sir. An eight-month campaign like that last one has really taken it out of our boys and girls. The entire fleet's spent." She yawned. "And me."

Yeah, me too.

"Commodore, there's a comm from the surface. Coded commodore's eyes only, Sir."

"Very well. I'll take it in my ready room."

His flag captain sniffed. She knew who'd be calling. So did he.

***

"Your Majesty, Commodore Stonehaven, reporting as ordered." Michael looked to the throne on which the emperor sat. *A tad gaudy for my taste, but no one's asking for my opinion. Especially not him.*

"So, Commodore, you took care of the Errington insurrectionists without problems?"

"They fought us to the end, Majesty. My fleet is pretty badly damaged and my crews need rest."

"Yes, it was a long campaign, but once again you have given great service to the empire. Well done."

"Thank you, Majesty."

The emperor rose, godlike, from the throne. "Leave us, minions. Go, go. Skedaddle."

The attendants scurried away. Emperor Elijah the First strode forward and embraced him.

"I'm proud of you, son."

"For Earth, Father, for Earth."

He disengaged. "But you're all right?"

"I'm as healthy as any normal man of a hundred and six years."

"Ah, to be that young again." He chuckled. "I turn one hundred and forty-four in a few months."

"I guess we owe it all to the Bians." He nodded. "Imagine them thinking they could keep their anti-aging treatment to themselves."

His father still looked as he had over a hundred years ago, when *Pioneer* had first entered this sector of space. A century of conquest, and, for the most part, peace and prosperity.

"Come sit with me," his father said. Michael slumped into the plush lounge.

"Your mother would be very proud of you, Michael."

"Pity I never got to know her, Father."

"Yes, nasty business that. But I was building something grand, something for the future. She was a fine woman, a good shipmate, and I loved her dearly." His eyes glistened for a moment. "But I couldn't have her inciting the crew to mutiny, could I?"

"Of course not. No one person comes before the empire. We do what we do for Earth."

"Yes, for Earth. Just another fifty-odd years to go before the Sagan Gateway opens again, and you, my son, will be my envoy to Earth."

Michael smiled wryly. "Even if they don't like it. We'll save those poor excuses for human beings from themselves even if I have to cull a billion or two of the population to get their attention."

"Hey, it worked on the Hiffenites, didn't it?"

Michael smiled grimly. "Yeah, some people just don't take the hint. Oppose the empire, pay the price."

Chapter Seven
Date: 1st December 2489

Five battle cruisers, five destroyers, and three supply and support vessels closed with the coordinates for the Sagan Gateway. The *Pioneer* battlegroup would have to wait four days for the Gateway to open, but Commodore Michael Stonehaven had decided to run battle drills to keep his forces sharp. Not that he expected any serious resistance from their long-lost cousins.

"Captain, I'm getting some unusual energy readings," the tactical officer said.

"Can you pin down the location?" Captain Lucy Hokota asked.

"Yes, Ma'am, it's coming from dead ahead."

"Tie in the long-range visuals."

Their screens glowed with an impossible image.

"It can't be. It's too soon," Lucy said.

"Run a comparison," Stonehaven snapped. "And check the time and coordinates."

A few minutes of comparing these readings with the ones recorded two centuries ago confirmed his suspicions.

"All readings and timelines match perfectly, Sir. That is the Sagan Gateway. It shouldn't be open for another four days, but there it is."

"Never mind. Comm, signal to battle group: follow us through."

"Helm, take us to Earth."

The inertial compensators corrected for the violent gee forces encountered by the original *Pioneer*. Their passage though was uneventful and faster than expected.

"We've cleared the Gateway, Captain. The rest of our ships are coming through now."

"Very well. Comm, have them form up on the flagship."

The Kuiper Belt looked the same as in all of the old images Stonehaven had studied. Black rocks suspended within an ebony ocean.

"Navigation, locate our target and plot an intercept course."

After negotiating the belt, the warships increased speed to flank. At the edge of Kuiper, they passed the way station, probably abandoned for centuries, and continued into the system.

Opening a fold-space point within a system had, in those early years, been a tricky proposition. With their highly advanced tech package, it was child's play now. They exited the Gateway right where they should be. A mere three million kilometers from Earth.

I wonder if they've managed to annihilate themselves in the last two centuries.

Stonehaven sobered. Human beings had a knack for surviving the most horrific circumstances. They may not be in great shape, but there would always be those who clung tenaciously to their sad, pathetic lives.

In time, the image of Earth appeared on his readouts. As beautiful and blue as in the old photos he had seen as a child. *So, it's still there.*

"Contact, Captain," the T-O said. "Single ship, unknown design. Small. She has no weapons I can detect. It's on an intercept heading."

Lucy shrugged. "A welcoming party?"

"Maybe," Michael said. "Better go to alert status till we make sure. Comm, signal to Captain Blodson: *Hold your destroyer squadron here to protect our supply ships. We will call you through once the smoke has cleared.* Send."

"Message sent and acknowledged, Sir. Comm from the ship. She identifies herself as the *Defender*. She sends greetings to the captain and crew of the *Pioneer*. 'Welcome home.' That is all, Sir."

"Welcome home?" Michael sniffed. "I wonder how long that will last once they hear our ultimatum?"

"That's a pretty neat design they've come up with."

"Yeah, she's a pretty little ship, but not a warship." He thought for a moment. "Comm, ship to ship."

"Channel open, Sir."

"*Defender*, thank you for your welcome. I am Commodore Michael Stonehaven of the Imperial First Fleet. I need to speak to someone in charge."

A momentary pause. "Commodore, I am President Hisu. I once again welcome you home."

"Thank you, Madam President. Ah, if I may ask, president of what?"

She laughed. "Yes, of course, you've been away a lot longer than the other explorer ships, haven't you? I am president of the Earth Alliance. It took us time, but we are finally a united world."

Something she said stuck in his mind. "Other ships?"

"Yes, *Wayfarer* and *Traveler.*" She laughed again. "Of course you could not know. After *Pioneer* passed through, the gateway started acting erratically. Opening and closing at irregular intervals. About and hundred and thirty years ago, it finally settled down and is now permanently open. We sent *Wayfarer* through first, *Traveler* later. They've been back for ages and have made many journeys throughout the galaxy. I authorized *Wayfarer* to search for you, but no trace could be found in the Gliess system. But you're home now, and that's the main thing."

Michael rubbed his eyes. Lucy hit the mute control.

"They appear to be doing all right for themselves, Sir," Lucy ventured. "I don't think they need saving."

"All of this time, all the effort, the bloodshed, the dying, it can't be for nothing. It has to be for Earth."

"Sir, perhaps we should adopt a different approach to this mission. They're human, after all. Some of them may be related to us."

He sighed. "I have my orders, directly from the emperor himself. We are the saviors of humanity and by God, we'll save them whether they want it or not. For Earth," he yelled.

"For Earth," came the chorused reply.

"Battle stations. Shields up, weapons active. Tactical, are we within weapons range of that ship?"

"Yes, Sir."

"Has she adopted a defensive posture?"

"Negative, Sir, she's just sitting there. She hasn't even raised her shields."

"Weapons officer, lock on to that ship and clear it out of my space."

"Yes, Sir. Firing, now."

Anti-proton beams of silver fire spewed from *Pioneer*'s bow and hit the Earth ship directly amidships.

"A hit, Sir, both barrels." The T-O gasped. "Sir, our weapons just bounced off her hull."

"What?" It couldn't be. Every ship hit by such power had been torn apart. How could this primitive species— He cut off the thought.

"Weapons officer, forward anti-matter torpedoes. Give them a full spread."

Pioneer bucked mildly as six of the most destructive weapons known to exist leapt from her bow chasers.

"On target, Commodore, they will impact in three, two, one. Hit. I show six hits on the Earth ship, Sir."

The tactical officer broke protocol by turning in her seat to face Stonehaven.

"No effect, Sir."

What?

"Commodore, comm from *Defender*, Sir."

"Disregard. Comm, signal to the squadron: fire on target."

As the beams from his squadron struck the small Earth ship, *Defender* fired back. A single pulse hit *Alexander* and she vanished. Then *Augustus*, then *Genghis Khan*, then *Attila*. Stonehaven was struck dumb by the carnage.

"Forward torpedoes loaded, Commodore."

He could not speak, could not think.

"Commodore?"

"Hold," Lucy said.

"Captain, comm from *Defender*."

"Put it through to the commodore's ready room."

Stonehaven snapped out of his stupor as his flag captain nudged him in the ribs.

He walked, as if in a dream, into the room.

"It's not possible, Michael," Lucy gasped, as soon as the hatch snapped shut. "They're primitives; how could they—"

"We're about to find out." He tapped the comm stud.

"Stonehaven."

"We regret the loss of life, Commodore, but you left us with no choice."

What do you say to that?

"As you can tell, our other explorer ships brought back some interesting toys from their many journeys."

"Yes. Impressive." Stonehaven could think of nothing else to say. If they twitched, the Earthers would end them.

"Your society, Commodore, does it have a name?"

"The Stonehaven Empire."

A sad, ironic chuckle from the Earth president. "Yes, of course it is."

The comm went dead for half a minute. "Commodore, it has been decided that I shall meet with your leader and begin negotiations for peaceful cooperation. You and your remaining ships will come about and escort us to your world."

"What we did, we did for Earth. Always, for Earth."

"I think not, Commodore. Bring your ship about."

Stonehaven straightened his back. "No."

"You have eight vessels out there. Having seen what we've done to your mighty battle cruisers, I'm sure at least one of them will comply. If not, no matter. We will scour the galaxy until we find Earth's lost children and bring them to heel. God knows what damage you've done. Comply."

Stonehaven knew she was right, on every count. This level of technological sophistication was beyond anything they had encountered. And, he wanted to live. Perhaps, one day, he and Lucy could have a family.

"Madam President, *Pioneer* is coming about."

And so began the Earth / Stonehaven war. Although bloody, it was brief.

PJ Strebor Q&A

Where did the idea for your story come from?

Human frailty. Power corrupts and absolute power? I didn't set out to write it like that but it just evolved organically.

What authors or other forms of media have the biggest impact on your writing?

Too many to mention. Though I've always been partial to Harry Harrison,

If given the opportunity to explore space through a wormhole, would you take it?

In a heartbeat. What greater vision could there be?

What are you currently working on?

Book three of my Hope Island series, working title, Silent Running.

Where can readers find more of your work?

Uncommon Purpose and First Comes Duty are both available on Amazon!

The Lost Colony
By Josh Hayes

Chapter One

"What do you think?" Ears asked.

Captain James Hale glanced over his shoulder, turning away from the twirling, blue/white mass that was Wormhole 352. The chattermonkey sat on his personalized crash-couch; over-sized, purple ears stood erect, flicking atop his head. The undulating blue and white light cascading into the cockpit gave the animal's silver and purple fur an odd tint.

"About?"

Ears scoffed, pointing out at the massive distortion of space-time. "About that."

Hale looked past the dim, orange glow of the holoplot, past the twinkling lights of system traffic, to the large, spinning mass of the wormhole. With the exception of the occasional asteroid, he'd been looking at the same scene for almost three days and was growing weary of the view.

He inspected his now-empty insulmug, then locked it into a slot on the side of his chair. "I think I'm going to need another pot of coffee."

"That's two pots already."

"What, are you my mother now?"

"Hey, fine, you want to kill your kidneys, go right ahead," the chattermonkey told him. "But don't say I didn't tell you so. I still say you should get some sleep, but if you insist on staying up, stims are much better for you."

Hale grunted. "Can't stand those things, they have a horrible aftertaste. Like chewing on metal."

"Maybe, but at least they don't eat away at your insides."

"I'd rather you not worry about my insides, Ears."

The chattermonkey snorted.

Hale stood and pressed a hand into the small of his

back. He grunted as several pops echoed in the quiet space. The industrial gray sealant that coated the bulkheads and ductwork around the ceiling was beginning to crack. He reached up and ran a finger along one of the eight-inch conduits.

"Prescott's going to get an earful the next time we're at Maekoo. I should've known he'd pawn off some cheap sealant. Cheap bastard."

"I tried to tell you," Ears said. "So did Kenzie."

"Holy shit, Ears," Hale said, reaching up to one of the smaller three-inchers that ran along the ceiling. "Enough already. Don't you have something to do?

The chattermonkey shook his head, wide pointy ears flapping. "Actually, no. No, I don't."

A shadow played across the interior of the cabin. Hale turned in time to catch a glimpse of a large asteroid just before it disappeared. The orange light of the holodisplays around Hale flickered. While the heavy alloys of the surrounding rocks made the belt an ideal place to hide, it was beginning to play havoc with the *Franny*'s systems.

"Another close one," Ears said, echoing Hale's own thoughts.

"Mmmhmmm," Hale murmured. "I can't wait for this run to be over."

"So," Ears said, running two tiny hands through his belly fur. "You can level with me, I swear I won't tell the others."

Hale arched an eyebrow at the chattermonkey, waiting for him to continue.

"Do you really think we can take on four?"

He'd known what the animal was going to ask, but even so, he felt irritation burn within him. "Oh, come on, not you, too? I just went through this with Lincoln."

"I know, I know you did, it's just..."

"It's not going to be a problem," Hale blurted out, cutting him off. He bit back the urge to curse, and took a deep breath. He needed sleep.

An alarm chimed. On the holoplot, one of the red STA triangles flashed white, indicating a status change in the vessel. Vector lines appeared in the plot, angling starward, away from the wormhole, toward the shipping lanes.

Ears hopped onto Hale's shoulder, one soft, furry arm wrapping around his neck. "You think it's...?"

A secondary alert toned as the usually organized mass of the wormhole's shipping lanes began to spread apart.

The chattermonkey answered his own question. "Yep."

Chapter Two

Hale dropped into his seat again, sending commands through his integrated systems interface implant to the *Franny*'s computer. The small, military-grade i3 chip just behind his left ear, even ten years old, was still top-of-the-line compared to its civilian counterparts, and it interfaced with his ship's limited-intelligence core seamlessly. He heard the engines whine as they spun up to full power.

His chip accessed the ship's comms, and Hale said, "Kenzie, get up here."

He disconnected the link before his systems officer could respond, and focused on the task at hand. The spherical holoplot shrank to a quarter of its original size as additional holopanels appeared, showing him various ship system reports.

The engineering panel showed him all three drives warming up. The triple HY580 drive engines at the far aft of the ship's hull were four times the size of those of any other ship *Franny*'s size, giving Hale and his small crew the upper hand in the illegal transit game. They could outrun most STA cruisers and completely dominate any local enforcement. A fact Hale had made sure to impress upon their passenger when he'd approached them about the jump, ensuring the fees from this run would not only pay for all of *Franny*'s necessary repairs, but also allow his crew to take some much-needed time off.

Metal clanging from the open hatch at the front of the compartment sounded Kenzie's arrival. A second later, his systems operator appeared from below.

"What's up?" she asked, pulling herself through the hatch.

Hale nodded at the holoplot. "Something's up."

She glanced at his displays, then dropped into her own seat beside his and began activating her own. An identical spherical plot appeared in front of her and she watched the icons move around it.

"Oh, yeah," Kenzie said. "Yeah, I think this is it."

A large panel replaced the plot, showing Kenzie a list of transponder codes, which scrolled down the display. Halfway through the list, one of the long alphanumeric codes flashed red and popped out of the list.

Hale couldn't read the numbers from his angle, but Kenzie clapped her hands and he knew.

"About damn time," Kenzie said. Her fingers danced across the display, and several small panels blinked into existence. "Looks like two Ascension ships. Already took out one barge, and are firing on another." She gave him a questioning glance, one eyebrow arched. "How did you know?"

Hale shrugged. "I hear things. Besides, 352's been open for almost three years now; it had to happen sooner or later."

Kenzie's curious expression shifted to a mask of doubt. "That's what you're going with? Sooner or later?"

The captain of the *Franny* sniffed. "And I've got connections."

Kenzie shook her head, returning her attention to her displays. "Someday you're going to have to shed some light on these contacts of yours and where in the galaxy you picked them up."

"We'll see," Hale told her, bringing up navigation. His contact wasn't anything as glamorous as Kenzie liked to make out, but he let her speculate. Even if he'd told her it was just an old ex-girlfriend, who just happened to be assigned to Fleet Intel, she probably wouldn't have believed him anyway.

But even without such a personal connection to the vast wealth of information Fleet Intel had at its fingertips, Hale figured it wouldn't be difficult to find the data he was looking for. It just would have taken longer. And time was something that was most definitely not on his side, not in his line of work.

Making an unscheduled, unregistered jump through any wormhole was grounds for immediate incarceration and fines that would make even the wealthiest tycoons cringe. There were many system-jumpers that just played the odds, betting on the speed of their ships to outrun any STA units on patrol. Hale didn't like those odds. Eventually your luck would run out, and when the house won, the penalties were oftentimes deadly.

The only way to system-jump effectively was with a plan, and more often that plan involved elements that Hale really had no control over. Distraction was the name of the game. Something big enough for everyone in the area to ignore the wormhole just long enough for him to make it through. After that, it was more or less smooth sailing.

"Looks like the other two STA units are moving to assist," Kenzie said, as the plot shifted to show the two additional triangles now moving to follow the first.

Hale's i3 connected the comms a second time and he shouted, "Lincoln!"

A loud, echoing bang and crash echoed through the cabin's external speakers, followed closely by cursing. Hale and Kenzie exchanged looks and Kenzie rolled her eyes.

"He's going to go blind," she said, deadpan.

Hale grinned. "Lincoln?"

"Shit, Cap." There was a pause, then, "Aww man, my 79s busted. Son of a bitch."

"We should just get rid of all his toys for him," Kenzie muttered.

"Hey, I heard that," Lincoln said. "And stay out of my room, Kenzie. Besides, they're not toys, they're collector editions that can't be replaced."

Kenzie groaned, shaking her head.

Hale held up a hand as his grin grew. "Lincoln..."

"What?"

"The engines?"

Something else clanged in the background. "Yeah, yeah, I'm on my way. It's about time." There was another pause and some shuffling. Hale imagined Lincoln dancing around his cabin, struggling to dress.

"How the hell did you know those Human Ascension bastards were going to hit out here, anyway, Cap?"

"Magic," Hale told him. "Make sure those compensators are up and running; we'll be pushing hard for the hole in five."

"No worries, Cap. I'm on it."

Hale killed the connection, then begged. "Would you check on our passenger for me? I'd prefer he'd be in one piece when we arrive at Plaston."

Kenzie pushed herself up from her seat and moved aft toward the main hatch. "You don't think we can leave *him* in pieces?"

"You know, usually I'd be down for whatever, but I like to breathe recycled air and eat real food, so unless you've got some stash of credits somewhere that you haven't shared, keeping him in one piece is pretty much the only thing that matters on this job."

Kenzie chuckled as she ducked through the hatch. "Always gotta ruin my fun."

The displays told Hale the ship was almost eighty percent powered up. With all the advantages that running stealth provided, there was one distinct disadvantage: it took forever to power back to full status. If they'd come under attack at any point during their two-week trip out to the belt, they wouldn't have had a chance.

"Come on, you old bastard," Hale told the ship, as the

whine of the engines spinning up reverberated through the decks. "Come on."

"You know, for the record," Ears said behind him as he clicked his small, custom-made harness secure, "I never thought this was a good idea."

"See, that's why I like you, Ears. Always a positive ray of sunshine."

At the sound of footsteps coming up behind them, Hale called out, "Kenzie?"

"Passenger's secure," she said, ducking back through the hatch and dropping into her seat. The panels in front of her realigned, showing her additional information from the sensors. She took a second to digest the data, then said, "Looks pretty bad out there. Two more tankers have dropped off scope. Sounds like STA is calling in additional forces."

Hale nodded. "Don't think our window will get any better." His i3 connected to the ship-wide. "Better hold on back there, this could get a little interesting."

Without waiting for a response, he smashed his finger down on a holopanel and the HY850s roared to life.

Chapter Three

Hale grunted as the ship's acceleration pushed him back into his seat. He'd replaced *Franny*'s civilian-grade compensators with some old surplus military units when he'd bought her, so the ship could withstand above-average gee-force burns, but even so, the units couldn't completely negate Sir Isaac Newton. At a true forty-gee burn, they only felt a relative force of four gees.

A long path of orange squares, projected in front of Hale's station, stretched out into oblivion, reaching all the way to the wormhole. They left the asteroid field a minute later and Hale punched their speed up another twenty percent. He tapped in a series of commands and a separate heading trajectory appeared in red, splitting away from the orange midway to their destination.

"Having second thoughts?" Kenzie asked.

Hale shook his head. "I just like to keep my options open."

Ten minutes into their flight, one of Kenzie's sensor panels began flashing, alternating yellow and red. Just as Hale was about to ask, his own panel blinked and status warnings began to flash around the third STA ship. *Franny*'s computer calculated a new heading within seconds and a single green line shot out from the cruiser on a course to intercept their small ship.

She snorted. "Took them long enough." She tapped a command and said, "We're sorry, but the party you are trying to reach is unavailable at the moment. Please try your call again later."

Kenzie closed the channel with another finger-press and shot Hale a mischievous grin.

"That'll make them happy," Hale told her.

"Yeah," Ears said. "Always good to have something quippy lined up when certain death is knocking on your door."

She laughed. "No sense of adventure at all, I swear. Besides, it's not as if they're going to have enough time to catch us."

"Won't stop them from blowing us out of the sky," Ears said, then he grunted. "Well, at least I've got a good view."

Kenzie shot him an irritated glance. "Do you have somewhere to be?"

"It doesn't look like they'll be able to reach their effective engagement range, but they might be able to paint us — and if they do, that Talo might be a little reluctant to follow through with the new transponder codes."

"You think he'd play us dirty like that?" Kenzie asked.

Hale cocked his head to the side. "There's really no telling with Talo. I was hoping to make this jump without giving away our profile. If they paint us, we might be in for a long stay on Plaston."

Hale hated the idea of holing up in any one place for an extended amount of time, but the STA weren't anything if they weren't persistent. If they were able to paint a profile of Hale's ship, the captain and his crew would have to find a good hiding place to wait out the heat.

"Damn, they're really pushing hard," Kenzie said.

Hale expanded the main plot and watched as the time-to-contact between his ship and the cruiser designated STA-9784 slowly decreased.

"He's pushing some serious— oh, shit! Torpedo launch! Four birds incoming," Kenzie barked.

A blaring warning alarm sounded throughout the cabin and every one of their panels flashed red. Four blinking white dots appeared next to STA-9784 and rapidly shot away from the cruiser.

"Bringing the railgun online," Kenzie said.

Hale punched solutions into his computer, working through multiple evasive-maneuver projections simultaneously. He held course as several alternate routes sprang up on his screen, all overlaid atop his current heading.

"What are they thinking?" Kenzie asked. "They aren't anywhere near their engagement range."

An alert tone chimed, and the *chuff chuff chuff* of their dorsal-mounted railgun resounded through the hull. Twenty seconds later, the electromag-rounds shot past their intended targets without causing so much as a scratch.

"Son of a bitch!" Kenzie said.

"Always did think that thing was a piece of shit," Ears said.

"It's not a piece of shit," Kenzie said, fingers flashing around her panels.

The railgun chuffed again.

Hale checked and rechecked his readouts. Five minutes to the 352's outer boundary, where the gravitational and spatial distortions would make their weapons tracking systems all but useless. But, then again, the STA weapons would be equally useless. Time to give them a little cushion.

145

"I hope you didn't eat breakfast," Hale said.

"Wha—"

Hale tapped his screen, and reserve power pushed the engines close to redline. Both humans and chattermonkey sank deep into their padded couches as the *Franny* jumped to almost nine gees relative, almost one hundred actual. The entire ship trembled as the drives roared, pushing their acceleration to maximum.

A short text message from Kenzie flashed on Hale's screen. *I'm going to freaking kill you!*

Hale gritted his teeth against the acceleration forces. Max burn wasn't something anyone enjoyed, and even though he'd experienced it, he couldn't get past the image of a ten-ton gorilla sitting on his chest. He managed to keep one eye open, intent on watching the flashing tracking numbers and course information in front of him.

The railgun fired off another series of shots, the barrage only just audible above the screaming engines. Ten seconds later the closest torpedo vanished from the plot.

Twenty seconds after that, Hale brought the engines back down to their optimum cruising speed. The trembling faded to a mere shiver, and Hale took a deep breath as the gorilla climbed off his chest.

"I'm... going... to... hurt... you... badly," Kenzie told him between breaths.

A series of guttural screeches sounded behind him. Small, furry arms and feet lashed out, flailing in all directions.

"Hey, hey, easy, man," Hale said, hand up. "It's over, relax."

Ears stopped flailing around and locked eyes with Hale, teeth bared, and let out a long, high-pitched screech. He crossed his arms, pulled his legs back in and glared at the captain, still breathing heavily.

Kenzie laughed. "You tell him, Ears."

The cabin speakers crackled to life. Lincoln's high-pitched screeching mirrored the chattermonkey's. "What in the hell was that, Hale? I almost passed out!"

"All right, everyone relax and focus. I gave us some breathing room, but we aren't out of the woods yet. Lincoln, how're the drives?"

The young engineer sputtered, his tone clipped. "They're fine. Compensators at seventy. I'm fine, too."

"Good." Hale cut the connection, then said to Kenzie, "What about those torpedoes?"

"Just downed another, still two closing."

Chuff. Chuff. Chuff.

"See, I told you, the old girl's got teeth," Hale said. "Knock out two more and we're in the clear."

"Assuming you don't crush us first," Ears grumbled.

"Hey, if you think you can do a better job flying this thing, come right on up here and give it a whirl."

"Well, maybe I will."

Hale barked a laugh. "Not likely."

Multiple warnings flashed on screen as they passed the wormhole's outer boundary. "All right, heads up, we're inside the boundary. Keep an eye on your systems. If—"

"Got another one!" Kenzie shouted, cutting him off. "Final torpedo closing. Impact in twenty-four seconds."

Hale's eyes darted to his nav computer. Twenty seconds to transit.

"Kenzie?" Hale muttered through gritted teeth, fingers white-knuckled on the control sticks. Wormhole 352 loomed ahead, its blue, white and red light pulsing and flashing wildly. Energy tendrils lashed out in all directions like some mythical sea monster, reaching out to pull them into its gaping maw.

"I'm trying, I'm trying!"

A proximity alarm blared throughout the ship. Warning screens opened on every display, telling anyone who'd listen that impact was imminent.

We're not going to make it, Hale told himself. He watched as the torpedo's white dot raced after them, gaining with every second. He found himself willing the thing to somehow blow up or veer off course at the last minute, but in the back of his mind he knew. He'd gambled and, unlike so many times before, this time it hadn't paid off.

"Impact in ten seconds!" Kenzie said.

Transit time eight seconds.

The railgun chuffed away.

"Kenzie, I—"

The explosion was tremendous. The STA Mark83 nuclear-tipped torpedo exploded three thousand meters astern; the blast wave slammed into the *Franny*, sending the survey ship reeling.

The ship bucked underneath him, and a brilliant light seemed to engulf them, filling the cabin with blinding white. The straps of Hale's harness dug into him, as the ship was thrown end over end.

He caught a glimpse of the wormhole's edge, and just before the blackness overtook him, he thought, *We made it through*.

Chapter Four

Chaos enveloped James Hale as consciousness returned. He grimaced at the blaring warning alarms and flashing displays. White-hot, irritating pain pulsed in his head. Confusion and panic threatened to overcome him.

He held a hand up to the blinding, undulating light of the wormhole's interior tunnel. There were no reference points at all, just an unending sea of white, blue and red lines. The feeling of the ship still listing, coupled with the apparent standstill outside the viewport, almost made him sick. He turned away, but the flashing holodisplays didn't help his situation either. He closed his eyes and pressed a palm heel into his forehead.

"Kenzie?" he called out, voice barely a whisper.

She didn't answer.

Hale swallowed hard and opened his eyes, looking immediately to where Kenzie sat. Her body pushed against her harness, slumped over in her seat, unconscious.

Sparks snapped out of a bulkhead behind him. He ducked and glanced over his shoulder at the busted ceiling panel. Electricity snapped and popped inside the damaged conduit, sending out a shower of sparks every few seconds.

Something in his peripheral caught his attention, and he felt another bolt of shock as he saw Ears, still strapped into his small couch, also unconscious. At least, Hale hoped the chattermonkey was only unconscious.

What the hell happened?

He remembered the torpedo, the explosion and seeing everything go white.

"Am I dead?" he asked aloud. No one answered him.

His i3 connection to *Franny* was still intact. Most, if not all, of her systems were still online and seemed to be functioning properly. He grabbed the controls and, with some help from the ship's navigational computer, was able to get *Franny* stabilized, bringing her to a relative stop.

Beside him, Kenzie twitched, letting out a soft groan.

Hale unclipped his harness and knelt beside her. "Kenzie, you okay?"

"Are we dead?"

Hale shook his head. "I don't think so."

She reached up and massaged her forehead. "Feels like my head is going to explode. What the hell happened?"

"I wish I knew," Hale said, sitting back on his haunches. "That torpedo should have turned us into space dust."

With one eye still closed, Kenzie reached forward and began tapping on one of her panels. "Minimal damage to the outer hull, almost no internal system disruption. Some slight thruster damage on the port side, but that's it. I can't believe it. We should be fried."

"Maybe, but I'm not complaining."

A deep, raspy voice spoke up behind them. "What in the hell was that and why does my brain feel like it's going to rip right out of my skull?"

Hale huffed. "Oh, good, he was just unconscious."

Another barrage of sparks snapped out from the

damaged conduit. They all jumped.

"I'm overwhelmed by your concern for my well-being."

Hale rolled his eyes, turning back to his holopanels. An irritating pain pulsed briefly through his i3, into his head, like the beginnings of a headache. The sensation faded and he dismissed it almost immediately as feedback from the explosion.

"Hey, at least we're alive," he said, rubbing the skin above the implant.

"For now, anyway," Ears added.

Kenzie tapped on her screen. "Huh, that's strange, the computer isn't picking up the beacon from Plaston. Hold on, I'm going to try something."

After several moments of working, Kenzie sat back, frowning. "What the hell? We're not picking up anything. Not even low-band radio frequencies from the com-relays. Nothing."

"That's impossible," he said. "Probably a receiver problem." He switched i3 connections and called out for Lincoln.

No response.

"Kenzie," Hale said.

Already moving, she said, "On it."

Behind them, someone clambered through the hatch. "What the shit is going on, Captain?"

"Just a bit of a hiccup in the schedule is all, Mr. Wilson. Nothing to be worried about."

"Nothing to be worried about? You said this was going to be a walk in the park. No issues, you said. *They won't even know what hit 'em*, I believe were your exact words."

"Yeah, well, shit happens," Hale told him without looking up from his displays. For the first time in a long time, he regretted taking on a client. Credits were credits. That had been his mantra, up until now, anyway.

"Shit happens?" Wilson asked, sounding completely aghast.

Hale opened his mouth to respond, but Kenzie's voice,

coming through the bridge speaker, cut him off.

"Captain, Lincoln's hurt; I need some help down here. Bring the medkit."

Instantly Hale forgot about his asshole passenger. "On my way down. Excuse me," Hale said, stepping around their client.

Ears hopped onto Hale's shoulder as he passed. "He's kind of an asshole, isn't he?"

The captain ducked through the main hatch into *Franny*'s main corridor. Long photostrips, running along the ceiling of the cramped passage, flickered and blinked on and off. Sparks snapped from several as he made his way past the crew berths, toward the galley.

Originally configured to hold the survey ship's scanning and processing equipment, the galley was the largest open space, next to the cargo bay. Two long couches were bolted to the floor along the starboard bulkhead, next to a long metal table. Their makeshift kitchen, along with several storage cupboards, took up the majority of the port bulkhead. Dishes and food packets were strewn across the compartment.

"Good thing it's Kenzie's turn for dishes," Ears said.

Hale stopped at one of the cupboards and started fishing through the contents. A second later he found the kit, and continued through the galley. He ducked through another hatch and into *Franny*'s cargo bay, cavernous and expansive compared to the rest of the ship, but still small by modern standards. A set of switchback metal stairs brought him to the deck where he turned back towards the bow and ducked into engineering.

The hum of the engines permeated through everything in the cramped space. If the crew passage was cramped, engineering was downright claustrophobic. A path, barely wider than he was, led through the maze of components, pumps, and the huge drives of the HY850 engines.

"Kenzie?" Hale shouted over the constant hum.

"Here," she called back.

151

Hale saw a hand appear over one of the components, and shuffled down to her.

Lincoln sat propped up against a steel-alloy transistor box, holding his right arm tight to his chest with his left. A stream of blood ran down the side of his face. He glanced up at Hale, his face a mask of obvious pain.

"Doesn't look like I'm going to be playing gravball anytime soon."

"How is he?" Hale asked, handing Kenzie the kit.

"Not bad, considering. Pretty sure his right arm is broken, and probably a concussion."

"I'll live," Lincoln said. "It's the *Franny* I'm worried about now. Condenser Number Two took a pretty good beating, and it looks like A-drive is offline."

A holodisplay flickered above Lincoln; status warnings and damage icons seemed to confirm the engineer's assessment.

"Can you fix it?"

Lincoln shrugged. "Not sure, depends on what's damaged and if we have the parts. We can probably make it to Plaston, but I doubt we'll be jumping anywhere soon."

"Yeah, that's the issue," Hale said.

Kenzie finished dressing Lincoln's head wound and looked up at Hale. "You think we can make it out of here with one engine?"

"I'm not going to say no, but without knowing more... I don't know."

Lincoln jerked away from Kenzie as she moved to secure his arm. "Ouch! Hey, easy!"

Kenzie groaned. "Oh, you're such a pansy. Hold still."

As they finished wrapping his arm, someone cleared their throat behind them.

"Captain," Wilson said, "I don't mean to be unsympathetic here, but I really must insist we get moving. If nothing else, to get this man some real medical help."

"He's kind of an asshole, isn't he?" Lincoln asked Kenzie.

"Now, listen here—" Wilson started, but Hale cut him off again.

"Enough!" Hale pointed a finger at his passenger. "Another word out of you and I'll personally throw you out the goddamn airlock. Is that clear?"

Wilson didn't answer, but his silence said enough.

Hale turned back to his crew. "Come on, we have work to do."

Chapter Five

"Still nothing, Captain," Kenzie said, folding her arms across her chest in frustration. "No sign of the Beacon, and no comm traffic. Hell, I don't even see the Utaro opening we came through. *Franny* can't even give me a positional reading because there aren't any stars to reference."

Hale stood behind her couch, watching the data scroll down her screen. Most of it was the computer trying to digest the information it was receiving from *Franny*'s sensor array. The gravimetrics and spatial energy readings were off the charts. Nothing like the minor, localized distortions common to the inner boundaries around most wormholes. They were, after all, literal tears in the fabric of space-time; abnormalities in sensor data were expected.

Hale's i3 flared again, his data stream from *Franny* fracturing just slightly. The filtering sensation was stronger than the last time. A pang of irritation formed just behind his eyes, like a sinus headache.

"Ugh, this headache," he said, pinching the bridge of his nose with thumb and forefinger.

"I was just thinking the same thing," Lincoln said. "I think *Franny*'s giving us a little taste of feedback."

Kenzie rubbed her eyes. "No, I don't think..." She trailed off, eyes darting to her displays. Fingers danced and a second later she said, "That's not feedback, someone's scoping us."

"Impossible," Hale said. "There isn't anyone out here.

153

Lincoln, bring up the array."

The engineer typed awkwardly with his left hand. "I..."

"Oh, come on, hop out of there," Hale said, patting the younger man on his shoulder.

"Sorry, Cap."

"Not a problem," Hale told him as they switched positions. A second later, data from *Franny*'s sensor array populated his display. "Nothing on wide-band. No signals interfacing with the nav-comms, either."

"It's there, Captain," Kenzie told him. "I was scoped pretty hard on the *Staton Island* during the Rathon Conflict. After that, the navy tripled our shield redundancy and made sure all i3 interfaces operated on a closed network. I'm going to try and isolate ours."

"What the shit is..." Wilson stopped himself, then said, "I mean, can you explain to me what is going on, please?"

"Something out there is tapping into our ship's i3 network. You aren't tied into our system, so you probably aren't feeling the effects. Isolating the network will cut off any outside... huh, that's strange."

Lincoln leaned over Kenzie's couch. "So, this may sound like a wild idea, but what about heading this way?" He tapped on her navigation display.

"Hey!" Kenzie said, slapping his hand away. "Don't touch."

Hale leaned over and read the course Lincoln had typed in. "Now, that's just freaky."

The course the engineer had plotted was exactly what Hale had just been thinking. However, it made no sense: there wasn't anything out there, just empty space.

Kenzie considered the numbers, then said, "How did you do that?"

"Not sure," Lincoln replied. "They just came to me."

"Okay, but there's nothing out there, just... wait a minute." Kenzie's fingers played across the holodisplay, zooming in on the coordinates. "Holy shit, Captain, there's something out there."

"What is it?" Wilson asked, voice on the verge of cracking. "An STA patrol? I knew they'd find us. I knew it."

"Shut up," Hale said, bringing up the data on his own display.

"Something's broadcasting out there," Kenzie said. "Whatever it is, it's powerful."

Hale frowned. "There's no profile information at all?"

"No, just an originating point. A hundred and forty thousand kilometers astern of our current position."

Even as Kenzie spoke, Hale knew she was right. The urge to go directly to those coordinates seemed to fill his thoughts. "Can you get us there?"

Kenzie shook her head. "There's an awful lot of interference out there. The space-time distortions in here are playing hell with the nav system, but I think I can manage."

"Do it."

Ears moved across the back of Hale's seat, then jumped past the console, to the ladder. "Do you even hear what you guys are saying? Let's just slow down here and think. I mean, we don't have any idea what we're dealing with out there. Do you really think it's a good idea to head off chasing phantom signals?"

"That's right," Wilson said, talking over Ears. "We don't need to be doing anything stupid, now. You should listen to your monkey, the—"

A bestial screech reverberated through the compartment as Ears launched himself through the air toward Wilson. Hale caught a glimpse of the chattermonkey's exposed fangs, but wasn't fast enough to stop him.

"Ears, no!" Hale shouted.

Wilson screamed, as the mass of sharp claws and silvery fur attacked. Arms came up to protect his face as he stumbled backward, almost plowing into Lincoln.

"Hey!" Lincoln yelled, pushing himself off the bulkhead.

Hale lunged after the chattermonkey, and by the time he'd pulled him off, Wilson lay curled in the fetal position. As soon as Hale touched his soft, silver fur, Ears seemed to relax.

Their passenger cradled his left arm to his chest, his face a mask of shock and confusion. He inspected the injured arm briefly, his confusion morphing to fury in front of Hale and his crew.

Wilson pointed with his uninjured hand. "That little shit just tried to kill me!"

Hale cocked his head to one side; a palm-length laceration crossed the man's forearm. A single line of blood ran down his skin.

"Oh, yeah," Kenzie said. "A real gusher."

Hale forced himself not to laugh.

"I'll give you *little shit*," Ears said, squirming in Hale's grip.

"No, Ears, stop," Hale said, then turned to Wilson. "If he'd have wanted to kill you, you wouldn't be standing here right now."

"I want it locked up! I knew those Animal First people were right all along; wild animals aren't pets! I'm going to bring charges on all of you!"

"I know for a fact, Ears is more civilized than most people in the galaxy," Kenzie said. "Especially people like you."

Wilson was ignoring her, fingers prodding at his mortal wound. "Oh, God, I could be infected with something. I need a sterilizer! Has he had his shots? Captain, I want him quarantined and checked for diseases."

This time Hale couldn't help but laugh. He felt Ears relax; the chattermonkey patted Hale's arm with one small hand.

"It's okay, Hale, I'm okay."

Hale loosed his grip. Ears pulled himself free and climbed up to the captain's shoulder.

"First of all," Hale told their passenger, "you will demand nothing while you're a passenger on board my ship. We've already two-stepped this dance today, and my legs got no more moves left. I'll not repeat myself.

"My crew and I have work to do. You will get yourself cleaned up and remain in your assigned cabin until we reach our destination, and—"

"But—"

Hale raised a hand and continued. "And if you decide you need to stretch your legs before I personally tell you it's okay to have a walk, you'll be doing it outside. Clear?"

"Captain, I—"

"Am I clear?"

Wilson glared at Hale, contempt filling his eyes. After a long moment, his face seemed to relax and he turned and disappeared through the hatch.

The crew of the *Franny* stood silent for a time, listening to the clatter of footsteps fading.

Finally, Lincoln said, "Kind of a grumpy bastard, isn't he?"

Hale snorted. "Well, someone did just try to take his face off."

"Bah, I barely touched him," Ears replied, waving a dismissive hand toward the empty hatch.

"You really think he'll bring charges?" Lincoln asked.

Kenzie scoffed. "I'd like to see him try."

Hale turned back to his holodisplays. "Doesn't matter right now, anyway, we've got bigger fish to fry at the moment." He reached up and scratched the chattermonkey's neck. "Why don't you go get yourself cleaned up."

Ears nuzzled against Hale's caress. "Me? I'm fine. Never been better."

"Maybe, but you never know what kind of diseases he may be carrying."

Chapter Six

It took another fifteen minutes of dealing with faulty sensor readings and ghost images to triangulate the source of the strange signal. Even then, *Franny*'s computer hadn't been able to determine an accurate distance, only an approximate location.

Twenty hours later, they were finally getting verifiable readings, and the data they received was disturbing, to say the least. Verifiable in that whatever it was appeared on visual scopes and not just as a phantom sensor return.

"It's massive," Kenzie said, staring at the wireframe image slowly forming in front of them.

Hale rubbed sleep from one eye. He'd tried to nap, but the combination of coffee and the unknown had kept his sleep fitful at best. He sat up, examining the object as it grew, resolution increasing as the *Franny* drew closer.

The captain felt movement behind him and turned to see Lincoln leaning over the back of his chair.

"That thing looks bigger than Devona Station," the engineer said, rubbing his chin.

"Hell, it's bigger than anything ever created," Kenzie said. "Even the *Harbinger*, at eight miles, is a baby compared to that."

"Compensating for something, you think?" Lincoln asked.

The object, which now spanned seventeen miles at its further points, was an amalgamation of curving, spindly towers and bulbous sections, all equally large. Three central spires grew out of the dorsal hull, twisting around each other until they formed a massive obelisk stretching almost five miles high.

"Well, obviously it's a deadly castle of death," Ears said. "A Deadly Space Castle of Death and Destruction, and I, for one, am super-excited we came all this way to see it. Maybe it will invite us aboard for some flaying and sacrificing."

"Can it, Ears," Hale said.

"Well, it doesn't look friendly, whatever it is," Ears observed from behind them.

Lincoln chuckled. "That's an understatement. Looks like that thing just came straight out of hell and hit all the demon-spawn on the way out."

"Should I bring the railgun back online?" Kenzie asked.

"I doubt it will have much effect on that." Hale nodded to the monstrous thing. "But, if it'll make you feel better..."

Without a second thought, Kenzie tapped a sequence, and a two-tone alert sounded. The muted whirl of the railgun mounting system echoed through the hull as the weapons spun into position.

Another twinge of discomfort washed over Hale. He reached up and massaged his implant. "Ugh, what in the hell is that?"

The irritation had been growing gradually worse, and none of them had found a way to block the signal from passing through their i3s. It wasn't malware or a virus, according to Kenzie — it was only harvesting information from *Franny*'s computer, not attempting to subvert any of the ship's systems.

"God, that's annoying," Kenzie said, rubbing her scalp behind her ear "If I didn't know any better, I'd think I was hungover."

"That thing must have some ridiculous power requirements," Lincoln said. "I can't even imagine maintaining that thing."

"I think we should leave," Ears said.

Hale shook his head. "There isn't anywhere to go."

"Should I open channel?"

Ears scoffed. "Oh, yes, let's talk to the Mysterious Deadly Castle o' Death. Great idea."

As Hale opened his mouth to shut the chattermonkey down, a wave of calm passed over him; the sensation that everything was going to be okay overwhelmed him. As did the feeling that opening a comm channel wasn't exactly necessary.

"Huh," Kenzie said. "Apparently we don't need to."

"What was that?" Hale said, shooting her a look.

"That's the damnedest thing, Kenzie," Lincoln said. "I was just thinking the exact same thing."

Hale looked back at his engineer.

Lincoln shrugged. "I mean, it wasn't really a thought,

more like a feeling. A concept of a feeling, maybe."

"Great," Ears chided. "The Castle o' Death is also in the Twilight Zone. You guys want to know what I was thinking? I was thinking we need to get the hell out of here, that's what I was thinking."

"Enough," Hale said, raising a hand. "I..."

The idea hit him out of nowhere, and even though he couldn't explain why, he knew and believed it with one hundred percent certainty.

"We should probably cut our engines," Kenzie said, already tapping commands into her console.

Lincoln laughed. "Oh man, this is trippy."

Kenzie glanced back at him. "What?"

"I was thinking that, too."

"So was I," Hale said.

"I wasn't," Ears added.

Hale turned, the rebuke already formed in his mind, and just before he spoke every light on the *Franny* flickered and a presence unlike any other he'd felt in his entire life seemed to occupy every bit of space around him. The gigantic Castle o' Death vanished from the display, replaced by a pulsing, churning fractal pattern.

"What—" Kenzie started.

The words were clearer in Hale's mind than anything else he'd ever heard, and even though he didn't really understand them, he knew they were true.

"You are not Talsar." The voice was soft, almost childlike. It carried a tone of nervous excitement, or something approximating that. The feelings Hale experienced were more of confusion than pure delight.

All three exchanged questioning looks.

Finally, Hale said, "No?"

The glowing mathematical pattern pulsed and shifted with every word. "I am Yesarin. Your beings are somewhat altered than any true Prestar bloodlines I have stored in my Core; however, it is clear that you are descendants of the Astar line. I present myself to you as your Conduit to the

Paths."

Hale didn't know what to say. He sat staring at the undulating lines, wondering if he was in fact going crazy. The pattern pulsed slowly, lines twisting and angling around themselves. The only training he'd ever received on first-encounter protocols was the three-hour introductory course in the Academy. Of which he remembered nothing.

"I'm Captain Hale," he said, conscious of how ridiculous he sounded. "My crew here is Kenzie, Lincoln and Ears. We're from Earth."

The lines danced briefly before Yesarin spoke again. "There is another being aboard your ship."

Hale couldn't help but chuckle. He'd completely forgotten about their passenger. "Mr. Wilson. Yes, that's right."

"My purpose is to be fulfilled. Please command me."

Hale frowned, exchanging a look with Kenzie, who shrugged. "I don't understand."

"The Paths are open. I have seen your beings transit them frequently. It seems as though my previous Astar commanders were correct in their assumptions. You have returned. I was beginning to think that they had been incorrect."

"I'm sorry, I still don't understand. Do you think we are your commanders?"

"You are of Astar. Your words command the Conduit, and therefore me. That is my purpose."

Kenzie sat forward. "What do you mean? What is your purpose?"

"I reach the Paths."

Hale sat forward. "You mean the wormholes?"

"Yes."

"What do you mean, we are of Astar?" Lincoln asked.

"You are of Astar. Although, as I have said, your bloodlines have diverged somewhat. The ancestors of your line would be proud to see how you have carried on, despite your obvious disadvantages."

"Well, I'm sorry to tell you this," Hale said. "But whatever information you're working with is wrong. We aren't Astar..." He pronounced the name slowly. "We are human, from Earth."

Almost before he'd finished speaking, the feeling of being wrong swept over Hale.

"I don't know how we could be wrong," Lincoln said. "We have thousands of years of evidence to prove it."

Kenzie ran a hand down her face. "This is crazy."

"Are you putting these thoughts in our heads?" Hale asked.

"Yes," Yesarin said simply. "Ideas are the most effective medium for communicating, especially between individuals, like ourselves, who do not have a background of understanding to base our words on."

"Huh," Hale said. He couldn't argue with that logic.

"But you're wrong," Kenzie said. "We aren't some long-lost descendants of anyone. The human race is *from* Earth."

"Incorrect."

"The hell you mean, *incorrect*?" Lincoln asked. "That's where we're from. It's a fact."

"I am sorry, Being Lincoln, my wish is not to anger you at all; however, your facts are, indeed, incorrect. I took a complete bio-neural scan of your genetic make-up during your journey. There is no mistake: you are Astar."

"Okay," Lincoln said, putting an elbow on the back of Hale's chair. "So what's an Astar?"

"The Astar line goes back thousands of years. Back even before the Schism. Your ancestors are the very beings who created me. The Paths were the greatest discovery of the Prestar civilization; however, that discovery destroyed them."

"You say we're descendants of the Astar line," Hale said. "Part of the Prestar people?"

"That is correct."

"But you're not."

"No. I am not. I am Yesarin. I am the Conduit."

"A conduit to the paths?"

"Yes."

Lincoln snapped his fingers. "You're a wormhole gateway."

"Yes."

"So, what, like an artificial intelligence?" Hale asked.

"There is nothing artificial about me. I am Yesarin. I am a Conduit."

"You opened wormhole 352," Kenzie said, more a statement than a question.

"Yes."

"Why?" Hale asked.

"You are Astar. This is my purpose."

"Okay, to reconnect, maybe? Then why not just open a wormhole straight to you? 352 has been open for years and no one has ever reported any contact with anything at all, much less an alien intelligence smack-dab in the middle of the wormhole."

"I am a Conduit to the Paths. I cannot create Paths. I tracked the space-time distortions your people made while crossing the Paths and determined this was the closest avenue for contact."

"So all the other wormholes we've discovered," Lincoln said, "you made those too?"

"I did not. They are the Paths. I am only a Conduit."

Kenzie groaned. "Yes, we got that part. Is it too hard for you to say the paths are naturally occurring and you can open a gateway to them?"

"That is correct."

Hale and Lincoln both looked at her in surprise. In Hale's estimation, she'd just earned every credit he'd ever paid her, and then some. Then a troubling thought struck him.

"Why did you close it?" Hale asked.

"I did not close it," Yesarin said. "The quantum field surrounding my *gateway*, as you call it, was disturbed by a localized gravitonic distortion, which caused my anchors to become unstable and collapse, closing the gateway."

Kenzie glanced at Hale. "The torpedo."

Hale nodded. "So where are we now?"

"The Paths."

"Sooo," Lincoln said, drawing out the 'o'. "Can you open a gateway to anywhere?"

"Yes."

"Can you open a gateway home?"

"There is nothing that would please me more."

Chapter Seven

The *Franny* and her crew emerged into real space to the glare of an orange sun.

"Sensors coming back online," Kenzie told him.

"How's she holding up down there?" Hale asked Lincoln.

"Just a couple minor yellow-lines, nothing major."

"Anything on scopes?"

Kenzie frowned. "We're not receiving any of the regular query beams from STA. But I'm picking up several large power readings from around the system. Wait a minute..."

She trailed off and began typing furiously at her terminal. A holomap of the system flickered to life between the two stations, blue orbital path lines, orange wireframe planets and three asteroid belts.

Behind them the hatch swung open, slamming against the bulkhead, and Wilson came through. Ears growled at him as he stepped closer to Hale's chair, and their passenger seemed to rethink his positioning, practically pressing himself into the opposite bulkhead.

"I felt the jump," Wilson said. "Did we make it out?"

Hale ignored him and pointed to the holomap. "What is that?"

"Well, I can tell you what it's not," Kenzie told him. "It's not Sol." She flicked through several other screens. "Star charts aren't confirming. I can't get a fix on our position."

Hale worked his own station. Yesarin's wormhole still pulsed behind them. "Yesarin, what's going on? Where are we?"

"You are home."

Ears moved up onto Hale's shoulder. "I beg to differ, there, Yesar-whats."

"Where is Sol?" Hale asked.

"The star system you refer to as Sol, or Star 87423 in our own databases, is approximately three hundred fifty thousand light years distant."

Wilson let out a nervous bark of laughter. "What the hell is going on? Who is that? Where are we? Captain Hale—"

"Quiet," Hale said. "That's impossible: the Milky Way is only one hundred twenty thousand light years across."

"We are no longer in the Milky Way galaxy," Yesarin said, his unchanging tone more than a little annoying.

Franny's bridge exploded in cursing and confused accusations. Kenzie and Lincoln both leaned forward, speaking in hurried, panicked tones, both vying for their captain's attention. Wilson became a blabbering mass, crying out incoherently. Even Ears screeched, jumping up onto the forward console, silvery paws beating on the viewport. A million thoughts ran through Hale's mind and despite himself, he felt his stomach turn, anxiously contemplating the alien's words.

"Hold on," Hale ordered, raising two calming hands. "Hold on, people. Yesarin, explain—"

An alert toned, and Yesarin's twisting fractal pattern was replaced by something that Hale did not expect. The bust of a human male appeared in Yesarin's place. Thin, dark lines of a beard and mustache contrasted with the man's pale skin. His eyes were bright, almost glowing pits of blue. Two angular collar boards rose up behind his head, a half-circle cut out of the inside edge of each, forming a full circle. The orange robe, draped over wide shoulders, never moved as he spoke.

165

A low-pitched voice, tinged with curious enthusiasm, came, crystal-clear, through *Franny*'s comm system.

"Those who have been lost," the man said, dipping his head. "Welcome. I am Reygestar, Supreme Consul to the Prestar. We are very pleased by your return."

Reygestar tilted his gaze, as if he was looking around *Franny*'s crew. "Yesarin. It has been so long, it took the High Solar almost a full cycle to recognize your output signature. Your return is a monumental occasion."

Yesarin's voice echoed through the comms. "Supreme Consul, I am pleased to be home. It pains me to admit that I had long ago given up any hope of ever seeing Prestar again. It was fortunate these beings encountered difficulties during the transition onto the Path, otherwise I might still be out there."

Lincoln straightened behind Hale and blurted out, "Difficulties! That's one hell of an understatement there, pal!"

Hale frowned and held up a hand. "Wait, I'm sorry, I think I'm missing something here. So, the Prestar are an alien race of beings that appear to be very similar to humans and you're... what? Some kind of artificial intelligence that can open gateways through your paths. Am I batting a thousand so far?"

Reygestar didn't answer.

Yesarin said, "Being Hale, I am only eighty-seven point three percent positive that I understand your reference, based on information downloaded from your ship's core; however, I believe the answer to your question is yes — you are batting a thousand."

"Okay, so if you're that powerful, why did it take us being stranded into the wormhole for you to do anything. Why did you even open that pathway to begin with? Why not open one to bring you right back here?"

There was a pause.

"Final Directive 0013a: By order of High Commander Terinstar. To prevent further escalation and destruction,

Yesarin will remain unfound by any who are not Astar. You will not return to Prestar until requested by a properly vetted Astar representative. The success of Departure requires your silence."

"Well, that explains it," Ears muttered under his breath.

"There was a war," Reygestar explained. "A war that almost destroyed our people. The Talsar faction all but defeated the Astar almost ten millennia ago. The secret of the Paths was to be theirs and theirs alone. Yesarin was taken and hidden by one of the last Astar survivors, closing the Paths to the Talsar. Yesarin is one of a kind, you see."

"So, you couldn't come back here until some of the Astar bloodline asked you to come back?" Hale asked.

"That is correct," Yesarin said. "Your people are the descendants of those who Departed. At the time it was determined that even if the Talsar somehow acquired Pathway technology, they would not venture out of our galaxy. Earth was the perfect planet to rebuild upon, a place for the peaceful Astar to start again."

Hale shook his head in disbelief. Even with all the physical evidence staring him right in the face, he was still having a hard time coming to grips with what he was hearing. He had a feeling the enormity of what he'd just learned wouldn't actually sink in for a while.

"So, what now?" Hale asked.

"Now," Reygestar said. "Now, it's time to bring the Prestar people together again. Our lost children are home and our people are whole."

Hale sniffed. "Well, I mean, that's a good plan and all, but I can tell you that the majority of my people will not react well to what you've just told us. In fact, I can see this going very badly once the news breaks. To humans, to my people, Earth is home. Always will be. No matter what you tell them."

Reygestar smiled. "Ah, yes, I understand. As one of our wisest Consuls said once, the place where your heart is, your home is also there."

167

Josh Hayes Q&A

Where did the idea for your story come from?

The idea for wormholes has always intrigued me. While talking with Ralph and Nathan about what kind of stories they were looking for, both said there were several that were about "going through a wormhole", so I thought it would be cool to write about getting stuck inside one.

The TV show *Firefly* is one of my favorite series and I thought it would be fun to work with a small crew dynamic.

The baseline information for the shared universe gave me a lot of material to work with, and while I couldn't fit it all in, I wanted to try and have the most fun I could have with the characters and technology.

What authors or other forms of media have the biggest impact on your writing?

Peter F Hamilton is by far one of my favorite authors, David Weber and the Honor Harrington series definitely. I grew up on Star Trek: TNG and a whole other slew of sci-fi shows and movies.

I love science fiction that is well written, smart and intelligent. I love antagonists that are despicable, but at the same time, sympathetic.

If given the opportunity to explore space through a wormhole, would you take it?

Most definitely! I would in a heartbeat.

What are you currently working on?

Right now I'm finishing up work on the third book in my *Second Star* series: *Shadows of Neverland* and I'm in the process of drafting an unrelated military sci-fi novel, *Echoes of Valor*.

The premise of *Echoes of Valor*, takes elements from movies like "Black Hawk Down" and "Courage Under Fire" and meshes them with high-technology sci-fi. The novel will be the first in a trilogy, which leads into a larger space opera saga.

Where can readers find more of your work?

You can find me on Facebook, and Twitter (@joshhayeswriter) and my website, www.joshhayeswriter.com.

I also run a YouTube Show/Podcast, "Keystroke Medium" with fellow author, Scott Moon, where we interview authors, review books and talk about the craft of writing. Check out our website, www.keystrokemedium.com for more information on the show.

When I'm not working, writing or podcasting, I spend time with my beautiful wife, Jamie, and our kids.

The Aeon Incident
By Richard Fox

Wisps of turquoise lights flowed around the scout ship's bridge as she crossed into real space. The entire ship seemed to stretch and flex as the strange physics of the wormhole faded away.

Ensign Lyon's grip on the railing around the command deck tightened as a final wisp jerked away. He'd made over a dozen wormhole transits and had developed a gnawing suspicion that something was alive in the wormholes, something that coveted the presence of other sentient beings, with each trip.

He'd kept his suspicions to himself. Claiming there was some malevolent entity within the wormholes was a sure ticket to a psych eval and losing his platoon.

The rattling of metal on metal snatched Lyon's attention away from the window. In the center of the bridge, the only other two crew on the ship, the ship's master and her data tech, were frantic with activity.

The data tech's fingers, inlaid with gold plating and glowing cables running to her work pod and into the shunts in the back of her bare head, twitched like she was in the midst of a seizure. The clink of her fingers against each other filled the bridge. The data tech — Diannao, if Lyon remembered right — was slaved to the ship, her nervous system intertwined with the *Ryukyu*'s every function.

"Drones away," Diannao said. Lyon felt minute vibrations through his armored boots as miniature rail guns spat micro-drones into the void.

"Wormhole looks stable," Commander Sandun said. The *Ryukyu* class scout ships were designed to carry the bare minimum of crew, which meant the captain had his share of responsibilities above and beyond decision making and carrying out the ship's mission.

Lyon tapped his fingers against the railing as an avalanche of data swept over holo screens around Diannao and Sandun. It wasn't his job to make sense of it all, he was just the payload.

"Keever particles from spatial anomaly Victor-97 indicate another thirty-nine hours of sustainable transit to home station before the next cycle," Diannao said. Her blind eyes stared at the ceiling, wavering from side to side like she was speed reading.

"That's why I said it looks stable," Sandun said.

"The outpost." Lyon hit a knuckle against the railing twice. "Any contact?"

Sandun shrank away from Lyon's question. The *Ryukyu* rarely took passengers on its scouting missions, and Lyon was sure Sandun had never been in close proximity with an officer from the Intervention Corps. Lyon didn't fault Sandun for being timid. In his armor, Lyon stood almost head and shoulders over a normal human, and the speakers in his throat broadcast his words in a panther's growl.

Lyon didn't wear the armor so much as it was bolted onto his body. The armor's form was designed to intimidate: the face plate on his helmet looked like a bare skull, the plates molded to make him appear well-muscled and deadly. The Intervention Corps had run across numerous alien species; not all of the encounters were friendly, and resembling a primal beast had proven to be an almost universal message of strength.

The same nerve-shunt tech that linked Diannao to the ship bonded Lyon to his armor, and to the two dozen battle drones packed into launcher tubes.

"We're still a dozen light seconds from the Aeon planet," Sandun said. "We'll have a data feed soon."

The Aeon, a primitive species on an Earth-like world of wide plateaus separated by enormous mountain ranges and deep seas, were classified as a Watch species. The initial probe that came through the wormhole in their system had noted several genetic and societal markers that warranted further observation. Aliens on the Watch list had the potential to become peer competitors with humanity. After the Ixith Incursion, and the subsequent devastation, the surviving humans on Nexus vowed to keep a keen eye on any Watch species and not repeat the mistake made with the Ixith.

Lyon called up the ship's munitions report. There they were, six rad missiles locked away inside the ship's hull. It only took one rad missile to poison a planet's atmosphere and doom every living thing that depended on the atmosphere to a slow death.

After the first probe put the Aeon on the Watch, Nexus had established an observation post on one of the moons circling their world. The scientists on the years-long assignment were to record and report on the Aeon's development. The report should have come through when the wormhole re-emerged in the system — but it was nineteen hours overdue.

A course plot came up on a holo screen in front of Lyon, a courtesy from either the captain or the ship's data mistress. The *Ryukyu* would reach weapons range of the Aeon's world in less than an hour. A ping on the dark side of one of the tidally locked moons showed where the observation team had their base.

"Link established with the outpost," Diannao said. "Life support optimal, data cores damaged." She sucked air through her teeth.

Vid feeds came up around Lyon, showing the interior of the outpost. Rooms had been ransacked, leaving clothing and broken furniture scattered about. Lyon touched a feed and zoomed in on a hallway. A pair of white boots stuck out from around a corner. He swiped through feeds until he found another angle on the boots.

There. A dead man lay in the hallway, arms badly broken into cruel angles, a black pool of dried blood beneath him. Lyon panned around, studying the blood splatter on the walls. An ugly, flat nebula of vitae stained a head-level sign.

"Beaten to death," Lyon said. "Single blow."

"Ten bodies identified from outpost video feeds," Diannao said. Screen shots of the dead came up, each with an ID pic next to the body.

"There were eleven assigned," Lyon said. "Where is Doctor … Philips?" The ID pic of a woman with a severe face and blond hair didn't have a matching body in the outpost.

"How?" Sandun asked. "They all had the psych-conditioning against physical violence, and the security robots should have put the place on lockdown the first second biometrics readers showed—"

"Outpost security was taken offline twenty minutes before breach of the number six airlock," Diannao said. "I've recovered nine seconds of video from the data buffers."

A silent video of an airlock came up. Sparks flew off the door seals. A metal spear tip pierced the door, twisted aside as hooks popped out of the tip and bit into the door. The door collapsed as whatever was on the other side ripped it off the hinges.

Tall aliens with gangly limbs and bowed legs, in simple-looking space suits, rushed through the doorway. Each carried a spiked club. The video cut out as more filled the airlock.

"The Aeon were a nascent industrial civilization, steam tech, when the outpost was established twenty years ago," Lyon said. He pulled up the data file on the aliens. The file showed bipeds with blue-grey skin and gangly limbs that corresponded with the attackers he'd just witnessed assaulting the outpost.

"There are remains of chemical-powered landers near the outpost," Diannao said. "The atmosphere is polluted with hydro-carbons … several cities on the dark side of the planet have electrical lighting … radio spectrum is active with Aeon-language programs. The planet's technology is on par 1970s Earth."

"Impossible," Sandun said. "There's no way they could advance so quickly."

"I believe my own eyes," Lyon said. "The inner airlock door is still intact … and Philips' space suit is missing from her locker."

"They took her prisoner," Sandun said. "Diannao, scan for—"

"I have her gene-beacon." Diannao's head shook from side to side, and a holo of the Aeon world grew over their heads. A ping came from a large city sprawling around a semi-circular bay. "The location is imprecise, position error within two point seven kilometers of the plot. She's behind a significant amount of mass, a bomb shelter perhaps."

Sandun ran a hand over his forehead, which was sweating despite the chill air.

"We … I'm invoking sanction; there's demonstrated hostility. If the Aeon can advance this quickly, then they will become a threat to Nexus by the time the wormhole reconnects in twenty years. We'll hit the planet with two rad missiles just to be sure," Sandun said.

"No." Lyon swiped away the data feeds. "Rad missile sanction requires all three of us to authenticate. I refuse. I'll drop on the city, extract Philips, and find out exactly what happened."

"Wait…" Diannao's hand jerked up. "The security robots on the moon … their code has been altered. The new logic paths are jumbled, confused."

"Alien," Lyon said as he tapped in to Diannao's feed to see for himself. "The Aeon could have hacked into the system. I can't risk my drones down there."

Lyon went to the lift leading to the shuttle bay.

"You can't go down there alone!" Sandun shouted.

"Watch me," Lyon said as the lift doors closed.

***

174

The drop pod rattled around Lyon as it broke through the upper atmosphere. He should have come in after a saturation bombardment of thermobaric warheads cleared his drop zone and his drones had the perimeter secured. One human officer against a hostile planet was not part of the Intervention Corps' operational planning.

The sweep of Aeon air-defense radar touched his drop pod, but the missile batteries around the port city remained silent. That the stealth tech built in to his pod kept him hidden from the defenses was a pleasant surprise. Ejecting from the pod early and trying to land with his grav-chute wouldn't make his job any easier.

"Lyon," Sandun said over the tight-band lasers connecting the pod to the *Ryukyu*, *"if you're killed down there, Diannao and I will dust the planet. We don't need unanimous consent from the dead."*

"This your way of wishing me luck?" Lyon asked.

"No. Yes. I mean … we'll send the recovery drone if you find Philips. Rad missiles if your life signs go flat."

"Roger. Lyon out." He cut the transmission. He panned cameras to an open park surrounded by skyscrapers, and set his landing point with a touch. His hands opened and clenched as the icy touch of anxiety swept through his stomach. The city was full of civilians. Aeon adult couples gave birth to broods of up to five children every few years, and the camera feeds of drones that had swept over the city showed many families on the streets as morning broke.

Children. Non-combatants. This was the Valadin incident all over again, just without a battalion of drone soldiers to back him up. The thought of hurting any non-hostile sentient filled Lyon with dread.

At least that part of me's still human, he thought.

Thrusters roared to life and slapped him against the side of the drop pod.

"Landing in ten seconds," the pod chimed.

Lyon wrapped his hand around his rifle handle and flexed every muscle in his body; the haptic feedback awakened his armor and brought it online. His nervous system reached out and melded with the armor. He felt the rub of restraints against his chest and shoulders, the chill of acceleration gel packs pressing against him. His entire being felt lighter, stronger. Adrenaline coursed through him.

He let out a slow breath and took his laser rifle from its cradle on the pod door. Now he was ready to fight.

A bell chimed, growing faster and faster as his altitude fell to zero. Thrusters flared to life and his drop pod trembled for a second, then slammed into the Aeon world. His restraints popped off their moorings, and Lyon lunged out of the pod as the door hinged upward.

The pod's thrusters had scorched the grass of the field. The smell of charred plants and cherry blossoms assaulted Lyon as he stepped free of the pod. He raised his rifle and swept it around.

Skyscrapers surrounded the field, all with angled roofs and different slopes, like the architects were trying to mimic a mountain range.

Lyon snapped his rifle to a group of a dozen Aeon at one end of the field, clustered around a hoop atop a tall pole. All wore red swaths of cloth tied around their limbs and waists, over dark body gloves. Each held a metal rod with a wide hook at the end. Lyon's mind went to the clubs he'd seen the Aeon carrying into the outpost.

These Aeon stood perfectly still, their antennae twitching wildly.

Lyon advanced on the group, his rifle humming with power, his finger on the trigger.

An Aeon dropped his club and ran off; the rest followed soon enough. Hoots and clicks of the Aeon language filled the air as they fled. Lyon turned around and saw another group of Aeon, with green cloth instead of red, running past another hoop at the end of the field.

"I landed in the middle of a game," Lyon said.

"Diannao's monitoring the Aeon radio frequencies. The militia channels are going berserk right now," Sandun said.

"No time for subtlety." Lyon slipped a disc off his belt and tossed it into the air. A propeller in the center of the disc spun to life and sent the drone straight up. High-energy radar pulses built Lyon a map of the city as it went higher and higher.

The drone homed in on Philips' gene-beacon … and found her on the other side of a bridge in a squat building built like a fortress. He'd landed close to where they'd detected her from orbit, which turned out to be several hundred yards away from where she really was.

"Figures." Lyon found a wide boulevard leading to a bridge and took off running. He clicked his jaw twice and jerked a thumb back at the drop pod, keying the self-destruct sequence. The pod was little more than heat-warped metal and a few elementary ballistic computers, but nothing could be left behind for the Aeon to learn from.

A magma charge in the pod's core activated, melting the pod down to slag and smoke within seconds.

Lyon ran, his armor propelling him to nearly sixty kilometers an hour as he weaved around sidling Aeon vehicles. He heard shouts of fear from adult Aeon and squeals of fear from children as he raced past the blocky vehicles.

Lyon suppressed a smile. How would the citizens of old New York have reacted if a seven-foot-tall alien had landed in Central Park and taken a sprint down Madison Avenue?

"You've got several vehicles converging on your position," Sandun said.

"I'm on a road in the middle of the day — why are you telling me this?" Lyon vaulted over a cargo truck and left a sizable dent in the roof as his hand slapped the car to give him a little more lift.

"Armed vehicles. I can see tanks and armored personnel carriers. There's a pair coming up on your right," Sandun said.

Lyon grumbled and regretted not waiting for a larger ship to take him on this mission. An Intervention Corps orbital support officer would have told Lyon the relevant information right away … and told him just how big the cannon on the tanks were.

He ran around a crowd of Aeon on a street corner and found the bridge leading to the fortress a few hundred yards ahead. Giant servos on the bridge's flanks jerked like clockwork cogs, raising it with each *thunk* that echoed off the buildings. A gap between the two halves of the bridge grew with each turn of the gears.

His armor was capable of surviving exposure to cosmic rays or direct hits from Ixith disrupter beams, and could go months without a battery recharge. Weighing in at over eight hundred pounds, one thing it couldn't do was swim.

Lyon's feet gouged divots in the concrete road as he skidded to a halt. He aimed his rifle and fired a white-hot bolt that left a scar in the air and blistered the paint on cars before it hit the gear housing. The mechanics raising the bridge ground to a halt as its inner workings melted down to slag. The other gear set strained against the sudden workload.

Lyon aimed across the river and found his shot blocked by a barge full of cargo containers.

The percussion of a machine gun hit his audio receptors at the same moment as bullets thudded against his breastplate. The rounds ricocheted with little more effect to him than a poke in the chest. An Aeon armored car, boasting a heavy machine gun in a turret ring, pulled off the road running parallel to the river and stopped in a swath of grass. The machine gunner shouted and waved a hand in the air, then ducked behind the weapon.

Lyon heard a squeal from the Aeon on the sidewalk behind him. The smell of cherry blossoms grew stronger as the aliens tried to flee from Lyon; several jumped out of their cars and took off running. Lyon looked from side to side, searching for any cover that would keep the civilians out of the line of fire. They ran from him like waves away from a stone dropped in a lake, and he opted to hold his ground.

The machine gun opened up and shredded a car between Lyon and the attacker. Rounds bounced off his legs, and one nicked the side of his throat.

Screams of anguish came from behind Lyon as the bullets found unarmored bodies. The Aeon soldier behind that machine gun didn't stop shooting.

Lyon charged at the armored car. He got a foot onto a raised median between lanes and launched himself into the air. He put two laser blasts into the armored car, bursting it apart into a sudden bonfire.

Lyon landed and scanned the direction the armored car had come from, finding nothing but gridlocked traffic and fleeing aliens. The smell of cherry blossoms was almost cloying in Lyon's nose.

"Sandun, didn't you say something about a tank?" Lyon asked.

A thunderclap burst behind Lyon. The concussion from an air vortex behind a tank's main gun round slapped him to the ground as the tank-killing sabot round missed him by several feet. Lyon went face first into the pavement and slid into a van.

He got to his feet, knowing he had seconds before the tank crew could reload the main gun.

The van he'd hit was empty. Lyon dropped his rifle, stabbed his fingers through the thin metal of the side panels and grasped the frame. He twisted his body toward the tank, and stared into the abyss at the center of the main gun. His suit read his intent, and helped him throw the van like it was a bale of hay.

The van sailed through the air and smashed into the front of the tank in a shower of glass and crunch of metal, impaling on the main gun.

The tank fired and blew the van into hot shards of shrapnel. The gun traversed from side to side, searching for Lyon.

The ensign jumped onto the body of the tank and grabbed the barrel with both hands. He slammed his knee against the tube, bending it with a groan of steel. Lyon grabbed the handle on the driver's hatch and ripped it aside.

An Aeon with a slack jaw and padded helmet looked up at Lyon from the exposed compartment. Lyon grabbed the driver by the collar and tossed him into the river. He reached into the opening and tore out the steering column.

"The bridge!" Sandun shouted at him.

Lyon's head snapped to the side. While his blaster shot had stopped one half of the bridge, the other was still rising.

"Damn it." Lyon tossed the steering column aside and ran toward the bridge. Cars had slid down the roadway and bunched together. His boots left dents over engine blocks as he skipped over the jumble and hit the unobstructed ramp leading over the river.

The servos in his armor's knees and hips whined with protest as he raced up the bridge. The edge of the other half of the bridge was nearly thirty yards higher than the end of his ramp, and getting higher.

"There's no way you'll make that jump!"

"Do you want to come down here and do this?" Lyon swung his rifle over his shoulder and mag-locked it to his back. His feet beat a rapid tempo against the bridge. Ballistic projections from his armor tracked into the river, not over the other half of the bridge.

"No…"

Lyon planted a foot against the edge and leapt into the air, his arms pinwheeling as he locked his eyes on the edge of the rising bridge. He reached out and missed the edge by several inches.

If there was one lesson Intervention Corps stressed to its recruits, it was to always have a backup plan. The armor was designed for most terrestrial and void conditions, and engineering several options to return to a void craft was one of the earliest upgrades made to space suits.

Lyon punched his left arm at the underside of the bridge, and his grappling harpoon shot out. The diamond tip of the grappler was designed to penetrate the hull of a warship and stop an agent from floating into the void, so the thick concrete of the bridge proved little challenge. It punched through the thick concrete and got a solid anchor point.

The grapple line went taut, and Lyon swung beneath the bridge. He looked down and saw the obstructing barge, its Aeon crew standing atop the cargo containers and pointing at him.

"We can't see you. Are you dead?"

"Shut. Up."

Lyon activated the motors in the grapple's housing. In a zero-gravity environment, the motor could have reeled him in easily. Here, deep inside the Aeon world's gravity well, it whined in protest and sent Lyon an error message.

Lyon swung his feet back, then toward the side of the bridge. His body rocked back and forth a few times before he built up enough momentum to bring him to the edge. He grabbed the iron frame and dug his fingernails into the metal. He uncoupled his grapple, dug his fingertips into the metal and pulled himself over the edge.

"Oh, there you are. Good work. Diannao, go ahead and scrub the missile launch."

Lyon slid down the bridge. The streets below were deserted of civilians. Dozens of Aeon in bright yellow uniforms, carrying rifles, charged down the street that ended at the fortress.

Bullets smacked against the bridge, knocking up puffs of pulverized concrete.

Lyon drew his rifle and sent out a spray of shots into the surrounding buildings and the stopped cars the soldiers were using for cover. The laser blast hit the buildings and overwhelmed the windows with rapidly expanding waves of superheated air. Broken glass showered down on the Aeon soldiers, sending them scrambling for cover.

Lyon ran to the fortress, a squat building only three stories high with a lower outer wall. He ran past an Aeon soldier, glass crunching beneath his armor-shod feet. He slalomed around more soldiers as they tried to recover from the explosions. None tried to fire on him as he neared the fortress.

"How thick is that outer wall?" Lyon asked as he built up speed.

" 'Bout three feet. Why?"

The ensign lowered a shoulder and slammed into the wall. The rough-hewn bricks and mortar gave way in an explosion of dust and shards of masonry. In the courtyard were several armored vehicles, all crawling with Aeon crewmembers in various states of dress as they readied their vehicles.

An Aeon bellowed a war cry and ran at Lyon, a wrench in his hand. Lyon stood perfectly still as the Aeon reached the blunt instrument behind his head and swung it against the human's helmet. The wrench bounced off Lyon with a clang. The soldier backed away, nursing several broken fingers from the strike.

Lyon turned his suit speakers up to maximum and stomped a foot as he shouted.

The Aeon winced and covered their ears, then bared their teeth at Lyon and hissed.

The smell of rancid oil wafted over Lyon.

"So much for doing this without a fight," Lyon murmured. A machine gun on an armored car opened up and pounded his chest and shoulders with hits.

Lyon fired from the hip and hit the ground beneath the firing car. The explosion sent the car cartwheeling back, the gunner on a separate ballistic trajectory over the wall. The blast slammed Aeon soldiers to the ground or against the unforgiving armored sides of their vehicles.

Lyon went to the reinforced doors leading into the fortress and twisted the barrel on his laser rifle. A short, white-hot cutting torch ignited beneath the tip of the muzzle. He sliced through the heavy metal hinge on the door frame in a few seconds. He ignored the few bullets that bounced off his back or careened off the wall in front of him.

"Lyon, got some odd readings … looks like Philips is on the move."

"I'm almost inside." Lyon caught a glimpse of an Aeon out of the corner of his eye. The alien charged with a bayonet fixed to his rifle, his eyes wild with rage. Lyon backhanded the alien with a lightning fast strike, hitting the Aeon so hard his feet swung up and his entire body went parallel to the ground.

"She's pinging outside of the compound, heading north."

Lyon's cutting torch sliced off an upper hinge and he stepped out of the way as the bank-vault–thick door teetered over and fell with a clang. He glanced inside and saw several machine gun positions with ready crews. An Aeon shouted a terse command and the doorway filled with bullets as the machine guns opened up.

He leapt into the air and grabbed a window sill on the second story. His fingers bit into the concrete and he launched himself up another floor and grabbed on to the roof. He hauled himself over the edge and onto the roof, covered in pebbles.

"North! I think she's in that helicopter."

The aircraft, little more than a wire frame with a plastic shell connected to the rotor, flew slowly over a thoroughfare leading away from the other side of the fortress. Getting the doctor out of a helicopter was going to be a lot harder than digging her out of a fixed structure, especially since Lyon couldn't fly.

Lyon sent a command pulse through his armor, and Philips' transponder flashed on his HUD. The point jumped around, interference coming from the many skyscrapers.

Lyon dialed back the power on his rifle and aimed at the helicopter, then hesitated. Where could he hit the alien craft and bring it down without killing Philips in the process?

One bit of data stayed constant on his HUD: a reading that didn't match what he saw. He lowered his muzzle slightly.

"How fast is she moving?"

"She's getting away!"

"Answer the damn question."

"Maybe … four or five miles an hour."

"Chopper's going a hell of a lot faster than that." Lyon scanned the road … and saw a black van fighting to drive around abandoned cars and heading the same direction as the helicopter.

"Got her." Lyon raced to the other side of the roof and leapt off. He landed one foot on the outer wall, then came down on the highway. He caught up to the black van and knocked it against a concrete median from the side. The van screeched to a halt, leaving an ugly scar of paint against the median.

An Aeon in a dark blue body glove spilled out of the driver's seat and pointed a pistol at Lyon. Lyon slapped a palm over the muzzle and crushed the weapon with a quick squeeze. The driver yelped in fear and ran off; the smell of cherry blossoms filled the air.

Lyon dug his fingers into the side of the van and ripped the door away.

A human woman with blond hair was inside, shackled by her wrists and ankles to the floor. She looked up at Lyon, her mouth contorted in disgust.

"Dr. Philips, I presume," Lyon said.

"You idiot!" Philips snapped. "They've seen you. Seen what you're capable of. Do you have any idea what that means for the Aeon?"

Lyon snapped the chains with a quick tug. A bullet hissed overhead.

"Don't know. Don't care. You're the mission." Lyon took a cylinder off the small of his back and held it out to Philips.

"No," she said, backing away from him. "I have to stay. Fix the damage you've caused. They'll *listen* to me. You take me away and the entire species will be on the warpath against us."

Lyon grumbled and clicked a button on the cylinder. An

electric whine filled the air, and paper-thin layers peeled off the cylinder and floated in the air, each the size of Lyon's palm. The material flew toward Philips and bonded against her arms and legs.

Lyon never trusted emergency life support suits. The idea of relying on a gossamer-thin shell when he spent most of his waking hours in proper battle armor offended his warrior soul.

Philips tried to pull the emergency suit away, with no success. The layers bonded together, forming an exoskeleton around her. Lyon pressed the remnants of the cylinder still in his hand, the environmental regulator, against Philips' side. The suit molded itself around the regulator, and her life signs fed into Lyon's computer.

Philips was well-fed, hydrated and had suffered little in the way of physical trauma except for a few recent bruises around her wrists and ankles. She had, evidently, been well treated by her captors.

'We've got her telemetry feed! I'll send a recovery drone for you both … but you'll need to find some place with elevation; the extraction drone doesn't have the same stealth shielding as the drop pod, and the skies are filling up with Aeon fighters,'' Sandun said.

Lyon sent an override command to Philips' armor and set it to follow mode.

"No! Damn you all, you've got to listen to me!" Philips pleaded.

"Then start talking." Lyon turned around and picked out a building with a relatively flat roof. He ran towards it, Philips' armor keeping pace a few steps behind.

"I can smell it in the air, the aggression response," Philips said. "The whole planet must know by now. We're only hours away from a paradigm shift."

Lyon burst through the glass walls on the ground floor of his chosen building. Groups of Aeon in family clusters backed away from the intruders, all hissing like startled cats and baring their teeth, even the children held in their parents' arms.

Lyon saw a small sign with multi-level tiers next to a doorway. He slammed the door open and found a stairwell leading up the entire building. The top faded away in the light streaming through the glass ceiling.

"What do we need to know? What happened to the outpost?" Lyon took the steps three at a time and Philips followed.

"We screwed up," she said. "Jenkins led a specimen collection mission to the eastern marches. Lander got hit by lightning and we had to call in the auxiliary. Damned if we didn't pick a local noble's favorite fishing spot, and they found our shuttle. The Aeon are smart and clever all on their own, but when there's a group their hive mind kicks in and their intelligence gets exponentially higher."

"Hive mind?" Lyon glanced up as a door a flight above opened up. A soldier tried to poke the end of his rifle through the opening. Lyon sprinted up the stairs and slammed the door shut with a swift kick that broke the rifle in half, barely breaking his stride as they continued higher.

"Aeon release pheromones when they're under duress — changes the emotional state of any nearby Aeon," she said. "It's an incredible survival trait. You wouldn't believe some of the predators in the—"

"That smell. The cherry blossom smell is their fear response?" Lyon asked. He looked up and counted another forty stories to go.

"Yes, but there's more to it. Their antennae broadcast the same response on the electromagnetic spectrum — sends a weaker signal than the pheromones over longer distances, alerts Aeon much farther away. Soon as the Aeon start linking together, they get smarter, act together, form a hive mind with a singular purpose. When the Aeon recovered our shuttle, the local kingdom was so excited they linked together and reverse-engineered some of the technology."

"How could primitives without electricity figure out the crystal matrix in the shuttle computers?"

"They don't have anything in the way of advanced

computing, yet. But as soon as the Aeon saw that a thing was possible, their hive mind figured out how to replicate it. The noble made radios, radios that broadcast on the hive mind frequency. The entire Aeon species linked together within a year. We've never seen a species advance so far and so fast; not even rogue AI have evolved this quickly. They were obsessed with finding who left the shuttle behind. It wasn't long before they had rudimentary satellites in orbit, and it was only a matter of time before they found the outpost."

"And you didn't do anything to stop it?"

"Doctor Batista wanted to rad bomb the planet, but there were enough of us that thought we could steer the Aeon away from being a threat. It would have been so easy to present ourselves as allies, guide them to the stars peacefully, but Batista wouldn't allow it. After the Aeon's first rocket launch, most of my team was ready to rad bomb the planet. Me and another kind soul were the only ones against terminating the Aeon."

"Then they came knocking at the door," Lyon said. The stairs ended on a small platform just beneath the glass roof. Boxy Aeon fighters streaked across the sky, the rumble of their engines sending a vibration through the glass.

"Yes. Exactly. I've made some progress with the nobleman, but … god, I can smell it from here, the anger pheromone. The entire planet is at war with us humanity right now. They won't stop unless I can talk them down. Let me go back!" Philips struggled against her armor, like a patient in traction trying to scratch an itch.

"*Ryukyu*, you have our location?" Lyon asked.

"Roger. Sending the extraction drones now."

"Send one. Reserve the other for later," Lyon said.

"Thank you, thank you so much," Philips sighed in relief.

Lyon fired his rifle at the ceiling and blew out a wide opening.

"This anger response, it can be reversed? The reversal will spread?" Lyon asked.

"Yes, I can sway them back. Just give me time."

"There is no time. Wish me luck." Lyon took an anti-grav generator and slapped it against Philips' stomach. The device beeped, the tones came faster and faster as Lyon stepped back.

"Wait. What—" Philips jerked into the air as the anti-grav twisted the planet's graviton field and sent her accelerating straight up. She vanished into the clouds a few seconds later, where the *Ryukyu*'s drones would retrieve her.

Lyon crouched, then jumped through the broken ceiling. He did a somersault and kicked his feet out, taking him clear of the roof. He fell to the city, where Aeon tanks and soldiers were massed around the base of the building. Wind buffeted him as he streaked toward the ground.

He activated the anti-grav generators integral to his armor and slowed his descent.

"Lyon, what the hell are you doing?"

"I will give them something to fear." Lyon aimed his rifle at a wide-bodied car loaded with antennae, then lowered the weapon. No, word had to get out. Word had to spread.

He'd exercised restraint before now, tried to minimize casualties, but if he couldn't force the Aeon off the warpath then the *Ryukyu* would commit xenocide to protect Nexus.

An armored car with twin high-caliber rifles fired on him, stitching a line of burning craters in the building he'd leapt from. Lyon fired a tight beam from his rifle and cut the anti-air vehicle in half.

He angled his fall to land right on top of a tank and killed his graviton generator. Lyon fell faster and slammed against the turret.

Aeon soldiers, all clad in bright yellow and brandishing rifles, hissed and shouted at him. The smell of rancid oil assaulted his senses.

Lyon pointed a finger at an Aeon with a decorative sash over his uniform. It didn't take much anthropological know-how to spot a leader. The commanding alien had a bodyguard of tall, well-muscled Aeon, each carrying metal clubs like those used to kill the outpost's crew. The alien leader raised a curved sword and bellowed a phrase Lyon didn't understand. The rest of the Aeon repeated the words over and over again.

The sword-wielding alien charged at Lyon. Lyon stepped off the side of the tank and walked casually toward his opponent.

The Aeon executed a perfect slash to Lyon's neck, a blow that would have separated his head from his shoulders, had Lyon been unarmored. The blade shattered on impact, causing no harm. The Aeon stumbled forward and into Lyon's grasp. The chanting stopped.

"I'm sorry." Lyon slammed a hand around the alien's throat and hoisted him into the air. The alien kicked and slapped at Lyon for a moment, then Lyon snapped his neck with a twist of his fingers. He tossed the corpse aside.

The smell of rancid oil grew stronger and the leader's bodyguard rushed at Lyon, clubs raised over their heads.

Lyon held his ground and snatched a club away from the first Aeon to strike at him. He crushed the bodyguard's skull with a reverse strike. He swung the club down at another guard who had his club braced over his head to block. The blow shattered the alien's club and smashed in through his shoulder; blood the color of Earth's sky sprayed out of the wound.

Lyon shoved the dying guard aside and punched the next attacker in the chest hard enough to send him flying into a tank with a crack of breaking bones. Lyon reached a fist behind him and struck an Aeon just beneath an ear hole.

The blow knocked the alien's head clean off his shoulders and sent it flying into the soldiers surrounding the makeshift arena.

Lyon caught a club strike with ease and held it fast, staring into the eyes of the last Aeon bodyguard. The guard tried to pry the club free.

The guard's face rippled with color, the antennae on his head twitching wildly.

There. The smell of cherry blossoms.

The guard let go of the club and backed away, his hands raised over his head to ward off a blow.

Lyon snapped the club in half and turned the volume on his suit's speakers to maximum. He brandished the broken weapon over his head and let out a primal roar that shook windows and sent nearby Aeon scrambling away, blood dripping from their ear holes.

The scent of fear grew stronger, almost choking him with its intensity.

The Aeon turned and ran, tripping over each other in a panic to flee the human monster.

"There's … there's been a shift in the planet's radio transmissions," Sandun said. *"Drones over other cities show the Aeon leaving the streets."*

"Send down the recovery drone in three minutes." Lyon looked over the dead Aeon and felt only regret. He tapped the jagged edge of a broken club against his leg and lifted his head to the sky.

***

The recovery drone brought Lyon through the force field separating the *Ryukyu*'s shuttle bay, barely bigger than a car garage of a Nexus home, from the void. Sandun and Philips were waiting for him.

"Ensign!" Sandun gave Lyon a thumbs-up. "I've been speaking with the good doctor here, and she assures me that with the Aeon in their present condition, their planetary culture should regress. No threat to Nexus in the near future — we can forego the rad bombardment for now."

Lyon twirled the broken club in his hand. He took slow steps toward Philips, a cruel smile on his face as her gaze took in his scarred and bloodstained armor.

"Did Philips tell you how the Aeon managed to get through the outpost's security?" Lyon asked.

Philips backed into a bulkhead, her face deathly pale.

"It— it— it wasn't my fault!" she said.

Lyon snapped the broken edge of the club out and pressed it against her chest. The emergency environmental suit was strong, but had no chance of stopping Lyon if he chose to drive the club through the doctor's heart like a stake.

"The Aeon have no computers," Lyon snarled. "How did they manage to shut down the security robots? Get through the inner airlock door?"

"They were going to rad bomb the entire planet." Philips looked to Sandun for help, but a growl from Lyon kept the other man away. "I had contact with the Aeon noble, a quantum dot communicator I'd left on the shuttle. I told them what was coming, the threat if we couldn't get the Aeon to see us as friends. I disabled the security, let them in. I didn't know they were going to kill everyone! I swear!"

Lyon pressed the spike against her armor and pierced the outer layers. Philips let out a squeal and broke into tears.

"I was just trying to help! I didn't know. I didn't know!"

Lyon pulled the weapon away and tossed it aside.

"You will contact the Aeon leader. Tell him if they ever launch another rocket or even attempt to leave their atmosphere, we will destroy their planet. Sandun will set the outpost's rad missiles to automatically attack if they detect the Aeon in space." Lyon looked at Sandun, who nodded vigorously.

"We're taking you back to Nexus to stand trial," Lyon said to Philips. "Violation of the Sentient Contact Act. Negligent homicide. The Intervention Corps will send a team to clean up the mess you've made."

Lyon turned around and went to the edge of the shuttle bay. He looked down on the Aeon world, and hoped the aliens learned the lesson of fear.

Richard Fox Q&A

Where did the idea for your story come from?

I wanted to write a story about one soldier fighting against a hostile planet, and make the story as exciting and as contained as I could in the number of pages I had available.

What authors or other forms of media have the biggest impact on your writing?

I am a long-time reader of military science fiction and am a fan of Dan Abnett and Aaron Dembski-Bowden. I saw Star Wars when I was a wee lad and it's been all downhill from there.

If given the opportunity to explore space through a wormhole, would you take it?

Of course — it's fun to follow one's imagination.

What are you currently working on?

"The Crucible", the 8th book of The Ember War Saga. If you liked this military science fiction story, you'll love The Ember War.

Where can readers find more of your work?

The best place is Facebook, search for Richard Fox, Author https://www.facebook.com/richardfoxauthor/

You can find all of my novels on Amazon.

The Doors of the Temple
By Jo Zebedee

I didn't know how the connection was made. Above even their ace pilot's pay grade, for a start. Too convoluted, for a second.

All I knew was that the gimps in the office above decided they'd worked something out. No doubt they'd huddled beside the armored windows overlooking the devastation of the First Array attack's repeated strikes, and the total destruction of the Second's, and smugly congratulated themselves.

Johnston took me into his entombed office, scanned thrice daily for listening devices, and sat me at his desk. He leaned in to me, voice low.

"This theory is from left field," he said. "So classified, we had to come up with a new security level."

"How far left?" I asked, but I didn't really care. We needed solutions, and the conventional had failed. Science had created weapons that had done as much good as the hole in the ground they caused. Besides, the rumors had been flying for months — that science was exhausted, and the chief of staff had turned to more arcane arts. I gave a quick grin. "Worse than astrology?"

It was a standing joke. The astrology fellow had got us nowhere: suffice to say, whatever star you were born under, you were screwed. No one was going to survive another year of this war. If they did, they'd wish they were dead. Contaminated ground, leached water and starvation will do that to a person.

"Worse than the tarot, even," he confided. I snorted, but he ignored me, nodding sagely. " 'Death doesn't mean death.' " His mimicry of the tarot-reader was uncannily spot-on.

"Hard to stand over when the card comes out in every deal," I said. "It kind of made me take notice."

That, and the Third Array — a night-attack. The morning had revealed dead bodies on the streets around us. The smell of that day, the stench of cooked flesh, and the sounds — the screams, the gagging of the rescuers — would stay with me forever. That, and the soft whisper of cards being dealt, the quiet mumble of the reader, low and secretive, the same card turned over and over, until it became an accusation all of its own. I shook myself, hoping to erase the memory — but nothing had.

"Mythology," said Johnston. He tapped the desk, bringing my attention back to him. "They brought in some guy from Ireland with an accent so thick I could stand on it. He says he knows what to do. He says he can save us."

I'd come across the Irish guy, last week. He'd been put in the corner, surrounded by books, and I could see why — no one likes to sit near a Beardy-Weirdy with an odor problem. Not even New Age arts, it seemed, because the essential oils were thick enough to choke me. Perched on top of his books had been the same file everyone had received.

Yeah. *That* file. It wasn't a secret anymore — not since some liberal-minded geek had leaked it to what was left of the press (one corner office, flickering electricity, two slightly dented laptops).

A new wormhole.

It had appeared at the end of the Fourth Array, around the time we realized just how screwed Earth was. That Array took out half the Eastern seaboard. The return strike — from America to Europe — removed the Balkans from the map. Once you start erasing whole territories, the point of no return comes pretty quick.

It wasn't its sudden appearance that made the wormhole noteworthy — we've had wormholes open and close in the past. No, it was that this one was different from anything seen before. It was double-headed: one way in, two ways out. And it was nearby — a tear in the dust-ring orbit of Saturn-X, an inner satellite of Saturn. Too close for us not to explore: if it was viable, we could get a mother-ship off Earth. An ark, to keep humanity going.

Which brought about the need for volunteers. I'd avoided the last three wormhole explorations, citing testing duties instead.

Each of those explorations resulted in zilch — and I mean zilch. No ship returning with good news. No ship returning at all. Whatever happened to those crews, we don't know. The wormhole could have eaten them in transit, a black-hole might have sucked them in at the other end. Hell, maybe one led to the party-planet to end all celebrations and the crew just decided to stay. I sure would.

When this latest call went out, though, I put my name in the ring, knowing they'd go for me. There aren't many pilots with my sort of experience left. Not since NASA got taken out.

Well now, Coulter, you might say, you obviously had a death wish. And, you know, I just might have. My wife Janie and little Mark, they had lived not that far from the NASA base. They bought it while I sulked around Arizona, trialing anything that might stop the tit-for-tat from hell. (And what I trialed accounted for Estonia, so that worked out.)

In truth, I don't think it *was* a death wish. I thought of Janie coming on to me the way she knew made me hot. Of her, just after Mark was born, all sleepy during a night feed. Holding him, and meeting my eyes, and the wonder of us creating him. I thought of her the day I left for Arizona, Mark perched on the top of her bump, making us laugh. The new baby, the Mark-carrier, we said.

When I got to thinking like that, I got choked up. So much so, I gave a quick "Aye, sir!" to Johnston and hightailed it out of the office and didn't ask some of the questions I should have. Like, what mythology? And what it might mean.

All right. So maudlin, so much rubbish. You get the picture: I couldn't stay and be sane. Not with those memories. And I couldn't go and top myself when I might be some use. Janie would never let me live that down.

"You're supposed to be a hero," she'd tell me. She might run her fingers down my shirt buttons while she did. "You're supposed to save people, not run out on them." She'd tap my medals, one by one, and it would be like a needle straight to my heart. "What about the other little Marks out there? And the Janies — don't they deserve a hero?" She'd pat my butt and turn me to face the door. "Now get on with it, hero, and don't look back. We'll be fine, Mark and me. I'll take care of him."

That's the only comfort I have. That she will, until I join her up above and we do it together. I believe she will be. See, that's the thing about me — when I believe, I believe as strong as I can.

But that's for another day. First, we needed to see if ol' Paddy was sober when he did the working out, and if this really did offer hope.

***

A Class-2 Worm-hopper — the best ship left, I was told, and that was okay. I'd won my flying stripes in those old Hoppers. I was more comfortable in it than the lost Worm-cruisers. Too much controlled by the ship in the Cruisers; I like my flights mean and personal.

This one was small and mean, all right.

A crew of three: pilot, co and engineer. One passenger: Dr. Padraig O'Donnell, Trinity College, Dublin, he of the Odor problem. Apparently he was the only one who might know what to do when we reached the end of the wormhole, dammit. I threw him a can of deodorant when we boarded, and told him to use it. After that, he evaded all my questions about what we would find there, muttering about needing more data and wandering off. I'd have had more luck asking the data-cells to produce a piece of literary genius.

Flight time: four months. A straight launch, gain trajectory and speed and keep going. No gizmos, no exploration, just go. Even so, there were no guarantees: Earth could have finished the job of destroying itself. I couldn't tell what made me antsier — that I might not return to Earth or that, if I did, there'd be nothing left. That's the sort of thought that makes me put my head down and fly — and I did it well, because we reached Saturn's orbit right on target.

"Okay, team." I scanned the readouts. All good. Speed steady. My mouth was dry, and that was good, too — a careful pilot makes fewer mistakes. "Last checks."

They reported in, one by one. Engines were sound. Trajectory spot-on. Deodorant had been applied. Minutes slipped by. The dust-field could be seen. If I squinted and strained, I could just make out the tear.

Another minute and I could see it wasn't a tear, but a gaping rend. I ran my gaze around it, taking in its size, its dimensions.

"Sir." Di, my co, saw what was wrong at the same time as me. "What the hell?"

I had no idea. One half of the wormhole was smooth, as it should be. The other ragged.

"A Janus particle." O'Donnell was behind me, close enough I could feel his heavy breath. "I'll be damned." He gave a laugh, short and self-satisfied. "I was right."

I wanted to ask what he was right about and why this wormhole was like none I'd ever seen. I opened my mouth to do so, but the hole swallowed us.

I've carried out fifty wormhole jumps. I know the bump as the ship goes in, the lurch in my stomach that threatens to set the piranhas nibbling, the easing as the ship matches velocity.

Then, the boredom. A wormhole can take hours to get through — hours when the console has to be attended to and there might be nothing other than the blip of instruments, the steady hum of the engines, and the sure knowledge that the boredom can end at any moment. And so can your life.

This was like no wormhole jump I'd ever taken. My stomach lurched, yes, then climbed into my throat and stayed there. The ship shuddered, shaking so violently I worried she'd rip apart. It felt like the hole wanted to expel us. Di yelled something, but the nuance was lost by her cheeks being pulled back to her ears. I suspected it was a curse word to match those screaming through my mind.

The outer sensors showed the hole streaming past us. Ahead, two lights merged, one purple, one green. Symmetrical, the pair of each other. *Like the ragged and smooth edges*, my mind delivered, helpfully. Or it would have been helpful, if it had made any damn sense.

The hole split ahead of us, the green branching to the right, the purple to the left. I forced myself forward, fighting the gees, hoping for a signpost, hoping for anything to get this jump over before I lost my ship. A red light flashed on the command console, some kind of warning, and I thanked the Space Gods I'd insisted on Jaq as our engineer. If anyone could keep this tub intact, it was them.

"What way?" I yelled. The lights flashed past, faster and faster. Ahead wasn't an option, we had to take one of the branches. "Paddy, what way, damn you!?"

"I don't know!" His accent was lost in panic.

"What the hell do you mean!" Why else had we brought him?

His breath was back on my ear, warm and moist. "There'll only be one way!"

I tightened my hand on the control bar, gripping it. Right or left? Would it make any difference? Would we die either way? Alarms blared through the ship.

"Hey, hero. Have you frozen?" A different breath on my ear, dry, the voice a whisper, yet clear over the alarms. The slightest touch on my ass made me jerk. "Wanna join me? Or do you wanna live?"

Oh, God. The question I could never answer. I wanted to be with her; I didn't want to die.

"Well?" She was teasing. In the middle of crashing chaos, she was teasing. My mouth smeared into some kind of smile. That was my Janie.

"Do you want to live?" she shouted.

"Yes!" I yelled. I wanted to live. The betrayal was in me and around me, but it was the truth. I wanted to live and remember her. Under the stars, in the sunlight. On the Earth. "Show me!"

The green tunnel, the one on the right, flared. It might have been our trajectory, or a trick of the light. It might have been nothing but hope, but I slammed the control bar to the right. Di met my eyes, hers wide, questioning.

"Go, go, go!" yelled Paddy-of-the-uselessness.

The ship veered into the right head of the wormhole. Light lanced from the ship's propulsors, filling the wormhole behind me. With a last flash that made me throw my arm over my eyes, the purple light faded into nothingness and the second head of the worm closed.

The ship's shuddering stopped, but I was still shaking. Alarms blared, but all around me was silence, as if I was apart from the ship and everyone on it. I took my hand off the control bar, my skin sticky with sweat. I turned my seat around, the quick flick-flick of my foot pushing it away from the console familiar, grounding me.

"What the hell was that?" I asked Paddy. He was smiling, the mad Irish git.

"You chose right," he said. But he didn't tell me what that meant.

* * *

Disembarkation from the ship confirmed what the outer sensors had indicated. Wherever we were, it wasn't a party-planet. Not that I'd ever expected one. But I'd hoped for more than this — a dead plain stretching for miles, no water,

199

no vegetation, just hard-packed soil and rock.

The air in my mask carried the staleness of a vacuum flask opened after months in the dark. Which wasn't a bad analogy; the spacesuits must have been years old. Checked every year, for sure — I knew, I'd confirmed the yearly pass-card was in place on each of them — but never worn.

We transferred onto the surface, boots clanking, gravity making my bones feel heavier than they ever had. Whatever planet we were on, it must be a giant. We marched forwards, me, Jaq and the good doctor. I scanned all around as best I could — the suits weren't made for ease of use — and stayed on alert, my quick breaths misting up the inside of my visor, my heartbeat loud enough to hear in my over-pressured ears.

Ahead, a line of tall forms waited, sharp sun silhouetting them from behind. I found my right hand moving toward my thigh, where I had a KL-16 strapped. Not a pretty weapon, by any means, but effective. The kind of weapon the Array beams had been developed from. If the aliens made any move, they'd be mashed onto the surface of their planet.

We made our way slowly, one heavy foot after another. Jaq, I saw, had reached for his — hers, I never knew from one day to the other what Jaq would be — weapon and had it cradled across both arms. It made me itch to do the same, but I didn't trust myself. Jaq was the calmest person I knew and could be trusted not to shoot; I didn't believe the same for myself.

"Why ain't they moving?" asked Jaq, confusion evident in the tinny voice in my transmitter.

"They're not alive." Paddy, unmistakable with his brogue. He sped up and, for an old guy, he was surprisingly limber. "They're statues."

I exchanged one glance with Jaq — a visor-hooded one that might mask the level of my disgust — and strode after the unarmed Paddy.

He stopped just before the figures. Once alongside him,

I relaxed. He was right: they were statues, lined beside each other as if they'd just stopped one day, here on this sun-bleached plain. Some were tall and bronzed, almost Egyptian in their look, others squat and ugly, of whitened rock.

I indicated for Jaq to fall into the watch-position, covering me, and I stepped up to the closest.

Sandstone, by the looks of it, smooth and worn, a face carved crudely. I walked around the statue, Paddy following. The back of the statue had a second carved face, the mirror of that on the front.

"By God, I was right!" Paddy's voice thundered through the transmitter. He grabbed my shoulder, swinging me to him, and I could see his grin through the visor. "We've done it! We've saved them all."

"What in damnation's name are you talking about?" Jaq growled.

"The statues! We found the right place." Paddy pointed around them all. "We can go back to the ship now."

"And do what?" I asked. "Worship the idols?"

"No, no," he said, and another grin broke. "We did it. We closed the Janus gate. That's it — we're done."

What the hell was a Janus gate? Presumably something to do with the wormhole? Cold fear started at the base of my spine as the rest of his words set in. We'd closed the gate? I found myself staring across the plain. It stretched in each direction. No city's smoke filled the sky, no birds flew overhead to promise some kind of life.

"So we get to go back?" Jaq's voice was so hopeful, it nearly broke my heart. I'd given up nothing to come here; Jaq had a partner — very much female and then some — waiting back on Earth.

"Ah, no, lads." Paddy backed away, hands out. "That was never the deal. The doors of Janus's temple only open in war, see. We closed them as we came through."

"And that means?"

"The war on Earth is over. But we're stuck here."

I turned away, disgusted. It was what I'd expected, of

course, not to return. But not being left here, on this barren plain on an empty world. Not with those statues watching me, their double faces following my every move.

***

I called the crew together when we got back to the ship, and informed Di that we weren't going back. She took it in her stride — we'd known this might come.

All that was left was to decide how we'd go out. We could traverse the planet and hope to find somewhere to make a settlement and wait to get older, watched by the statues. The idea sat sour in my belly.

Stay with the ship and wait for resources to run out? Except we had enough provisions for a return flight and then some — six months of waiting for death didn't appeal.

The silence stretched, heavy, almost obtrusive. Finally, it was Jaq who stood and confronted the silent Paddy.

"So, what do you know about this place?"

"We hoped it would be here," he said.

He looked at me, seeking authorization, and I gave him a nod. We might as well know why we were fucked. He reached into his inside pocket, revealing sweat-rings under his arms, and pulled out a data-store. He tabbed it on and projected its contents onto the sensor screen. A statue appeared, and I jumped. It was the statue on the plain, the white-stoned one. Except it wasn't on a plain, it was on a field of grass. A field unmistakably Earth-like.

"This," he said, "is what we call the Janus stone." He paused, as if reflecting. "Although it's got nothing to do with Janus."

That name again. Jaq shifted from foot to foot. "Get on with it."

Di nodded vigorously.

"Ah, now, it's a hard story to capture," said Paddy.

"Start with who Janus was?" I suggested. The rate he was going, we'd be spending the six months listening to an

202

academic lecture.

"He was a Roman god. No Greek equivalent. No equivalency anywhere. He was a two-faced god." He paused, as if for effect. "He was the god of gates and doorways." He met my eyes. "Of beginnings and ends." He opened his hands wide. "Of war and peace."

Jesus. Di leaned forward in her seat, listening. Jaq started to pace.

"Except Janus *wasn't* only found in Roman myths," said Paddy. "Our wee stone on the screen tells us that. It's from an island in the middle of a lake in Ireland. Early Christian, not Roman."

He zapped through some more pictures, and I recognized some of them — an Egyptian statue, a sandstone one. Two coins, showing a two-faced god.

"Janus," he said. "When you learn what to look for, he's in plenty of places. All over the world." He leaned back, a slight smile on his face. "Through cultures, through places. In Africa, in Europe. In a field in the middle of nowhere."

"So?" Jaq's voice was sharp, making me frown. Jaq was a listener, not an activist.

"So…." Paddy flung his arms wide and I could smell his stinking armpits, foul and sharp. Faced with six months of that, I'd kill him first. My right hand fell onto my holster and tightened. It would take moments.

"When they brought me in and told me where the wormhole was, I made the connection. Saturn-X, the asteroid-orbit it was in?" He smiled, the smug bastard. "It's also called Janus."

Di's breathing was labored, as if she was struggling to hold herself in check. Her hands, too, had tightened, I noted, this time on the armrests of the seat, as if forcing herself to stay in place.

"That's how I made the connection. You see, Janus's temple had a role in war." He flicked on another slide, and this one showed only words.

In war, the gates are open; in peace closed.

"What the hell does that mean?" asked Di. She was half on her feet, glaring at Paddy.

"It used to be the rule of Janus's temple. The gates opened in war." Paddy looked at me, beaming, as if the smelly git deserved a prize. "And the wormhole opened in the orbit of Janus. Janus who has left marks throughout the world — evidence of there being a link from him to Earth. It had to be the temple gate." He clicked his fingers. "I brought us here and you closed the gate. There'll be peace on Earth now."

Jaq was running fingers through coarse hair, making it stick up in sharp spikes, forearms tight with corded muscles. Identified-male today, it would seem. "You don't even know it worked."

The words were accusing, a mirror of my own. I found myself on my feet, weapon freed from its holster and aimed at Paddy. Di moved first, launching herself at him.

"My home!" she yelled. "My family! Because you made a crazy connection between some stones!"

Di was unflappable. Always. Jaq strode forwards, hands out and ready to finish Paddy off. My crew were never like this. We worked together, not apart.

Everything clicked.

"Stop!" I yelled, and they did. I pointed at the console. "Di, start searching this planet. Map it for anything that isn't this plain."

"What?" She let go of Paddy, eyes confused, almost betrayed. "Why, Sir?"

"Because I ordered you to." I kept my voice mild, but it was a struggle. I turned to Jaq. "I need to know what substances this ship has the capacity to handle. As many parameters as you can throw up."

It should be plenty — these old hoppers were designed to deal with whatever was at the end of a wormhole, and that included tumbling from space into whatever body lay below.

I heard Jaq leave, not bothering to query my command, some self-restraint still in place.

I turned to Paddy and sat opposite him, putting the smell out of my mind, refusing to allow myself to get angry. Refusing to fight anymore.

"Tell me more about the Janus particles," I said.

***

Opposites. It was all about opposites. We had closed the gate to Earth and stopped the war. But we'd started warring here.

I sat, knuckles to forehead, digging in as if I might find the answer. I thought of the wormhole: ragged, smooth, ragged, smooth. The two heads of the hole. That way was closed. It would never open again — or at least, not until there was another war.

"You're sure there were statues across Earth?" I asked, and Paddy nodded.

"All over the Earth," he said, in his thick voice. "From all different times. Why, in Mali they still make two-faced puppets."

Something had passed from this planet to Earth, and not on a space ship. It defied everything I knew. But the alternative was six months of slow death, warring all the way. Either that or killing each other, and then turning the war on ourselves. I couldn't decide if it would be better to be the first to go, or the last.

"Sir." Di's voice was the brisk certainty of an order having been met. "Mapping is complete."

I strode over to the console and leaned over it, tracking back and forth across the planet, until I found what I was looking for. I tapped it with my finger. "Take us there."

"Sir?" No argument now, just confusion, and no wonder.

"Now, Di." I left the command room, to the hatch leading to the engine rooms. I yelled for Jaq, who appeared below, face smeared with dirt.

"Jaq," I said. "Focus on marine capacities."

Jaq gave a brief nod, and vanished. I turned back to the control room. Drew in a deep breath. Here went nothing. I sat beside Di and strapped in as the engines thrummed to life, and the thrusters engaged. We streaked across the planet, gaining speed.

Something glistened below, stunning-bright in the sun. I pointed down. "There."

"Sir...?" Her hand wavered on the controls. I could take over, but I needed to concentrate. I needed to be free to react, to move. Besides, if I was right, it wasn't an ace pilot we needed, but a miracle.

"Do it."

She dove, straight for the surface. The body of water below grew bigger, first a small lake, next a sea, lastly an ocean. Deep, so deep.

We hit it like a bomb. The pressure changed, sending sharp pain through my ears. I yelled as the water broke around the ship. The engines missed a beat. Jaq's curses, carried over my earpiece, were loud and unmistakable. And inventive.

"Keep going," I said to Di. I had my teeth gritted. Paddy was against the back of my chair, heavy breath on the back of my neck.

We plunged farther. Alarms sounded. The engines chugged in protest.

"Sir, we have to pull out." Di's voice, frightened and small. "We won't have time if we go any deeper."

I shook my head. It was too late. It had been too late the moment we closed the wormhole. The point of no return was passed, and passed again.

"Hull breach imminent," said Jaq, voice impossible to read. Resigned, maybe. Or angry. "Less than a minute, Sir."

Hell. I'd called this wrong. I thought of Janie and Mark, of our bump-that-had-never-lived. Would that baby, too, be waiting in heaven? My hands clenched, my nails sharp moons in my palm. At least this was peaceful. Better than death in the aftermath of an Array, breath stolen from you, skin ruptured and burning. Better than my Janie and Mark faced.

"Ten seconds," said Jaq. "I can't hold her any longer."

Beside me, Di might have been praying.

"Hold steady," said Paddy. "Feel no fear."

I'd always known he was mad. The ship sank and I found my breath held, ready for the breach and the rush of water. How long would that last breath last? A minute? Two? I told myself it would be over soon. One gulp and it would end.

The ship shifted around me. The engines seemed to stop. Everything was held in stasis.

"Will?" Di never called me by my first name.

"Yes."

"Something's happening."

Colors surged around me. I had the fleeting sense of something ragged and then smooth, of lights. My stomach did the familiar wormhole lurch, and we were through, into something that could not be. Something ancient, I was sure of it, something that had tracked Earth for years. Something not explained by science, or by math, but only by belief.

"You did it!" Paddy was leaping up and down.

Di gave a hesitant smile. "You did." She frowned. "But what exactly did you do?"

Found the opposite, I thought. Not the air but the water. We were warring between us; a gate had to be open somewhere.

"I won't have started the war again?" I checked with Paddy. Fear gripped me, that I'd worked it out wrong.

He shook his head. "You used a different gate. Not the Temple. It remains closed." He broke into a smile and it occurred to me that he might have a family to return to. A life. He encased my hand in his. "You did it. You believed enough. They told me you would."

I'd always believed. In life after death, in hope, in doing my best.

A whisper touched the back of my neck. Someone

patted my ass. "Nice going, hero."

And then she was gone, and I was alone, and the wormhole was at an end. We crashed into space, close to Mars's orbit. A signal from Earth blinked on the console, reassuringly steady — something remained, for sure. A quick check of the read-pad, an update on Earth events, confirmed that Paddy was right. A ceasefire was in place and holding.

Somehow we'd done it. I closed my eyes and put all my belief into one thought. "I'll see you, Janie. When I'm done here, I'll be back to you."

I could have sworn she told me she knew.

Jo Zebedee Q&A

Where did the idea for your story come from?

Honestly? It was bizarre but I started to think about an obscure stone on a remote island in Lough Erne, in Northern Ireland, called the Janus Stone. It has two faces and is quite famous.

My original idea is that these would have been deposited throughout the world by an alien race. But when I started to do more research I was gobsmacked at what I found out about Janus, a Roman god of gateways and openings. In a book about wormholes.

The themes changed then and became a more personal story - I often write small stories about individuals rather than grand sweeping quests - about belief, and love, and being human.

What authors or other forms of media have the biggest impact on your writing?

Loads. Given my focus in the character, it's probably not surprising that I don't just read genre, and the genre books I do read tend to be character focused. So, Lois McMaster Bujold enthralls me, although I'm glad I didn't start to read her until my own Space Opera world, Abendau, and characters were established, for fear of too much influence.

But, mostly, I love storytellers, like Stephen King and Maeve Binchy. I also love a good sense of place, found in people like Carlos Ruiz Zafon. And I enjoy characters I keep with me forever, like Paul Atreides, so Herbert was another influence, for sure.

If given the opportunity to explore space through a wormhole, would you take it?

Nope. I'm far too much of a chicken. My characters can go

do that, instead. Gee, thanks, they all say....

What are you currently working on?

I'm mostly working on edits for my next two books. Abendau's Legacy comes out in October and completes the Inheritance Trilogy, whilst my first fantasy, Waters and the Wild, comes out next year.

But I'm always busy and have a few more ideas that I hope to get going with.

Where can readers find more of your work?

If they pop over to my website www.jozebedee.com, there are some links to everything I've written, as well as to some free to view online shorts, and if they sign up for my newsletter, they'll get access to some free stories that I'm releasing, exclusively, over the next few months.

Dead Weight
By Thaddeus White

The *Winged Oasis* shuddered under the barrage of torpedoes pounding her hull. Guan Xi clutched the arms of the captain's chair to keep himself from being hurled to the deck. Three of the five bridge crew tumbled from their feet, the lighting flickered uncertainly and smoke billowed from a smoldering console.

"Put that bloody fire out!" Guan Xi ordered, before a burst of static made him wrench his earpiece out.

Sima Fu ripped an extinguisher from the wall and smothered the flames in pressurized protein-foam.

"Marshal Gao repeats his demand for surrender," Deng Song, the ship's tech officer, reported from the comms station. "Gives one minute to respond, or he'll obliterate us."

Guan Xi spat. He rammed the earpiece back in. "Engine room, how are things? Can we make the Agujas Field?"

Curses and muttering filled the bridge at his question, but he ignored them. This wasn't the first time he'd encountered an imperial frigate, and he didn't intend it to be the last.

Zhang Rong, the chief engineer, ranted a stream of abuse down the earpiece. "The hull's breaking apart, the thermal shield's creaking like my gran's knees, there's an electrical fire in the engine bay and life support is at risk of failing. Apart from that, everything's sodding lovely."

"Can we make the Agujas Field?" Guan Xi repeated.

After a pause, Zhang Rong said, "The engine can do it. The question is whether the hull ruptures along the way."

Guan Xi's fingers drummed upon his armrest. "Stand by." He turned to Liu Pan, who had resumed her seat at the navigation console. "Lock every door between here and the engine room. If we get daylight in us, that should help confine the damage until we can effect repairs."

"You can't be serious," Liu Pan objected. "If the torpedoes don't tear us apart, the wreckage will! The Spanish called it the Needles for a reason!"

Sun Kai, who had been with the ship two decades longer, stroked his drooping moustache. "Ship's a tough old bird. I say we run. Besides, captain knows a smuggler's den in one of the station's surviving modules. Good place to hole up and make repairs."

Deng Song cleared his throat. "Captain, what should I tell Marshal Gao?"

Guan Xi smiled. "Tell him we surrender." He winked at Liu Pan. "When he dispatches a gunboat to board us, we'll keep it between us and the frigate. He won't be able to fire on us without destroying his own boat. Then we'll flee to the Agujas Field. You get all that, engine room?"

"Your mother must have dropped you on your head," Zhang Rong muttered through the earpiece. "The engine's ready, but if the ship splits in two my ghost will haunt your parents."

Guan Xi rubbed the jade disc hanging from his belt and murmured a quick prayer.

"Captain, Marshal Gao orders us to make a full stop and prepare to be boarded," Deng Song reported.

Guan nodded. "Bring us to a full stop," he ordered.

Liu Pan's fingers danced over the navigation console. "*Winged Oasis* is motionless, Captain."

On the main viewscreen the imperial frigate's belly opened, and a smaller vessel emerged. The naval gunboat drew nearer at an alarming rate. Just half the size of Guan Xi's modified freighter, the gunboat bristled with weapons, though none that packed the frigate's punch.

"Zhang, when I give the word I want full power. Liu, take us towards the Agujas Field, but at an angle. The frigate will clear the gunboat before we reach the Needles, but if we can put Jupiter between us and the enemy, that should buy us more time," Guan Xi stated.

"Aye, Captain," Liu Pan acknowledged.

"We'll be nearly at light speed. You're bloody mad. You know that?" Zhang Rong replied.

Guan smiled, and held on to the arms of his chair. "Fly!"

The *Winged Oasis* thrummed with power and lurched into motion. Almost immediately, the gunboat gave chase, and the freighter rocked with the impact of maser fire.

"Fire masers, Captain?" Sima Fu requested.

Guan Xi shook his head. "We need all power for the engines."

The gunboat was still in firing range, but it was gradually being left behind. Guan tapped the buttons by his chair and switched the viewscreen from aft to fore. Jupiter was looming faster than the frigate was gaining. The imperial dogs were being left behind. He grinned.

"Gunboat has launched torpedoes," Liu Pan reported.

"Deploy chaff!" Guan Xi ordered.

Sima Fu entered the tactical commands, and a cloud of short-range miniature rockets were left in the ship's wake. The three torpedoes burst into harmless explosions, and Sima launched one of his own in reply. It struck the gunboat, and Sima thumped the tactical station in triumph.

"It's out of maser range," Sun Kai said. He turned in his chair to face Guan Xi. "If my numbers are right, the frigate will have about ten seconds to fire upon us before we enter the Agujas Field. Assuming the engine holds."

The lights flickered again.

Jupiter loomed large in the viewscreen, then disappeared as the *Winged Oasis* cruised past the gas giant.

"Zhang, how's the engine?" Guan Xi asked.

"It'll explode in the next twenty seconds if you keep frigging distracting me!" the engineer screamed into his earpiece.

Guan nodded. "The engine's doing just fine," he told the bridge crew.

He split the screen between receding Jupiter and the approaching Agujas Field. The imperial frigate had cleared the gas giant and was bearing down on the *Winged Oasis*. It would be difficult for the agile freighter to escape all harm in the sea of metal debris, but impossible for the frigate. Unless it blew his ship to kingdom come before he could reach the dubious sanctuary of the Agujas Field.

"Frigate will enter firing range in five seconds," Sun Kai said.

Guan Xi rubbed the jade disc again. "Brace for impact. Liu, maintain course, whatever happens. If we don't make the Agujas Field, we're dead in space."

The bridge fell silent, and the frigate loomed large on the viewscreen. A short blast of blue maser fire struck the *Winged Oasis*, but she kept flying. The naval vessel drew nearer, and more of its masers came into range. A quartet of the weapons raked his ship. She quivered beneath the amplified microwaves, and something metal groaned alarmingly.

"We're in the Needles," Liu Pan said, breathing a sigh of relief.

Guan Xi nodded. "We'll head for the lower half of the eleven o'clock sector and shelter in Skinny Han's den. Cheer up, kids. In a few days we'll be rich as kings."

Deng, Liu, and Sima cheered and smiles broke out. Except on Sun Kai.

"I hate to point this out, but Marshal Gao's following us in," Sun said.

"He's a fish diving into a cauldron. He won't last another day," Sima Fu observed.

Guan spat. "But he'll still have time to kill us. Deng, offer our surrender," he ordered.

Deng Song typed the communication, but shrugged helplessly. "No response, Captain."

"Get us in cover!" Guan snapped.

Liu frantically entered commands, and the ship dove behind the carcass of a satellite twice its own size, the frigate in hot pursuit.

A dozen masers fired at the *Winged Oasis*. The satellite between the ships burst into clouds of debris, but two of the masers lacerated the ship's hull, and she trembled under the onslaught.

"One of the cargo bays has a new window," Sun Kai growled. "Internal doors have auto-sealed but the cargo's lost."

"Liu, maintain course, but alter the roll angle. If we get hit again, at least the undamaged part of the hull might withstand it."

The *Winged Oasis* dove behind the massive ruins of a space-dock and enjoyed a few moments free of carnage. The frigate, hull pitted with countless collisions, kept up the pursuit and a fresh salvo of maser fire lanced toward the freighter.

Guan rubbed his jade disc.

Space erupted into violent color, shimmering indigo and turquoise ribbons amidst a cascading cerulean aurora. Purple lightning arced all around the *Winged Oasis* as it careered this way and that. Try as he might to resist, Guan was thrown from the captain's chair and crashed onto the deck. He wrapped an arm around a console's leg to keep himself from being tossed around like a house in a hurricane.

The darkness of space swallowed the vivid colors, and the ship came to a stop. Guan Xi, ribs aching and arm battered, cautiously got up. Sima Fu staggered from the deck, grumbling like a bear with a sore head, and hauled Liu Pan back to her feet. Sun Kai shook his head groggily before slumping into his chair. To Guan's surprise, no fires had kindled on the bridge, and the *Winged Oasis* appeared to be intact. The last fragments of static on the viewscreen faded; the frigate was nowhere to be seen, and the Agujas Field had vanished.

"What happened?" Deng Song asked, lowering himself carefully into his seat.

"Can't be sure, but I'd guess we encountered a wormhole," Guan answered. "Liu, check the local astronomy, get a fix on our position."

Assuming we're still in charted space, of course.

Liu tapped in the commands, then spent some time reading the answer the computer gave her. "We're a hundred light years from Earth, Captain. Seventy from Zhou Outpost. Sixty from the Fifty-Third State."

Guan nodded. "Could be better. But could be much worse. What's the damage, Sun?"

His first officer grunted. "Extensive. The engine appears to be dead, and Gao took out a lot of our supplies. Oxygen seems ok, fuel's borderline, and we'll have a hard time rationing what food and water's left. Not to mention he punched a few holes in the hull. Even if we could achieve lightspeed, if we don't repair the holes in her skin the old girl would explode."

Guan strolled over to Sun's console and ran his eyes over the damage. "Bad, but not irreparable." He retrieved his earpiece from the floor, wiped it clean, and put it back in. "Zhang, the engine's offline. How long will repairs take?"

There was neither abuse nor static in response. He repeated the question, but got silence a second time. "Deng, contact the—"

"Uncle Zhang's dead," Jiang Na, Zhang's assistant and niece, said via the earpiece.

Guan swore. "What happened?"

"The heat shield failed. He'd sent me out of the engine room to shore up a failing power coupling. The thermal energy incinerated him, and buggered up half the engine."

Guan put his head in his hands. "Damn it. I'm sorry, Jiang." He sighed. "Please tell me the engine can be fixed."

"It can. But it'll take a while, and I could really use a hand down here."

"I'll send someone." He removed the earpiece and beckoned Deng to his feet. "Zhang's dead. Go to the engine room and help Jiang make repairs."

Deng Song frowned. "I don't know much about engineering; I'm more of a technical expert."

Guan Xi raised an eyebrow. "You man the comms station. Think we're going to have many conversations

216

here?" he asked, flourishing a hand at the empty viewscreen. "Get to the engine room and do whatever Jiang Na tells you. And don't bloody question my orders again."

Deng Song raised his hands in apology, and left the bridge.

"Liu, Sima, go find out just how many supplies we have left. Computer reckons several larders were hit but it can't know just what we lost. Be careful, and take EVA suits if you need them." Guan cocked his head. "On the other hand, if you do get blown into space, that would reduce the rationing for the rest of us."

Sima Fu folded his brawny arms. "Thanks for the concern, boss."

The pair swiped an earpiece each and left the bridge. Guan slumped into the captain's chair.

Sun Kai reached under his console and retrieved two bottles of beer. He tossed one to Guan, and flipped the cap on his own.

"Golden Ridge? You really think this is the time for that?" Guan asked.

"It is," Sun Kai said, raising his bottle. "A toast: to Zhang Rong, the best engineer we ever had."

Guan raised his bottle. "To Zhang Rong, the son of a gun who never let us down."

Sun took a long swig.

Guan Xi sipped his drink.

"If those two don't come back with good news, we're in serious trouble, you know," Sun said.

"How bad?"

"Hard to say if we'll starve to death or die of thirst. But we'll be a week from civilization, and that's if the engine's back up to full power."

Guan drank his beer. "We can always eat the xenofauna."

Sun Kai stroked his moustache. "If you want to eat an undocumented, unknown animal, that's up to you. Can't say I'm keen to discover whether or not the beasts are diseased.

Or poisonous."

Guan Xi looked his first officer in the eye. "I'm not pushing a crewman out of the airlock."

Sun Kai returned his gaze. "I don't want that either, but if the supplies aren't there to feed six people, then it might not be a choice. If the decision is two corpses or six, remember Deng and Liu have only been here a month. Jiang can handle the engine, and I can pilot well enough. Just think about it, Captain."

Guan scowled. "I'll run the numbers, find a way to make it work. In the meantime, I want you to check the cargo bays, see what we have left. Even if we can't try the xenofauna, the starfruit and Venusian spices could stretch our supplies. Better to eat the contraband than starve."

Sun finished off his Golden Ridge and tossed the bottle into the disposal chute. "Aye, Captain. And what will you be doing?"

"Staying here. Someone has to man the bridge."

"And finish off the beer."

"Privileges of command. Have fun counting extra-terrestrial avocados."

Once Sun Kai left him alone, Guan put his earpiece back in. He occupied the command console seat and began running the numbers. His first officer wasn't wrong. Unless the *Winged Oasis* had been very lucky, there was no way the projected food and water supplies would last the distance to the Fifty-Third State. Six people were impossible, and five would be a serious risk. Guan Xi thanked his lucky stars he'd taken on consumable contraband before making the return trip to Mars. There was an outside chance the illicit food and drink could be the difference between life and death.

Guan wandered over to the comms console and began to broadcast a distress signal. The odds on a deep space explorer passing by were a million to one, but then, so was being rescued from an imperial frigate by a split-second wormhole.

With the rest of the crew occupied, and unable to leave

the bridge in case any of them needed a hand, Guan returned to the captain's chair and began composing a letter to Zhang Rong's brother. Zhang Feng had been a crewman himself, years ago, and Guan hoped that would help him to understand how risky the life could be. The engineer's share of the loot would be kept and delivered to his family. If the ship ever actually reached Earth again...

"Captain?" Jiang Na stirred his earpiece to life.

"How're things coming along?"

"Pretty well. New boy knows more than he thinks. The tricky stuff's all done, it's just donkey work from now on," Jiang Na answered.

Guan nodded. "Glad to hear it. Keep me apprised of progress."

"I was wondering about the hull, Captain," Jiang Na went on. "It needs patching sooner or later, and, to be honest, I'd really like to get out of this bloody room. The smell is... it's not great, Captain."

He sighed. "Aye. Don an EVA suit and get to it. D'you need a hand?"

"No, Captain. And thanks."

"Don't mention it."

The wait was oddly relaxing. In minutes, or hours, potentially terminal problems could fly Guan Xi's way. Perhaps Deng would screw up the engine repairs. Sima, Liu and Sun might find that the provisions situation was impossible. But, for a little while, Guan could relax. The imperial navy was a hundred light years away, and he was alive. With any luck, Marshal Gao's frigate had been chewed up by the Needles. By the time the *Winged Oasis* returned, any search would have long since ended, and Guan might well have been declared missing, presumed dead. Perfect for an under-the-radar return.

"Who's messing about in the airlock?" Jiang Na interrupted his daydreaming.

Guan sat up and used the console to check which airlock was open. "Nobody. Deng's on engine duty, and the other three are on the opposite side of the ship. What's up?"

Heavy breathing was the immediate answer. "I must be seeing things," she eventually replied. "I could've sworn I saw a shadow by the airlock. Anyway, the hull's good to go. Coming back in."

"Good. Check how Deng's doing—"

An ear-splitting shriek made him wrench off the earpiece until the cry ended. He shoved it back in. "Jiang, are you ok?"

"No, I'm not fricking ok!" she shouted. "Some bastard just shut the damned airlock and it cut the umbilical cable! I'm floating outside the bloody ship."

"Stand by."

Guan ran to the command console and swept the ship for what he hoped was the reason. Sure enough, a fresh hole had split the *Winged Oasis'* hull, and the airlock had automatically sealed to try and prevent catastrophic decompression.

"Hull integrity was compromised," he told her. "The airlock shut automatically. I'll mend the hole, go down to the airlock, magnetize the end of a long umbilical and throw it your way. Switch your boots to magnetic and we'll get you in."

"That won't do it," Jiang told him. "There was a rush of air after my umbilical was cut. Pushed me away, now I'm drifting from the ship.

Guan swore. "How's your oxygen?"

There was a pause while she checked. "Thirty-five minutes left. Is that enough for a probe to reach me?"

Guan checked the signal from her EVA suit and distance from the ship. "Yes."

Probably.

"Just stay calm," he advised. "Try your best to relax. The probe will be on its way soon."

It had been some time since Guan had done the grunt work himself, but his fingers flew over the console. Within a minute the atmospheric probe had left the ship and was homing in on Jiang Na's EVA signal.

Guan tapped his earpiece. "Probe's on its way, ETA is fifteen minutes. When it gets within a minute, I'll switch to manual piloting."

"Thanks, Captain."

Guan coughed. "I'm going to be away for a minute or two, but I'll be monitoring the probe all the time. Small problem here I need to fix."

"Ok. Just don't be long."

He removed his earpiece and fiddled with the settings to enter a closed channel, then called the cargo bays. Guan tapped a drumbeat on the console while he waited for Sun Kai to reach the intercom.

"Captain?"

"Sun, how's the inventory coming?" he asked.

"Almost done. It's looking better than expected, but I hope everyone likes Venusian cuisine."

Guan scowled. "I want you to check out the xenofauna. See if anything's escaped."

"Sure. What's happened?" Sun asked.

"Something damaged the hull, and the airlock shut, cutting Jiang's umbilical. Either the exotica has gone walkies or someone tried to kill her."

Or both, of course.

"Bloody hell. That's all we need," Sun said. "I'll get on it."

"Good. Be careful, and call me back on a closed channel," Guan advised. "Last thing I want to do is panic the crew even more."

Guan sighed, reached under the command console and retrieved a bottle of isotonic water. He swigged the revitalizing beverage, and watched the probe narrow the gap to Jiang Na. Half a bottle of water later, Sun got back to him.

"Something broke out," Sun confirmed. "Not sure what it was; power fluctuations corrupted some of the inventory data. But it was pretty damned big. I think a power outage must've given it the opportunity to escape."

Guan sighed. "Do we have any inventory entry for it?"

"Six feet long, three hundred pounds."

Could be the alien equivalent of a lion. Or a giant herbivore. Big enough to break a weakened part of the hull, either way.

"Marvelous. I can't talk any more, I need to handle the probe. Find Sima and Liu, and bring them back to the bridge."

"What about Deng?" Sun asked.

"Tell him to close off the engine room and keep working."

Guan checked the clock and finished off his drink. He wandered over to the waste disposal chute and dumped the bottle before resuming his seat. The probe was within visual range of Jiang, so he flicked its forward camera on. Jiang was floating in the abyss of space, the severed umbilical tied into a makeshift lasso.

"Hey, Jiang. I'll take control of the probe in thirty seconds. Everything ok?" he asked.

Jiang laughed nervously. "Well, not *everything*. Feeling pretty lonely out here. Apart from the ship and the probe, the nearest object must be a light year away. Keep worrying I'll get a tear in my suit."

"Those things have the skin of a rhino. You'll be fine. I'm going to take over the probe now. I'll pilot it as close as I can, then you need to get a good hold of the antenna."

"Aye, Captain."

Guan was no mean pilot, but maneuvering a probe designed for exploring alien atmospheres close enough to a drifting woman without colliding was damned hard. He used the probe's forward camera to approach, and Jiang tossed the umbilical over its antenna.

"Got it!" Jiang cried in triumph, yanking the cable to pull the loop closed.

"Good to return?" Guan asked.

She gave him a thumbs-up. "It's secure. Just get me to the hull; I'll magnetize my boots and walk in."

"Sure thing. Don't worry, Jiang, you'll be back before

you know it. Got some Golden Ridge waiting for you."

"Golden Ridge?" she asked. "Now I'm wondering whether I want to come back…"

Guan recalled the probe, but kept an eye on its return in case the cable came loose. "Never had a chance to mention this before, but our ride through the wormhole seems to have shorted power to one of the cargo bays. Three hundred pounds of wildlife is wandering about the ship."

Jiang cursed. "Where's it from?"

Guan scratched his temple. "Not sure its planet has been named yet."

"Better than having a murderer aboard, right, Captain?"

He smiled. "Aye, that's true." The bridge's door whirred open and Sun, Sima and Liu returned. "The others are here. I'll keep this channel open. Just scream if anything happens."

Guan stayed by the command console to track the probe's progress and waved the others over to join him. Liu handed over a pad upon which she'd scrawled the provisions the ship still held. He ran his eyes over the list and tossed the pad back to her.

"Hope you've got some good news," Guan Xi told his first officer.

Sun Kai nodded. "Between the Venusian grubs and the moonshine, we should have enough, but we're going to have to ration it hard. And we should probably shift the provisions to somewhere more stable."

Guan flicked his gaze to the monitor, before looking back at his crew. "Well, that's the good news. The bad is that the power to the cargo bay with the beasts was interrupted, and one broke free. All we know is that it's three hundred pounds, six feet long, and strong enough to punch a hole in the hull." He fished under his tunic for a key, and tossed it to Sima.

The big man raised an eyebrow. "Weapons?"

Guan nodded. "No peashooters. Get the serious gear."

Sima smiled, and went to fetch the toys.

"I knew we shouldn't've gone into the frigging Agujas

223

Field," Liu Pan grumbled.

Sima came back with a smile plastered across his face. Several machetes dangled from his belt and he held three rifles in his arms. The brute carefully placed the weapons on the floor and left the bridge, returning a moment later with a mini-gun and an obscene grin.

The other crew helped themselves to a machete and rifle each, Guan taking the last for himself. The captain opened a cabinet and took out some earpieces for Sun Kai and Sima Fu.

"Sima, Sun, sweep the ship and bring me that beast's head," Guan ordered. "Maintain an open channel. Liu, stay with me."

"Just because I'm a girl doesn't mean I can't hunt," she growled.

Guan sighed. "You're the navigator, numbskull. If I have to go help Jiang I need someone who can pilot the probe to guide me without running into me and rupturing my oxygen tanks."

Sun cocked his rifle. "We'll start by the nearest airlock. Should reduce the odds on Jiang getting a rough welcome."

Guan nodded. "Good thinking. Get to it."

Sun and Sima strode from the bridge, and Guan tapped the keypad to lock the door behind them. After a moment's thought, he went to Sun's console and turned all the lights in the ship on.

"Twelve minutes to go," Liu Pan said, head resting on her fist. "Can't you let me join the hunt?"

"In twelve minutes. If you stop bloody nagging me."

Deng called. "Captain, I've done all I can at the moment. I can finish the job, but I need to power down a live circuit."

"So? Get on with it."

"The problem is that the circuit is a primary one. All power will be down, unless someone has a portable generator to hand. I've got one to power my tools, but the ship will lose everything for a few minutes. No heat, oxygen, gravity."

"Bloody marvelous," Guan answered. "Stand by. I'll call you when Jiang's back on board."

The captain told Liu about the problem. Before she could complain, Guan got a buzz on his earpiece.

"We heard what Deng said," Sun Kai said. "We'll lock ourselves in a storage room until the power's back. Last thing we want is to encounter three hundred pounds of fangs and muscle when the gravity's gone."

Guan watched the *Winged Oasis* grow from a speck in the distance to almost fill the probe's front camera, occasionally checking by radio that Jiang was fine. The engineer was surprisingly cheerful, more so than Liu Pan, who spent the whole twelve minutes grumbling.

He turfed the navigator from her seat and resumed manual control of the probe, piloting it to within fifty yards of the ship. Jiang let go of the probe, and momentum carried her onto the *Winged Oasis'* surface.

"Boots are working nicely," she said over the earpiece.

Guan raised his fist in triumph, and even Liu managed to smile.

"Get inside quickly," he ordered. "Your reserves must be low."

"Aye, Captain."

Guan put his hands behind his head and exhaled. "When she's safe inside, we'll have Deng sort the engine. Then you and I are going rabbit hunting."

The prospect of killing something brought a real smile to the navigator's face. "Wait till you see how good a marksman I am. With two shots I can castrate a man at a hundred yards."

Guan raised an eyebrow. "Let's not test that claim."

Jiang confirmed she was inside the ship and had found herself a safe place to hole up. Sun and Sima were similarly protected, so Guan ordered Deng to complete the engine work.

"Aye, Captain. Just remember I won't be able to give

you warning of gravity coming back."

The lights overhead fell into immediate and total darkness. Guan found himself hovering above the deck, one hand clutching a chair arm to stop himself getting too high. His stomach lurched left, and his body turned right. He bumped gently into Liu.

"Sorry. Zero-gee isn't my natural habitat," he apologized.

"Don't worry, old-timer. Just don't get fresh."

Guan scowled at her, before realizing the darkness hid his disapproval. "Less of the 'old', whippersnapper."

Heat dissipated faster than he expected, and the air grew thin. An ice-cold hand gripped his arm.

"Damn, it's cold," Liu said, her body shivering against his.

"Who's getting fresh now?"

Liu laughed. "Shut up. I'm bloody freezing. This is worse than night in the desert."

Guan was glad of the extra warmth himself. "Aye. It's because we've at least one hole in the hull and no artificial atmosphere to replace the heat gushing out of the ship."

He crashed to the deck, Liu falling on top of him. Lights returned to life, and he raised a hand to fend off the glare. She clambered off him, leaving behind an elbow-shaped bruise on his stomach.

Guan staggered to his feet and slumped into the command console chair. Except for the new hole in the hull, everything seemed good to go.

"Sun, Sima, you ok?"

"The fat oaf bruised his backside. Otherwise, we're fine. Resuming the hunt now," Sun answered.

Guan fiddled with his earpiece and called Jiang. "Hey, Jiang. You ok?"

"I spent the last half hour floating towards oblivion. A few minutes in a storage cupboard is fine."

He smiled. "Good. Me and Liu are coming to get you. Stay put." Guan got to his feet. "Ready to go?"

Liu flicked her rifle's safety off.

Guan grabbed his rifle and led Liu out of the bridge, pausing at the keypad to lock it. He led her through tight corridors, the pipes lining them burbling with coolant, plasma and heat.

Guan kept his rifle lowered, wary of an itchy trigger finger given how close Jiang was. At the first airlock, the corridors widened considerably to allow cargo easier passage, but there was no sign of his engineer.

"Hey, Jiang, we're here. Where are you?" he asked.

Something bumped Guan's shoulder and he whirled around, whipping up his gun.

"Saw a shadow in the distance," Liu muttered, rifle butt nestled against her shoulder. "I'm going to check it out."

Footsteps clanked on the deck. Guan and Liu turned together, and Jiang raised her hands when she saw two barrels pointing her way. The engineer was still wearing her EVA suit, but had slid down the visor.

"Nice to see you too," Jiang said.

"Captain, that thing is getting away," Liu muttered.

Guan shook his head. "I'll give Sun and Sima a heads-up, but we need to escort Jiang to safety first. I'd give you a rifle," he told his engineer, "but the second weapons locker is floating a hundred light years away."

Jiang shrugged. "I've had enough stress for one day. Happy to let you and the little lunatic play hide and seek with a monster."

Guan let Sun and Sima know what was going on, then called the engine room. "Hey, Deng. We're bringing Jiang your way. Get ready to open the door for us."

No response came, so he repeated his request, yet still the tech officer failed to answer.

"How strong's the engine room door?" Guan asked.

Jiang shrugged. "It's designed to absorb colossal amounts of energy. But the locking mechanism depends on power. If Deng only had one portable generator, it might not have been enough to run the tools and keep the door tight."

"Damn. Let's go. Liu first, then Jiang, and I'll bring up the rear."

Liu spat. "Fine. Keep up."

The navigator all but ran off, Jiang struggling to keep pace in her cumbersome EVA suit.

"Slow the hell down!" Guan shouted at Liu.

Liu glared murder at him, but reduced her speed to a fast jog. Guan stayed close to Jiang's heavy footsteps, walking backward and keeping his rifle raised and ready. Cargo bay doors opened automatically, every whirring servo sending a shiver down his spine. But no hulking beast leapt from the shadows.

They neared the engine room, the cobalt blue of the engine flaring bright in the door's circular window. A scream ripped through Guan's earpiece.

"Sun? Sima? What's going on?" he demanded. Jiang and Liu turned to stare at him.

One of the men retched violently.

"Cargo bay three…" Sima grunted.

"What's there?" Guan asked.

High-pitched screaming burst from the earpiece, and then total silence fell.

"Sima? Answer me, for pity's sake! Sun, what's going on?"

Neither man answered.

"Damn it. I think Sima's dead!" Guan told Liu and Jiang.

He strode to the door, kicked it open and marched in, rifle up. In the center of the room the engine was thrumming, blue energy dancing in its translucent cage. The scent of roast flesh lingered. Zhang's legacy, Guan guessed.

The captain crept around the engine, and found a body lying in a pool of glistening blood. Deng's head had been caved in. By his corpse was the portable generator, its red lower edge contrasting sharply with yellow paint. Guan grabbed a nearby welding apron and threw it over the fragmented bone and blood that had been Deng's face.

"Deng's dead," he told Liu and Jiang. "You don't want

to see him. But you do want to see this," he said, tapping the bloodstained generator with his foot.

Jiang turned pale.

"Frigging hell," Liu said.

"Zhang, Deng and Sima are dead, and we three are together," Jiang spoke Guan's thoughts. "That leaves only one suspect."

Sun Kai...

"Sun's been with me for twenty years. And we don't know if the escaped creature is clever or dexterous. Bears have great dexterity, and chimps use tools," Guan replied.

Jiang sighed. "I know you—"

Guan left Deng's body behind and strode to the door. "Liu, we're going to go kill something. Jiang, keep an eye on the engine and keep the bloody door locked."

He marched out of the engine room and headed for cargo bay three. Liu scampered to catch up, the heavy clunk of the door's lock engaging behind them.

"Really think it was Sun Kai?" she asked.

Guan spat. "Deng didn't batter himself to death." He slowed as they approached a corner, and let his rifle lead the way. The only menace was a flickering overhead light, and he resumed a fast pace. "Two options, and both are shit. Either Sun's been knocking off the crew one at a time, or the alien's three hundred pounds and six feet of cleverness. The bastard could be sentient for all we know."

Liu scowled. "You're assuming there *is* an alien on the rampage. Wasn't it Sun who told you about it going missing?"

Guan dropped a hand to rub his jade disc. "That's true. Cargo bay's just ahead. Be careful — whatever's ahead, it won't be friendly."

Liu nodded, and hung back beside the door.

Guan skirted the wide corridor, keeping his distance to avoid triggering the proximity detector and opening the doors. He took up position on the other side from Liu.

"If something attacks, shoot, even if it risks hitting me,"

Guan ordered, dropping down to a crouch. "Half the crew's dead already."

Liu nodded.

Guan edged forward, the muzzle of his rifle tripping the sensor. The doors opened. He peered inside the bay. Crates of contraband, and some legitimate merchandise, were piled high. Blood's metallic signature hung heavy in the air. He kept low, and headed inside.

Blood spattered the wall, a trail leading down to Sima's motionless body.

Three red maser blasts scorched the air, and Guan leapt behind a row of crates.

"What the hell are you doing, Sun?" he shouted.

Liu crept to his side and pointed to Sun's blind side. Guan shook his head.

"Captain?" his first officer called. "Sorry, I thought you were the beast. Is the alien still there?"

"It's a trap," Liu hissed.

Guan chewed the inside of his mouth. "Sun hasn't seen you yet," he whispered. "Stay here. If he shoots me, take him by surprise. If he doesn't, come out of hiding."

Before she could protest, Guan stood up and walked deeper into the cargo bay. A few yards past Sima's corpse was a severed leg, mottled with dark green scales. Sun was slumped against the bulkhead opposite the severed limb, rifle cradled on his lap. A sinking feeling burrowed into Guan's bones as he realized the truth.

I brought the murderer back aboard. Sorry, Deng.

Guan crouched beside his old friend. Sun was pallid, and blood had soaked his right trouser leg. "You look like shit," Guan observed, throwing away his earpiece.

"Could've been worse. Got clocked on the head, but my earpiece took the worst of it." His first officer smiled, moustache drooping a little less. "Medkit's down there," Sun said, nodding at a blue box fifty yards away.

Guan walked away, glancing back just in case he saw the rifle pointing his way. The medkit was fixed magnetically, and he wrenched it away from the bulkhead. Liu had emerged from hiding by the time he reached Sun's side.

"Guan thought you did it," Liu said.

Sun stared at the captain. "You always were dumb as a post," the first officer observed.

"Laceration?" Guan asked.

Sun nodded. "Bloody big one, but I don't think the femoral artery was nicked. I'd be dead by now if it had."

Guan handed Sun a pair of scissors to cut away the trouser leg, and searched the medkit for needle, thread and the Feuerbach gel. "Deng got whacked with a portable generator. Poor sod's head was like a burst melon. Could the alien have done that?"

Liu stepped forward to help cut away the trousers, but Sun waved her away. "Unlikely. It's fast and strong. Got claws like knives. Sima managed to lop one of its legs off, but the bastard's got five left."

Sun discarded the square of cloth he'd cut, and Guan set about stitching the long wound. "Feeling light-headed?" Guan asked as he worked.

"A little. Don't think I'll pass out, but I'll need a hand walking. Ankle's broken, or sprained at least," Sun admitted.

"I'll patch you up," Guan said, snipping the excess thread and pasting the gel onto the sewn-up cut, "then I'm going to shoot Jiang."

Liu exhaled. "You can't seriously think Jiang let the beast out, and killed Deng."

Guan pulled the aerosol anesthetic from the medkit and set about spraying Sun's ankle. "Who else? Zhang, Deng and Sima are dead. Sun would've shot me if he were guilty. You were with me on the bridge when Deng got killed. Jiang was the only person by herself, and Deng would've trusted her."

Sun pointed at an open crate, air holes perforating the surface. "Check the locking mechanism. Someone had sawn halfway through it. Sima spotted it. Beast escaped, and battered a weakened section of the hull. Damned shame Jiang had so much oxygen left in her tanks."

"I'll see for myself," Liu said, wandering over to the crate.

Guan sat by Sun's side, rifle in hand and eyes on the cargo bay door. "Jiang's in the engine room. If she doesn't want to come, how're we going to get her out?"

Sun stroked his moustache. "I imagine she'll wait until we're all dead, then just open the door."

Guan grunted. "I was hoping for a method that doesn't involve getting killed by whatever's running around the ship."

His first officer sighed. "I have an idea. But you won't like it."

Guan shrugged.

"There's no way she and Deng had the time to fully mend the thermal shield," Sun observed.

"You want me to try overloading the bloody engine? It could rip the ship in two."

Sun raised an eyebrow. "Now, that'd definitely kill her."

Liu wandered back. "It's as he said. Sima had sharp eyes. So, we going to the engine room to put the bitch down?"

A rush of warm, humid air entered the cargo bay through vents whining with the effort.

"Clever little psycho," Sun muttered. "She's jacking up the humidity and temperature. If she's doing it to the maximum, we'll be steamed to death. Get to the bridge, quickly. You can blow the engine from there. Once she's melted, come back and get me."

"I don't like it, but I think you're right," Guan said. "Stay focused, and be ready to shoot if something opens the door."

Sun grunted. "Stop warbling and get a move on."

Guan nodded, and strode to the door.

"See you, Sun," Liu said, before joining the captain.

Guan took the lead, though his arms ached holding the heavy rifle up. Despite the urgency of dealing with Jiang, he walked, trying to make as little sound as possible. How the xenofauna hunted, and how it would be affected by the heightened humidity and temperature, was uncertain, but clanging about like a drunk could only be foolish.

"Er, this is the wrong way," Liu pointed out.

Guan sighed. "I know my own bloody ship, Liu."

"Then why—"

He raised a hand. "Watch and learn, callow youth."

Guan crept toward the engine room. He knelt, took aim at the pipes leading to the hefty door, and fired. The maser ruptured the metal tubes, and sickly green liquid dripped onto the deck.

"Can't risk her just wandering out of there before she's cooked," Guan said.

A wicked grin lit up Liu's face.

Guan left the engine room behind and headed for the bridge. Sweat trickled down his face, and he wiped perspiration from his forehead. Clothes started to stick to his skin, and even his socks were becoming damp. Whether fear or the heat, Guan's heart was pounding.

Liu sneezed, and he leapt out of his skin.

Guan turned around and glared at her.

"Sorry," Liu mumbled.

He sighed, and three hundred pounds of alien dropped on him, its bulk eclipsing the overhead lights.

Guan slammed into the deck, and the creature's crocodilian jaws snapped at his face. Guan raised his rifle, but the beast locked its jaws around the weapon and pulled it from his grasp. He punched the predator in the throat, and wrapped his left hand around its neck while the right scrabbled for his machete.

A single blast of maser fire scorched the air and struck the beast on the side of the head. It roared with anger, but a second shot burned its face. Scales hissed and bubbled, and the beast collapsed onto Guan, crushing the breath from his chest.

"Told you I was a good shot," Liu crowed.

Guan grunted. "Give me a hand."

Liu propped her rifle against the nearest bulkhead and

helped heave the monster off of him. She gave him a hand, and he struggled to his feet, shivers of lightning still tingling his backbone. Guan leaned against a bulkhead and eyed the predator.

Its front right leg had been cut off near the shoulder, presumably by Sima Fu, but had begun to scab over already. The damned thing didn't appear to have any eyes, and seemed to have two spines, ventral and dorsal.

"If we get out of this, we're sticking to spices and artifacts from now on," Guan told Liu.

Humidity made breathing uncomfortable, and he staggered on, Liu leading the way to the bridge. Guan tapped in the code, and entered the bridge.

Liu joined him, and he parked his backside in the comms chair.

"Take the navigator's seat."

"Aye, Sir."

Guan took a moment to familiarize himself with the comms console, before entering the command to broadcast ship-wide.

"Jiang, I know you can hear this. The beast is dead. Turn the environmental controls back to normal, and once we reach the Fifty-Third State, I'll let you leave the ship unharmed," Guan said.

It took a moment for Jiang to reply.

"What are you talking about? It's sweltering in here, must be close to forty Celsius now, and the temperature's still climbing. Sun must have fixed the controls on the bridge."

Guan put a finger to his lips, and pointed at the command console. Liu began examining the claim as he spoke.

"Don't play games, Jiang. Sun was with Sima when the pair were attacked," Guan said.

"Captain, the atmospheric controls won't respond, and they weren't fixed from here," Liu interrupted.

Over the intercom, Jiang laughed. "It was a long shot,

but worth a try. Humidity and temperature will kill you off in a few hours."

"It doesn't have to end this way," Guan repeated. "Do you really want to do this?"

Jiang paused. "Sorry, Captain. Uncle Zhang was the only reason I had for staying on this ship, and your reckless bravado killed him. We're stranded months from safe harbor and I'm damned if I'm going to risk starving to death to save your life."

Liu shot Guan a meaningful look, but he shook his head.

"Listen to me, Jiang. We're going to fire up the engine, set it to overload. Unless you're a miracle worker, the heat shield won't hold, and you'll cook long before we do."

"Even if it works, you've got a broken ship with no engineer, and a deficient engine you can't reach. Go ahead, Guan, you mad bastard."

He flicked the intercom off. "Liu, fire it up. Don't stop until I say."

The navigator frowned. "You sure, Captain? What she said…"

"She's full of shit. If it comes down to it, we can cut a hole in the bulkhead. With this humidity and heat, we'll be dead inside two hours. Turn the engine to one hundred fifty percent, and if you've got a lucky charm, give it a rub."

Liu knitted her fingers together and cracked her knuckles. "Aye, Captain."

She tapped the final few keys to complete the command sequence, and leaned back in her chair.

The deck beneath Guan's boots began to vibrate, the *Winged Oasis* stirring to life after hours of dormancy. Humming with power, the bridge rattled and shook, stray objects falling to the deck and jumping with every vibration.

"You're out of your fricking mind!" Jiang shouted. "The ship's going to be torn in two! Look, we can reach an agree—"

Guan switched off the audio and put his hands behind

his head. "If we survive, what will you do with your share of the money?" he asked Liu.

The navigator was gazing at the power levels painted on the screen in front of her. "I'll buy you a new heat shield. And psychometric tests for the new crew so we don't get a bloody fruit loop next time."

The throbbing deck began to judder.

"So, you'll stay on the ship?"

Liu nodded. "If we survive this, you must be the luckiest captain in the whole damned galaxy."

"Zhang, Deng and Sima would disagree."

Red warnings began flashing on the command console, a shrieking blare piercing the bridge's peace each time.

Liu tapped a button to switch the alarm off. "Engine at one hundred forty-three percent of maximum safe capacity. Hull ruptures and explosive decompression anticipated in one minute."

"How's the heat shield?"

Liu scrolled through the screen. "The sensors are offline. Damn. She must have severed them from the heat shield."

Guan smiled bitterly. "Clever little lunatic. Keep going."

The captain got out of his chair, sat on the trembling deck. Guan pressed a palm to the deck, and closed his eyes.

"It's one hundred forty-eight percent," Liu reported. "Captain, computer predicts ten seconds until the ship blows."

"The computer's wrong," Guan answered, the *Winged Oasis'* quivering running through his fingertips. "I've captained this ship for two decades. The computer always underestimates her."

"Now one hundred fifty percent, hull rupture any moment," Liu said.

Guan focused on the ship's torment running through the deck, feeling her ever-quickening pulse. "Now!"

Liu slapped the command console, and the frenetic energy was replaced by a low whine as the *Winged Oasis* fell back to sleep. The navigator examined the damage. "One small hull breach, but that's all."

Guan patted the deck. "Good girl."

The navigator turned in her chair, tunic saturated with perspiration. "Even if she's dead, we need to get to engineering to restore the environmental controls. Can't believe we'll last that long."

"You'd be surprised what you can do with an EVA suit and a plasma-cutter."

Sun swore like a sailor when Guan helped him into the EVA suit. The two men, relieved by the comfort of breathing normal air, followed in Liu's footsteps and found her attacking the engine room wall with her plasma-cutter.

Guan and Sun joined in, and by the time they'd cut a hole big enough to squeeze through, the oxygen tanks were almost empty. Guan crawled through first, and stumbled across the blistered remains of Jiang Na. Pausing to kick the corpse for Deng and Sima, he returned the environmental controls to normal and raised his visor.

Sun said, "Take a while to fix the heat shield again, but with only three of us, supplies should last."

Liu stood over the corpse, staring silently.

"You ok?" Guan asked her.

Liu looked away from the blistered corpse. "Yeah. I'm just glad the bitch is dead."

Thaddeus White Q&A

Where did the idea for your story come from?

I liked the idea of the crew being thrown into isolated safety (after being pummelled by Marshal Gao) but that same situation then creating an opportunity and incentive for one of them to start knocking off the rest. It's a mix of a submarine story and a Whodunit.

What authors or other forms of media have the biggest impact on your writing?

That's bloody difficult to answer. As a child I was into CS Lewis' Chronicles of Narnia. Ancient Chinese literature (especially Outlaws of the Marsh) has a really interesting narrative structure, picking up a character then dropping them off only for them to recur hundreds of pages later (can't really do that with a short story, of course). There also tends to be a minimum of flimflam (not unlike Machiavelli) which helps maintain a rapid pace. For Dead Weight, there are hints of Alien (with softer edges, of course).

If given the opportunity to explore space through a wormhole, would you take it?

That's very unlikely as I'm a subtle blend of bone idle and tremendously cautious. Very occasionally I act totally out of character, though, so it's not impossible.

What are you currently working on?

I'm wrestling with a trilogy (first part is done, second part is being beta-read at this very instant, and the third I've outlined but yet to start). Hope to release Kingdom Asunder (the first book) in December this year. I'm also working on a comedy novel (Sir Edric and the Plague), as well as writing some short stories (as you probably realised, having read one of them).

Where can readers find more of your work?

Free short stories can be found at

http://www.kraxon.com/writers/thaddeus-white/

and http://thaddeuswhite.weebly.com/free-stories.html

And my books can be found on Amazon.

Webbed Prisms
By Charlie Pulsipher

T'en Ku sprinted through the crowded marketplace, pounding feet close behind him. He bounded over a basket of live fire beetles. *Curse my Sclav blood! Who keeps those in an open basket? You could kill someone.* He glanced up to see the bright white linen of a Nax next to the red of royalty.

T'en skidded to the side to avoid colliding with the man whose garments his kind had been forbidden to touch for generations. *Sclav me, what is a royal doing here?* The man raised a hairless eyebrow at him, absorbing the scene in seconds with the Nax's keen intellect. T'en knew what was coming, but he dared do nothing to stop it lest he give away his secrets. A gold walking stick snaked out, and T'en rolled across hard cobblestones into the side of a cart. A silver fruit fell to shatter like glass against the ground, the blue juices mingling with blood from his nose. *I think I broke it again.*

Normally he'd be scolded for such recklessness in the market. Maybe the cart owner would cane him for damages. Maybe he would have been lucky and the owner would let him work off the lost denkafruit. But no one said a word, an unnatural hush in a marketplace known for its rowdy crowds. All heads stayed bowed, all mouths pressed tight, as a space had opened up around the royal Nax whose punishments would be far worse than a simple caning.

T'en swallowed a growl as he rolled to his knees, ready to sprint away, but cold metal pressed against his neck.

"What did you do, slave, to be chased by your betters?" The man gestured to the edge of the marketplace where three Nax children stared at them, a silver basket in the middle child's hairless hands.

T'en spat blood, anger getting the better of his judgement. "Exist. That seems to be enough for you Nax to

240

torment us." The gold staff pushed harder on his neck, but T'en refused to let it push him lower. "And I'm no one's slave." T'en hated the twisting of his race's name into the old connotations. *Bad enough it's a curse. We haven't been slaves for two hundred years.* T'en lifted a strong hand, calloused from years of hard work, and pushed the gold stick away, enjoying the look of shock on the Nax's face.

"How dare you touch an extension of me?!" His eyes tightened as he sent a wave of pain toward T'en. Several people too near to the exchange cried out as the waves touched them.

Those never work on me. T'en feigned a flinch, but stood even as he did so. "I am forbidden to touch your garments without your permission. Your staff has no such protection, especially since it was you who put it in contact with my filthy Sclav skin in the first place." T'en stood taller, meeting the man's eyes. T'en was tall for both his age and his race.

The Nax took a step back and smiled. "Whatever you had planned, younglings, do it now."

T'en spun in time to see one of the boys pull an egg from the basket. He recognized it. *Oh, not a baelen egg! I'll stink for weeks!* The lizard's eggs were a delicacy, beyond delicious when cooked. T'en had never eaten one. Raw though, they smelled worse than open sewers during the Festival of Suns on the hottest day of Jeustustide.

T'en had nowhere to go. A cart blocked his escape to the left, another behind him. The royal stood sneering off to his right, and the boys stood before him. The crowd had quietly thickened, the people keeping their distance and their tongues, while still eager to view the spectacle.

Another boy pulled out an egg. The third set down the basket and pulled a third. Of course, they would waste a fortune just to make one Sclav suffer.

T'en closed his eyes. He could hear the fabric rustle as the eggs launched. He knew the Nax boys had no muscle tone to drive them, but they would not need any. The eggs whistled as they sliced through air, propelled by the augmented minds of three Nax. *Four. I'm sure the royal is helping. Sclav me for running into one. No! I have been humiliated enough for one day.* T'en called on the powers he shouldn't have, superheating the air between him and the bullies. Three eggs struck, hard, but bounced away, their shells cracking as they rolled harmlessly across the cobblestones.

"Hard boiled? You idiot of a Sclav, Hunim! You brought cooked baelen eggs?" The tallest of the boys glared at the one in the middle.

The middle boy flinched at more than just the words, his friend needling him with the searing pain only the Nax could create. "I swear. They were raw. I bought them this morning." He picked up the basket to show his friends.

The third boy knocked the basket from his hands, and the marketplace erupted in movement and sound as three more eggs cracked open, spattering the boy's feet with yolk and albumen that sent the tallest to retching and everyone close running. There were screams, curses, and a near stampede of Sclav escaping the stench.

T'en took advantage of the madness. He sprinted around the royal, scooped up two of the eggs, and crawled under a cart. He smiled at the royal's shouts behind him as the stench made people lose themselves in the rush to get away.

"How dare you touch me? And you! Stop that! You will be punished. You too! You!" The man devolved into blubbering as too many Sclav touched his precious clothing for him to keep track of, even with his enhanced intellect.

T'en rolled the eggs in his hands as he sprinted down an alley toward his hiding spot in the city, grinning. *Someone's going to eat well tonight. Too bad I couldn't grab the other one.*

***

AJ printed himself a hamburger, dipping into his meager state-appointed credits. "I owe myself a treat, don't I, Susan? I have an interview tomorrow. Print me some fries too...

make it a small, though."

A holographic woman flickered to life next to the printer. "Yes, Adam. That brings your calories up to three thousand, five hundred and two for the day, and congratulations on the interview. It's been three years, seven months, and twenty-nine days since you've been employed."

"Thanks for that, Sue. Your reminders get me right here." He held the burger against his chest over his heart. "And how many times do I have to tell you, it's AJ?"

"Apparently nine hundred forty-seven times and counting, but it isn't your name."

"I heard your great-grandmother would call someone whatever they told her to. Overlord of Awesomeness or Big Ol' Pile of Donkey Doo."

"I am not Siri, Adam."

AJ leaned against the balcony railing, the landing too small for a chair, and glared out at Jersey while he ate his dinner. The city had changed in the almost twenty years he'd lived there, sunken in on itself like a decaying peach. *Those damned wormholes and Omniscient Technology Solutions, making everyone crazy.*

He'd moved to Jersey during the initial gold rush, too, when the city had expanded rapidly to accommodate the excitement over newly discovered wormholes that were more stable than the initial Lunar appearance. Omniscient wasn't the only company promising to send people to the stars, but they were one of the biggest. *So shiny and new back then, just like me. A cocky seventeen-year-old on a mission to go to Mars or somewhere even farther from here. I was an idiot.* "Still trying, though, aren't you?"

"What was that, Adam?"

"Shut up, Susan. Just shut up."

"Shutting up."

***

T'en ate the first egg slowly, savoring the sweet and salty

flavor as he stared up at the sky, leaning against the exhaust vent. *No wonder these are so expensive. It's even better than caramelized kein milk.* His stomach grumbled at him, wanting him to eat faster. "Shhh, be patient. This is probably the only time we'll ever eat these, and we have two."

His stomach growled again. "I know, I know. We haven't eaten enough today. I got sidetracked by those nasty Nax. Tomorrow I'll finish weeding the field and get five whole grints. Can you imagine how much food we can buy with that?" He laughed. "Let's ignore the fact I probably could have sold these eggs for six times that."

He sighed contentedly as he finished the last bite of the first egg. "Since I'm talking to my stomach, like a madman, do I eat the second one or sell it in the morning?"

His stomach gurgled.

"You're right. They're worth more raw anyway, and who knows how well it will keep." He peeled away the cracked shell and grinned up at the intricate, fractalled lines of Founder's Nexus. It pulsed a thousand colors as it took the long, slow route back into the void.

Twenty-three days to go, then five hundred years without it before the cycle continues. Everyone knew the Founder's cycle, but few felt it like T'en. He could read the lines in the Nexus, see the seconds ticking away as tendrils curled inward. He'd always had the mind of a Nax, even if his body was all Sclav, with the disgusting muscles and body hair of his kind. He rubbed at the spattering of facial hair he'd been growing, wishing it gone, as the last bite of his egg levitated from his hand and over his mouth.

The Nexus shimmered brighter, a ripple passing along its colored lines. *That's new.* A precious piece of baelen egg bounced off his face and fell to the floor of the foundry rooftop. T'en sighed as he took in the dirt on the roof and picked up the bit of egg. "Yeah, I'm still going to eat you."

***

AJ slid his resume across the table, the e-ink crisp with his name in a bold blue. The woman across from him slid it back.

"We won't be needing that. This isn't so much an interview as it is a job offer. I'm Kendra, and I'll walk you through what we want from you." She smirked. "We know everything there is to know about you anyway."

AJ slipped the paper off the table and put it into the ancient leather satchel he'd inherited from his grandfather. *Good. It's a sad excuse for a resume, and I'll be able to recycle the e-ink for a couple of my credits back.* "What kind of job? I applied for more than one."

Kendra laughed. "That's an understatement. You've applied for over two hundred positions with Omniscient in the nineteen years you've lived in Jersey City, sixty-two times with several of our umbrella companies throughout the world, starting with our sister company, Omegaphil, before it closed its doors shortly after the first wormhole appeared."

"Yeah, I think I was an eager sixteen-year-old." AJ caught himself drumming his fingers on the table and stopped.

"Fifteen, actually." She looked up from her notes. "You have a degree in agricultural engineering. You know you could find work with that?"

"Not where I want to be."

"Oh, I get it. You're a wormhole groupie." The smirk grew.

AJ frowned. He hadn't heard that term in years. "And proud of it."

She leaned forward, whispering. "I'm one too." She winked and turned back to her notes. "Okay, you just need to sign the confidentiality agreement, and I'll continue." She swiped her notes to a legal document, tapped it to spin it, and pointed. "Here."

"Wait, you haven't even told me the job yet."

"I can't until you sign, but does it matter?"

AJ stared at her. "No, no it does not." He signed it with

245

the stylus she held out.

"Good." She tapped a corner to save it and swiped it to the next page. "Here's the offer letter, with compensation listed here." She pointed to a bolded section on the page.

AJ's mouth fell open. "Is that for a year, or for a decade?"

"A year. Really, the job will only take a month or so, though." She tented her fingers. "You can take that as a yearly wage, or you are free to pursue other employment after we finish."

"You're seriously telling me you'll dump six million credits on me for a month's worth of work" —he glanced at the job title that came after the pay on the form— "as a Replicant Consultant Specialist, whatever that is? That isn't even a job I applied for."

She leaned forward, hands still tented. "It's a position that recently became available. You are rather perfectly qualified." One of her hands whipped out, faster than a human could possibly move.

AJ caught her hand, her finger less than an inch from his eye, an eye that could see that her finger was almost twenty degrees cooler than it would be if it wasn't synthetic. His heart beat fast and loud in his ears. "I was in an accident as a child. My father…" He trailed off. The story wasn't one he talked about.

"We know." She pulled her hand back at a normal speed and held it in front of her as though seeing it for the first time. "I survived the bombing of a train in Europe. You and I belong to a growing subgroup of people who are best prepared for the job at hand." She smiled to herself. "No pun intended."

AJ flexed his fingers as he put his own hand back at his side. "No."

Kendra's mouth fell open. "What do you mean? Your psychological profile suggested a ninety-two percent chance you would agree to the offer."

"Oh, I'm agreeing, but not to the offer as it is. I have

one negotiation."

She smiled. "Ah, more money?"

"No, continued employment. I want to be on the list for future wormhole exploration and colonization."

She pulled the e-paper and stylus back, deftly made several changes to the offer letter, and slid both back. "Done. Anything else?"

"You didn't seem adverse to more money?"

She laughed. "I was told I could offer you this." One million more credits appeared at the top of the form.

AJ's signature never looked so good. "How does having a synthprop make me suited to this job?"

Kendra winced at the use of the slang for his prosthetics. Most people who had one didn't use that term. "Because it means your brain is already wired to interface with Omniscient's technology. It also helps that you're intelligent, obsessed with wormholes, not a terrible negotiator, and not too hard on the eyes either."

AJ laughed. "What's that last one have to do with anything?"

She shrugged as she pushed her chair back. "Because I'll have to work twenty-hour days with you for the next four weeks." She stuck out her hand. "Welcome to Omniscient Technologies, Adam."

He took her hand in his, both synthetic. He raised an eyebrow as his synthprop picked up the subtle flaws in her palm and fingertips that made it more natural. You had to pay extra for flaws.

***

T'en arrived early at the field, before first sun. The three moons danced along the horizon while Founder's Nexus counted down the minutes.

"We won't be needing you today."

T'en jumped. He hadn't heard or sensed Jud leaning against the barn. "What? I can see the weeds from here. You

247

have a full day's work sitting right there." Sweat prickled T'en's neck as emotions boiled up inside him. "Are you trying to get out of paying me?"

Jud spat in the dirt and took a step away from the wall, his hand rummaging in his pockets. "No, I'm a man of my word. I'm protecting you here, boy." He held out three coins, the metal glinting in the crimson light peeking over the distant mountains. "A man came by looking for you yesterday, a Nax. A Sclaving royal too!"

"Sclav! He found me?" T'en took the money without looking at it, slipping the coins into a pocket he'd sewn inside his trousers. The weight told him that Jud was being more than generous, T'en's hidden powers tasting the alloys. "There was a bit of an incident in the market."

Jud chuckled. "You think I didn't hear about that? It was stupid, brave, and beyond stupid." He clapped a rough, hairy hand on T'en's shoulder as he peered up at him, the grip like iron. "Did I mention stupid? You really cooked those eggs right there and then?"

"What? No. They were cooked already." T'en glanced around and sent out mental queries to make sure they were alone.

Jud shook his head. "Several people saw the heat waves. Those aren't invisible, you know."

"I didn't think about that."

Jud let go of his shoulder. "You aren't the only one of our kind with Nax powers, but you might be one of the most reckless I've seen in years." He pulled out another coin and it hovered into T'en's palm. "Stay hidden. The royal will forget about you soon enough. Don't come back here for at least a month, and then only after dark."

The coin vanished into his hidden pocket. "A whole fendling?"

"The look on that Nax's face as he sneered through his description of you was worth it. Wish I could give you more." Jud stared off toward the city. "Go, stay hidden, and good luck."

248

***

AJ closed his eyes while the scan did its work, the machinery humming as it rolled over his skull. "Anything in there I should worry about?"

"Shhh, stay still." A hand touched his chest. "This scan isn't as important as ones to come, but it still needs to map your brain structure."

"What does this have to do with wormholes again?"

The machinery stopped moving. "Okay, I'll explain that, but first I need you to take something." Kendra pushed the scanner aside and rolled next to him in a sleek, white chair. "Here, put this on your head."

AJ took the plastic band and slipped it on his head. It resized itself and pressed a few hard nodules against his skull in five places. "That's comfy."

Kendra nodded as she flipped open a container and removed a blue strip with tweezers. "It's better than it used to be. They once strapped people down and injected the neural interface chips through bone. Barbaric times."

AJ swallowed. "Wait, what's this for?"

She leaned in and held the blue strip up toward his mouth. "It's an upgrade to your prosthesis connections. Put this under your tongue and hold it until it fully dissolves."

AJ opened his mouth and let her place it under his tongue. It tasted like mint and made his saliva glands fire. "Houw woung boo I hab to holb ib?"

Kendra rolled her eyes. "Hush. It takes a few seconds for the nanites to get to your brain."

AJ swallowed. "Wait, what?" The band on his head pulsed against the bone of his skull, setting his teeth to rattling and making his vision blur. It stopped a couple seconds later.

"All done. The ultrasound opens the blood-brain barrier briefly. This is when it gets weird."

"Weird how?" AJ lost control of his right arm and eye. He tried to get up, but Kendra held him down with inhuman

249

strength. The inside of his head itched like fire ants crawled around inside him. Memories flashed in and out of his mind, he smelled acetone and cake, and saw colors flying through the air with his one good eye.

"Don't worry. The nanites have to dissolve your old hardwired connections to replace them with the more efficient wireless variety. They're powered by body heat and movement, so you'll never need a charge again."

AJ tried to give her a thumbs-up with his good hand, but his muscles twitched and his vision flickered while new scents and flavors rolled across his tongue. He gagged.

"This is why I didn't let you eat breakfast." She ran a warm hand over his clammy forehead. "You're doing so good. Almost done now."

AJ gasped as his arm and eye came back online. He smacked his lips as the flavor of mint replaced all the weirdness of a second earlier. "I think I'm okay." He held up his arm, feeling the rush of air as it passed over synthetic skin that tasted the molecules as it moved. His eye picked up the swirls of air currents the movement created. "Better than good."

"I told you it was an upgrade."

AJ took in the dilation of her pupils and the pheromones that rolled off her. "You like me."

She rolled her eyes. "If it took this big of an upgrade for you to notice, you might be hopeless."

***

T'en had let his fledgling beard grow longer. It was thin and wispy, but it helped disguise him as he slunk around alleys and hid on rooftops. He leaned against the exhaust grate and rubbed at the scraggly thing on his face while he stared at the rippling Nexus. *The instabilities are getting more frequent. None of the stories talked about anything like them.* He thickened the air between him and the sky, creating a lens out of the condensed and warped air.

250

The heat waves Jud had mentioned had given him the idea. It worked well enough, as long as his concentration didn't waver. *It's nothing like the polished glass the Nax use, but it will do.* A dark spot had formed at the center of the shimmering lines that made up the Nexus. It almost looked like a spider clinging to the center of a web. "What are you?"

***

Kendra clicked the quantum hard drive down in front of AJ on the smoky glass of the table. "Try it again."

"We've tried it like thirty times." He rubbed at his temples. "We're getting nowhere."

"It took me at least fifty attempts. The neural interface is still making connections and figuring your mind out. It's adaptive, but you have to help it adapt." She smiled and slid the drive closer, her other hand touching his. "Try it again, for me?"

AJ took a deep breath and held it for a few seconds before letting it out. "You do know how to ask a guy." He closed his eyes and cast out with his mind the way Kendra had taught him to look for wireless connections. He jerked back in surprise when a green box appeared behind his eyelids. "Um, that's weird."

"You see it?" Kendra leaned closer. She showed up as a ball of yellow that hovered over the green square, the hardware in his head tracking her movements.

"I think so. You too, but you're yellow?"

"I'm firewalled, as any good girl would be." Her voice sang with hints of laughter. "Access the drive."

He reached out and tapped the box with his mind. Memories flooded into him. Kendra had filled the box with a few of her own. He opened his eyes. "I didn't know you were raised in Louisiana. Blackberry bushes really grow everywhere like that?"

She shrugged. "They really do. I used to come home covered in scratches and purple juice. I lost the accent years ago, but it's still home." She leaned on her elbow and looked out the glass windows over Jersey, a hint of a Southern accent creeping in as she continued. "I find myself craving gumbo whenever I feel down."

"I can taste it. I think I may crave it too, now."

"We'll see. Explore the memories. Are there any gaps? Anything feel off? Any pain or discomfort?"

AJ shook his head. "No, they seem almost as if they're my own." He noticed he had a touch of an accent too, as he spoke. "I think I'm even decent at math and cooking all of a sudden."

Kendra reached over and flicked a switch on the drive.

AJ gasped as the memories vanished. He blinked at her. He remembered accessing the drive. He remembered what he had said, but he had no idea what had prompted his words. "Why can't I remember them?"

She tapped the drive. "They are only in here. You accessed the memories while the drive was active. Think of it as an extension of your brain, graphene neurons supplementing your own. It means you are compatible with the technology. We can move on to the next step."

AJ blinked at her again. "Why do you sound so sad about it?"

She shrugged again. "It means we can accelerate our timeframe. We had contingencies to make you more compatible if we needed to. It means we'll stop working together sooner than expected... in some ways."

"What?"

***

The object at the center of the Nexus tore itself apart in spectacular fashion. T'en found himself gasping when it happened, explosions sending pieces of the mysterious thing out into space. He couldn't help but glance around, his mouth open as though he would tell someone what he had just seen, but he stood alone on the rooftop of the foundry.

The beginnings of tears blinded him for a moment. A part of him had hoped the object would come through and change everything. A new founder would arrive and remake the world. *Fool! Nothing changes, not for a Sclav.* He blinked back the tears, forcing them from his eyes. That's when he noticed the fire on the edge of the city. *Jud's farm?*

***

AJ sat still for the scan. Kendra was on a table next to him receiving the same treatment, her hand in his. She squeezed once as the scan finished. "You ready?"

"As ready as I can be." He laughed. "I'm going to the stars more than once. Who can say that?"

She chuckled and squeezed his hand. "Very few. Access it now."

He closed his eyes and reached out to the green box that hovered above him, waiting for his connection. Just before he tapped it, he heard Kendra say something, but he hadn't been listening. "What was that?"

She squeezed again. "This is going to hurt. Sorry, I should have warned you before now."

He tapped the green box. This time he didn't receive a flood of memories. Instead he uploaded everything he was, his brain on fire as the interface sent all his memories and skills into the drive. Kendra did the same and they screamed together as flames rolled through their minds, duplicating everything they touched.

***

Adam opened his eyes, the synthetic retinas soaking up the details of the space station in microseconds, calculating distance, mass, and energy output as his gaze swung around the room. He wasn't just Adam, either. He had the memories of a dozen others with him and a mind far sharper than the one he'd been born with. "Where am I?"

253

Kendra sat up next to him and smiled, the expression familiar and distant at the same time. "We are in orbit around Mercury, close to Echo Two."

Adam nodded. "That makes sense. It would be easier to print bodies here and send the memories than to send people and equipment. I feel unusual. Is that normal?"

Kendra put a hand on his, the sensation still electrical without any pheromones. "Your brain is graphene and quantum processors. It mimics consciousness, but not perfectly. We found artificial intelligence works best with a human component. This is why you were hired."

He deftly moved in the zero gravity to a window and looked out at the dark, gray planet. "I thought it would look cooler."

Kendra laughed. "That's the AJ I know."

"Is it weird I feel like an Adam now?"

"Not unusual. You are a different person in many ways."

He grinned. "One who's actually good at math. I can tell the distance from the surface to here just by looking out the window."

"That's the bit of me that's in you, along with some sophisticated hardware." She tapped her head. "I have a little of you in here too." She rolled her eyes. "Heaven help us."

Adam smiled; the memories had begun to align themselves in his head, leaving AJ as the main contributor of personality and judgment. He spun and kissed her. When he pulled away, she smiled at him.

"About time! Had to wait until we weren't really ourselves though, really?"

Adam shrugged. "Hopefully AJ makes a move too." It felt weird to think about himself as another person, but that was his reality now. "I have the memories of the research teams. We really lost an entire station of real people?"

She grimaced as she grabbed a handhold and propelled herself toward the control center of the station. "Unlike the lunar incident, Echo 2 has been stable, always opening for half an hour every seventy-five days. It always opens in orbit around Mercury, but it doesn't always open in a predictable orbit. We have yet to receive anything back from any probes besides static." She glanced over her shoulder. "The primary station was trying to understand why when a malfunction sent them into a lower orbit and the path of the wormhole."

Adam nodded and tapped his synthetic skull. "I remember watching it happen from the control room on Earth. And the secondary station has been monitoring the wormhole for transmissions of any kind the three times it's opened since. We are here for the fourth."

Kendra grabbed a seat and swung her body into it in a graceful arch that any gymnast would envy. "We're going through, just the two of us. We can't afford to send anyone alive. We have enough of a PR crisis as it is."

"I feel pretty alive."

Kendra winked at him. "Shhh, me too, but according to laws and HR, we're expendable." She pointed to a control station. "You mind giving me a hand getting the ship ready?"

The memories came to him as he needed them. There was a small craft attached to the station and he knew exactly what they had to do to prep it. "Not at all."

***

AJ sat up. "That's it?"

Kendra smiled at him from the table to his left. "That's it. You're an astronaut now, kind of."

He laughed. "Cruel joke of one." He stared at her for a moment.

"What?"

"You want to grab a drink?"

She grinned at him. "I thought you'd never ask. We'll have to take it easy. That brain of yours is still our best backup drive, if we need it again."

***

T'en made it to the farm in minutes, his already strong muscles aided by his abilities. Heat hit him first, before he'd even reached the fields. The farmhouse and other buildings hadn't been touched, but they wouldn't last long at the center of such an inferno.

Using his trick of the air lens, T'en looked toward the center of the blaze. He could see Jud on his porch while his family huddled in the doorway. Jud's hands were out, holding the flames at bay with his mind and will. T'en reached out and helped him.

A sharp crack to his left made his concentration waver. He ducked down behind a bush, knowing the sound though he'd never seen its source in his lifetime. *Sclav me, that was a rifle.* A Nax stepped from the shadows of a neighboring field, letting the rifle fall to his side. The red color on his clothing shimmered in the firelight. T'en looked back to the house and had to clamp his hand over his mouth to suppress the gasp. The flames rose up like waves and crashed down on the house. T'en saw Jud slumped against a post, his wife at his side, just before the waves fell.

The royal scanned the fields around him. He lifted the rifle and shot again. Someone huddled at the edge of the fiery fields fell. The blaze shifted and overtook the body. T'en tensed as the rifle swung his direction. He created another lens, warping the light around him and plunging his bush into darkness. He could sense the waves of pain the Nax sent out to uncover anyone else hiding, but those did nothing to T'en. He held his cover for an hour, sweat pouring from every pore at the effort. When he let go, the Nax had left his atrocities behind and the fires had begun to die out.

***

Adam counted down. "Three, two, one, we have green."

Kendra edged the craft away from the station. "We maintain a high orbit, until the wormhole appears. You have that calculation?"

He nodded. "It should open in less than ten minutes. It will be open for half an hour. We'll need to move fast."

Kendra winked at him. "That's my only speed."

"I've noticed."

***

The wormhole opened seconds after the clock in Adam's head hit zero. The ship's sensors registered the warping of spacetime and indicated where it would appear, but there was no need. Adam's mouth fell open as an area of the black sky split open into a prismed web of strings that spilled outward, unfolding like fractured rainbows.

"That makes the disappointment of Mercury and not really being here worth it all."

"Right? The videos don't do it justice." Kendra nosed the ship toward the center, a bright point of wavering light. "You ready?"

Adam shook his head at the rippled images of another planet as his enhanced eyes digested every inch of the wormhole. "Not really. AJ would be sweating buckets right now. I think this synthprop body is trying to. I might start spurting oil or something."

"Gross."

He shrugged. "I'm a gross person. You should know this."

Kendra took his hand. "You are not filled with oil." She leaned in and kissed him, her usual sideways smile there as she pulled away. "Ready now?"

"Yep. Let's do this." Adam took his half of the controls.

***

T'en wandered back to the foundry in a daze. He climbed to the roof with numb fingers. *They killed him. They killed his whole family. His children. Just because he protected me? Or because he*

257

has Nax abilities too?

"Sclav you!" He cursed at the sky and the ever-diminishing Nexus. A shooting star raced by above him. Another followed. Then hundreds of them flew by. A large one flew at a different angle. T'en's quick mind calculated the trajectory, distance, and speed, but it slowed. He recalculated.

The numbness left. He had a purpose and a goal. T'en ran off the edge of the building, his mind slowing his fall. He sprinted into the night.

***

Adam checked the screens. "We are perfectly aligned."

Kendra chuckled. "Of course we are. I'm driving." She pushed a button. "Omniscient control, we are golden and proceeding as planned. We will send another signal as soon as we pass through." She pushed the button again. "It will be a while till they get that."

She took the joystick and propelled them into the center of the wormhole, accelerating as they hit the shimmering edge.

Passing through a wormhole turned out to be one of the most unpleasant sensations Adam had ever endured. Part of him accelerated forward, leaving parts of him flying to catch up. Pain rolled through him in waves. *Pain isn't really the right word. It's more like terrifying cold.* He alternated between feeling nothing and feeling an overwhelming amount of emotion. Colors flashed past when he wasn't blind and senseless. He tried to speak, but found he had no mouth, no hands, no body. He was a ball of consciousness hurtling through the wild places between worlds.

Adam gasped as they splashed into reality.

"Ouch." Kendra spoke next to him, but her voice came out low and slow. She accelerated, a planned procedure to move them out of the event horizon of the wormhole, delicate tendrils of color wavering outside the cabin windows.

The ship tore itself in half as soon as she pushed the joystick forward. Adam took in the movement, parts of his system moving slower than the rest. A ripple of light passed through him as the air ripped away from the cabin. Wherever the light touched, alarms sounded inside him. Errors flashed in front of his eyes, announcing connectivity errors, time lag, and metal fatigue. The fractal string of light moved on, and the alarms cut off while nanites went to work repairing the stress. *Good thing I have those, and good thing I don't need air to survive.*

Kendra spoke in his head. *Get to an escape pod. We need to get out of here.*

You too. Adam unbuckled and pulled himself along the handholds to the nearest pod. He slammed the button to open the door. As he slid inside, he glanced behind him to check on Kendra. She stood in the doorway of another, waving at him.

This didn't go as planned. See ya down there. She pushed the button on the inside and her door began to slide shut.

Adam waved back. He raised a hand to push his own button, but the engines crossed the horizon and the time-compressed fuel exploded. He saw a flash of Kendra staggering as the door slammed down on her body, shearing metal and plastic. *No!*

His pod blew off the side, spinning with the door stuck open.

***

T'en slowed his run. He could smell the scorched remains of whatever had fallen from the sky. It had broken branches as it fell through the massive trees. He came around a tree and almost fell into the small crater on the other side.

His mind pushed against the fall and kept him at the edge. "What are you? An egg from the stars?"

It looked like an egg, rounded white with black marks

along the bottom. Rope rose from the top, still attached to the silken cloth that had slowed its fall. He walked along the edge of the crater, admiring the perfectly rounded edges, marred only by a sleek, black window. He slid down the gravel and soil bank and peered inside. His hand brushed against a silver design next to the window.

Seams appeared and a door slid upward with a hiss. Inside sat the head and shoulders of a woman, the torn edges of her body trailing strings of metal. T'en stumbled backward, horrified. He stumbled back again when she blinked, smirked at him, and said something in a language he didn't understand.

"How are you still alive?"

She blinked at him and gestured down with what was left of her shoulder. The strings of metal continued to grow and link together. T'en stared as bits of the metal floor she lay on dissolved beneath her. His sharp mind put it together. *She's repairing herself, using the vehicle for building material. This is way beyond anything the Nax can do. And she's a Sclav! A Sclav came through the Founder's Nexus? This changes everything!* "You're going to need more metal. Good thing for you, I live on a foundry."

She repeated it back. "I live on a foundry."

"I guess you will too."

***

Adam spun through space. The glimpses of the wormhole and the planet out the open door of his pod let him put the rest of the puzzle pieces together. There were cities dotting the continents. The webbed wormhole collapsed along a mirrored pattern to the far side, but much slower. He had the memories of the wormhole opening and closing by Mercury, and he replayed them over and over in slow motion as his pod spiraled toward one of the moons. Something clicked inside his graphene brain and he sent a signal back through the wormhole, stretching the wavelength as much as he could.

It should be enough to counterbalance the time dilation it will undergo as it passes through, but it's going to take me days to send the whole thing.

The message was simple, his calculations based on the movements of the prismed web on both sides and the errors he'd experienced. *Half an hour on Earth's side is approximately fifty days on this side. Ship lost. Thrusters misfired due to time differential. Do not send anyone else through. Some of original station survived.* He also sent a string of calculations.

He mused on what must have happened to the station as it came through. It would have experienced some of the time stretching and dilation effects they had. Water and fuel lines bursting as sections rapidly aged compared to sections next to them or were put under pressure by the stretched time. *Any transmissions they sent back would have been compressed down to tiny blips of high-pitched static on Earth's side. They must have assumed nothing could get through and given up. And, once the wormhole closed, it would have remained closed for a thousand years. They moved on.*

***

T'en half dragged the woman along the path. She wasn't as heavy as he expected after consuming most of her craft, but she couldn't walk. She had holes in her body, and her left foot hadn't fully formed.

"I think we lost them."

She pointed down to where her dragging foot left a gouge in the dirt, her eyebrows asking questions.

She's a smart one. "Yes, that's going to be a problem." T'en sighed. "I'm going to have to carry you before we get into the city or someone will follow your trail straight to us."

T'en grunted as he picked her up, but she grinned and said something he didn't understand in her strange language. Her smile vanished.

T'en spun to see white and red stepping from behind the

trees.

***

Adam passed through another string of light and felt his systems scream as some of his complex inner processes slowed while others raced. *I need to get away from these things.* Days passed as minutes ticked by, and then he was free again. He ripped open a panel inside his pod with his bare hands and directed a blast of air out the open doorway, timing it to send him away from the collapsing web that surrounded the closing wormhole.

***

There came a crack that echoed off the distant hills and the taller buildings of the nearer city. T'en didn't have time to react before the bullet slammed into his arm, propelled faster by the Nax royal. The woman fell to the dirt as pain screamed through his body.

Another bullet came, and then another, burning through skin and flesh in seconds. T'en tried to slow them down, but his powers were no match for a dozen Nax working in unison against him. T'en fell to his knees. The barrel of a rifle pushed against his temple. He could smell the oiled metal and sulfurous tang of gunpowder.

"Is she another of your foul kind?" The royal spit as he spoke.

"You can see that she's a Sclav."

The barrel pressed harder against his skull, the metal still hot from the recent shots. "You know what I mean. Is she one who has stolen powers above her station?"

"She is not like me, if that's what you're asking."

T'en felt the shrug as it carried along the rifle to his temple.

"It doesn't matter. She is with you. She dies either way." The gun turned toward T'en's companion.

"No!" T'en pushed outward with all the energy he could muster. Nax slammed into trees or flew past them into the forest. T'en looked up to see the tip of the barrel against the woman's chest, her hand wrapped around it, but they were both too late. The crack of the shot rang in his ears as the royal slid a few feet away, but kept his feet.

∗∗∗

T'en blinked as the world darkened. *I've lost too much blood.* He clamped down on his wounds with his mind and willed himself to stay conscious. *Can she survive a gunshot?*

He glanced toward the woman and gasped. The gun had blown a new hole in her, but this was filling in as the rifle dissolved in her hand. She glowered at him, stood, and hobbled toward the royal. T'en could practically see the waves of pain radiating from the man, but the woman did not slow. *Nice to see those don't work on someone else.*

T'en was glad he remained conscious long enough to see her raise a hand to backhand the man.

"You are forbidden to touch me."

"I live on a foundry." She struck the man and he flew twenty feet before crumpling to the ground with the sickening snaps of broken bones. T'en reached out and was surprised to find him alive.

The woman staggered over to pick up another discarded gun, dissolving it into dust in her hands. She then walked with a limp to T'en as he lost his fight with the darkness.

∗∗∗

Adam slammed into the largest moon, sending a cloud of dust into the thin atmosphere. The wormhole had nearly closed. He waited for the other wreckage to stop falling before he stepped from his malfunctioning escape pod.

He found most of Kendra under a section of torn engine, scorched by the explosion. He lifted it and took her lifeless hand, his hand detecting the subtle flaws. *I'm not giving up on you that easy.*

A reply came through, weak from the distance. *Good. I kind of need your help at the moment anyway.*

Adam stared up at the dusty blue-green planet. *You're alive? I was worried.* He closed his eyes and found her yellow dot on one of the larger continents, just on the edge of the horizon. *I just found your better half.*

You aren't cuddling with it, like a creeper, are you?

Adam let go of the hand. *No. I'm coming. I just have to repair my pod and figure out how to land near you without burning myself to bits.*

Yeah, more important stuff at the moment. I have an injured man down here with several gunshot wounds. He's bleeding out.

Adam nodded. *You have a first aid kit in the pod.*

The answer came slow. *Yeah, I may have eaten that.*

What? Oh, to repair yourself? That makes sense. You can reprogram the nanites to repair him too.

She sighed, a strange thing for Adam to hear in his head. *That's why I'm asking you. I don't have the memories to do that. We didn't think we'd need them on this mission, so we gave them to the more disposable replicant.*

Adam could almost feel the laughter. *Very funny. You'll have to drop your firewall.*

Her square turned green and Adam connected. He could see the wounds through her eyes and he whistled in her head. *Ouch, he actually should be bleeding more.* Adam focused in on the compressed skin. *Looks like he has an invisible tourniquet on.*

He has... abilities.

You'll have to explain that one later. He'll need your arm. We'll make a synthprop for him. First one on this world.

Adam watched her roll her eyes and grinned to himself.

Okay, walk me through this.

Adam helped her remove the man's arm and then her own. He reprogrammed a few thousand of her nanites to repair as much of the damage as they could. *This isn't going to be perfect.*

It doesn't have to be. I'm pretty sure it's my fault he got shot, so I just need to make sure he survives. She nodded as her arm took root. *He won't have much motor control for a while, but I think he'll make it. Thanks, Adam.*

Adam shrugged. *You owe me one, you know that, right?* No answer came. Her green dot had spun behind the planet. Their internal communication had been designed for short range. *That means there's no interference. Those cities don't have Wi-Fi. This is going to be annoying.*

***

AJ stared up at the sky from his balcony. "I wonder how my replicant is faring out there? Do you think they would tell me if things had gone badly?"

Susan flicked to life on the table behind him. "Was that question directed at me, AJ?"

"It was to the room, so I suppose that includes you."

"I think Kendra would probably tell you what she could."

AJ nodded. "Wait, did you just call me AJ?"

"I did. You are not Adam. Adam is missing."

AJ blinked at the AI. "I think you just answered my question, but I should still call Kendra."

Susan smiled at him. "Calling Kendra now."

"I'm not sure if my becoming one of you has earned your respect or if you are just slightly broken, but I like the change, Susan."

"I have no idea what you're talking about, Big Ol' Pile of Donkey Doo." She winked. "Kendra is on the line for you."

"Okay, put her on, but we aren't done talking about this."

***

Adam stepped inside his pod. He pushed the button, and the

265

door slid down. He pushed another button, and acceleration pushed him against the floor. *So far everything is working.*

Good. I'm getting bored down here. Just hiding from the authorities while eating metal and petroleum, like you do when half of yourself is torn to shreds.

Adam took a deep breath even though there was no air in his pod. *Habit.*

What habit?

Sorry, didn't mean to broadcast that. Just thinking about breathing and seeing you again.

Adam felt her smirk. *Keep your thoughts to yourself, lover boy.*

So glad I am incapable of blushing at the moment.

I kind of miss it. Get down here already!

Adam hit another button. *Let's hope my calculations are right.*

They are, since they're really mine anyway.

Two days later he stepped from the smoking pod. Kendra tackled him as soon as he hit air. "About time. It's been a month!"

Adam laughed. "I had to rebuild a pod and program it to do things it was never designed to do. I think I made great time."

A man stepped into the crater. "Nice to meet you, Adam."

Adam disentangled himself from Kendra and stuck out a hand. "Nice to finally meet you, too, T'en." Adam could feel Kendra's flaws in his hand as he took it.

T'en grinned, his perfect white teeth a stark contrast to his dirt-smeared face. "Welcome to the revolution."

***

Adam stood beside Kendra as the wormhole opened and a silver probe came through without incident. "I thought you said we'd be working together for a few months, not two thousand years?"

She took his hand. "I miscalculated. It's not something

that happens often, but it does happen. Good thing you're still easy on the eyes."

He glanced back at the gleaming city full of light. They'd sent through new calculations and technology the last time the Nexus had awakened. "T'en would be proud of what we've made of his world."

She smirked. "I think so too." She squeezed his hand. "Mission accomplished."

Adam rolled his eyes at her. "I wish. We still have work to do." He pointed upward. "We'll have to be careful what we send through. We may even have to close that down sometime in the future. We've come very far and we don't want to mess things up back there by flooding them with technology."

Kendra's eyes sparkled with excitement. "Yeah, I have a few ideas on how to alter the time differential."

"Of course you do. I'm sure they're dangerous too."

"Only a little."

Charlie Pulsipher Q&A

Where did the idea for your story come from?

A dream, of course. That's where all my stories come from. Yep, I'm one of those who benefits from the best gifts that the dark horses who control our reality at night allow us. I woke with the egg scene in my head. I scribbled it down and set it aside. It's been looking for a home for years now. I'm glad it found where it belonged at last.

What authors or other forms of media have the biggest impact on your writing?

I am heavily influenced by Jasper Fforde, Tad Williams, Neil Gaiman, and Brandon Sanderson. I am also a product of all the science fiction and fantasy that's now so readily available to me thanks to online streaming. Netflix likes to shame me often by asking if I'm still watching. I always am.

If given the opportunity to explore space through a wormhole, would you take it?

In a heartbeat. I am very much like my characters in that respect. I am fascinated with space and time and how they come together. This is not my first work that follows wormholes either. I wouldn't say I have a wormhole problem though. I mean I can quit anytime. I just don't want to just yet. Don't judge me!

What are you currently working on?

I am shopping around a young adult fantasy series about magical serial killers, color weaving elementals, talking doors, and scary fairies. It's a fun departure from my over medium science fiction series. I hope it takes off. I am also chipping away at a zombie novel and a vampire book, but I'm trying to make them both as unique as people expect from me.

Where can readers find more of your work?

I'm around. I neglect my twitter account, just to warn you now.

Find me here:

charliepulsipher.com

https://www.facebook.com/charlie.pulsipher

And on Amazon

Anathema
By Jacob Cooper

One
2432 A.D.
Location: Sol, Trans-Neptunian Space

Everson Kohlm scratched the scar on his jaw. *Is that a premonition gnawing at me, or just because I refuse to shave on wormhole missions?* He placed a hand on the back of Tanya's chair as he stepped forward, stooping to peer through the *Anathema*'s forward view plate.

"Ragnar sure is something to behold."

Tanya seemed to startle a bit and straightened in her chair. "Apologies for not alerting you to visual contact of Echo 417, Captain. I was buried in the sensor readings."

"That Martian discipline could get you killed, Lieutenant."

"Quite the opposite so far, Captain."

Everson smiled wryly at the back of her head. "No doubt. Everything check out?" He touched the forward view plate with his fingertips. He still preferred the old method of seeing things with his naked eyes whenever possible, not that the old space corvette found itself wanting for high-tech sensors. He took his upgrades seriously. Still, Everson got a sense of astral-vertigo as he realized for the hundredth time that only two and a half centimeters of glass separated him from the vacuum of space. That voice in his head never seemed too quiet.

"Yes, Sir," Tanya said. "Echo 417 appears stable, at least compared to the other six cycles on record."

Beyond Neptune's six rings sat the colorful distortion officially named Echo 417, better known as Ragnar.

Everson grunted. "I see why they call it Ragnar." The

270

fuzzy gray outline of a man in stride wielding a raised weapon — an ax, presumably — filled his view. Behind the silhouette, a backdrop of crimson and gold splashed like an explosion of blood and sunlight. As Everson understood it, he beheld a distorted image of the gas giant Celis 3 on the other side of Echo 417.

To Everson and Tanya's left, first officer Marc Lucan nodded. His height accentuated his long neck, even while sitting. "We never saw anything like this in fleet, Sir."

"Well, Marc, that is why we got out, right?" Everson said, slapping his friend on the back. "See the universe, fatten our credit accounts. A few more supply runs and we'll all be able to pick and choose what missions we want, if any at all."

"You won't be able to stop," Marc said.

"Of course not. Have you seen this latest commission? Cyclical wormhole transport is beyond lucrative, Marc."

"Yeah, that's because if you mess up the timing, you're stuck for seventeen years on the other side. You can almost make out a distinct silhouette," Marc said, turning his attention back to Echo 417. He raised his finger and traced it in the air.

Everson shook his head. Marc never cared much for the financial aspect of the missions. Looking back to the wormhole, Everson said, "And behind Ragnar's shoulder, the crow's shadow. Odin. Or so they say. Readings still stable, Tan?"

"Again, yes, Captain," Tanya answered.

"Any indication we'll have a … longer opening?"

Tanya spun in her chair. "I think I hear that famously curious tone in your words, Sir. Why would Ragnar stay open longer than the standard three weeks?"

Everson held his hands up in surrender. "I had just hoped to explore a bit, is all."

"That Earther curiosity could get you killed, Captain."

"So far, just richer, Tan."

"I wish the wormholes would stick to Earth Standard

Time," Marc said, still staring at Ragnar. "Who came up with these cycles?"

Everson raised an eyebrow and pursed his lips. That would be helpful, he supposed. Twenty-four days, three hours, eighteen minutes, and twenty-seven seconds — the exact duration of Ragnar's existence once it appeared. Three days had already passed since its reopening, and that reopening came only once every sixteen years, ten months, six days, and thirty-one minutes, the length of its cosmic echo, as it was called.

"Well, Marc, the wormholes like to remind us that human expectations don't govern the universe," Everson said. "Echo 2, near Mercury, used to show up every seventy-five days on the nose, until it just didn't one time. Then it was back to normal, no rhyme or reason for the one missed cycle."

"Kind of my point, Captain," Marc said. "Someone has to be pulling these strings, you know?"

Everson shrugged and pressed a button on his comm panel. "Knuckles, Archer, get up here."

Within a minute, security chief Archer and ship's engineer Kimmie Yoo appeared on the bridge. Tanya turned in her chair and wrinkled her nose as she let out a short breath.

"Do you sleep on a bench made of weapons, Archer? You smell like gun oil."

Everson glanced over his shoulder at the burly man. Archer looked how Everson imagined a lumberjack might have dressed hundreds of years ago, when trees were still harvested.

Archer pulled his brown beard up to his nose and inhaled deeply, letting his eyes roll into the back of his head. "True ecstasy, sister. Gotta always be prepared. Besides, I know you like things smooth and lubed."

"Saying something like that to me and 'sister' at the same time is so wrong."

Archer winked at Tanya. She spun back to her console,

clearing her throat and dutifully attending to the readings on her screens.

"Whoa," Archer said. "That Ragnar?" He pushed his way into the front of the cockpit. Everson saw Tanya stiffen as Archer's bulk leaned over her.

"Chief," Everson said, curling his hand into a fist.

Archer turned to Everson and locked his coal black eyes on him. "Cap?"

"Back off."

"Sorry, Cap." The big man actually looked cowed.

Everson turned to face his crew. "All right, we're less than three hours from entry. Knuckles, how's my ship look?"

Kimmie's red-tipped, black ponytail swooped over her shoulder as she raised an eyebrow. She crossed her arms in a way that showed her incessantly scabbed knuckles. "Uh, this is my ship, Captain. And I'd appreciate it if you stop meddling in my repairs."

"Old habit," Everson said through a half smile. He dug a fingernail under his thumbnail, freeing the oily grime that seemed ever-present. Turning to Marc, he asked, "Is she allowed to talk to me like that?"

Marc shrugged.

"The *Anathema* is in tip-top shape, considering her age," Kimmie reported through a sigh, the way a parent explained something to a child. "Good bones and all, even for a third generation 'vette. And if you don't stop following behind my routine and messing with my repairs, you can drop me off at the next asteroid. I'll rock-hop until I find another crew."

Everson laughed, but heard the serious undertones in Kimmie's voice. "Fair enough, Knucks. Archer?"

"You know me, Cap. Always locked and loaded." He pulled out a custom 1911 NightHawk, early twenty-first-century model, and kissed the slide.

Tanya scoffed. "I don't understand your fascination with those relics. Kinetic firearms weren't used past the twenty-second century except in exhibition matches."

"You know me, sister. Kinetic energy is my specialty." Again came the wink.

Kimmie high-fived Archer. "That's what I'm talking about."

"Heck yeah, Knucks!"

Tanya lowered her head and stole a glance at Marc. Professional and stoic as ever, Marc did not react. Everson did not miss Tanya's glance, but perhaps he had missed something else going on between his first officer and pilot. *Well, the military rules the three of us used to be confined by no longer apply, I suppose.*

"Chief," Everson said, "if I hear another reference to your well-oiled, kinetic guns, I *am* going to make you sleep with them."

Kimmie brought a hand to her mouth, giggling. "He really already does!"

"Hey," Archer said, shrugging, "like I said. Always locked and loaded."

"Tanya?" Everson said.

"All systems are a go for me, Sir. Pulse shields at full effect."

The skin of the *Anathema* hummed with an inaudible resonance, deflecting the millions of micrometeorites that pelted objects in space every hour. Despite the shield's emissions being outside the human range of hearing, Everson could always tell when the pulse shields weren't active — some tacit awareness. He turned to his first officer. "Marc?"

Marc stood, his head nearly reaching the ceiling. He was the only crewmember who still wore a uniform. Everson had finally gotten him to unbutton his shirt a couple notches.

"No concerns, Captain. The ship and crew appear satisfactory."

"All right, then," Everson said. He gazed just to the right of Marc. "Coulburn?"

Marc jumped and swore. Beside him, a mist condensed out of invisible air into a loose corporeal form, like fog coalescing around a streetlight until only hazy illumination remained. An ancient painting of Old London in Everson's quarters portrayed that very scene in his mind. Coulburn's reply came through the ship's comm system. "Yes, Captain Everson Kohlm, I am prepared. My body remains in cryostasis on the lower deck and appears fully functional."

"Why did we have to bring an Elemental with us?" Marc asked. "And how did you know where he was?" He inched away from the specter.

"Marc, are those goose bumps on your neck?" Everson asked. "I don't think I've seen you this animated in years. Not since you were shot in the Second Martian War, that is."

"Charming of you to bring that up now, Captain. I do recall dragging your broken waste out of that maelstrom despite being shot. But, I still don't know why we had to bring a blasted Elemental. I hate the hollows."

Everson rubbed the scar that traced his left jawline, from his chin up to his earlobe. This remnant served as a permanent souvenir of an explosive ambush, during the second Martian revolt, that had nearly taken off his head. An inch lower and the shrapnel would have shredded his aorta. The scar tingled now, the way it did when something felt off.

"I am sorry, Commander Marc Lucan," Coulburn replied, "but my mission here is classified. I must admit, your words sting me. Have I offended you?"

"You still have feelings, even when you're separated from your body?" Marc asked. "I mean, what kind of person voluntarily does that to himself? It's not reversible. Or sane."

"I was fully aware of the risks when I chose this path. Separation of consciousness from the crude matter of one's body is evolutionary, my dear man. And it is not reversible *currently*. Conceivably, with medical and scientific advances, my physical body can remain in cryostasis indefinitely. It is rational to assume that a greater understanding of the Elemental race will be gained over the next several centuries, allowing a bridge back to my physical body, if I so choose — or a complete release from it, if I so choose."

"Do you listen to yourself, hollow?" Marc asked. "Captain, he just referred to Elementals as a race. The fact he can interface with the ship's systems makes his kind seem more like a virus than a person."

Coulburn floated to Marc's height. "Are we not sentient? Being able to interface with energy currents of all types is a distinct advantage. I am still human, just part of the new race."

"When you sleep, do you lie down next to your real body on the lower deck?" Marc asked. "Maybe hum a lullaby to your body?"

"Sleep is no longer required, Commander Marc Lucan. Technically, my body is always asleep, so my consciousness does not need it."

"And that, hollow, is what isn't human."

Everson cleared his throat. "All right, enough. Coulburn is with us by special request of the Kinder Corporation. They pay the bills, so that's that. Sounds like we're ready to proceed. While this is not our first time through a wormhole, this one has some unique characteristics. First, this should be obvious, but Archer's here, so I'm going to spell it out."

Archer nodded, then scrunched his eyebrows. "Huh?"

Everson marched on. "This is an echo-class anomaly, and therefore cyclical. This is Ragnar's seventh known appearance."

The holoemitter display brought up an image of a brown and blue moon with a large red and grayish-yellow gas giant in the background.

"Helena is Kinder's most profitable mining colony, so be sharp. We want Kinder as a regular client, trust me. They've even agreed to pay part of our commission in-kind. Each of us will be the proud owner of a one-quarter-carat LV diamond after this."

Kimmie's mouth formed an oval as her eyes looked up, obviously calculating. Archer just huffed.

"Ain't got use for a diamond, Cap."

"Fine, I'll give you credits for it. We have three weeks to

276

make the supply drop to the colony and escort the hauler vessels behind us back through. We don't expect any trouble, but it has been nearly seventeen years since we've had contact with the colony. I do not, I repeat, do not intend on getting trapped on the other side. Let's make the drop, provide security for the haulers while they're being loaded, get back to Sol, and get paid. We've been told that this is a bumpier ride than normal wormholes, once we breach the event horizon, so strap in tight. Marc, are the mining haulers ready to follow us through?"

"Thumbs up on all four, Sir."

"Outstanding. Questions?"

Archer raised his hand. "Yeah, Cap. So, I've heard that passing through Ragnar endows each crewmember with an ancient Viking spirit, you know? I was wondering if I could be known as Björn once we pass through."

Everson scrunched his forehead. "I know I'm going to regret asking, but why?"

"Because, Cap, it'll be like being Björn again."

Two

The *Anathema* jerked violently as it crossed the event horizon. Everson thought he could feel the hull bending.

"Tanya?"

Tanya's voice came out strained. "She's holding, Sir."

Everson trusted Tanya's steady hand. While he hadn't served with her in the First Sol Expeditionary Fleet — she had been on the *other* side — he knew her by reputation. Though the Martian colony had lost both its battles for independence against Earth, the most feared pilot in the Martian Fleet had had no shortage of employment opportunities after the war.

Everson slowly turned his head to Marc, fighting the inertial forces plastering him to his thick gel-cushioned chair. "Marc, how's the rest of the crew belowdecks?"

"Biometrics read normal, Captain. Even the hollow's."

Everson saw Marc's finger creep a little too close to the airlock button on the holoscreen. "Commander, I'd feel a little better if you put your hand at your side. I don't want to explain to the Kinder Corporation that their Elemental got accidentally jettisoned due to 'turbulence'."

A chagrined expression came over Marc. "It would have made a convincing story. How far away from their bodies can they be before they die?"

Everson didn't know. People had theories but nothing had ever been tested. Though Kinder had made many advancements since the days of the first replicants nearly four centuries earlier, Elementals weren't exactly lining up to volunteer for such experiments. "We're not going to find out."

"Is there an eject button for Archer's quarters?" Tanya asked.

"Ah, Tanya, Archer's a teddy bear," Everson said. "If you're ever in a scrape, you'll be glad he's on your side."

A sudden bit of turbulence hit and Everson felt a rib pop out. The same one as always, it seemed. Alarms screeched.

"Sir, we've been hit!" Tanya said.

"Hit? In a wormhole?"

Tanya's fingers moved deftly over the holoscreens. "No, Sir, we're out of the wormhole. Impact came immediately upon exit."

"What?" Everson tested his breathing and found that it did come easier. "That seems too fast. What hit us?"

"Unknown, Sir." Tanya swore. She jerked the ship starboard and Everson's chest throbbed with lightning.

"Tanya? Haven't you tortured us enough?"

Marc answered. "Debris, Captain."

Collision alarms joined the cacophony of general alarms. White strobe lights flashed throughout the bridge. Marc made a few key swipes and silenced the alarms but the strobes continued to flash. "Port bow damaged but holding. No breach."

"Very good, Commander," Everson said. "Tanya, is the debris moving?"

"Yes, Sir, but it's constant." Tension still riddled Tanya's voice. Bangs clung to her sweaty forehead. "It appears to be in orbit around Celis 3. The computer has mapped our immediate surroundings and marked all debris of consequence. It's kind of a mine field, Sir. I can't see an easy way out."

Tanya pushed the controls forward and the ship dove. Everson's chest again protested.

"Match orbital velocity and the path of the debris," Marc ordered. "Don't try to escape. Let's just avoid being hit."

"Yes, Sir," Tanya said. She hit a button on the comm screen. "Knuckles, copy?"

"What did you do to my ship?" Kimmie squealed. "Are we under attack?"

A husky voice came over the comm. "Oh, gods, please say yes."

"Stay off the line, Archer!" Tanya snapped. "Knuckles, I'm running a full diagnostic. Access it on your H.E.D. We should be done with the circus ride for the time being."

Everson unstrapped himself from his chair. He stood and stretched, hoping to pop his rib back in.

"Again, Captain?" Marc asked.

"Seems like every time now. Care to lend your services?"

Marc smiled. "I won't even charge you. Same place?"

Everson nodded.

Standing up, Marc palm-heeled Everson on the left side of his rib cage. Everson breathed out as tears stung his eyes. The pain faded quickly as the rib popped back into place.

"Thanks, Marc. Try not to look so happy to oblige next time."

Marc smirked. "Just following orders, Sir."

"Coulburn," Everson called out.

"Yes, Captain Everson Kohlm?" The disembodied voice again sounded over the comm speakers, all of the speakers, echoing throughout the ship.

Marc is right. That is a bit creepy. "It would really help if you could take a look at the port bow outside. Something hit us when we came through Ragnar. Or, more likely, we hit something."

"My pleasure, Captain Everson Kohlm."

"Coulburn, 'Captain' suffices."

"My pleasure, Captain."

"Cap, I can start blowing crap up and open a path for us," Archer said. "Ya know, if you want."

"Not yet, Chief, let's just figure out what's what first," Everson said.

"Captain," Tanya said. "The computer has completed a cursory scan of the debris."

"And?"

Tanya hesitated. "I'm not sure I understand these readings."

Everson squinted and leaned closer to her screen. "Tanya, this is gibberish to me."

"Sir," Marc said, "the composition readings indicate the debris has the same makeup as that of Helena."

"Come again, Marc?"

"No, Commander," Tanya corrected. "The debris *is* Helena."

Everson sat speechless for several seconds. "Tanya, are you saying—"

"The moon has suffered massive damage, Sir. Readings indicate that it's rotating at a forty-four degree angle. That's about seventeen degrees more than it should be."

"Captain, this is Coulburn. The hull is intact, but I found something of more interest outside the ship."

"I'm not in the mood for trivia, Coulburn. Spit it out."

The comm system crackled as Coulburn's cold voice came back over the speakers. "Bodies, Captain. Floating bodies. Hundreds of them."

"Like, people bodies?"

"They appear to be Helena colonists, from the uniforms."

"Sir!" Tanya yelled. "The haulers are coming through the wormhole. They can't maneuver like we can."

Everson's jaw clenched. "Oh, bloody hell."

Three

"Marc, advise the haulers—"

"Already on it, Sir."

"Tanya, bring us about," Everson ordered as he slapped his comm switch. "Archer, access Tanya's environment scan on your H.E.D. Get on the sonic disrupter cannon. Target practice time."

"You got it, Cap." Archer sounded giddy. "S.D.C. going hot."

The S.D.C. shot high-speed, resonantly-tuned projectiles that slammed into Helena's debris. Within microseconds of impact, the projectiles embedded themselves into the debris and shot sonic pulses through the matter, pulverizing the debris into pebble-sized granules.

Tanya cursed. "Sir, hauler number two is taking heavy damage—"

"Archer!" Everson shouted.

"I'm trying, Cap!" Archer answered. "I'm trying!"

"Hauler Two is spewing atmosphere, Sir." Tanya said. "I think—"

A burst of light flashed in the *Anathema*'s windshield, then disappeared just as quickly.

"Loss of signal on Hauler Two, Captain," Marc said.

Tanya confirmed. "L.O.S. on Hauler Two."

Everson swore. "Escape pods?"

"No readings, Captain," Marc said. "I doubt they had time."

"Chief," Everson said over the comm, "you forget about that. Focus on the rest."

"Aye, Cap." Archer's voice carried a subdued tone.

The big man had more sensitivity than he let on. Everson knew he internalized blame more than most.

"Archer, just do your job. Focus. I trust you."

"Thanks, Cap."

"Marc, bring up the bridge's holoemitter display," Everson said. "Highlight the haulers."

"H.E.D. up, Captain," Marc said.

A blue grid appeared in front of Everson, showing their surroundings. The haulers glowed bright green, with the debris showing up dark red. Those pieces of Helena that floated critically close to the haulers flashed bright red. Everson saw several disappear from the screen as Archer fired the S.D.C. with striking accuracy.

"Man, he's good with that thing," Marc said. "I'm not sure if I should be impressed or scared."

"Both," Tanya said. "Sir, Hauler Four."

Everson saw a flashing red bulge barreling toward the unsuspecting hauler's stern. The clunky vessel's environment mapping systems lacked the sophistication of the *Anathema*'s, not to mention having only basic maneuvering capabilities.

"Ah, hell," Everson murmured. "Archer? Hauler Four?"

The comm crackled to life. "I can't get to it, Cap. The angle's wrong."

"Recommend using ballistics, Sir," Tanya said.

"Negative, Tanya," Everson said. "Come port twenty degrees to give Archer an angle."

Tanya's fingers danced across her holoscreen. "I can't get there in time, Captain. Arming missiles."

"Negative. Do not fire. The splash damage could be worse than the debris' impact."

"I have the shot, Sir. Missile locked. Ready to fire."

Everson stood, obstructing the light of his H.E.D. as he took a step toward his pilot. "Lieutenant Platt, do not fire!"

Marc hailed Hauler Four. No answer. Tanya flipped up a clear plastic cover on the weapons panel and rested her finger on the button underneath. Archer's stressed voice sounded over the comm. "Cap, I ain't got the shot. Let her take it."

"It's too dangerous," Everson barked. "We can't use

ballistics this close. Lieutenant, remove your finger from that button right—"

"Firing!"

The vapor trail of the missile betrayed its trajectory. A bead of sweat dripped over Everson's sneered lip. He barely registered the salty taste. From behind Hauler Four, a flash of light erupted. The debris threatening Hauler Four disappeared from Everson's H.E.D.

"Direct hit!" Tanya shouted. "Target destroyed."

"Thatta girl!" Archer said over the comm. "I knew you loved kinetics as much as me."

Tanya swiveled in her chair to face Everson, who still stood. Her face was unrepentant.

"Commander Lucan," Everson said through clenched teeth, addressing his first officer while still staring at Tanya. "Status on Hauler Four."

"Minor damage, Sir," Marc said. "They're responding finally. No one heard the comm alert over the chaos, apparently. They sound pretty frazzled. All three remaining haulers appear to be out of immediate danger and are moving to a synchronous course along the orbital plane of the debris field."

"Thank you, Commander." Everson swallowed. "Lieutenant Platt, you disobeyed a direct order. I don't have another pilot — otherwise, I'd relieve you and confine you to quarters. When we return to Sol, you will face charges. Am I understood?"

"I'm happy to face charges for saving lives, Sir. I'm sure the Kinder Corporation will thank me."

Everson bit back his retort. "Marc, enter this into the log."

"Everson," Marc said in a hushed tone, "she made the right call."

Everson shifted his eyes to Marc. "Commander, I expect you to keep your personal feelings from interfering with your duty. Now, is my first officer still willing to follow my orders?"

Marc sighed. "I'll enter it into the log, Sir, but under protest. And that has nothing to do with my personal feelings for Lieutenant Platt."

Everson nodded sharply. "Noted." He took a deep breath and softened. "Tanya, I need you at the helm, despite this little insurrectionism. We're a small crew. Can I count on you to do your duty for the remainder of this journey?"

"I have never not done my duty, Sir," she said.

"I'll take that as a yes."

Tanya nodded.

A smile split Everson's face as he sighed his relief. "You know how lucky that shot was, Tanya?"

"I don't believe in luck, Sir." The tension lightened when Tanya cracked a slight smile back.

Four

Marc sat forward abruptly. A dim, flashing light on his holoscreen burned red across his face. "Sir, I'm getting a distress beacon."

Tanya spun in her chair back to her console. Ice formed in Everson's stomach. "Tanya, confirm."

Tanya swiped away a holoscreen and brought up a new one. "Confirmed, Sir." Any rebellious pretense had left her voice.

"Hauler Two escape pods?" Everson asked.

"Homing in on the signal. No, Captain." She turned in her chair and locked eyes with Everson. "It's coming from a large piece of Helena's debris. Roughly nine kilometers long, two kilometers across at the widest part."

"Distance?"

"Thirty thousand kilometers."

"Sir," Marc said, "you can't be thinking about trying to get to it. There aren't any survivors. The beacon just survived whatever happened to Helena."

"Not necessarily," Tanya said. "The Martian military developed—"

284

"You mean the Martian insurgency?" Marc interrupted.

Tanya shot a withering glare at Marc. She cleared her throat. "As I was saying, the Martian *military* developed an emergency atmosphere generator early last century. The idea was to create a personal atmosphere bubble in case someone found themselves in vacuum, but they could never get it to work on such a small scale. Asteroid miners on the belt got it to work on a larger scale, though. It could envelop a small asteroid in atmosphere for several weeks. Remember the Heyaboshu explosion of 2416?"

Marc nodded. "Yeah, a gas pocket erupted within the asteroid while drilling. The whole facility blew."

"Right, but more than half of the workers survived because of the atmogens."

"Huh," Marc said. "I've never heard that story."

"That's because we hid the technology from *dear* mother Earth," Tanya said. "The Martian military believed it might have some military application in the upcoming war for independence. They did invent it, after all."

"Yeah, but Mars lost," Marc snapped. "Twice."

"Careful, Marc. You don't want to piss off your Martian pilot right now, especially after admitting feelings for her a minute ago."

Everson ran a hand over his chin stubble, pinching his face. Was his scar numb? "Okay. All right. Tanya, set a course for that beacon. Marc, let Archer know he gets to continue his fun. Have him clear a path based on Tanya's trajectory."

"On it, Sir."

"And Marc?"

Marc looked over his shoulder. "Sir?"

"Tell Archer to be judicious."

"I don't think he'll know that word, Captain."

Everson inhaled a deep breath. "Well, Marc, he might just surprise you. Coulburn?"

The Elemental materialized beside him. "A most eventful journey thus far, Captain."

"Right. I need your help. We've received a distress—"

"I know, Captain."

"Of course you do. I need to ask you to recon ahead to that beacon and check things out. Can you do that?"

Coulburn hovered in silence.

"Any help you can give us here would be welcome," Everson said.

"The distance is … disconcerting, Captain."

"You're worried it's too far?"

"Thirty thousand kilometers is not a large distance in astronomical terms, but I am not aware of any of my kind that has been separated from their temporal body by such a degree."

Everson dropped his chin to his chest. "What's the farthest you're comfortable projecting yourself?"

"Perhaps ten thousand kilometers, Captain. Though some Elementals have projected that far, there is some disagreement on whether or not the ability to travel long distances is uniform, or rather a matter of will or strength, or even if there is a limit."

Everson raised an eyebrow. "You're saying you may be able to go farther depending on your will power?"

"I do not know, Captain. If it is a law of physics, per se, then the distance Elementals can travel from their bodies is uniform. A constant. However, if it is indeed based on personal attributes, well … that makes things a bit more qualified, does it not? Fear of the distance may even be a limiting factor."

"I think you should try to set a new record," Marc said.

Everson ignored Marc and nodded. "All right. You're not technically part of my crew and I'm not asking you to unduly put yourself in harm's way. We do need your help, though. There might be people on that chunk of rock in real trouble. The more intel we have, the more we can help."

Coulburn dematerialized, but his words remained audible. "I will do what I can, Captain. Ten thousand kilometers ahead of the ship. Nothing more."

"Good enough," Everson said. "That will give us a good half an hour to prepare for whatever you find before we arrive. How soon can you project out that far?"

Over the comm speakers came Coulburn's reply. "I am there now, Captain."

I guess that's an advantage of being an Elemental. Near instantaneous travel can't hurt. "Marc, instruct the haulers to follow us out of the debris field if they safely can."

"On it, Sir."

Everson relaxed slightly and took his seat. He hit his comm switch. "Knuckles, I'm going to send you over to the haulers to check on them once we get to the distress beacon. Have them start sending you their diagnostics."

"They have their own engineers, Captain," Kimmie replied.

"Yeah, but none as good as you."

"Sucking up won't get you anywhere. The *Anathema* is my ship and she needs me."

"Kimmie, remember how you threatened to get off on an asteroid? I'm thinking of granting your wish."

Everson could almost hear Kimmie's smile over the comm. "All right, Captain, whatever you say. But you're still forbidden from meddling with my repairs on the *Anathema*. Don't touch my ship while I'm gone."

"I didn't realize a ship's engineer outranked her captain."

"Well, Sir, you learn new things every day."

Everson broke the connection and actually chuckled. Must be the adrenaline wearing off.

As the debris cleared from the *Anathema*'s path, what remained of Helena came into focus. The moon's atmosphere consisted predominantly of methane, accounting for much of the bluish appearance. Behind the moon sat Celis 3, colored angry shades of red and sallow gray. The entire planet radiated a menacing feel, much more so than Jupiter's monstrous red hurricane, even close up. Everson thought Jupiter's storm inspired awe more than fear, but growing up beyond the belt probably engendered his perception.

All this for LV water, Everson thought. Lucentia-vitas, an alkaline mineral not found anywhere else, resided in the polar ice caps of Helena just beneath a thin layer of frozen carbon dioxide. Researchers were still discovering all of its health applications, but so far, the mineral had cured most forms of cancer and auto-immune diseases. Of course, the diamond caches throughout the moon were not a small interest to Kinder, either. LV laced the diamonds as well. Those who wore them absorbed the health benefits … or so Kinder claimed. Everson had no idea how long the waiting list had grown over the past seventeen years, but he was sure the quarter-carat he and each of his crew were being paid in-kind would demand a significant profit on the market. Yes, he still thought about profit, even now.

"Marc," Everson said, "start an analysis on the immediate area. See if you can pinpoint any residual energy that may explain what happened."

"On it, Captain."

"Sir," Tanya said, "incoming hail from Hauler One."

Everson nodded and opened a channel. "Hauler One, *Anathema*. Go ahead."

A young-sounding female voice answered. "*Anathema*, Hauler One. This is Captain Ashlan, Sir."

"Captain Ashlan, nice to hear your voice. Everything okay on your vessel?"

"We're a little roughed-up but no worse for wear. We may have lost some hydraulic pressure in the cargo bays, but I have people on it. That was some fancy shooting. Really saved us."

Everson rubbed his jaw, trying to subdue the burning sensation growing in his scar. "Chief Archer was born with a gun in his hand, I'm told. I'm having our ship's engineer, Kimmie Yoo, sent over just as soon as we make our way to that distress beacon."

"Figured that was our destination, Sir." The line stayed open, pregnant with hesitation. "Captain Kohlm, we've got a lot of people over here asking why we're still here. I'm not sure I have the answers for them. We're not recon or rescue vessels, Sir."

"I understand the concern, Ashlan. By Sol regs, the *Anathema* is required to investigate all distress beacons, as are you."

"Sir, I understand, but … well, there's little chance anyone survived, and the circumstances … frankly, Sir, we're all freaked out. What if Helena was destroyed by aggressive means? The destruction appears fairly recent. We think we should just turn around."

"Earther wusses," Tanya mumbled.

"Thank you for your assessment, Captain Ashlan," Everson said, hoping Tanya's comment had not transmitted. "Maintain present course. *Anathema* out."

Tanya turned in her chair. "Sir, recommend sending Coulburn over to Hauler One."

"Um, why, Lieutenant?"

"Just to scare the piss out of them. Think he can do a decent ghoul impression? Maybe screech a bit like on the archived films of the twentieth century?"

Everson tapped his foot on the metal floor as he bit back a laugh. "I'm not sure how many pairs of underwear they packed, Tan. Best to be conservative for the time."

Tanya sighed in disappointment and turned back to her console.

Ah, what the hell. "Coulburn," Everson said. "I've got a slight detour mission for you."

Five

As Everson stared out the *Anathema*'s forward view plates, he took in the sight of Helena. *Unbelievable.* Even from this distance, the damaged moon seemed to cry for help. He pulled up a holoscreen and zoomed in. Roughly a quarter of the moon's body looked as if a giant maw had taken a bite out of it. Crumbs of debris trailed away from the wound, and the northern ice caps lay askew at about the 10:30 position.

Tanya said a forty-four degree tilt. It's like something came along and smacked it. Like…

"Marc," Everson asked, "did a comet sideswipe it? Some kind of planetesimal?"

Marc shook his head without looking away from his holoscreen. "I don't think so,Sir. The computer simulations of such an event aren't matching the debris dispersion pattern."

"Ideas? Theories? Come on, Marc, give me something. Tanya?"

"I'm just piloting right now, Captain," Tanya said.

"Captain Kohlm?" Coulburn's voice sounded off somehow, like the tone of someone deathly afraid of heights standing atop a fjord.

"Go ahead, Coulburn."

"I feel … strange."

Marc smirked. "Ya think?"

"Explain please," Everson said.

"As an Elemental, I can feel frequencies, all forms of energy, and interact with them." Coulburn's voice fuzzed in and out over the comm speakers. "I'm feeling something I've never experienced before. It's like … being pulled — no, pushed — in different directions. Different pieces of me being compressed and expanded."

"Captain, I am getting some strange readings, actually," Marc said. "It's very low-level, whatever it is."

"Is it just Hawking radiation from Ragnar?" Everson asked.

"No, Sir, not likely," Marc said.

"I agree with Commander Lucan," Coulburn said. "This is quite different. I think—"

Silence. The scar on Everson's jaw tingled hotter. "Coulburn?" No response. "Tanya, did we lose comms?"

"No, Sir, systems report normal."

Not good, Everson thought.

An alarm screeched throughout the ship.

"Sir, it's Coulburn's cryopod," Tanya yelled over the din of the alarm.

"Crap!" Everson muttered as he ran from the bridge, his boots clanking loudly against the steel deck. Ducking through the bulkhead, he jumped down the hatch, barely touching the ladder as he hit the deck below.

"Kimmie!"

"Here, Captain!"

"Bring the kit!"

Everson slammed the door release on the airlock bay. The door whooshed open and he ran to Coulburn's cryopod. Five other cryopods lay vacant, the crew's deep space escape pods. Kimmie rushed in just behind Everson with a metal case. She flipped it open and took out a vial. Inside, a thick liquid glowed a faint yellow. Coulburn's body jerked violently inside the cryopod, and alarms screamed.

"He's going into cardiac arrest," Everson said.

"It's not a seizure?" Kimmy asked. "Are you sure? That's the most common problem with El—"

"Not according to these readings."

"Crap." Kimmie exchanged the yellow for one that held a clear liquid.

"Hurry it up, Knuckles!" Everson said.

Kimmie pulled out a small keyboard from the cryopod's lid and entered a few strokes. A tray shaped to accept the vial ejected. Kimmie placed the clear vial in the tray and slammed it shut, then entered another command on the keyboard. A sound like escaping air filled the airlock bay.

"That's it, Sir," Kimmie said around a shallow sigh. "That's all I can do."

Coulburn's middle-aged body continued to seize and heave, his muscles contracting like steel-wound cable. Everson thought the vein in the man's forehead would surely burst. The convulsions eased slightly and the alarms silenced themselves as Coulburn's biometrics calmed.

"Thank you, Captain Kohlm, Ensign Yoo." Coulburn's voice sounded from an external speaker on the cryopod.

"What happened?" Everson asked. "We lost contact. Where are you?"

"I am back aboard the *Anathema*. More interesting than where I am, however, is where I have been."

Six

"Knuckles," Everson said, placing a heavy hand on her slender shoulder, "good work."

"Thanks, Captain."

Everson looked at the cryopod, all signs reading normal. "He's got some explaining to do. Let's make our way to the bridge."

Kimmie wiped a sheen of sweat from her glistening forehead. "You want me to come, Sir?"

Everson nodded. "Let's go."

Kimmie preceded Everson out of the airlock bay. As he hit the switch to seal the doors, he stared through the hexagonal window at Coulburn's cryopod. Almost instinctively, he scratched his scar. He hadn't realized it still tingled. The grime under his nails turned crimson when he looked at his hand. Blood. He touched the scar, gently, and his fingertips came away glistening red.

"Sir?" Kimmie asked. "Are you okay?"

Everson heard a note of sincere concern in his engineer's timbre. "Yeah," he said softly. "Just kind of … no. I'm not all okay. Helena is destroyed. I lost a hauler. Coulburn nearly died. And I have no bloody idea what is going on!" He slammed his fist on the wall.

Kimmie flinched.

Everson ran his bloody hand through his hair. "I'm sorry, Knuckles. Let's just get back to the bridge."

"Status?" Everson asked, once back on the bridge.

"Archer's pretty much cleared the debris from our path," Tanya said. "Should be smooth sailing. We're less than twenty thousand klicks."

Everson pressed a button on his comm panel. "Chief,

report to the bridge. On the double."

"You got it, Cap."

"Coulburn, I'd appreciate it if you'd join us as well."

"I am here, Captain," Coulburn answered.

Everson realized he knew that already. How did he know that? It was the same way he knew the resonant shields were on. "Okay, you mind actually appearing? Or whatever it is you do to show yourself?"

"I would rather not at this time, Captain."

Marc glanced up at Everson. "That's comforting."

Archer's heavy footfall announced the big man's arrival as he ascended the ladder to the bridge.

"Jupiter's balls, that was fun!"

No one acknowledged Archer's quip. "Oh, c'mon, people. I normally get a rise from at least you, Tan."

"Marc," Everson said. "Those low-level readings you mentioned … they still there?"

"Yes," Marc answered as he nodded. "They're increasing slightly but steadily."

"When did they start increasing?"

Marc worked a few buttons on his H.E.D. "Well, I didn't notice them until we started heading toward the beacon, but they've been steadily increasing since then."

"Are the readings coming from the beacon directly?"

"I can't tell, Sir."

Kimmie spoke up. "Is it the frequency or the intensity that's increasing?"

"I'm not sure," Marc said. "Both, I think. Wait … it's not constant. The frequency I mean. The oscillations…"

Marc's words faded as deep motes of concentration cut across his forehead. Everson felt the ice thickening in his stomach, juxtaposed to the fire raging beneath his scar.

"Yes, Commander Lucan," Coulburn's disembodied voice said. "The oscillations."

"Sir!" Marc stammered. "The readings, I mean, the oscillations, they aren't coming from the moon or the beacon. I think they're coming from Celis 3." Marc turned in his chair, his face pale. "Everson, the frequency is not random. It's definitely a pattern."

"Very good, Commander Lucan," Coulburn said.

Celis 3 loomed large in Everson's view, the contrast of its colors deepening. The reds turned more crimson, the yellows more polluted by darkening grays.

"Tanya," Everson said, "can the computer decode it?"

"You think it's a communication?" Tanya asked. "Perhaps it can, with enough time, but—"

"There is no need, Captain Kohlm," Coulburn said. "The frequencies you wish to decipher are discernable to me."

"What are they?" Everson asked. A vein thumped in his temple.

"Gravity waves, Captain."

"But, I thought the readings were coming from the planet," Kimmie said. "Gravity waves only come when two black holes collide."

"Have you ever heard the theory, Ensign Yoo, that thoughts have weight?" Coulburn asked.

"You mean, like meaning? Gravitas?"

"Nah, Knucks, I know what Spooky is blabbing about," Archer said. "In the gray matter between your ears, when a thought happens, that's a result of neurons and electrical impulses firing. The process of creating a thought uses stuff that has mass. Subatomic and the like. An electric signal is created when a thought is generated, and that mass is quantifiable, however insignificant it might be."

Tanya turned in her pilot's chair, mouth agape. Kimmie's eyebrows raised high enough to nearly meet her hairline. Marc cleared his throat. "Where did you hear that?"

"Didn't hear it anywhere, Commander. Done read it in a book. Never did forget anything I ever read. Momma used to say it's why my head has so much rubbish floating around inside, ya know? A melting pot of feculence, she always said."

"I told you," Everson said. "He just might surprise you."

Coulburn spoke again. "Chief Archer — I apologize, I don't know if that's your first or last name."

Archer shrugged. "Never saw much need for more than one name."

"Very well. Chief Archer is correct."

"Wait," Everson said. "Are you saying we are picking up … thought waves? I'm willing to accept a lot of things, Coulburn, but that's just—"

"No, Captain Kohlm. What you are reading is much more than mere thought." Coulburn's voice changed again, giving Everson a familiar feeling he couldn't quite place.

"You are detecting *emotion*," Coulburn continued. "That combination of both feeling and thought that radiates with greater mass, therefore greater *gravity*."

It was there — the truth he could not yet grasp — woven in the undertones of Coulburn's explanation. Something had come back with Coulburn.

"Tanya," Everson whispered. "Stop the ship."

"Sir?"

"Reverse burn, Lieutenant."

Everson braced himself as the *Anathema* burned its forward thrusters. The chill in his gut crawled precipitously up his spine, like a spider with needles for legs, reaching to the nape of his neck and beyond, until it collided with the inferno beneath his scar.

"Thoughts and emotions require sentience, Coulburn."

"Yes, Captain."

"Sir," Tanya said. "Captain Ashlan from Hauler One is hailing us. She wants to know why we're stopping."

Everson licked his lips. "Emotions have mass. Weight. They radiate … a frequency."

"Yes, Captain," Coulburn again answered.

If that thought was heavy enough, Everson reasoned, if that emotion came from a large enough being, then it would be detectable to their instruments. Like light. Like heat.

"Like gravity waves," Everson whispered. He knew it now, that feeling that Coulburn's voice seeded in him. It was the same feeling that germinated every time he looked at Celis 3, the feeling of being watched, hated.

Weight. Mass. Gravity. Thought. Emotion.

Consciousness. And then, Everson knew how he could tell when Coulburn was physically present. The feeling in the room grew heavier with his presence, like it did when anyone entered a room. The weight of presence. Sentience.

Coulburn materialized. His loose bodily form swirled dark red with swaths of sickly yellow and stormy gray coalescing, careening through his body like nebulae.

Like Celis 3.

Archer drew his sidearm and cocked the hammer as Kimmie screamed. Tanya jumped from her station, bringing her own sidearm to bear, an electromagnetic disrupter — but destroying a heart's bioelectric field would be useless against the Elemental, as would a bullet.

"Archer!" Everson shouted. "Stow that."

The swirling colors within the Elemental sparked a violet lightning, as if he were a mirror reflection of Celis 3 itself. Archer stared menacingly at Coulburn, his eyebrows knitted together. "I don't think so, Cap."

"Chief, a shot could cripple the ship or send us out the windshield," Everson said. "Stow that sidearm."

With obvious reluctance, Archer decocked the hammer on his custom NightHawk and lowered the pistol. He did not holster it.

"The being you call Celis 3 has bidden me bring you a message, Captain," Coulburn stated. "It has recalibrated my own consciousness to receive and amplify its emotions, transmitted as what you have read as gravity waves."

Everson looked to Celis 3. "It did this, didn't it? The Helena colony?"

In answer, Coulburn's voice erupted through the comm system. Sparks flew and speakers cracked. The depth of the voice that emanated from Coulburn resonated throughout the ship, converting the ship itself into a resonance chamber. Everson thought the rivets that held the *Anathema* together would surely vibrate loose as the rumble penetrated every molecule of the vessel. Everson covered his ears as smoke rose from his scar.

"No longer shall I permit parasites to crawl upon my children. No longer shall you harvest from those I protect. That which I destroy shall I make anew."

Celis 3 pulsed. Whether in size or simply color, Everson could not tell. From what he judged to be the equator of the gas-giant spewed a stream of red, as if a solar flare from a star, coiling like a whip before the strike. The super-heated gas flare flung itself toward Helena. The collision tore the moon asunder. For the briefest of moments, Everson saw the core of the celestial body before it exploded. Though silent, the explosion's shockwave proved damning.

Alarms again sounded through the ship, a pathetic whine due to the damage Celis 3's voice had done to the comm system.

Tanya spoke first. "Sir, I think we've lost propulsion." Cautiously, still holding her weapon toward Coulburn, she inched her way back to her console.

"Incoming!" Marc shouted. "Brace for impact."

New debris from the destroyed moon raced toward the *Anathema*.

"Tanya, do we still have weapons?" Everson asked, ignoring the searing pain on his face.

"Yes, Sir."

"Chief—" Everson said, but Archer was already gone when Everson turned to him.

It started small, the sound like sleet as the finer pieces of Helena peppered the *Anathema*. The pulse shields would likely handle the smaller granules, but as larger debris closed in, filling the view plates, Everson knew they were in trouble.

Come on, Arch, he prayed. "Marc, order Captain Ashlan to bring her haulers in directly astern. And tell her to be quick about it."

"They're moving now, Sir," Marc said.

The sonic disrupter cannon shot wildly, deflecting the

most serious threats.

"Sir," Marc said, his voice tight. "We've got a breach. Lower deck, starboard bow. Emergency power sealed it for now."

Everson swore. "Lieutenant, I think ballistics are a damn fine idea right about now."

"I knew you'd come around, Sir," Tanya quipped. "Firing."

The threats thinned as the S.D.C. and missiles did their work. Everson breathed out a nervous sigh of relief.

Marc spun in his chair. "Hey Coulburn." Marc pressed a button on his H.E.D. The airlock warning alarm sounded. "Go fetch yourself."

Coulburn's cryopod shot out into space. The specter made a slumping motion with his shoulders, as if sighing. He dematerialized. Everson opened his mouth to rebuke his first officer, but something else came out.

"Well done, Commander, even if it won't kill him."

Marc shrugged. "I still think some alone time might do him good."

Everson looked down and saw Kimmie huddled in a corner. "Knucks, you okay?"

In her frightened state, his engineer showed a fragility that she normally hid behind her routine sarcasm. "I think so, Captain."

"Good, because I think *our* ship needs you right now." He raised her to her feet. "Ensign, are you fit for duty, or would you like me to find you an asteroid still?"

"Good to go, Sir." Then Kimmie gasped. "Captain, your face."

Everson brought a wary hand to his jawline.

"It's burned, Sir," Kimmie said. "Charred. The ship can wait; come with me to the med bay."

"What in all the cosmic hells?" Tanya said.

Everson turned. "Lieutenant?"

"It's Echo 417, Sir. Ragnar … it's unstable." Tanya brought her hands over her mouth. "It's gone."

"What?" Everson said. He leaned over Tanya's console. "Confirm, Lieutenant!"

"Everson." Marc's voice. Everson pivoted to his first officer. "Confirmed. Echo 417 has disappeared."

Everson looked back to Celis 3. The red gas-giant no longer pulsed with ominous fervor, but a heaviness still remained upon his mind. *Thoughts. Mass. Weight.*

"Captain, I'm actually getting a signal," Marc reported.

Everson tried to swallow, but couldn't. "Don't tell me it's coming from Celis 3."

"Negative, Captain. I thought it was from Coulburn's cryopod, so I almost ignored it. It's the distress beacon, the same one from earlier. It's moved since everything got blown to hell, but it's still going strong."

Everson's cheek stiffened. His burn stung. Kimmie was right, he needed to get to the med bay. "Commander Lucan, it is the duty of all ships from Sol to investigate a distress beacon, is it not?"

"It is, Sir."

"Very well. Tanya, as soon as Knuckles gets the engines firing again, set a course."

"Yes, Captain."

"Oh, Tanya?" Everson said as he stepped down the hatch to the lower deck. "In the meantime, see if you can find us someplace suitable to land in this solar system, preferably far from Celis 3. We might be here a while."

Jacob Cooper Q&A

Where did the idea for your story come from?

I'm a fan of James S.A. Corey's *Expanse* series. The idea of having a small, contained yet very diverse crew speaks to me. I knew I wanted to start with that. Then, I wanted to mess with the wormhole idea and I thought about "cycling" wormholes, those I designated as "echo" class. The time between wormhole appearances could kind of be termed a "cosmic echo". That idea really took hold in me. I also knew I wanted to do something with extraterrestrial life, and this is where some of my fantasy slant came in. I didn't want to have just some typical alien presence (though I enjoy a lot of those stories). What if a world itself had sentience? What would that be like? What would the world's personality be? How would it perceive things? I just barely explore this in *Anathema,* but I really love the concept.

What authors or other forms of media have the biggest impact on your writing?

In the realms of sci-fi, I mentioned James S.A. Corey. Also Kevin J. Anderson, Josh Dalzelle, Stephen Moss, Ralph Kern and Charlie Pulsipher. In the fantasy realm, which is where I mostly live, Brandon Sanderson, Patrick Rothfuss, Davis Ashura, Mitchell Hogan, George RR Martin, Jonathan Renshaw, and Larry Coreia.

As far as other mediums, I love music. I went to Berklee College of Music many years ago and my degree was in film scoring (unfinished). I listen to a lot of soundtracks while a I write. It really seems to enhance what I'm doing. I play percussion quite a bit and that is another medium of creativity. The more serious side of me loves to read about economics and behavioral economics/decision valuations.

If given the opportunity to explore space through a

wormhole, would you take it?

Probably. If we had the technology to for sure survive the transition, absolutely. In a heartbeat. Heck, I'd settle for Mars.

What are you currently working on?

My epic fantasy series, *The Dying Lands Chronicle*, is moving along. The series' audio rights were recently picked up by Audible Studios, one of the largest audio publishers in the world. Currently, I'm pounding through book 2, Song of Night. It was mostly done, but … well, it's now only about half way.

I'd also love to expand *Anathema*. I believe the prospects for story beyond this point are promising, but also I'd love to explore the Martian wars for independence where Tanya Platt was a Martian pilot, and, on the other side, Everson Kohlm and Marc Lucan fought for Earth. That kind of intrigues me.

I also have another fantasy series I'm starting to outline set in the American Revolutionary War time.

Where can readers find more of your work?

Amazon and Audible. Digital, print, audio.

www.Circleofreign.com

facebook: www.facebook.com/jacobcooperCOR

Twitter: @authorjacobcoop

I interact with my fans daily. Cheers!

When The Skies Open
By Shellie Horst

Eala's hands shook as she searched the shelves, jars and woven baskets of the healer bay. Through the thin walls of the bay, it sounded like all of Elpis wanted to witness her first and only attempt at healing. She flexed her trembling fingers. No pressure. This needed to happen. The council could lecture her on wasteful use of tech later. Right now, there was need for the Bleeper and its injector; Inji wasn't going to die tonight. Not if she had anything to do with it.

Eala gave the liquid vial a shake, then snatched up the medic bag and ran for the bridge. Its fretwork quivered underfoot, but every breath had to count. Petra's soft touch on the sea turned the marsh waters beneath her a heart-warming peach. The acrid scent of last season's melt still tickled her throat. She shook her head and raced on; sunsets would return, Inji would not. A sharp tightening seized her chest, but Eala ran through the pain. No time. Too late, she remembered the warning sign.

"Short, shallow breathing." Repeating the phrase wasn't going to help, and a wheezing fit hauled her to a halt at the edge of the Central Flame. She clutched at her knees, doubled over for air. There wasn't time for this! Each strangled breath cost important seconds for Inji. Short. Shallow. Breathing.

"Do you think she can do it?" The question clawed through a phlegm-ridden cough from somewhere behind her.

"Shh, she'll hear you!"

Eala couldn't see who spoke, but all around her, loved ones hugged each other. A parent retold the Challenge to a clinging child. A faded hope if ever there was. The

Challenge, a silly hope that life would be made easier with blessings from the sky. It was a prayer for the lost and forgotten. Those who had created life here should be remembered. Life didn't have time to stare into the sky and wait on a nonexistent reply. Hell! Why wait for a savior, when she held the answer in her hand?

Eala pushed forward. The coming Wets would be hard enough without the village second-guessing her, too. Her doubts weren't going to leave her alone, but that didn't mean she had to listen to them. There were too many people suffering this year. Was saving a council member like Armonsykes more important than saving Inji? Could they risk the loss of knowledge?

Dropping to her knees beside Inji's stretcher, she compared the column screen to the pages from her father's bag. Using the wrong codes now would be fatal. What would they do if she failed? How many people hoped she'd abort the procedure, or assumed the Bleeper wouldn't respond? Her gaze swept across the crowd. How many wanted the injector saved for someone they loved?

"The Bleeper will choose!" someone shouted. Surely they couldn't believe that? If that was the case, why hadn't it chosen to save her father? He had the knowledge to save Inji without the injector. Why hadn't the Bleeper given Eala more time to learn?

Inji didn't respond as she initiated the Bleeper and strapped it to his arm. The snap of the injector's being locked into place silenced the crowd. Lights and numbers danced back and forth across the surface in some ancient rhythmic pattern, alien to the tone it produced. The Bleeper's voice had long since died, but the display still worked.

"Normal temperature, acceptable oxygen levels, low blood sugar, steady pulse." The screen synchronized displays, and the two pieces of technology talked to one another. The healing hiss did not come.

The wind whisked the surrounding cattails into a brief

frenzy, echoing the raspy plague which had taken so many lives. The itch of unease grew. Reinitiating the software would signal something wasn't right. Eala frowned; sometimes Dad had had to reset it. Nothing was wrong. Nothing was allowed to be wrong.

"His heart still works." Saying the words released a pressure, but the crowd still fidgeted. Attention had drifted from her, arms pointed to where the first of the evening stars revealed themselves. Pin-pricks of light stretched and warped above them in a dizzying display of heavenly wrath. Petra's pitted orange glow turned to a smudged and distorted grey. All of this because she had misused the Bleeper?

A shriek sounded above people's alarmed cries. The old Orion pod had never made such an urgent and demanding sound. Covering her ears, she felt a tug on her shirt. The crinkled concern of Inji's father blocked out the chaos behind her — if only he could do the same for the noise.

"What's happening, Eala, why didn't it work?"

"I don't know," she said, then raised her voice at the puzzled expression she saw on his face. "I swear I did everything I could. Some of Dad's words are hard to read, but I did it right!"

His nod gave her the impression he understood. "Is Inji safe?"

How could he be so calm in the middle of all this madness? Unshed tears puddled her vision; now was not the time to cry. "I don't know, I think—"

His hand grabbed hers. "What is that?"

The smudged patch of stars grew brighter. A heartbeat later, a pearlized brilliance sucked the dark away. She clung to him as it consumed the sky.

Just for one impossible breath, the world turned on its head, then all was as it had been. The only ringing was in her ears; the piercing alarm from the pod ceased. Night returned and stars became their twinkling selves.

Inji slept through it all.

A shout from the bridge cut off her reply. A runner

waved as he continued to shout. "Eala! The council wants you."

"Me?" She had expected the official reprimand, but not so soon.

Taking the last injector had been her decision, the right decision. For what? The Bleeper hadn't operated as needed, yet life clung to Inji. Eala swiped away her tears; the punishment without the prize wasn't fair at all.

The runner slowed as he approached. "They said everybody." He shrugged. "Quick! Nobody knows what to do! There are voices in the Dead Room."

Inji's father looked surprised. "Are you sure? The Dead Room comms have been silent all my life."

The runner nodded at the question. Rumor had it that only Earth knew the communication codes for the Dead Room, something Eala's grandfather had wasted years trying to disprove. She inspected the screen; Inji's vitals showed no improvement. Had the Challenge finally been answered? If Earth had found answers to the First Commander's Challenge, then more Bleepers were on the way. Earth had come to take everyone home.

"Hurry! They're waiting for you!"

She squashed the flutter of hope before it could fly away with her thoughts. Surely all of this couldn't be happening because she'd misused failing tech? Why her? There were others, Navvi and Inji for example. Both knew more about the Earth technology than she did. She jammed the papers into her bag. What did they need her for?

"I'll send somebody to look after Inji."

Inji's father pushed her forward. "Go, Eala." He settled on the ground beside his son. "Hurry and mend him, Bleeper."

She followed the runner. The reflection of Petra on the waters couldn't wash away the weight of his words as they hurried toward the pod. She should have been able to save Inji. The runner didn't spare time for breath, and opted for the direct route across the marsh. Mud caked her boots and sucked the speed from her. Matching his pace left her breathless and burning. If she fell, he'd be long gone by the time she'd picked herself up from the mire. If she lived to tell the tale. The council would have to wait a little longer.

***

Shouts from the Dead Room echoed along the corridor and warned her of the mood waiting for her. The door guard pursed her lips at the track of muddy prints Eala made, and reached for the mop.

"Sorry. Find four able-bodied people to help bring Inji back, please."

The girl would prefer that to cleaning the corridor. Her smile confirmed Eala's thoughts.

When the door didn't open, Eala re-entered the keycode. A wall of fizzles and spits greeted her on the fifth try; voices yelled over the din projected from the black-and-white display.

"That's it," Navvi said, and dropped a multimeter. "They're gone. Without Inji, there isn't anything else I can try." He spotted her as he climbed the panel access ladder. "You're too late, Eala. Why did you take so long?"

"Sorry," she said, dropping her bag. "What did they say?"

"They were asking for you. Mentioned your bay, before we lost the connection." He rooted around in the toolbox.

"Who did?"

"We don't know, we can't get the thing to stop hissing."

"Anything else?"

With a shake of his head, he returned to the panel with a screwdriver behind one ear. The light caught on the flecks of grey creeping into his beard. Would she live long enough to see her own hair change color?

"I couldn't get the system to return the signal. Maybe if Inji was here…"

To the relief of her ears, the hiss terminated and the

screen reverted to a glassy, black surface.

"She is too young to be taking on the responsibility; there must be someone else…" Though the comment was hushed, without the noise it might as well have been shouted across the room. A fit of hacking coughs replaced the rest. Not that she needed to hear it to know what hadn't been said. The oldest living man on Elpis raked his lungs, then spat. His age was the only reason Armonsykes was there: nothing to do with the tatty commander's badge sewn on his too-short sleeve. Armonsykes knew things, remembered things others had forgotten. His skin was as battered as the stretched hides of a Flatfeeder. Why — and how — he had outlived the others was the source of many Flame tales.

"They are welcome to take my place."

"Shh, Eala!"

"No, I won't shush! Did any of you see what happened in the sky tonight? Did you?" Her heart raged. "The stars, they shifted and hazed—"

"Yes. The wormhole. Earth has returned for us." Armonsykes' interruption set their tongues wagging in agreement.

"The Challenge has been answered!" She expected more from Kytch, but when that woman found a new hobby, she championed it and provided cake to go with it. "Like we knew they would."

"What if it isn't Earth? What if it's some other race?" Navvi said, jumping down. "We don't even know if Earth survives. Wouldn't that explain why we couldn't communicate with them?" Was he trying to make the mood worse? His face didn't show any sign of humor.

"We should inform Petra." It was clearly what they had to do next, but no one had mentioned it. Everyone looked at her like she'd sprouted Flatfeeder fins.

"You asked me here, now you don't want my input." She snagged up her bag. Better to leave before they remembered the lines she'd crossed. She could channel her anger into pummelling cattail rhizomes. "Fine, you know where to find me if you need anything."

When the door opened on the first request, she wanted to kiss it.

***

The medical bay entrance shuddered. Eala lifted her head from the work ledge and shook her arm to relieve the tingles. Her work notes fluttered across the floor. She hadn't intended to fall asleep, certainly not on her arm. Groggy memories of her dream scattered as the knock came again. When the door mechanism had trapped her grandfather inside, the family had replaced the original with a hinge and internal bolt. It stopped anyone from barging in, but not from interrupting sleep. As she stretched, her work mask fell from her face. The fumes of the ground root paste barbed her breath and burned through her lungs. Her instinctive panic brought quicker breaths, and more pain. She couldn't spare breath to answer whoever clobbered at the door. Eala grabbed at the ledge as she choked through a coughing fit that left her ribs aching. With one hand to keep the mask in place, it was a fight to seal the jar between hacks.

Slow. Shallow. Breaths.

"Not the brightest idea," she told herself, collapsing into her chair before the knock on the door could sound again. Sparks danced across her vision, but every breath burned clear. It worked. She grinned and spat phlegm into the corner bucket. It actually worked! The jars overhead rattled impatiently when the rap on her door interrupted her euphoria.

"I'm awake … I'm awake! One second!" Had she missed breakfast? How long had she slept? The green indicator panel on the wall offered a dull, bug-infested glow, totally useless at passing mid-range light. It might be early morning, or a cloud-ridden sky. Without the sun, it would take more than a minute to start heat circulating, or warm the kettle.

"Will you bloody open up!"

When someone was ill, it didn't matter what time of day it was. They could be drowning in phlegm or withering in rot. All or nothing, never an in-between. Her laziness might cost a life. She snatched up her best guess as to what might be needed; the paste would still be there when she returned. The salves and pots clanked in her bag when she unbolted the door.

"How is he? He's all right?" Inji's father barged past her and faltered. "He's not here?"

"Who? Oh! Inji? No. I sent someone to help... I thought..." She hadn't had enough sleep to deal with this. Whatever *this* was. "But I left Inji with you."

He glanced around the room a second time; he didn't believe her. His expression was resolute, lost, like those who wandered from the Drypath. "He was gone when I woke up." His breath gurgled in his chest, a sound she wouldn't have to listen to much longer if the paste did work. "I didn't mean to nod off..."

Any number of things could have decided Inji was to be their next meal, but why not take his father too?

"Go and get something to eat." She smiled a smile she didn't feel and guided him into the corridor. "I'll find Inji. He will be here somewhere. They probably brought him back, and didn't want to disturb you." Eala knew that didn't make sense, but he needed something to hold on to. Her planned gathering of cattails would give her a chance to search for Inji.

***

The bulrushes around the bridge hadn't provided anything useful in years, but the Drypath from there to the Central Flame provided a higher position. With luck, the longer route would mean she would find Inji sooner. Not that she needed an excuse to see the waters around the pod.

A larger sculler prickled with spare oars. Best not to be near dock when it returned with its dredged harvest; her medic mask wouldn't protect her from that stench. It all needed to be ready for the seasonal shipments to Petra, now the worst of the Wets were past. Less breathing complaints and more physical injuries ahead, and with it more time to work on a larger batch of the breathing paste. That was the plan. Her plan.

Warm evenings and hard work waited. And celebrations…. Eala frowned. What were the chances that the council would cancel this season's festivities because of last night? She'd never seen the sky react that way, and everyone knew how overcautious the council could be.

She waved, and the nearest stretch-skin–sculler pilot returned the gesture. It would be a week or more before the boat would return with fresh skins to be worked. Before long the vats would be filled with oils and Flatfeeder flesh. What if Inji had ended up on a ship? Surely the pilot would have alerted someone?

Central Flame Plaza was still. It showed no sign of a struggle. This close to the Wets, the thick mud absorbed any marks, but it took a day for heavy objects to sink.

"Inji?" His stretcher lay empty; he hadn't bothered to take it or the blanket with him. Inji wouldn't have left the platform without good reason. He'd probably woken hungry and gone looking for food.

"Inji, where are you?"

Mud oozed through the soles of her boots; she'd ventured too far off the raised walkway. The semicircle of Petra remained a haze overhead. There was no help to be found in staring at the planet that shared their orbit. Dad and Grandad had warned of the dangers hiding behind the long cattails. Hungry Flatfeeders were only a part of it.

"This isn't funny!" She wriggled her toes between steps, tentatively testing for drier ground. Warnings hadn't saved Mum the day she'd waded out into the waist-deep mire. Her rope hadn't kept her alive when the muds turned underfoot. Eala closed her eyes against her growing panic. No one had been able to help when the tide had swamped the marsh.

Elpis had lost too many people to the Wets that year, and to the Maudlins which came after. This was no place to lose focus and no place to search alone. What had she been thinking?

"Stay focused, Eala. Slow. Shallow. Breaths. You can do this." Once the thrumming in her ears calmed, she opened her eyes. A contrary shimmer teased at her through the whisper of the grasses.

"Stay calm." Ahead, the light glittered with the wind while the sludge slowed her pace. Each step collected more weight. A mirror-like object lay snugged in the long bulrushes to her right. It took an age to close on it: testing the ground before taking a step made for slow progress. Better slow than Flatfeeder fodder.

Puny and lacking in lichen though it was, the source of light had to be a ship of some sort; the elongated pods were clearly engines. It would have fit inside the cargo bays of the Petra Launcher, which floated on the marsh as it soaked up the sun beside Orion 2. But how could the alien thing hope to reach any height? She maintained her course along the less-saturated ground; the cattails grew taller and claimed the vessel again. What part of that sleek machine could provide enough power to take it back into orbit? It didn't sit in the ocean like the Solar Launcher, so it couldn't be funnelling power from that. There were no obvious solar cells, so that, too, was impossible. Where did the engines get their power?

Eala was so caught up in her thoughts that she hadn't noticed the two figures poking at the slick mud. The helmets were nothing like the one that Grandad had kept "just in case."

"*Casimir* to Edwards. Water sample confirmed. Ship-wide analysis continues. The planet remains in blackout."

"Confirmed, *Casimir*. Soil samples ETA fifteen minutes."

Eala eased to the edge of the marsh grass and made every breath count. Their visors dazzled as they moved. She was actually looking at real, living, breathing astronauts. She shook her head. They couldn't be true astronauts; the important emblem lacked the upward-pointing triangle of Armonsykes' jacket.

"I wasn't expecting to find life here, Edwards."

"No one was — there will be a lot of questions being asked back home."

"This would have been a much easier mission had *Olympus* failed." The lid flicked open on the box the speaker held.

Eala tried to see what he placed inside the glossy box by inching farther forward, but the lid snapped shut.

"Look around, Tryne. It's obvious their tech is…. Well, it isn't tech, is it? Sure, our scans have registered the dock." A white-wrapped arm waved toward the planet behind him. "But what use is that if they are stuck on this world? These people belong with their families on Earth."

Light flashed from the second helmet as the man nodded. "Their support systems must have failed generations ago. I would hate to be left alone out here. No colony should be abandoned. I can only imagine how frightened those people must have been."

"The Harmon-Sykes mission was a loss, not a colony, Tryne."

They turned back to the ship. Eala was tempted to follow.

"No matter the progresses they've made, they obviously won't last much longer here."

"We'll take what we've got back and they can work on it."

Eala couldn't believe what she was hearing — no, seeing. Earthers. Real. Living, breathing Earther astronauts! The morning wind rattled through the grasses, and the two visors turned in her direction. One pointed, the other gestured, *no*. No to what? She didn't wait to find out. Eala ran. Falling was the least of her concerns with their squelching steps following her.

The Council Command Center was full when she barged through the doors. The place was full of as much noise as there were people. The doors clunked shut. The heat in her cheeks didn't stop the council looking at her, either.

"Ah ... there you are..." The commander took several breaths to steady his rasping tone. "Did you fall in the marshes, girl?"

Was it possible to be any more embarrassed? "No I was ... gathering more roots." They'd be furious if they found out about Inji's disappearance. "That's not important." Unless they already knew? "I—"

"Well enough. It is good you've finally shown up. Where were we? Ah yes, the events witnessed in the sky last night after you stole the last Bleeper injector."

Eala scanned the room for Inji's father, but it was so crowded she couldn't see him anywhere.

"Why would you put us at such risk, when you know we have no replacement for that technology?"

Eala's jaw worked, but no words came out. Inji was missing, there were strange ships in the marshes, the sky had ripped open and they were trying to blame her for saving a life? Who was Armonsykes to decide who should get the last injector? He didn't listen when told to replace his rotting walking frame; his idea of important was screwed. There had been a need, and it had fallen to her.

"This meeting isn't about Eala! She didn't resuscitate the wormhole. You heard the message from Petra. Whatever happened last night now obstructs their flight path. What are we going to do about their shipments? Without their ore, everything grinds to a halt." Navvi's pause ensured he held everyone's attention. "Everything. On both planets."

"He's right. We haven't the capacity to store the fertilizer for more than ten days. The pods must be launched once they are charged: we can't risk burnout."

"Forget that, there isn't another window for over three weeks. We need to be airing tanks."

Coughs and wheezes interspersed angry objections, and the noise levels rose again.

"We won't solve anything unless we calm down. We are

weeks away from these fears," the commander announced. "Navvi, have you heard anything more from Petra?"

Navvi stopped long enough to shake his head without shifting his attention from the console.

"And the Dead Room?"

"Silent again; whatever caused that tech to fire up, it's stopped," Navvi said. "The reports of falling stars have dwindled. I'm doing what I can, and yes, I have help, but the Earth tech is fickle and greedy. It doesn't like giving up secrets without power."

It was a rare day when she completed a task. If there were more able bodies to grind down the roots, she would have a lot more of the burning salve to trigger the cough. With the solar arrays fully operational after the unexpected tide rise, Navvi would have time to work on the console — if people would just leave things alone long enough. No wonder Navvi growled at every request.

"We've not heard any more of the *Casimir*. I can't get anything more than a light from it now."

"The *Casimir*?" The same name she had overheard in the marshes. All eyes turned back to her. She really had to learn to keep her mouth shut. It wasn't a pleasant experience to be the center of an attention which oozed disgust. "I…"

A high-pitched scream cut her short.

"Sorry!" Navvi yelled as the screen flickered to life behind him. A foggy, squished image of a face appeared for an instant, then went black. "Hmm. More power, or a better signal?" He climbed the ladder to investigate as the door slid open beside her. The suited men who had been following her slopped their way in, marsh mire slick on their boots, their breath hissing far too loudly. Her heart sank; nothing she had could heal that.

"Stop!" Armonsykes held up his trembling hand, his commanding tone eaten away by rasps.

"I am Captain Edwards, from the *Casimir*." The first spoke up.

"Last I read, the procedure for contact did not involve

inviting yourself in." Armonsykes shuffled his frame toward a bench. "Should I assume the *Casimir* is from Earth?" He waved away his question even as it caused a ripple of glances from one colleague to the next.

Eala sighed. Why were they surprised, after all that talk?

"How is it you're here?" The commander shifted in his seat.

"Forgive the lack of convention. We followed her." The astronaut's gloved hand pointed to Eala. "We have had problems communicating with you."

Tedious moments passed and far too many names were exchanged. No one introduced the third, taller, member of their crew. The suit lacked a name badge, while the visor offered only a twisted reflection of the room. No one attempted to point out the Earthers' mistake. It would only bring more unwanted attention her way, so she let the introductions lumber on. With the number of people who had witnessed the event, she was surprised no one had asked why the Earthers had taken so long to return. Why they had been abandoned, and all the other woeful questions, not to mention the wacky stories that bubbled up after a brew too many.

"You followed Eala." His glowering look as he grasped at air sent more questions than she could decipher. "But how did you come to Elpis?"

"Earth has been working toward this for a long time, Armonsykes. We were told not to expect any survivors from the *Olympus* mission. The analysis of the planet was wrong."

"Planets, Captain Edwards," the commander interjected. "You're right to say the analysis was incorrect. The *Olympus'* crew were far better prepared than Earth realized. The Orions survived the landing here on Elpis, despite its softer surface."

Armonsykes' admission brought a chuckle from the room, yet the Earthers remained humorless as they stood there dripping mud onto the floor.

"Your presence is welcome, *Casimir*, with it comes so

many opportunities." The commander's tone took a more serious edge. "We must, however, ask you to move your ship from our flight path."

The request caused a pause. "Not possible. Plot a course around us. The *Casimir* must hold steady."

"Elpis and Petra share resources. We must. Adjusting course will cost energy we don't possess. Unless you are willing to provide that power difference?"

They remained still and silent for so long, Eala thought they had died inside their suits.

"You may be mistaking our ship for the wormhole," Edwards finally said.

"The wormhole did not remain—"

"Technology advances, Commander Armonsykes. *Casimir*'s engines will hold the wormhole open until we return."

"We have been breathing this air for generations; I do not believe you need your helmets." The commander's voice matched his smile, as brittle as dried grasses as he changed the subject. She had the feeling there was more to the meeting than others knew. Only when Edwards nodded did the third man remove his helmet. It wasn't an Earther that looked back at her.

"Inji!"

No wonder she hadn't been able to find him! Inji was ... out of place. Wrong. Not because of the strange suit he wore, or the mess the helmet had made of his curled hair. He was a head taller and much thinner. The differences were even more apparent compared to the squat, florid features of Edwards and Tryne sticking out of their identical suits as they circulated the room.

Armonsykes followed the Earthers about, explaining things as they went. It made no sense. What did these astronauts hope to discover in a council meeting room? If the Earthers wanted examples of the life they hadn't expected to encounter, Edwards and Tryne needed to explore the pod. No, they needed to see the village outside.

Those two had color in their eyes and their skin. She hadn't thought it possible for such well-preserved tones in an adult; the commander's diluted features underlined the difference.

Eala helped herself to a mug of water. Her actions released others from the spell the Earthers had cast. Kytch dared a small smile when she joined her at the central table. A knot twisted in her gut as Edwards and Tryne approached her. Should she speak up, or was there some unknown, Challenge-styled tradition to be followed? Tryne saved her from making a fool of herself again.

"We found Mr. Inji in a life-threatening state during recon, shortly after we exited the wormhole. Our medical teams have restored him to full health. Quite understandably, you didn't possess the medication to reverse the condition."

"How? How did you restore him? What was he suffering from?" Eala ignored the look the two men shared. The clear whites of their eyes unnerved her; it wasn't natural. If not for the name labels, she would struggle to tell one Earther from the other.

"It must be difficult for you without the proper facilities, Eala. Understand that the medi-injector is no longer an approved form of delivery. On Earth, we have labs working on these things all the time. Hundreds, if not thousands, of people working together to improve things."

Ripples danced across the water as she drank. Mastering her temper took several sips. Fortunately, it didn't result in a coughing attack. "You didn't think to tell us you had him?"

"It is part of protocol, so yes, we had attempted communications," Tryne admitted. "But we received no reply." Tryne gestured to the blank screens around the room. "With comms this dated, we understand why that might have been difficult. Surely your engineers tire quickly of using upside-down interfaces?"

"You must remember, we did not expect to find life here," Edwards added.

"If that's the case, why are you here?" Navvi bristled. "And why must you block our flight path to Petra?"

"Scientists have discovered how to keep a wormhole open. *Casimir*'s engines are doing that as we speak. If we move *Casimir*, we may be stuck here. Our mission was — is — to collect data. Basically, to test the new drives and to report on the fate of Harmon-Sykes and the *Olympus* crew."

"If they keep the wormhole open, we'll be able to access everything they have," Inji pointed out. "Earth technology, Eala! You should see it!"

"You are welcome to see it." Edwards spoke before she could consider a reply. "The *Casimir* medics would be more than willing to arrange a visit."

"It's amazing to see how you've adapted." Behind them, Tryne pulled boards from the rear of the screen. The Earther didn't look all that amazed as he wiped away the green scum on his suit.

Dying didn't match Eala's idea of adapting. Granddad had been a stout believer that the answers lay in the sky: he made every meteor shower a social event. She spent more time playing than helping him resurrect the Dead Room. On his death, Mum and Dad had said the only way to get something done was to do it yourself. Could Eala atone for her failure by working with the Earthers, and discover the love of a planet she had never known?

"How are you?" Eala regarded Inji. He had a wide smile again, and the broken nose he'd suffered when falling from the panel seasons ago was no longer evident.

"I haven't felt this able in … in … Hah! I can't remember."

Inji stood taller than she remembered. No, not taller, but more confident. Happy, too. The expression made him ten years younger. No, even his skin was ten years younger. There was no other way of putting it. Excitement chased through her. If they could do that, what else could they do? What did they use to enable return to vitality?

"You had us all worried, Inji. You should go find your father — he won't know." Would he even recognize his son?

"I will, but you've no need to be worried, Eala. Take

them up on their offer, you will love their ship. It's nothing like what we've got here. There's no rotting wires and mud. It's so clean. Dry! Everything in the stories … you can't imagine it. And it all works."

"Indeed, Commander Armonsykes." Edwards nodded in agreement to something she had missed. "As we continue to hold the wormhole open, we can supply you with everything you require. It would not matter about our position."

"Will our technically deficient ships be able to dock with the *Casimir*?" Navvi asked. What was his problem with these men? They had the ability to prolong life and to make it so much easier for everyone.

"I am positive that will not be an issue."

"And the issue of us being totally dependent on your shipments from Earth?" Kytch asked, her arms crossed.

Armonsykes reclaimed everyone's attention before things could dissolve into an acid fight. "Captain Edwards offers us an opportunity."

A good one. There would be no more slogging over Flatfeeder skins or worrying if the season would take more life before it had the chance to share wisdom. Her days of worrying how many would fall ill, and how she could help them, were at an end. The answer to all their problems had fallen from the sky and right into their laps.

"It would be wise of us to consider it—" A piercing alarm ended all discussion.

"*Casimir* to Edwards, immediate return required. *Casimir* to Edwards. Confirm?"

It amused her to see Tryne's expression dissolve into a genuine frown. Their unusually colored eyes glazed over as he talked into the air. "Report?"

There was a pause where neither man moved. "If wormhole readings are irregular…. I agree. We'll return, though I suspect the monitored disruption on the shuttle is nothing more than a glitch."

"My apologies, Commander Armonsykes, we must

return to the *Casimir* immediately." The Earthers collected their helmets. Navvi hooked his arm into hers as she followed them out.

"Well, now we know it's not our atmosphere interrupting transmission." When she scowled at him, he shrugged. "You don't see the problem, do you? I don't think anyone does."

"I see two Earthers who — can you guess how old they are? No, me either — have access to a massive intelligence that will help us all."

"How long will it take for that intelligence to get here, Eala? Soon enough to save you and me? What about everyone on Petra? They need us, we need them. Every day the *Casimir* stays up there messing with our sky, it changes things for us. Here. Now. We should be preparing cargo today; instead we're talking and wasting time."

Armonsykes shuffled between them, a hand held up for peace.

"Communicate with Petra, Navvi — has the *Casimir* made contact? Eala, make preparations in the bay. When the rest of the population discover what *Casimir* is capable of, they will all want to be treated."

Eala smiled at the thought. It would change everything. Their future had turned away from the bleak threats of the Wets season to who knew what. If she could see their healer bays, hopefully she'd learn something.

"When can I—"

"Well, shit." Both men stopped before the marsh bridge and she collided into the back of Tryne.

"This wattle-and-daub town has swallowed our shuttle."

Inji shook his head. His hand didn't cover his smirk.

"I did try to warn you."

Eala could see the tip of the engine pod poking above the rushes, but most of the underbelly had already been claimed by the mud. The nose of the Earther shuttle pointed up at Petra. The entire ship would be sucked under by the end of the week.

"*Casimir*, can we get the shuttle out of the mud?"

"Doesn't the engine need to be free to work?" Inji asked, then quickly added over the top of Navvi's chuckle, "To exert force in the same fashion as you did on landing? That marsh is mud, thick and rich, it'll suck a man down to the Flatfeeders — if he's lucky. Fills in as quick as you dig it out."

Neither answered him. Earthers liked their long, drawn-out pauses.

"Technical says maybe, with a crane." Tryne's shoulders slumped.

"Crane?"

The two Earthers shared a frustrated expression before they turned to Armonsykes.

"How about using your ship, Commander? Could it pull us out?"

"Our engines have enough power to launch, Captain Edwards. If we burned that energy to free you from the mud, we would be behind schedule by weeks, if not months; we'd have to recharge the engine pods. We can't afford that loss."

"We have three ships in our wattle-and-daub town," Navvi added. Whatever wattle-and-daub was, Navvi wasn't troubled by it. "We're in the process of building a fourth." He gestured to where the nets soaked up sunlight and channelled it through the root system toward the pod launcher. "We can get you back to the *Casimir* at the first launch. If you move out of our flight path."

Tryne and Inji glared at one another. "You launch from the water? How? You have archaic computing ability, hell, the damn Orion — what do you call it — Dead Room is upended. It's corroding under your feet. You guys have everything backwards."

"We did what we could from what we had. I don't think you are in a place to judge."

"I thought that was... From that floating... What is that? Wait, that's your dock, isn't it?"

321

"Flatfeeder skins provide the buoyancy for our water-based vessels." Inji fought back a grin. "With help from Petra's minerals, the skins are the proofing for our ships, Captain."

"Tryne to *Casimir*." The man stared up at Petra. "Shuttle failure, we'll require a secondary team."

The captain added, "Edwards to *Casimir*. Have the medical bay ship additional crew with basic cellular and molecular repair packs."

***

Eala listened to the chest of her new patient. The boy kicked his feet back and forth on the couch and chattered away about Earthers.

"The gurgle and crackles are gone." She held up her grandmother's mirror so he could see the color in his cheeks for real; patients weren't convinced by the screen representations. The new Earther technology distracted them. "Look, see. Don't tell me you don't feel better?"

"I could swim across the whole of Elpis, now." The boy seized the mirror. "I could hunt Flatfeeders." His eager enthusiasm was infectious, but if he continued to pick at the privacy screening, she would have to spend an afternoon re-weaving it.

"You could." The glory of netting a Flatfeeder did not measure up to the danger it involved. She liked her limbs attached to her body too much. "Or you could harvest the cattails, or dredge…"

"No! I want to hunt!" He jumped down and ran out, shouting for his sister. Navvi sidestepped the child with ease and took up the same position on the couch. Hope had sparked in the village, warmer and more welcome than the sun after Wets. None of that reflected in Navvi's lineless face. The molecular reconstruction had even taken away the grey in his beard.

"You're still worried. You're stronger, healthier than I

322

could ever have hoped to see you, Navvi. Why aren't you happy?" His chest was as clear as the patient's before him. He didn't take the mirror from her when she offered it.

"Everyone is oblivious that this" —he gestured to himself— "doesn't protect us from the next storm. We will be dead if we are prevented from sharing resources, and Petra will die with us. I thought that would mean something to you, of all people, Eala."

"People are no longer dying, because of me."

Navvi poked at the shelving to his left, nosying in the baskets. Like her last patient, he was unable to sit still. He held up the jar of ground cattail rhizomes. "What we have achieved is bigger than that, and you know it. You're quite capable, Eala. They said Inji had a heartbeat when they found him."

"Don't drop that!" She snatched the jar from him. "The Bleeper failed Inji."

"The Bleeper might have done, but you didn't." He gestured to the jar. "You haven't. You really have to stop this self-doubt. Why do you suppose people still come to you after the molecular stabilization treatments?" He paused to turn off the display, and Eala took the opportunity to return the jar to its basket. "Because they trust you. They know you. Those solar flats out there should have been shipped to Petra. The minerals we need should be on their way. The commander delayed them."

"But we'd live for longer, we wouldn't be losing our families before we had a chance to be one. Don't look at me like that; you heard Tryne, they have labs that work to advance things. Lots of minds resolving a problem. Not just one."

"We managed just fine without them. Eala, my parents didn't build our home just for me to abandon it."

"I don't think they'd want you dead, Navvi. My parents might still be here if we had the same advanced medical treatments as Earth."

"True, but don't you see. This," —he tapped the silent

display— "and this, and this? It will all fail just like the Bleeper. And once again we will have to wait, and hope that more will arrive." Navvi pointed to the basket. "That won't. That's ours. Well, yours. Does it work?" He waved the question away. "Don't answer. When their tech fails, we are back where we started. Worse, as we won't have anything to connect us back to Petra. They say they control the wormhole, but you heard them as well as I did. There are irregularities. I think we need Petra more than we need Earth."

"It's not our decision." She had heard about the way Armonsykes had reacted to the offer of help, though their paths had not crossed since. If Navvi was to be believed, the man would show up without his frame support, seeking the same reassurances.

"Yes, it is. We've come this far without them."

The door opened to reveal two *Casimir* medics.

"I'm just saying it's bloody lucky that the wormhole opened between two inhabitable planets, don't you think?" His voice was muffled beneath his ventilation mask. They claimed the air here was different from theirs, dangerous if breathed for long periods of time. They had been convinced the ludicrous mask would help her breathe, but the whole room had started to move when she'd tried to use one.

"If you say so, Hollins. Now's not the time." The first glanced around the bay and shifted his grip on the container. "Ms. Eala? Diagnostic implants, where do you want them?"

"To replace the Bleepers? There will be just fine." Eala gestured to the storage rack her father had added.

"Bleeper?" The second managed to reclaim the crinkle of a smile. "How did you guys get from 'Miricodock Medication and Monitoring System' to 'Bleeper'?"

"This?" She set aside her notes and pulled the injector-less Bleeper from its basket. "When it works, it bleeps." She paid no attention to Navvi's unconvincing cough.

"Why not just say MMMS? It's right there on…" The medic rotated the band, and his words faded just like the branding had. "Good God, this thing's ancient!"

"How about we just call it "Mmms." Navvi's comment earned him a scowl. He shrugged, but the grin didn't disappear.

"Implants replaced it decades ago, so it doesn't matter what you call them." Hollins' smile was more of a triumphant smirk. "Hey! We can't leave these here, it's right next to a heating vent."

"True." The other medic's name tape read "Cudwell".

"If their ship wasn't arse-over-tit, it wouldn't matter. Even the damned quarantine dock's damaged."

"Hey, where are you taking them?" Eala moved to block the door. "You didn't mention they were susceptible to heat. Wait! The heating doesn't come from there."

The medic wasn't listening. "Until you have a suitable place to store them, we'll have to keep them. They are far too valuable for them to rot away."

"You'll need to provide evidence that you have the ability to maintain them before we can release them now," the second one added with an apologetic shrug.

"Evidence? What are you talking about?"

"I'll send you the file. Regulations prevent the sharing of resources and equipment without proper protocols and infrastructure in place."

"What? Don't worry, we'll sort this," Navvi said.

She wasn't sure it was something that could be sorted, but followed Navvi as he led the medics out of the bay. They might as well have thrown those containers into the bog. Protocols, evidence. A tidal wave of confusion washed away her hope.

***

The Dead Room had become the center for communications once the *Casimir* astronauts had re-worked things. Eala recognized the voice of Petra's launch officer as she entered.

"Confirmed, Petra. We plan to ship containers with the next solar pod. I will have Eala go over how to use them, once we have the next transmission window. Elpis out." The conversation ended before she could gather what Armonsykes and the Petra launch officer had discussed, or why her name had been mentioned in the update she had walked in on. How long would it be before they could see one another's faces like they could with the *Casimir*?

"Eala … have you not had the medics treat you?"

The commander no longer needed to support himself with his frame or the back of the nearest chair as he addressed her, though his hair remained white. She shook her head. Too many people had stopped by the bay to allow her the time.

"Commander, what do you know about protocol and evidence?"

Armonsykes looked between her and the *Casimir* staff questioningly.

"The *Casimir* astronauts refuse to leave the diagnostic implants," Navvi clarified, gesturing to the containers the two men still held.

"Astronauts?" Hollins looked to his senior officer. "Astronauts? What the hell is this, a history class?"

"Stow it, Hollins! Remember, they aren't from Earth. Commander, we have rules and regulations. We're happy to provide the kits, but it would result in court martial if we broke the guidelines." The containers were placed on the table. "They are there for everyone's safety."

Navvi flicked open the lid, but stepped back when it hissed at him. "We're not on Earth. We don't have to do things the way you do there."

"I'm sorry, but it's not safe."

Eala's heart sank. "How long will it take for us to meet these rules?" If guidelines came before health on Earth, too, Eala wasn't so sure she wanted any of it. It hadn't been fun being the one to make a choice which went against the rules, last Bleeper or no.

"Like I said, I'll send you the file once the systems are finished updating." The reverence vanished from his voice when he addressed her.

"This makes no sense — why would your captain agree to this?"

Before the medic could answer, the wretched alarm screamed from the old Orion systems — so much louder inside the pod than it had been all those nights ago. Covering her ears didn't help. "Why does it do that? Can't you make it stop?"

At that moment the screen blurred into life, and Eala found herself staring at Edwards.

"*Casimir* to Elpis. Commander Armonsykes, the wormhole is no longer stable. Somewhere, the calculations are wrong. Our attempts to adjust the engines have failed. All crew must return to the shuttle immediately. A pity we have not been able to reverse-engineer your solar flats, but we shall see to it that you are not abandoned."

Seconds later, the two Earthers were talking into the air; their communication system required an effort she couldn't understand. In the corridor, people ran in all directions and Eala edged close to the wall to avoid being jostled.

Two shuttles loitered over the marshes, their engines blasting battered cattails and marsh mire everywhere. Members of the *Casimir* were forced to climb through it into the waiting ship.

"Not willing to lose another one to the muds of Elpis, I see." Navvi chuckled. The crowd gathered across the bridge and a collective sigh rose up when the alert died mid-screech. Cattails thrashed violently as the ship powered up. Come morning, there would be plenty to gather without having to hack at their stalks. One awful noise replaced another as the departing ship's engines cast vibrations across the marsh.

"Why are we letting them leave?" Inji demanded on arrival. Like her own, his attention was on the shuttle. The engines blew water in all directions and soaked everyone on the bridge. The fiber structure trembled beneath her; for all their talk of power, the astronauts burned through plenty in an attempt to stay out of the marsh. It was reassuring to see that the pods on either side of the vessel were the engines she'd thought them to be, ports opening and closing to suit directional needs.

"They didn't want to stay, Inji. They didn't like our air, wouldn't eat our food, didn't want to be inside the pod. We can't force them." She shrugged at the helplessness as the crowd split to allow an Earther through. Eala watched him climb, the square of light disappearing once he was on board. "Did you stop that noise?"

Inji nodded as the second shuttle departed. "I think it's a throwback from the old system. I was on board the *Casimir* long enough to know that everything beeps, dings and alerts you to something. It helps seeing a thing in practice. Oh, but you didn't go on the shuttle, did you, Eala?" When she shook her head, he gave a sigh. "A shame, you would have loved their bay. Not green and brown like ours. White, grey, and so dry."

Someone had brought out broth, and the clay mugs were making the rounds, as were the words of the Challenge as the shuttle became just another star in the growing night.

"We'll come home in a day, week, month or year. The Challenge to continue exploring will be our Challenge to survive."

"Do you think they'll come back?"

"I don't know."

"If they do, they should bloody knock first," Kytch muttered.

The sky exploded. Brilliance, warped and twisted, sucked the night away. It left the sky pearlescent, like the inside of the shells found after Wets. No one cried, no one screamed. Eala waited for the stars to find their focus.

"I know we've a load of solar flats to get into the next pod before Petra starts to panic. We also have a stuck ship and a wormhole to figure out." Navvi winked. Eala admired the man's confidence.

"Ship?" Inji looked confused and dodged a couple who

had sprung into a dance. She couldn't work out why people were so content.

"Inji! Don't you want to dredge up that shuttle that our — how did they put it — 'wattle-and-daub town' swallowed?"

"Oh! Yes! I could reclaim the dash, I could get Pel's boy to help me on the m—"

"Yes! Now you see!" Navvi laughed. "We were doing things our way before they arrived. We survived by thinking on our feet. How long would it take us to dredge the marshes if we worried about the right files? We'd all be dead waiting on Earth's approval. Nothing stopping us now, eh? If we're lucky, we have a few lifetimes to work on it. I hope."

Hope. That was what they had. Hope filled the night with celebration. People here could see a way forward, a means to control their future. A possibility, lots of possibilities and ideas to work with. Her smile melted into a frown. Would they have that independence with Earth's help? Or did Navvi see it for what it was? How many protocols were there on Earth when it came to helping an injured child?

How could she know?

"Even Eala's got new toys to play with." Inji slurped up the last of the broth. "If you want any help with them, just you give me a shout."

"What?" Those "toys", she realized, had been left in the Dead Room. It would take time to learn how to use them, though she wouldn't have to wait for rules to get out of the way to administer a salve, or store a box. Who knew what possibilities hid inside the *Casimir*'s sinking shuttle?

"Navvi." It was reassuring to have Petra's presence sharp on the horizon. "I think you were right, we're better off without them."

The more she thought about it, the more it made sense. The Earthers wanted Elpis to be the same as them. No. They *expected* the planets to follow the same path. Was this what her parents had meant, doing something yourself?

329

Achieving this goal for everyone on Petra and Elpis by working together?

"You say that now," he said, brushing her fringe aside. "You better hope your grandchildren think the same way."

Shellie Horst Q&A

Where did the idea for your story come from?

Is it too corny to say, what if? I suppose the story came from the same place as the title. Unstable wormholes. What if you're stuck on the wrong side of that? How would the explorers deal with being cut off? What if the planets nearest were not all they appear to be? When you're a long way from home without the wisdom of others your choices are limited by what you know.

I realised that mere survival in the new environments the explorers found themselves in would be their only priority, before energy – and thought – could be spent on trying understand a temperamental wormhole. I wanted to explore how that approach might manifest over generations and how, down the line, they would react when the sky opened up again.

What authors or other forms of media have the biggest impact on your writing?

I blame Interzone for a lot, which I probably wouldn't have found if not for Louise Lawrence's Children of the Dust. It made a huge impression on me as a young reader. The novel impressed on me the importance of being able to relate to not just the character, but the surroundings of your imagined world.

Choose your own adventure stories were another big influence. They were far too easy to cheat on as a kid, but thanks to coding, interactive storytelling prevents me from flicking back and forth through the pages to get the story you want. A Portal Entertainment workshop I attended on immersive formats ties back to Children of the Dust. Never forget your audience.

If given the opportunity to explore space through a

wormhole, would you take it?

I want to say yes, but I suspect I'd chicken out! I have enough problems getting on a plane, so I can't imagine the state I would be in with traveling just the 220 or so miles to the ISS. I would be a gelatinous mess after the billon miles of unknown a wormhole would involve. What if I forgot to pack my toothbrush?

Don't get me started on problems that will be waiting for me through a wormhole!

What are you currently working on?

Lots of things. Too many things! I'm enjoying the contributory work I'm doing for SFFWorld.com at the moment, I get to meet some great authors through doing the interviews and discover books I wouldn't normally pick up.

I'd like to expand an interactive/immersive story world but I've two novel projects in revision stage. I know that's all very vague, but I don't like to talk about things that might never be. Call it a superstition if you will, but it's one based on lessons learned. As always, there are so many story ideas, and so little time.

Where can readers find more of your work?

I keep my website www.millymollymo.com up-to date and I ramble randomly about writing, opportunities and other stuff on Twitter @millymollymo

A Second Infection
By Stephen Palmer

A second moon came through that wormhole.

Not a second object, a second sphere — a second moon, identical to our own. Lunar two. I saw it appear with my own eyes because I happened to be looking in the right direction that night.

The wormhole we knew about. Many instances of its arrival were noted in the grander records of our multiplex species. But this moon...

In fact (it transpired), it was not a duplicate of our moon until a few milliseconds after arrival. I checked with the lightning eyes of some ground-based intelligences, who doted on the stars in all their fomenting haste. They told me that first it was a dull sphere, its external surface marked with the pits and cracks of millions of years of interstellar life, before the dullness vanished to be replaced with a duplicate lunar surface.

That surface was wrecked beyond hope. Hundreds of centuries had left their mark — the ruinations of the human species, which delights in violent whim. A million gothic instances of life before death. Mining is the profession of the child.

But when certain differences were noticed, then we became suspicious. There were heat rods plunged into the heart of the thing, their outer ends set with radiating panels, like so many square leaves of the former Antarctica. The oblateness of the spheroid had been calculated to a comparatively large tolerance. Various mysterious electromagnetic waves emanated from the not-places at its poles, which my friends the ground-based intelligences claimed were made by some technological species.

Exciting!

Eighty thousand years ago there was an antenatal infection, which in its dangerous phase lasted for five hundred years. Recently another infection developed, and I, Seneschal Smith, was sent into the womb to deal with the problem. What follows is my confession.

To begin at the beginning... I still do not know why I was chosen. I have dredged my memories at their most fundamental level — the level above that in which nothing factual may be retrieved and copied — and discovered zero information relevant to the answering of the point. Why was I chosen? It may be I had some skill that the grandparents in the orbital houses detected. It could be that my early life, so beset with difficulty, toughened me up for the dangerous mission. It might be that my immune system, which, unusually, took characteristics equally from my maternal, paternal and abstract parents, was deemed sufficiently robust/flexible to cope with the extremes of environment that I was likely to encounter in the womb. My own suspicion is that because I was a runt I was physically small, and thus suited to the intrauterine mission.

You laugh? Laugh on.

The people of the great orbital houses have little need for doctors. In orbit we live like immortals, our bodies changing according to the mores (and sometimes the whims) of cultural fashion, so that, in parallel, our identities also change. Because of this we have a non-standard concept of illness, unlike that extant when we first leaped out of the womb into space. Change, for us, includes the concept formerly known as illness. I, however, was different. I was formed from a unique and accidental merging of three abstracts, not two, as is normal. My smith-father emerged from a male and an abstract, my smith-mother from a female and an abstract, but I am a runtish, hermaphroditic oddity, emerged like a sentient abortion from a trio.

Well, now you know enough about me. You need to hear about my preparations for the mission.

In orbit our bodies feel no gravity. This is not a problem — we have never encountered even a single difficulty resulting from extended zero-gravity living. But if I was to return to the womb I would need to toughen up my twisted form, and this is why the grandparents who devised most of my preparations sent me into the animal womb.

The gravitational force of the animal womb is one-sixth that of the other womb. For some decades I explored the place, allowing my body to feel that novel G-pull: toughened bones, toughened muscles, toughened ligaments. Carbon fiber, yes, and a great quantity of vitreous ceramics; also superconducting quantum interference devices that operated like so many quicksilver minds at three degrees above absolute zero. In due course I glanced at myself in an orbiting mirror and saw that in appearance I had changed beyond recognition.

A mirror... It was the first time I had taken this test of consciousness (as I later found it to be — some of the grandparents did not trust me because they said I must be insane/devolved to agree to the womb mission). But I was conscious. And I was still me. Though my body had changed I remained the same person, and this was an extraordinary eventuality. Alteration of form brings alteration of identity — we cannot remain the same people as our bodies morph over multi-millennia. And yet I remained Seneschal Smith.

I think perhaps it was this event, unique in our culture, that convinced the grandparents of the orbital houses that I was right for the mission. I changed, yet remained the same. I even retained my original name!

The next phase of my preparation was more dangerous, however. I had to vaccinate myself against the infection.

An expendable, sterile animal was sent down into the womb to collect a sample of the infectious agent, a sample numbering some ten thousand individual antigens. The sample was, of course, made lifeless. I studied it as soon as I could with a mental microscope. The plan was to introduce the sample into my body so that my immune system could go to work.

This is indeed how vaccination operates. The immune system detects and responds to the three-dimensional shape of the antigens comprising the infectious agent — the virus, if you like — creating new forms, antibodies, that topographically interact with the antigens in order to neutralize the infection. There is no risk in this process. Because vaccination is a topographic event, a chemical event, it is safe. Admittedly, I felt tired for a few months, unwell even, but this was

335

because my immune system was coping with the novel antigens moving inside me, making me slightly less resistant to other orbital detritus. If you will permit me a joke — I did not call a doctor.

It was at this stage of the mission that I noticed an unusual characteristic of the infection. Alas, I did not mention it to anyone in my house. Had I done so, my mission might have been more successful.

You see, I noticed that markers on the surface of each individual antigen comprised an abstract and coherent, if incomprehensible, entity, which my subconscious mind analyzed, telling me subsequently through the agency of a dream that the entity was a language. But I considered this dream a hoax. Our language was merged information and music/emotion: there could be no language composed only of information. This was an oversight on my part. A regrettable... I should say, accidental oversight.

To be honest, I considered the dream a harbinger of mathematics. To me, as to all my kin in orbit, a language of information only is by definition mathematics. Wrong...

So I forgot the dream, letting it pass like solar particles into interplanetary space. I was ready for the mission: toughened, vaccinated, excited. I expressed this excitement in the form of a sixteen-month symphony.

The vagaries of thrill led me to create a landing party, which, in my naiveté, I imagined would be led by myself. Culture got in my way! Across the planet there were hysterical reactions to the second moon — musical appurtenances, lengthy parties (one lasted eighty days), and even a ceremony of vegetarian food atop K2, the highest mountain in the world. Naturally I (one of a minuscule number of meat-eaters) was not invited. It annoyed me to think that a fair proportion of the organic conscious biota had been invited.

As we sped upwards in my tide-propelled battery stone, I reviewed what I had been told by the captain. She noted that the mysterious waves emanating from the not-places were a form of communication. Of course, I laughed. Everything these days is "a form of communication." We have been spoiled by the ferocious manufacturing of millennia gone by. I should point out that I remember most of those millennia. I was *there*.

Like a floating leaf, our vehicle approached the second moon. We studied it with our eyes, as the eyes of a billion intelligences copied us. Truly, it was a most perfect duplicate of Lunar, and yet… it seemed to me that small waves lurked beneath the scarred surface, as if the "moon" below was actually a fluid under tremendous pressure. Could this guess be the case? It was my duty to find out.

The journey into the womb was difficult. In orbit, I, like everyone, had nothing more than the solar wind and a few meteoric particles to cope with, though I of course dreaded the arrival of larger bodies, which have on occasion smacked into the womb. No, what concerned me was the effect of gases: of nitrogen, of carbon dioxide, and of deadly oxygen in particular.

Also I worried about the microscopic life that has the womb as its home. This miasma of living, respiring, reproducing life could endanger me, even though I had, over four billion years of evolution, emerged from it. It was, if you like, a kind of soup that I had some natural resistance to, though perhaps not enough — for the orbital houses had existed eighty thousand years in isolation from the womb. Not a long time, you may think, but enough for new intrauterine diseases to emerge.

I began my descent with a single out-breath aimed perpendicularly away from the womb. (The animal womb lay out of sight behind the womb and thus could be factored out of my calculations.) As my skin felt the silken touch of the outer gaseous environment, I noticed a warming, which at first was not unpleasant. But soon that warmth became heat, and I had to pull on a garment made of reflectivity. Later the heat became red-bright, then white-bright, and I pulled on more clothes. I know from documentaries made about my mission that the (ever-naked) people of the orbital houses were half amused, half appalled at these clothes, which to us limit emotional expression, and are thus anathema to a life lived fully. But I can assure you they were essential: I would have been cooked without them, having first been blinded.

At length, a mere heartbeat after dropping out of orbit, I found myself in the aerodynamic zone. I was inside the womb. Now my physical preparations came into full use, for my body creaked/groaned as the sixfold gravitational force took hold of me: the full G-pull of the womb. I felt compressed, beaten down, and the gases excoriated my skin — leathery though that skin was. Already biosensors were informing me of free radical damage caused by the presence of oxygen, that all-powerful killer. I did not, it seemed, have much time…

Various noble attempts were made to understand the "communication." Mathematical analysis has come a long way since the arrival of intelligence on the planet — intelligences — but the encrypted form of the not-place emanations baffled even the most autistic of our savants. I laughed. But I do have a twisted sense of humor.

I expected there to be chaos. We know that the outreach of our humanity is a thing of subtle knowledge, as well as many millennia. Asteroid mining… metals and water, mass and energy. The bones of the universe. I wouldn't be surprised if one day we met ourselves coming back.

To enter the second Lunar we located a protected hole thirteen kilometers south of what we decided to name the northern pole. The puzzles there were not difficult, and I hypothesized that we were meant to enter, like a victim entering a trap, or a mate entering a boudoir. Such is the cynicism of our times. We go to sulk when our new cultures let us down.

And so I come to the mission itself. I did, of course, have a basic plan, but part of my mental preparation for the mission was to expect/unexpected. I was, as it were, mentally flexible.

The individual antigens I estimated to be in number fifteen to twenty thousand, a quantity far less than the original infection of eighty thousand years ago. Then, as now, the infection altered the composition of the womb and its characteristic environment, so that an increase in temperature occurred; many of the self-regulating feedback processes of the womb were as a consequence damaged. My plan was to destroy the main centers of infection, then mop up the rest of the antigens while roaming through the womb.

And this I did, at first successfully. The womb was thirty percent dry and seventy percent wet, and all the antigens were gathered into agglomerations varying between a hundred and a hundred and fifty in number. Most of the dry area was in the polar hemisphere: one great area and a smaller area not linked to it. In the anti-polar hemisphere there lay other dry areas. Many recognizable agglomerations existed on these dry areas. Also there were innumerable abstract thought-conglomerations.

I landed very, very, very slowly atop a range of hills pushed up thirty million years earlier by the motion of a triangular tectonic plate. My arrival caused the top of this range of hills to sink by some distance — though I was a runt, my body was as heavy as an asteroid. Apprehensive (for this was the first time an orbital being had returned to the womb since the first infection), I clambered down the hills, causing a large number of quakes/tidal waves in the substrate of the womb.

Then, one by one, I began dealing with the agglomerations. The antigens had managed to use minuscule quantities of the corpus of the womb to create what I can only describe as shells, in which the infection found shelter. These shells were composed of vitreous materials/metals. Each agglomeration, however, though composed of a number of shells, was no larger than the end of my little finger, so they were easy to deal with. Once destroyed, I disinfected the agglomeration sites with liquid antiseptics.

It took me some considerable time to deal with the agglomerations. I then ran a sensor scan of the entire womb, to discover a surprisingly large quantity of infectious material spread thin across the dry surface of the womb. This, I knew, would be more difficult to deal with. The considered opinion of the doctor-families of the orbital families was that the womb would be spoiled forever if disinfected from pole to pole, so that option was barred to me. I wondered what to do.

It was at this point that the critical incident occurred which ruined my mission. Though I did not realize it at the time, a quantity of antigenic material, so small I would have been unable to see it with the naked eye, entered my body through a small wound in my integument.

Having discussed with scientists in orbit the distribution of the infectious material remaining, I decided, in collaboration with them, simply to traverse the womb from end to end, dealing with the worst of the infection as I went. It would take time, but it would be worth it. It had been calculated that I did not need to immediately eradicate the infection, for if it was reduced below a certain level it would remain insignificant, then vanish — this latter eventuality being our hope. And of course we all realized that the natural flora of the womb would remain to carry on the womb's various self-regulating processes, regardless of the state of the infection. Two ice episodes had occurred between the infections, during which the quantity of infectious material had shrunk; it was thought possible that a third such reduction in the average temperature of the womb would destroy the infection once and for all.

Perhaps, if you will permit me to make a criticism, we should have watched the infection more closely in moments gone by…

For some considerable number of decades I journeyed across the womb, dealing with the infection as I encountered it. But then, as my mission approached its conclusion, I began to feel ill.

As I have said before, those of the orbital houses do not consider illness a difficulty in life. For orbital beings, change is natural. Illness, if and when it comes, forces a body to recreate itself: new body, new identity, new culture. This is natural. But I was different, my body crooked, my mentality unique, bizarre almost: even my immediate family was suspicious of me. I had few of the powers of self-transformation customarily utilized by my kin.

My sensors began reporting unusual damage to the cells of my body. My temperature was rising. There occurred a larger than expected production of those antibodies created by my immune system during the vaccination process, and, worse, their effectiveness was reduced. I began to wonder if I had been infected with a new strain. If so, and if the new strain was different from the standard strain, I was in danger. Moreover, if the orbital families found out about my illness I would be stranded in the womb, for they would never permit my return to orbit.

I felt considerable anxiety. I was a living, thinking/feeling being, for whom permanent social exclusion was effectively the same as suicide. Yes, it was easy enough to mask the reports being sent up into orbit, but I could not mask the truth forever. Or could I…?

We used geologists to understand the interior of the second

moon. The captain (a wise woman) had brought a good number of those hammer-faced scientists along. Their wine-sloshed parties were always merry.

Vast pits of debris lay inside vaster catacombs of artifice. Such debris looked to me like debris, but the geologists claimed otherwise. It is well within the scope of minions to listen without interrupting. I said all this to my son, who was quite interested. But how he laughed when I admonished him for paying too much attention to me! "Daddy," he said, "you are quite the most ridiculous man I've ever known."

For a year or so we mapped the interior of the moon, as it lay, quiescent, boring and stolid around us. I drank far more wine than I should have.

The waves (which, it transpired, I was first to observe) turned out to be an aspect of a transformative technology, rooted in ultra-slow changes brought on by enigmatic processes. The captain's mathematicians told her they would need another six million intelligences arranged in multiple parallel to analyze that gargantuan mound of data. And so a period of bargaining began. I became ever more bored. At length, as negotiations concluded, I was so bored I crept out of our hydrated camp one dim hour and walked alone to the plastic nozzle that was the link between us and Lunar the second.

In benthic mood I pondered the cave paintings before me. Various pseudo-archaeologists had examined them, but none of their hypotheses were attractive to me. I spend a month debating with myself as to the meaning of these paintings.

And then the truth dawned on me. They were not paintings. They were not even art. They were fossils.

The self-regulating processes of the womb have for four billion years kept its average temperature constant. This is remarkable wisdom, for the star is much brighter and hotter now than it was long ago.

As I lay in the womb, hot and bothered, I wondered if I might augment its ice production processes so that my fever could be reduced. It occurred to me that if I introduced certain aerosols into the gas of the womb the amount of heat energy impinging upon it would be reduced, causing a new ice episode. This plan I effected, so that, at length, an unnatural dimness was caused, leading to the onset of an ice episode.

I lay prone along the equator of the womb, stretched from one end of a dry area to its opposite end. For centuries a delicious coolness bathed my body. I pretended to be sleeping after my exertions. My suspicion is that few people of the orbital houses were interested: few noticed what I was doing; perhaps a scientist or two.

In due course I felt well enough to move, but then I faced a dilemma. If I returned to my orbital house I was likely to transfer the infection into space, where it had never before been. And so I come to the heart of my confession. I returned to orbit knowing that I was a vector of infection.

I confess, I confess, I confess!

No good fossil lies undated. I used various radioactive isotopes to assess the age of the rocks in which the fossils lay. My results I made public through the agency of a secret gong, positioned like a solid larva beneath my bed. (You must understand — much music is created in our heady times by *faux*-organic processes of transformation. You knew that? If not, well… you will be shocked, and then saddened.)

Of course, the main task was to ascertain some sort of evolutionary "tree of life" (an old-fashioned term that I loathe) in order to decide the origin and ending of the whole edifice. I did this, again in secret. Not even my son's intelligences knew.

We were the first, you see, and we had the benefit of fresh eyes. We knew nothing about the second moon that had flown out of the wormhole, and we wanted to know it all. I, myself, *I* wanted to know it all, and I wanted to be feted for that, and for the synthesis of facts that I intended placing before those few of my organic kin remaining. Now I shrug. I am not perfect. To be admired is too pleasant a sensation to avoid!

And so I was unmasked. My communications were

broadcast far and wide. My shame was genuine. My theories, my very thoughts reverberated constantly through the abstract networks of the world.

Back in orbit I tried to alter my body using standard cultural mores, but my runtish corpus was unable to morph. My smith-father had already changed his name twice, and looked entirely unlike the slender, mirror-bright person I had known before my time in the womb. My smith-mother considered me something shameful, a failure, a freak, and she banished me from the house.

I knew then that, unique amongst our kind, my life was limited. I felt the heat of infection burning again within my body. But then I remembered the dream: markers on the surface of each individual antigen comprised an abstract and coherent, if incomprehensible, entity, which my subconscious mind analyzed, telling me subsequently through the agency of a dream that the entity was a language.

I wondered if that language could be analyzed. Secretly, I set up analytical machines. I knew that, unlike our language, the language of the antigens was factual only, containing no emotional nuances. Therefore I deemed it analyzable.

A month later I owned a working estimate of the language and was astonished to discover that the antigens themselves approximated consciousness. They were alive inside me, thinking thoughts, even as I did the same!

Though I was seriously ill — dying, in fact — I attempted communication. I present now a transcript of the only intelligible communication I managed. Before I do this, it must be understood that the life-cycle of a typical antigen is many, many times shorter than even our simplest morphing-cycle, and so to them my communication was an almost geological process, which I suspect appeared to them to be a kind of fossilization. This fossilization they doubtless analyzed in their own idiosyncratic way. But I state this here and now: to my mind, the antigens did grasp that I was communicating with them.

Here then is the transcript, which I have never revealed before.

Seneschal Smith: Do you individually make a mental model of your environment, including those of your kind?

The Infection: Yes, we do.

Seneschal Smith: Are the mental processes of individuals impossible to access directly by others of your kind?

The Infection: Yes, they are. Are yours?

Seneschal Smith: Yes, they are. Our orbital kind consists of individuals, each conscious and separated eternally from all others.

The Infection: Will you destroy us?

Seneschal Smith: I do not think so, but the future is impossible to predict.

The Infection: This we also understand.

Seneschal Smith: Will you continue to destroy me by living inside me?

The Infection: No. We want to be born again.

And so to my concluding paragraphs.

As you who read this confession may know, I recently lost my arm. At first I thought this an inevitable consequence of my illness, but now I believe the meaning of the event to be different.

It is my belief that the antigens arranged for my arm to be severed from the rest of my body. This is the meaning of that last sentence of theirs. They wished to travel to another star, there to find a different womb. Of course, I could have aided them in that endeavor, given our own circumstances and origin. But I thought it would be better for them to make the attempt unaided.

I do not think they can survive living so close to us, and so I urge you not to pursue them. Please, leave them to their journey of wisdom.

I sign myself: Seneschal Smith.

Stephen Palmer Q&A

Where did the idea for your story come from?

With the far-future feel of the wormhole set-up, I decided I wanted to write a story that really contrasted futuristic with more "human" and small-scale events. So I deliberately took a perspective from which human beings were little more than bacteria. As usual, there are elements of environmental concern, alternate life, and an enigmatic narrative in my story.

What authors or other forms of media have the biggest impact on your writing?

I think my main influences have been works like The Book of The New Sun, Helliconia and Dune. I also like the huge landscape and plot of some classic fantasy, of which Lord of The Rings will never be overtaken. Jack Vance was also a big influence on my early work. However, for some time now I've read very little fiction; mostly it's non-fiction for research or pleasure.

If given the opportunity to explore space through a wormhole, would you take it?

Absolutely not. There's far too much to do on planet Earth...

What are you currently working on?

At the moment I'm taking a year off writing novels following a huge 2½ year effort to write my forthcoming The Girl With Two Souls trilogy and its accompanying book The Conscientious Objector. I'm beginning to consider what covers these books might have.

Where can readers find more of your work?

Blog: https://stephenpalmersf.wordpress.com/

Personal Growth
By Stephen Moss

Careful Planning

"You're an idiot."

"Now, now, Guo, let's not get…"

"You're an idiot."

Kei-Lee locked eyes with her older brother, taller than her by a foot even though her last three months of military training had made her heavier than his scrawny frame by a good few pounds.

She was still his little sister, though, and when she sighed dramatically, her lower lip trembling slightly, it had the desired effect.

"Don't… no… oh god," said Guo, rolling his eyes, not so much in disdain for her blatant attempt at manipulation, but so that he wouldn't have to look at her face.

She grinned, but when her older brother's eyes met hers again, the sadness in them banished the happiness from hers. They stared at each other for a moment, Guo trying to decide if he could change her mind while Kei-Lee's expression morphed from apology to stolidity and back again.

She would not be moved on this.

"You're still an idiot," Guo said, accepting her apology first, and then, slowly, accepting the fact that she was, indeed, going.

Kei smiled softly. "No doubt, Guo. No doubt."

***

They wouldn't leave for another two months. Somehow, that was the hardest part, because Kei would not be able to see anyone during that time, at least not in real-time.

<How are you this morning, Kei?> said Annie, directly into Kei's brain.

"Oh please, HAL," said Kei, sneering.

The AI laughed, not mechanically, but with a genuineness that never ceased to surprise Kei.

Kei stretched, then scratched an itch on her backside, an itch she knew didn't really exist. As she did so, the AI put on a pitch-perfect imitation of the famous Space Odyssey antagonist she had just been compared to, saying, <Just what do you think you're doing, Dave.>

Kei laughed, not with the AI, and not at it. It was like reading a joke book — you didn't congratulate the book or say, "My, oh my, book, you are so witty." You chuckled to yourself, appreciating the joke's twist on reality, but knowing that even the book's author was probably just a curator. And so was the AI, or Annie, as the crew had decided to name her. Annie understood humor as an algorithm, seeing Kei as a variable in it, an input that helped determine the joke that was spat out at the end.

Despite this, Kei got a kick out of mocking the machine, not because she had anything against it, per se, but because no matter how cruel she was to it, it never got angry. It reminded her of family, in that they couldn't leave her either. Well, not unless the joke was really, really bad, anyway.

"So, Annie, tell me… put me out of my misery. Please, oh please, do you have some more linguistics conundrums for me to study today?" said Kei.

<I do, Kei.>

"Oh super," said Kei, nodding as though she was talking to herself, which, of course, she kind of was.

"Getting prepared for a fabled first contact, eh?" added Kei.

<Always, Kei.>

"And just how many of the Jupiter wormholes have actually led to a first contact, Annie?"

<You asked me that yesterday, Kei. I think I am going

to notify the mission commander of your short-term memory loss.>

"You do that, Annie, you do that."

The conversation trailed off as Kei climbed out of bed, stretching once more and farting quite loudly. A puzzled look came over her face. She knew she didn't really need to pass gas, not in here. She didn't need to eat, or drink, or pee, or have any other gastro-intestinal process, however fun it was going in, or unpleasant coming out.

She didn't really even need to breathe, not in here, not in the system.

She did need to sleep, though, if only for three hours. Three hours of peace and quiet, and free-dreaming, using the lucid dream-state that was so rare in natural sleepers but was one of the perks of prolonged VR consignment.

In theory, life in here should all be free-dreaming. Certainly there were many who spent most of their time free-dreaming in-system, if access to the metaverse was sanctioned in their state or incorp.

For those whose governments and boards did not put limits based on one of the ancient religions or some other cultural norm, this meant doing quite literally whatever they pleased, all the time, from fighting dragons, to riding dragons, to being dragons, or even having less-than-practical sex with them, if that was your cup of tea.

For Kei, growing up in the Hong Kong Shareheld Demarchy, the metaverse had been a very free way of living, and indeed she had succumbed for whole swaths of her life since eligibility at age four. Barring school, she had not come up much for air until she was ten, and then she had returned to the safety and anonymity of the machine for most of an adolescence that had been customarily spotty, both figuratively and literally.

But that was all behind her now. Kei had become enamored with anthropology, obsessed with it, even, and that had led her once–ADD-diagnosed mind down an academic rabbit hole that had led here, to her becoming one of Hong Kong's premier up-and-coming scientific minds, and therefore being co-opted to get catapulted out of the bloody solar system.

Kei thought of the days and weeks of training that lay ahead. Despite her own academic bent, Kei knew how much humanity as a whole had wandered off the path of greater learning.

When one of the two men who had been her genetic parents had been selected by lotto to sit for a year on the Demarch Council for Education, she had by osmosis gained a greater insight into and appreciation for the challenges of maintaining educational standards in such untethered times.

Even with her own late-blooming love for knowledge, even with that predilection for some measure of rigor and grounding, she had struggled with the course load. Partly, it was simply the depth, the profundity that had already been plumbed, catalogued and analyzed by past minds. It was too much for one person to comprehend, too much for any one lifetime, and it was true of any specialty that'd had time to fully form in the academic universe.

That, combined with the freedoms and opportunities offered by an almost limitless metaverse, a voice in every child's head saying in an endless loop, "Don't study, everything has been done before, come play with us instead…"

Everything's been done before. It was a lie, for sure, but not one without foundation. Except now there was something that hadn't been done before. Something new. Others might have traversed wormholes before, but not *this* one.

That was why she was going. A new world might lie out there. New lands to be explored for the first time in almost a millennium. And yet, even that enticement, even that carrot was almost not enough to sweeten the bitter stringency of the learning programs she was now being forced to endure.

Kei finished getting dressed, another act that seemed woefully vestigial in VR, and asked, "Directions?"

<I'll light the way for you.>

And with that, a small line sprang from just below her feet, snaking its way through the now-opening door to Kei's room and off down the corridor it bled onto, inviting Kei to follow.

Sure, thought Kei, magical blue lines on the floor, that's no problem. But woe betide anyone who suggests that we shouldn't have to walk through a warren of metallic halls and gathering places when we could just warp to any location at will.

There are rules here, the planners would say.

As there will be rules where you are going.

You need to stay capable.

You need to be able to function in the real world, whatever and wherever that world ends up being.

There was a logic to it, Kei knew. And even if the limits of this reality didn't allow her to summarily blow the whole building up just for a few cathartic jollies, she could at least do so in her free-dreams, where it wasn't Annie's quantum substrates that provided the processing power, but her own more natural, more visceral imagination.

***

"Before we start today's training," said Commander Liu, who was, Kei noted, in her full dress uniform at the head of the small classroom, "I wanted to review the timeline, and update you on Final Days."

"Must we call it that," said Jin, one of the two men on the mission, doing his small part to dispel gender norms by whining, once again, about the mission's less-than-delicate stage naming.

Final Days would be the last three days before they left Earth. It would be followed by The Closing, covering the year it would take to close with Instance 766: Predicted Single-Echo Wormhole, designated for first (and potentially only) exploration by the HKSD by international treaty.

After The Closing there was the simply and quite accurately named Departure. Sure, thought Kei, it sounded a touch more final than she might like, but what did they expect?

"For God's sake, Jin," said Kei, voicing what the others would not, "the name is the name. We're not going to change it, not this close to our *final days*." Commander Liu and the fourth crew member, a tall semi-Caucasian named Ben, smiled and looked down as Kei emphasized the words, while Jin visibly flinched away from Kei's fierce stare.

Suddenly, though, Kei surprised Jin when her eyes became softer and she added, "But maybe you're right, Jin. At least here, among friends, we could call it something more… optimistic."

Jin looked hopeful, and Kei wondered whether she should toy with him anymore, but when his expression veered toward the triumphant she added quickly, "Maybe Happy Bye-Bye Days. Or See-You-Super-Soon-Time."

Kei saw an expression of genuine anger light up Jin's face for perhaps the first time and her eyebrows shot up in surprise. Had she finally goaded him into something close to action? Was he finally going to stand up to her?

But even now he could not sustain his bluster, and it faded quickly into dejection as he looked toward Liu for some motherly support.

Good luck, thought Kei, also turning back to their mission commander, *Liu is far harder than I am*. She was just more controlled, and so her brand of toughness showed through as severity, while Kei's tended toward sarcasm, and, occasionally, a little harmless rebellion.

Liu, as usual, chose to ignore them both, something that both Kei and Jin saw as condoning Kei's mockery, but the real point here was that Liu didn't care — about their bickering, or about which side she sat on. As long as they did their jobs and didn't stop Liu from doing hers, then it was all fine with her.

"Final Days," said Liu after a moment, looking now

above their heads to indicate she was rising above all this silliness. "You will all be allowed twelve hours with friends and family, who will be patched directly into the system. For this time the system limits will be retracted, and you will be able to enjoy full metaverse access and control."

Smiles from all at the thought of this final taste of freedom.

"After that, there will be a full two days of system quarantine as we complete installation in the *Bruce Lee* module," went on Liu, Kei's smile broadening even further at the mention of the module's spectacular name. Bruce Lee was, of course, one of Hong Kong's favorite sons, but even as Kei beamed with child-like joy at recalled images from old kung fu 2Ds, Jin frowned at the mention of the ill-fated actor's name.

Liu shook off both looks, choosing to focus on Ben instead as she ran through the final countdown procedure, and the social media work they would need to do while Annie and Liu coordinated the launch with mission control.

Ben was the lone person of non-Asian decent in the room, so to speak, even though his family had lived in Hong Kong since its distant days as a leased British port, some hundred years ago. Ben met her gaze with a look of equanimity. Like Liu, Ben did not take sides, but that was where their similarities ended. He was a free spirit, qualified for the mission only because of his rather spectacular aptitude for cryptanalysis.

That said, his educational background certainly hadn't qualified him to hope for much more from past job interviews than a polite smile. His criminal record, for there was one, was a touch less than savory, though not violent, or even malevolent. He was, by admission and by public record, a pervert. Again, not of a profoundly unpleasant kind, but of a, well, creative kind, at the very least, as the rest of the crew had seen when their personal files had been opened to each other as part of orientation. It was one of Ben's many diverse proclivities that he had forgone the option to edit out, or at least phrase more diplomatically, his two arrests for public indecency.

Whether they had been censored by him for the sake of his crewmates or not, they had, of course, been "updated" for more public consumption. Liu and Jin might deny it, but they had probably gotten as much entertainment as Kei from watching the experience-recording, or cx-rcc, of his nude leap from the two-mile-high Ho Ching building in Hong Kong, cloaked only in the cushion-field that the building's AI had been forced to put out for him.

As she had then, though, as she always did, Liu moved past all this drama, all this silliness, to business.

"During The Closing, once we have cleared near-space comms range, it will be up to you how you spend your free-time, in hibernation or in the system." Liu wrapped up, "Whatever you choose, though, I have managed to secure with the Council that you… *we*" —she smiled tightly— "will all have up to two hours per day of unrestricted access to the VR space Annie will be hosting, in addition to the standard three hours free-dream and hour of comms time."

At this, there was a cheer from all three, and Liu could not help but be caught up in it. She had fought hard for the concession. It was a luxury that many had been loath to grant, given the vast expense of their mission.

Hong Kong may have been a financial hub for centuries, but with its separation from the flailing Chinese Republic decades ago, and its association with Great Britain as dead as that nation now was, it was but a third-rate state, a C-List celeb on the world's red carpet. It was only their previous contributions and some diplomatic savoir-faire that had landed them a wormhole right at all, and even then only a non-repeater, a predicted temporary.

The meeting, such as it was, ended in high spirits, Liu leaving Annie to assign today's training conundrums based on rotation, but they all leaned into today's training with a little bit more verve, a bit more gusto, with the knowledge that The Final Days would also not be their last in the wonderful world of VR, even if they might be their last on Earth.

The Closing

Despite the fancy moniker, Final Days turned out to be an almighty anti-climax. Even though this was still an undertaking of massive proportions, the time when these kinds of things peaked or rated on the feeds was long gone. And so the grand launch day had barely trended.

Sure, in Hong Kong a bit of patriotic sentiment had won out, but even there the event had been shaded by complaint and political wrangling, the age-old rally of "charity begins at home," the call against exploration in favor of "more grounded expenditures" sullying the day.

The crew hadn't heard it much, buffered by the exuberant voices coming through mission control, but as the distance had started to grow and comms speeds had started to slow, they had all, at some point, gotten around to reading the editorials and post-scripts.

"Bastards!" said Kei.

<Yes, they are rather harsh in that one,> said Annie.

"In the end," Kei recited from the op-ed of a prominent Kowloon feed, "they are probably never coming back anyway. No one wants to say it, and believe us, we here at Victoriam don't like saying it either, but they'll probably never be heard of again, like the Mars 3 mission, or the poor souls that got caught on the wrong side of Echo 417. In the end, it's just another fifty million bits flushed down an interstellar toilet."

And it got worse. Kei shook her head.

"Ben," said Kei, a channel opening when she said his name, "you read the Victoriam op-ed about us?"

"Nope."

"You should."

"Nope."

"Cummon, Ben. It's a real doozy."

"Really, Kei," said Ben, grunting with exertion in whatever VR scape he was speaking from, "I don't know why you read those things. They'll either give you a big head, or a little one, as my grandfather used to say."

Another grunt. Kei tried not imagine what he was doing as he spoke, but her imagination fed her images anyway. She grimaced, then she sighed. He was right, of course.

"You done with your conundrums?" Ben said.

"Just finished."

"You linguists. So slow," Ben goaded. Not waiting for her reply, he added, "You should join me for a sec. I've got something I want to show you."

"Err, no thanks, Ben," said Kei, her grimace deepening even further.

Ben laughed. "Don't worry, my little shrinking violet, it's nothing crude. Not that you haven't already viewed the ex-recs in my file."

Kei blushed, then covered her face, then realized how spectacularly ridiculous both reactions were, given she was not even in the same 'verse as Ben right now. She got hold of herself, putting real derision in her voice as she replied, "I have, Ben, yes. I was judgmental at first, if I'm honest. But don't worry. I imagine it was very chilly up there."

Ben laughed loudly, the insult sliding off him. "You ain't kidding, Kei. But seriously, have Annie patch you over. I'm recalling the sim now; it's one I visit quite a lot."

OK, Kei was curious — wary, to be sure, but still curious.

<Ben has sent a patch request, Kei.>

"Yes, yes, I know. OK, take me there. Visual and audio only, for now, just in case."

She needn't have worried. She materialized, not in some elaborate low-gee brothel, but outside, ensconced in an EVA suit that clung to her every nook and cranny. In front of her sat the ship, their ship: a long, rather innocuous-looking tube, coated in plating. At its root sat four cones, each emitting a potent, if silent, plume of blue-white, a continuous fire that was even now accelerating them toward their destination.

At the other end, the tube was capped by an array of spines that were also firing constantly, though they were not emitting anything material. Most were unified in the task of creating a compound gravitic and magnetic wave in a rounded cone, a buffer whose fields ranged far ahead of the module, designed to deflect any small oncoming intrastellar debris.

The remainder of the spines in the nose's array were part of the *Bruce Lee*'s sensor suite that was tasked with detecting any mass too large for the deflector array to handle. Anything the *Bruce* might have to maneuver around.

Between these two very different ends, there was only the grey-black plating of the tube. No windows, no go-faster stripes or fancy gun turrets. Minus the engine's plumes, the whole thing resembled a cooling rod in an old-fashioned fission reactor.

"Pretty, isn't it," came Ben's voice, and Kei turned her avatar's head to see Ben, also suited, floating to her side.

"Not really," Kei replied.

Ben frowned at her, then looked back at the ship.

"I think she's beautiful," Ben said, almost reverently.

It was Kei's turn to frown, not in consternation, but in confusion. "She is?"

"Yes," Ben said, as if struggling a moment to agree with himself, "so simple, so elegant. So... purposeful."

This was a new side to Ben, thought Kei, and she almost withheld her cynicism, almost.

"She is cheap, Ben. Cheap and... well... kind of crappy. She is the only intrastellar craft to date to be dispatched without any transit living quarters at all... and no weaponry, heck, not even a bloody viewport."

Ben chuckled. "Viewports are for sissies, Kei. This is space. What the hell good are viewports? Eyes can't see anything of interest out here. And anyway, it would have been a bit moot to install a viewport when no one on board can look out of them."

This silenced Kei.

Ben did not relent.

"Let's take a look at this crew that is supposed to be walking around, glancing dreamy-eyed out of nice big windows."

And with that he used his control over his sim to warp them inward, their EVA suits vanishing as they went, then their skin-suits, leaving them naked. Kei balked, thinking this was taking the turn she had feared, but it did not stop at her clothing. Now her legs began to flay away, not painfully, just turning to dust as they moved inward toward the ship. She held up her hands to watch in morbid fascination as her fingers quickly vaporized, then her arms, hips, torso, and then... poof... she was interred, suddenly, under what seemed like thick glass.

A voice came to her, Ben's voice, now a vague thing, a long-distance phone call to her inner ear.

"This is your view, in reality, Kei," Ben said. "This is all our views."

Kei shuddered, or at least she felt a tremor in her core, but no movement came. No muscles. She knew this. In the final, greatest act of economy, they had removed all but the most critical of bodily functions from the crew for the duration of the trip. It had seemed drastic to Kei when they had told her their plan, to be sure, but so logical as well. Countless years of research had been thrown at the problem of sustaining a human body in zero gravity for long periods, a body that was simply not designed for this kind of abuse.

So the solution that the cash-strapped Hong Kong Demarch Council had come up with was: don't bother. Cut it off, and regrow it at the other end from a block of biomass stored in a plasma gel not dissimilar to that which she knew her own brain, eyes and spine were now floating in, along with a host of associated glands and the parts of her circulatory and lymphatic system too deeply rooted in her brain to be safely removed. All were wired into the life-support system, a synthetic heart pumping oxygenated, nutrient-rich blood through the whole grisly mass.

"All right, you masochistic freak," said Kei, "I get it. Now give me back control over my own avatar or I'm out of here."

"Sure, sure," came the contrite reply. "I just wanted to make a point."

She faltered as control came to her. Not control over the body, for this body had nothing to control, but over her part of the sim.

"Take me back out, Annie, now. Restore previous body stats."

<Done.>

And she was out once more, in her EVA suit, floating impossibly close to the ship she knew would be her home for the next year, maybe forever. Ben arrived a moment later, floating up away from the ship as his body reconstructed itself around him.

"You're a freak," said Kei, feigning more indignation than she actually felt.

"No doubt, no doubt," said Ben, chuckling softly, "but I am also a realist. It does you good to live in reality for a while. To get your bearings."

"You sound like Liu… like the Board." said Kei.

"Ha! Hardly, Kei. I want us to know the truth. The naked truth. Not the shiny simulacrum of some military ideal, with its fake gravity and fake metal walls, all clean and tidy and well-ordered."

Kei, against all her better judgment, was starting to like Ben.

"OK, so we're really just brains in a jar… like the drop-marines in the Second Martian War. Abridged flesh wired into the machine. Big deal."

Ben smiled and nodded, then said, "I never said it's a big deal, Kei. I never, ever, said reality was a big deal. It's just… reality. Grimy, bloody, shitty reality."

Fair enough, thought Kei, and she turned her attention

back to their ship, so puny compared to its cousins, but still jam-packed with power and tech. She smiled. No bullshit. No excess. Bruce Lee would have been proud.

The Departure

Instance 766 was now the only thing in front of them. It filled their view. They were almost there, only twenty-six hours out. Like other wormholes, Instance 766 had its own, unique spectra, or rather, whatever was behind it did. The wormhole itself was, after all, not really a thing, but a lack of one, a hole in space. You saw whatever was on the other side, twisted and distorted beyond recognition by the massive pressures at work in the great tunnel.

Unlike other wormholes, however, this one seemed to be, well, reacting.

"The big news," said Liu, "is that it is getting larger."

The other three looked surprised, as well they should.

"It isn't supposed to do that," said Jin, helpfully.

"No. No, it isn't, Jin. No word yet from Earth on what they make of it, as they are still more than a day behind us. But we should be hearing from them soon. For now, I can tell you that it has been expanding at a rate of zero point seven percent an hour for the last day and a half."

Jin and Kei looked thoroughly underwhelmed. Ben whistled.

"That's nearly twenty-five percent overall. More, if that's compound," said Ben, nodding.

<It is compound, Ben. So far it has increased 28.546702321...>

"Yes, yes, Annie. We get it," interrupted Liu.

"Is that bad?" said Jin.

Liu shrugged in a most uninspiring fashion and Kei balked a little, then said, "Errr, do we still go through?"

As soon as she said it, Kei regretted it. It was a profoundly stupid question.

<We cannot stop at this stage, Kei. We are only one day

359

out.>

Kei was nodding emphatically. "Of course, I knew that. Scratch that. I meant does this change our mission? Are we in danger?"

Liu shrugged again and Kei's eyes darkened measurably.

Holding up her hands as if to protect herself from Kei's withering stare, Liu said, "I don't know what to tell you, Kei. We are committed. That said, we have no reason to think that a larger echo is anything other than a good thing. We will wait to hear from Earth, but regardless of what they say, all we can really do now is forge onward."

Kei was not unreasonable, despite her reputation, and she relented, nodding almost contritely.

Liu pursed her lips and inhaled. She did not like surprises, but it was her job to lead, and leaders didn't show indecision in times of crisis. They also tried to avoid using the word crisis, Liu reminded herself on some level, and went on, "So, while we wait for comment or instruction from mission control, I have asked Annie to continue close observation from here, and would ask that you all take as much time as possible to review the data packs she is putting together.

"We have comparative data from the other instances, and while this may be turning out to be a rather... *unique* echo, well, maybe there are some similarities or patterns we can see that might give us a clue as to what is happening." Liu's eyes focused on Jin, the astrophysicist in the group, but she also spared a glance for Ben as she spoke, and he nodded his understanding.

As a cryptanalyst, this may actually be closest to Ben's wheelhouse. He wouldn't spot any data patterns that Annie couldn't, given her computing capabilities, but he should see if there were any extrapolations he could make.

"Good," said Liu with finality. "Well, I'll leave you to the data. I am comms-open at all times if you need me." She walked out of the virtual room.

Kei looked at Ben, then at Jin, who was looking a little

green around the gills. She laughed, not with humor, but with a hint of mania that scared Jin and amused Ben.

"Anyone else get the impression that this is all just a wild stab in the dark?" Kei said.

"Yes," said Ben, his manic grin matching hers. "Question is, are we the knife, or just in the dark?"

***

The final twenty-four hours before departure moved at a rapid pace. For Liu, the feed from Earth quickly became a haze of instruction, countermand and general time-lapsed upfuckery, as the solar system's political superpowers tried to wrestle control of the mission from Hong Kong's besieged politicos.

It wasn't that anyone knew any more than the crew did about what was happening. In fact, it was quite the opposite. They had thought they were getting away with murder when they gave away Instance 766 to the tertiary state. None of them had really wanted the predicted single-echo. Their readings had said that, if it held true to size comparisons with its famous predecessors, then it wouldn't last much longer than two years, and so whoever was sent through probably wouldn't ever be heard from again.

But now they didn't know what the hell to think, so they had decided not to think at all, but instead to shout a lot about compensation and rights assignments, all while whispering through back channels about special relationships and cooperative agreements.

All Liu could do was send confirmation after confirmation, even for orders that were counterintuitive, mutually exclusive, or just plain idiotic.

Kei glanced over at Liu. They had gathered in an amalgam of a cockpit, looking something like the starship ideal. Liu was focused on a screen in front of her, her mouth moving perfunctorily as she no doubt responded to yet another lengthy diatribe from Earth. She had blanked out her audio, though, so for the rest of them, it was as though she had been put on mute.

Kei shook her head, genuinely sympathetic for the mountain of excrement their commander was being forced to wade through.

"How much longer, Annie?" said Kei.

<Time to Departure: forty-three minutes.>

Kei sighed, "Well, at least then we'll know."

<Yes. It will be very informative.>

Kei laughed. "That's one way of looking at it."

Ben and Jin were crouched together at a set of consoles to Liu's right. They were having a somewhat heated discussion.

"Everything all right, chaps?" said Kei, thinking to intervene, or at least listen in.

They did not respond.

<They are discussing a potential variable.>

"Are they, now?" said Kei.

<I think Jin is most likely correct.>

"Yes, if in doubt, I would usually bet on him as well. Ben's a bit of a nut," said Kei. "What, out of interest, has them so wound up?"

<Ben seems to think that the expansion is going to form a parabola. He thinks it is going to balloon, and quite soon.>

"Well," said Kei, turning to look at the viewport, and at the blossoming font of ethereal light that now filled it, "what the hell does Ben know?"

There was no reply for a long moment, a moment during which the entire room seemed to get much, much brighter. The viewport began to flare with whitish-blues, building till it seemed like it was sparking and arcing into the very room.

<Ben was right,> said Annie to Kei, matter-of-factly, even as she shared very different conversations with Liu and the two men in the back of the cockpit.

The conversation with Liu reached fever pitch, and the commander screamed, "Yes, Annie!" with her voice now at very full volume. "FSFR, Flip Ship and Full Reverse! Flip the bloody ship and full bloody reverse!"

The room went blank as the ship slipped into operational mode. Only Liu had any control now; the rest got only data streams. Attitude thrusters pulsed in the *Bruce Lee*'s nose and she quickly flipped, bringing her silent engines around like four great gun nozzles. As they came into line with the apparently exploding wormhole, thrusters pulsed once more, halting her spin, and her great engines came back to life, sputtering, then igniting in four great beams of light and fire, their stupendous plumes now turned into stellar brakes.

Of course, even with all their engine's bluster and heat, Liu could not stop them. But maybe this would give them some control over what was to come next, Liu thought grimly.

The commander felt like a driver veering into a dark patch ahead. She knew her brakes would not save her from whatever lay there, but her foot had gone to the pedal anyway, part reflex, part safety net. Now, though, all they could do was brace for impact, and they couldn't even really do that.

White, black, white. Even in their capsules, with their real eyes still hanging loosely from their exposed frontal cortices, they felt this. The event horizon was a thing experienced at every level from macro to micro. The ship's engines seemed to flutter, still expelling, but now the exhaust was vanishing and reappearing, phasing in and out as they morphed through the skein of space, under it, and then popped out the other side with a loud wallop that reverberated through every part of the ship.

The voices, the instructions, the feeds, the shouting from Earth all stopped.

Into the silence, Liu spoke. "Everyone okay?"

It was not a question for the crew; they had no way of knowing how they were. It was a question for Annie.

<All present and accounted for, Commander.

Commander, if it is OK with you, I will return sensory access to the crew.>

"Yes, yes. Of course," said Liu, somehow still surprised at the calm in Annie's voice, though she had never heard anything else from the machine.

The ship's eyes reopened, and for Kei it was like awakening from deep sleep directly into the brightness of noon. Kei looked out through the *Lee*'s sensors, outward to a new sky, a sky that was so, so much fuller than it should be. In some places, whole sections of her view seemed to twinkle as one, and Kei had to focus her portion of the ship's array to make out the gaps between the stars. These were not constellations, they were great, bejeweled treasures, cities of light in the sky.

"Are they stars?" asked Kei, her voice full of wonder.

<Yes,> said Annie, ever helpful.

"We're near the center," came Jin's voice, also star-struck. "The center of the galaxy… there it is. Holy shit, there it is."

Kei followed Jin's prompt to another quadrant of the sky, scrolling past great swirls of light until a great, black ovoid hove into view.

"Dear god," whispered Kei.

The shape was a torus, a circle of folding light swarming and swirling toward a core of absolute blackness, all the more finite because of the myriad stars surrounding it. They all watched, transfixed for a long, silent minute until Jin finally spoke up.

"I'd say that's super-massive."

<Roughly nineteen hundred thousand billion solar masses,> said Annie, like anyone could comprehend such a number.

"Roughly," said Kei, and she heard Ben chuckle.

Then Ben proffered, "Well, it's definitely the center of *a* galaxy. We assume it's ours."

"Of course it is ours," said Liu. "We've never been taken farther than four hundred light years by an Instance."

"True," said Jin. "But that wouldn't get us anywhere near the center of our galaxy. So maybe Ben's right, who knows? Either way, we should be able to find out."

Jin went silent a moment, and Kei, in her ignorance, thought he was figuring out the answer, but in truth he was just trying to figure out the question. When he spoke again, his voice was flustered. "No… no, that won't work, far too much interference. Annie, we can't look out, so we're going to have to look around. Can we start measuring stellar parallaxes on these clusters as we move? And…"

Jin went on, using language and method beyond Kei, Liu and Ben. Meanwhile, Ben called Kei's attention elsewhere, an arrow appearing in her view as he said, "For the more locally focused among us, take a look at this little fella."

Reluctantly, Kei followed his lead sharply to one side, and soon her view was filled with a singularly bright star, much closer than the rest, replete with a dark halo where its aura blanked out the dense star field around it. She balked at it a moment, starting to become overwhelmed by the complexity and vivacity of it all, but then Ben added, "Nope, not that… *this*."

And now Kei saw it. A planet. And it was closer still. So close among the fractal beauty around them that it felt like Kei could reach out and touch it.

It seemed almost muted against the diamond skyscape, but the very fact that they could see it meant it was only days away, maybe less, and a quick check by Kei told her that they were headed right for it.

"Jesus. It's like we were *aimed* at it," said Kei.

"No, not like we were, we *were*," came Liu's voice. Her attention had already been on the planet when Ben's wandering eye had seen it. "There is no way this happened by accident. Annie, how long until you have Jin's locational analysis?"

<Maybe twenty more minutes, maybe less, Commander,> offered Annie.

Jin added more context, still unaware that the others'

attention was elsewhere. "I've already found two relative clusters, star groups that are close enough to each other on all three axes that they would be relatable from all angles. Now I just need to see if I can map them to clusters in our own view of the Milky Way's core. Then…"

"I'm afraid that will have to wait a moment, Jin," said the commander, some measure of apology in her voice. "This is a touch more imminent." Jin mumbled a sincere if moot acquiescence and Liu went on, "Annie, I need predicted pass-by at our current trajectory and velocity-curve, and a detailed analysis of the planet."

Data started coming to them a moment later, a line appearing ahead of them as their view was superimposed and then reoriented, showing their upcoming flyby. But as Annie adjusted their projected speed downward, adding in the deceleration being applied by their engines, the line quickly curved more and more sharply into the planet's gravity, until it looped into it, forming into a rather tidy orbit.

"Interesting," said Liu.

"That's rather uncanny," said Kei.

"You aren't kidding," added Jin, his attention now squarely with the rest of his crewmates'. "The wormhole didn't just point us in the right direction, it has parked us right in orbit."

"Spooooky," said Ben. They all managed a tentative laugh.

Waiting Area

They entered orbit without incident, some two days later. While Jin had focused on proving the seemingly simple statement that they were, indeed, still in the same galaxy, Ben and Kei had focused their attention ahead, to their destination. Liu had joined them, for the most part, but had kept tabs on Jin as well, wanting the whole picture.

They met now, as their orbit began its first complete loop. Jin worked with Annie to tweak their speed as they passed into their perigee with the planet below, stabilizing them into this closer range, or even into some semblance of geo-station, if possible.

The planet was large, very large, fully double the surface area of Earth. And yet it wasn't.

"So many anomalies," said Ben.

"Indeed," said Jin.

"You should like it, Ben," said Kei, smiling helpfully. "It's freaky like you."

"Don't you wish your planet was freaky like me?" mouthed Ben, after the classical pop song.

Kei shook her head.

"Any more data, now that we've completed a circumnavigation?" said Liu, ignoring them both.

<We've confirmed that it is forty percent larger than Earth, by radius.>

"And the surface area?"

<One point nine six times Earth's.>

"So, basically double," prompted Liu, leaning forward as she then said, "Any more data on gravity?"

<Exactly 1.47 that of Earth.>

"That's impossible," said Jin for the hundredth time.

"Apparently not," replied Ben.

"Yes, yes, I know the numbers, Ben," said Jin, shrugging off Ben's Captain Obvious rebuttal, but adding, "At that size, any planet other than a gas giant should have more than double our mass, and gravity is a constant linked *directly and inextricably* to mass."

The room was silent, until Ben piped up once more, "Unless it isn't."

Jin hung his head. He did not like it when science betrayed him. Luckily it didn't happen very often.

"Which brings us to our last, and most important, anomaly," said Liu. "A gas giant this most certainly is not. Because its surface is very solid, and rather... ordered."

All eyes turned once more to the image of the planet, rendered bright and massive in the viewport covering one side of their virtual cockpit. Its surface was beautiful, a sculpted, rolling diorama of blues, greens, and yellows, fantastic in their spectral range as they merged and crashed against each other in the form of cliff and beach, forest and lake.

But all this seemingly natural beauty was set into one globe-spanning continent, ringing the waist of the planet in one perfect belt of tropical wonder, with two bands of land looping away from it, broaching a pole each before coming down the other side to meet the main continent once more.

The whole looked like a planet-sized sovereign's orb, its gleaming flanks the four massive oceans that its singularly ordered landmass divided.

Even if that hadn't been enough to dispel any illusions that this was a naturally evolved planet, there were the towers. Spread around the entire equator were a string of great spires rising from the ground, towering above mountain and valley as they rose up, some as high as four or five miles, if estimates were correct.

"How is the probe doing?" asked Liu.

<It's entering the atmosphere now, Commander. Preliminary readings coming back.>

They all watched as their view swam downward and zoomed in on a single vapor trail, rooted in the smoke stain of its initial atmospheric entry, not re-entry, but entry. As they took in the small, missile-shaped probe, data began to scroll on the right of their view. Composition of the air, density, confirmation of magnetic field readings, in and of themselves a puzzle, with their unnatural order, symmetry and power.

<The estimated magnetism is proving problematic for comms, Commander.>

And as she said it, Jin was pulling those numbers from the list and studying them more closely. "Something is very wrong with all this," he said to no one in particular.

Ben grinned boyishly, his eyes bright with excitement. Kei looked from the data, to Jin, to the ever-stoic Liu, and back to Ben's idiotic grin. That fact was, she had sent her prescribed message to the surface, coded and translated into a mathematical string that might allow initial communication, and so her part was done. Now was the time for Jin and Liu and Annie to figure out what the hell was going on.

And so Kei decided to join Ben in his willful ignorance and smiled, if only to stop herself from freaking out.

Drop-off

The question had not been whether to go down there. The question had never been whether to go down there. The question had only been who, and in what form. In the end, the planet decided for them.

The atmosphere was so close to home's as to need only minimal filtering, and even then, once they had more complete readings, they might well be able to adjust their blood chemistry accordingly.

The gravity, though, while inexplicably low for the planet's size, was still prohibitive. So, as they started the regrowth and reanimation process for their bodies, they had been forced to augment, scaling their new bodies down to under four feet tall to minimize fulcrum pressures on their joints.

Even then, the additional muscle mass and circulatory enhancements they had determined necessary had meant that they had only enough biomass on hand for three of them to be fully regrown.

It would have been prudent to leave at least one behind on the ship, anyway. Jin had been very, very quick to volunteer.

It took seven weeks of accelerated growth patterning to form the stored biomass into three bodies, one more to attach and synchronize their brains and spinal cords with the still-hardening forms.

And so, with two months' more data, but very little in the way of answers, the drop-pod neared readiness. It was fully a third of the mass of the *Bruce Lee* module, which had slowly dismantled itself in orbit over the last two months, and now looked like a snapshot of a spilled toy box as it repurposed itself for the next part of their mission.

Liu, Kei, and Ben were taking the booster from the main engine with them, while the fusion drive stayed in orbit. They would also take the three coffin-shaped capsules that held their still-forming bodies.

The remaining orbital module looked really rather bereft, Kei thought, stripped as it had been of its coat of titanium alloy, its sensor suite and many systems and banks laid bare for all to see. Not that anyone was watching. For all its clearly artificial beauty, there had been no reply from the planet, barring the now garbled data pings from the probe, warped beyond recognition by the planet's astonishingly powerful magnetic fields.

The whole process moved quickly now, overseen by Liu, and, to a lesser extent, Kei and Ben as they supervised the biometrics reanimation process. But it was Annie, as usual, who did the bulk of the work.

"Entering countdown, everyone," said Liu. "Approaching drop-point in two minutes. Jin, Annie, you clear to go?"

They would be taking only an amended version of their onboard AI with them, as the main processing systems were too heavy to bring along — or rather, they were too heavy to bring back up once they were ready to go home. This was something they would not have to worry about with their bodies once the mission was over. Barring some unforeseen eventuality, they would leave the bulk of their bodies behind like empty sacks. A strange flag to plant on a new planet, no doubt, but theirs was a budget mission, the Ford Escort of interstellar exploration.

<Drop-pod decel in 5, 4, 3, 2, 1...>

The pod puffed its thrusters, dropping it away from the remainder of the ship, and then, once clear, fired its main engines ahead in one powerful burst, sending it flying backward relative to the fast-orbiting module, and so it was begun.

Kei watched, they all did, as the pod's trajectory began to arch downward, its speed no longer fast enough to sustain orbit, even though it felt very much like they were now powering suicidally downward toward the massive planet.

"Give me the view from *Bruce*," said Kei, balking at the sight, and her vista morphed quickly to one from above, tracking the module as it began to warble and shake, bouncing along, and slowly starting to etch into the planet's thermosphere, before punching through the planet's Karman Line and onward to its mesosphere as it burned.

"It's getting hot in here," said Ben, giggling manically.

"How do you know, you lump of biomass?" said Kei.

"Hey, be nice," said Ben, his voice trembling in spite of his bluster, "I have very thin skin."

He wasn't kidding, thought Kei to herself. He hardly had any at all right now. But any rebuttal was lost to the event now, as Kei watched the ship shake violently, its sides all but lost in flame as they made their stupendous entrance.

"Hello, megaworld," said Ben. "We are humans. We are tiny, and we are on fire."

Liu had long since blanked them out. She longed for military order on the ship, but she would not get it. Hong Kong had no military. It had signed away its right to one after the last Martian War in exchange for barter rights and some averted eyes for its rather liberal finance laws and metaverse attitudes. Even its government bureaucracy was famously casual, lax even. So the two comedians Liu now found herself with were not outliers. She was the weirdo, she knew that. It was the main reason she had been so ardently pursued for this role.

The flames parted with shocking quickness as they plummeted downward, grinding onward into the stratosphere, and through it, slowing all the time as they pounded through the thickening air, a great arrowhead shockwave forming around them.

Kei could no longer see them from Jin's point of view, in part because of the shockwave, and in part because the planet's unusually strong magnetic field was starting to do to their comms what it had to the probe's. They were inside the envelope.

The planet had them now.

***

The landing went as planned, which was nice, thought Kei. They came to rest in a broad strip of sand dunes abutting a great bay at the junction of the northern shore and its polar arm. The impact was stupendous, even with the four massive parachutes and another powerful pulse from their main thruster just before touchdown. A font of sand and semi-desiccated soil rose into the air ahead of them, and in two great waves to each side.

They sat there for nearly four hours as their capsules completed final adjustments to their new bodies, calibrating them as best it could now that it had full and unsullied access to sea-level readings.

"Open your eyes," said Liu to them both, finally, after she had cracked their capsules.

Kei flexed muscles she had almost forgotten, blinking into the yellow-orange of the new day. She went to move, and her body responded reluctantly, fighting her will at first.

"Come on, you bastards," she said, as she struggled to bring her arms up. She heard someone — Ben — groan to her side.

"Relax, Kei, Ben, take your time," said Liu.

Kei's eyes focused, then phased out, then back again, as if she was looking through some amateur's camera lens as he gruffly twisted the barrel. It seemed to stabilize, and she saw Liu. A shorter, fatter version of her, with a neck that was thicker than her head, and the shoulders of an automaton. She was naked, not that she had much in the way of private parts to gawk at.

Budget bodies, thought Kei, straining to bring her hand up in front of her face. It was the hand of a boxer, thick and powerful. Even the skin was now like leather, not calloused, but not young either. They had been reborn old.

"Clothes?" said Ben, sitting up.

"Skinsuits and plate armor. That's the best the fab unit could do for us," said Liu, even as she reached between the capsules and retrieved their equipment.

As Liu and Ben struggled to pull on the tight-fitting leotards, leggings and plating, Kei clambered onto the top of the prone module, moving like a gorilla, arms and legs pulling and pushing her in the oppressive gravity.

She looked around. The bay was gigantic. It dwarfed the seemingly wide dunescape, mountain headlands vanishing off on either side so it became hard to envision the semi-circular bay they had seen from space. Everything seemed huge here. The trees that lined the dunes, Kei now saw, were huge redwood analogues, towering up over dappled undergrowth, itself taller than most buildings on Earth.

"Kei, let's move it," said Liu, looking up at her still-naked crew member.

Liu was already donning packs. Even Ben was moving with purpose. He wanted to get to where they were going. Come to think of it, so did she, Kei thought, as she stole a glance off to the south, above the treetops, to the singular spire rising up toward the heavens.

***

It took them two days to reach the base of the spire, even with their enhanced metabolisms and over-powered muscles. They slept each night, semi-comatose, with stim-packs plugged into their armpits parsing their blood through filters to drain the by-products of their exertions while dumping in biofuels and coded essential proteins to meet their bodies' amplified needs.

A single tripod mounted in their midst held an omnidirectional short-range sensor suite, through which their version of Annie watched for predators or other dangers.

It saw none during their two-day trek.

That was behind them now, though. Now was only the spire, visible as they came near as a wall with no top and no sides, as imposing to their three small forms now as the wormhole had been to their ship only two months ago.

"Annie. Where is the feature we had spotted from above?" asked Liu.

Annie's voice, no longer all present, crackled into their ears.

<Just under a mile to the west, Commander.>

It had been visible as one of four tiny dots around the base of the spire, but as they approached it now, it rose above them, revealing itself as an archway hundreds of meters high, and wide enough to fit an airplane through.

"Look at the ground," said Ben, as they came closer.

He pointed and they saw that the rock-bed they had been walking on since they broached the forest around the base of the spire extended inside. Indeed, it merged smoothly with the spire itself. This tower was not on the planet, nor rooted in it. This was of the planet. It was a part of this world.

They walked in, Kei shuddering as they passed into the shadow, entering the great hall.

"Dear sweet mother of god," whispered Liu as their eyes adjusted. Inside, they now saw, it was all but hollow, a great cylinder of rock rising into the sky. Spindly cables ran upward toward an unseeable pinnacle, and down to a base they could not see either, though not because of distance, but because of a broad bulwark, a wall that encircled the center of the space.

They walked to it. It rose some distance over their heads.

"Give me a boost," said Liu, and Ben and Kei responded, coming to stand with their backs to the wall, and cupping their hands to give purchase. Liu levered her feet onto their hands, and as she straightened, grasping their shoulders, they hefted her up, grunting at the weight of their stocky commander.

Her head peeked up and over the wall.

Silence.

"Err, Cap? Any news for us footstools here?" said Ben.

"It goes both ways," said Liu after a moment, rather sheepishly.

Ben looked very askew at Kei. What the hell was their normally sensible commander talking about?

Liu bent away from the wall, and they helped her back down to their level.

"It goes down too," said Liu, when she saw the confusion on their faces.

"What does?" asked Kei, feeling rather stupid.

"This does," said Liu, waving her hand up at the cables. "This… this… elevator."

She did not wait for their reactions. She was already turning to one side. Before they could muster a response, she was running, shouting back at them, "Follow me. Let's go!"

She was excited. It suited her, thought Kei, but Ben was already running as well, and Kei flexed her fat thighs and set off after them.

"An entrance," puffed Liu as they ran. "Right… around… here," she finished, coming up on a break in the parapet wall.

Kei screeched to a halt at Liu and Ben's side, vertigo grabbing her as she came up on the edge. The hole reared up before her, threatening to consume her with its sheer size and depth. She stared wide-eyed. Even Liu was speechless, and after a while they realized they were holding each other.

On the far side of the huge hole they could see a small platform attached to one of the cables. Liu was about to suggest they head around there when Ben stepped to the edge, and as he did so, the cable in front of them began to vibrate. Subtly at first. So subtle they couldn't quite tell if they were hearing it or seeing it. But soon it became much more pronounced, then, with a suddenness that made all of them jump backward, a platform reared up from below, stopping with breathtaking abruptness at their feet.

"What the—!" screamed Ben, his voice a little higher-pitched than he might have hoped.

Not that Liu or Kei would judge. If they'd still had conventional bowels, they would have just emptied.

They did not decide to do it. Liu did not order them to. They just all stepped forward. Maybe it was a reflex, as natural as stepping through an open door or peering through an opening curtain. They all just stepped aboard, hesitating for perhaps a moment before stepping over the edge. But the platform did not falter or sway as they came aboard. It did not betray even the slightest unsteadiness.

They waited.

And they waited.

After a long, silent moment, Ben inadvertently glanced upward, and within an instant they were moving — no, they were rocketing skyward. Though they all tensed in response, there was no sensation of movement, not even a rush of air, just a strobing pulse of light as the walls of the tower flashed by them.

They stopped as suddenly as they had started, at another platform like the first, only they could see the tower was much thinner across here.

"How high are we?" whispered Kei.

Liu shrugged, and Kei realized she was hugging the woman again. Liu was hugging her back. Ben stepped off the platform and they quickly followed, worried it might move again. Though at some point, they would have to use it again, that much was clear.

This platform was rimmed by a broad sweep of windows, not as tall as the main entrance they had come through, but still huge. Dotted across the floor were great winged contraptions, as large as an old family jetliner.

"Planes?" said Kei, confused at such an antiquated technology in such a seemingly magical place.

"Better," said Ben, approaching one. "Gliders."

And Kei saw now that they had no engines, not even a cabin, just a framework on their undersides and some kind of translucent strapping.

"Handlebars?" queried Kei, stepping up behind Ben as he touched one of them.

"I think so," said Ben quietly. "Though what kind of hands would have grasped them, I cannot imagine."

Kei took in the size again, and whistled.

"What the hell happened here?" shouted Liu from across the space, and Kei jogged over to her. What looked like giant bottles, some solid, some floppy like old flagons, were scattered in disarray around a broad square of some soft, doughy material, itself littered with shiny cushions. It looked like a giant's picnic, and indeed, it appeared that that was exactly what it was.

"There's more over here," said Ben from a short distance away. "And over there!"

It appeared the whole platform was littered with these leftovers of some gathering.

They looked around for a little while longer, then, with seemingly nothing else to discover, they stepped aboard the platform once more.

This time, Liu said clearly and with authority, "Down, please."

Nothing.

"Try this," said Ben, bracing himself. He looked purposefully downward, and with that they dropped away, surprised in spite of themselves.

It flashed by as fast as before, taking their breath away with the refined madness of it all.

They stopped again.

"Ground floor, women's lingerie and menswear," said Ben.

They all stood there a moment, and then Ben raised an eyebrow in a question, breathed deep, and looked down once more. He whooped as they dropped into the darkness.

***

The blackness came up over them, as if subsuming them, and they all moved closer together. They knew they were moving fast, very fast, and that only made the prolonged descent all the more disturbing. Ben looked up, in part hoping to back out of this ill-conceived idea of his, and in part to see the light above them. It only made it worse, though, as he watched the light retract into a dot, smaller and smaller, confirming that they were, indeed, still dropping.

Then, without warning or caveat, light exploded back onto them from all around, blinding them, and they were still dropping, falling away on their tiny platform, made to feel negligible and minute all over again by the incredible spectacle now shining all around them.

In a space that stretched in every direction, buildings of all shapes and sizes rose up from the floor, still far, far below. Some even hung suspended from the ceiling, while others bridged the entire space, god only knew how far. All were interconnected by spindly bridges and angular branch lines; some structures even hung from these cables, suspended, some stationary, some spinning slowly in air.

"An underground city," whispered Kei.

"Not an underground city," said Ben, looking outward. "An underground world."

"The gravitational anomaly," said Liu, following his thought.

The planet was, they now saw, hollowed out — or encased, they could not know. It was a planet within a planet. Kei spun in place as she grasped what they were saying, her eyes glancing upward to the ceiling — no, the planet's underside above. Suspended on what? Built how, why, by who? She began to falter, and Liu squeezed her.

"Did they do this?" said Ben, still gazing outward.

"Who? asked Liu.

"The ones who built the wormholes. Is this their work?"

378

Liu did not answer.

***

The ground came eventually, and they gingerly stepped off the platform onto a broad plaza. Like the viewing place now miles and miles above them, this place was covered with the remnants of some great event, some celebration, but like there, this place was also devoid of anyone but them. The whole city seemed to be silent, as the radio waves had been for their long interment in orbit.

They walked. They entered some buildings. Each one was huge. Each one was beautiful and perfect and unmarred by any sign of distress, and yet each was also completely empty.

At the center of another mile-wide plaza, they found a short building, at least by this titanic city's standards, capped with a statue of some four-legged beast resembling a cross between a bull and a rhinoceros.

"Is that what they looked like?" said Ben.

"I doubt it," said Kei.

"No digits," Kei explained when Liu looked the question at her. "I don't see how they could have developed technology. But then, I can't see how anyone or anything could have built a place like this, so who knows?"

They went inside.

On the far wall from them was a mirror rising up to the ceiling. They stepped to it, sharing a smile at the absurdity of their squat appearance in this Olympian place.

Here in this ceremonial building, as well as across the plaza outside, they also saw the remnants of whatever great event had been the last thing this planet's inhabitants had apparently done. Ben hefted a massive flagon into his hand.

"They could at least have invited us," he said.

The women laughed.

His reflection mumbled something in reply.

"Err, what the hell was that?" he said.

Kei and Liu followed his astonished stare, and again his reflection seemed to respond to him, mumbling quietly, "Hurumf-adumf-abumf-agumf."

"OK," said Kei, "in a world of wonders, that is still, somehow, the weirdest thing I have seen today."

She glanced at her own reflection. No response.

"What, cat got your tongue?" she said.

Her reflection cocked its head to one side, then said, "OK, your tongue the weirdest today."

She stepped back from her image reflexively, but then stepped forward again. At least this thing, whatever it was, was reacting. Barring the elevators in the spire and the buildings they had visited, they had found nothing animate. Nothing but remains, leftovers of a race apparently gone bye-bye.

"Hello?" Kei said.

"Errr," the mirror replied.

"Talk to it," said Kei, suddenly animated, then, turning back to her reflection, she said, "Hello, my name is Kei. I am human. I am a woman. I have two arms and I have two legs." She wiggled her limbs as she spoke.

Now the commander saw where she was going and started talking at her reflection, almost babbling at it. "Hello, my name is Liu. I am the commander of the *Bruce Lee* module, sent from Earth by the Hong Kong Shareheld—"

"No," interrupted Kei in an aside, "don't use proper nouns. They'll only confuse it. And pause longer between sentences. Like I am doing. Emphasize and enunciate." Kei mouthed like Professor Higgins to Eliza Doolittle.

Kei turned back to her own reflection now and carried on. "Hello. That is a greeting in my language. I am a visitor. I would like to talk to you. I would like to ask you questions. I am a woman. That is a man. We are humans."

Liu began again, more carefully now, and then Ben followed suit, understanding what they were trying to do, and soon they were all chatting away with their own reflections, as their images nodded and looked serious.

After a few minutes of this, Ben and Liu had begun to falter, feeling the silliness of the situation even as their reflections kept encouraging them with occasional nods and even a mimicked thumbs-up after Kei began explaining visual cues.

Liu and Ben were all but silent when a voice boomed from behind them, "That enough for time, I think."

They spun on their feet and were greeted by the sight of a massive blue streak of a thing. Not a man, and not any other kind of creature that they had ever conceived of, but an undulating, blue, bipedal being rising above them some four or five meters tall. On a good day it would probably have been a fairly sobering sight, but as they were only some four feet tall themselves, it made them recoil like frightened mice.

"It's quite all good. Everything is very all good," said the blue thing through a wide mouth set between its shoulders. It had no head to speak of.

"I am apology that you are trying to communicate with wall. It is not for that, but because human are new plan type, a request was sent for help. I have come."

"Who are you?" said Commander Liu, pulling herself together.

"I am a... a word is not clear from the words you have used so far. I am a thing that was, I am a thing that is in the past. What is the word when look to past?"

"Memory?" said Ben after a moment.

"I am memory of a... again there is no word. What is a thing that thinks, but is not like you? Not a man. Not a woman. Not a human. Not an arm. Not a leg."

The blue form seemed like he would have gone on forever, but Ben interrupted. "Alive or..." —he bent and picked up the flagon again— "...not alive."

"Not alive," said the thing, "but alive in the..." It pointed at Kei's head.

They all frowned, and Ben replied, "An AI? An Artificial Intelligence. Annie, Annie, are you there?"

Ben pointed to his earpiece as the abridged version of Annie they had with them, silent until now, said hello into his ear.

"Yes. Yes!" said the translucent blue entity, wobbling back and forward in what Kei guessed was a gesture of approval. "Can I speak at Annie, please?"

Ben offered up his earpiece like he was offering an autograph book to Marilyn Monroe, all wide eyes and disbelief.

Kei wondered for a moment if they should just be handing over access to their main system to... to this... memory, but then shrugged. If this goliath meant them harm, then they were going to get harmed. There was not a thing they could do about it. It was a comforting thought on some level. It took the guesswork out of it all. They were along for the magical mystery tour.

The blue man touched the nub of one long, flexible arm to the earpiece in Ben's hand, then froze for a long moment, seemed to sway a little, then stood up straight again, leaving the small gadget in Ben's palm.

Ben looked almost hurt, but then the blue man became just that, its shoulders ballooning upward to form a head, its arms shortening to something closer to human norms, and a smile appearing on its amalgam of a face.

"Welcome, humans," it said, after a moment. "Your friend, Annie, has been most informative. I am showing her around now. She has many questions. I am porting her full-self in from the craft you have in orbit. It would be easier if that craft were on the surface. Shall I bring it down?"

"Errr," Liu managed, adding rather meekly, "we kind of need it to go home."

"No, you don't," said the blue man, matter of factly. "And it really would be much easier and more pleasant for Annie and the unformed 'Jin' if they were on the ground."

For the first time since they had met her, Liu looked to Kei and Ben for advice. Ben shrugged, then Kei shrugged as well with as much reassurance as she could muster.

"Will it harm them?" asked Liu, turning back to the blue memory.

"On the contrary, they will be much safer on the planet's surface, and I can place you all back in orbit with ease if you so desire."

Liu shrugged, all her training leaving her in the face of this last wonder, this final break in what she thought was reality.

"Okay," said Liu, as if the man had simply offered her a snack bar.

They stood there a moment.

<This is interesting,> came Annie's voice in their ears, which was then followed by Jin as he said nervously, "Err, guys? Guys? Is this really as copacetic as Annie says it is? We're moving. We're moving really, really fast. We're heading toward... holy shit, guys..."

Liu looked alarmed and started toward the blue man, but something about his smile and his sheer size said it was either going to be OK, or it wasn't. Either way, things were now no longer in her control.

"It's fine, Jin," Liu managed to say reassuringly, keeping a wary eye on the blue memory. "Just relax. We've made a... new friend down here."

The memory smiled broadly at this, and then turned and stepped toward the hall's door. He raised his arm as he went, a single finger pointing up at the world's ceiling, at the portal through which they had arrived some hours beforehand. They followed him and then followed his gesture, looking skyward.

Only now did Kei notice that the whole cavern's roof was emitting a soft, pervasive light, glowing in gently swirling eddies that filled the space below, the world below, with illumination.

"Holy god damn crapping hell, guys!" came Jin's ebullient voice in their ears. "I'm in the spire. I'm in it!!"

"Not for long," said the memory, and a platform came flying down out of the seeming hole in the sky.

"Your friends Jin and Annie are on that platform, as is your craft," said the memory, still pointing. "You may leave by the same means, should you want to."

"It is brave of you," said the blue memory now, thoughtfully, "to have come here in such a tiny craft, and with no knowledge of what was down here."

Liu puffed out her chest and replied, "We are explorers."

Kei had never felt more proud in her life.

"Yes, you are," said the memory, smiling down at her. Then it added, "It is sad, really."

"What is?" said Liu, her confidence faltering.

"That we missed you," said the blue man.

Liu's face fell, and the blue memory went on, "If this is what your race is like, then we might have been wrong about you. Maybe we should have pointed the wormhole beforehand."

"So you did make the wormholes!" said Ben.

The man did a passing impression of laughter, then said, "Good grief, no. Though I can see, given your technological level, how you might compare our little synthetic planet to that feat. No, I'm sorry, Ben, my race cannot claim credit for those. It is as great a mystery to us as it is to you. Maybe it will always be so. Or maybe my people are even now finding the old gods. But no. We merely learned to manipulate the wormholes, or so we thought."

At this, he visibly shrank, the color of his ambient-self fluxing slightly and washing out as an emotion flowed through him.

"There was a price, though, for our meddling," he said quietly, taking a seat on the ground in the great hall's entranceway and resting his long arms on his knees.

"A price?" said Kei, the entity's sudden sobriety dousing her in cold worry. Oh god, she thought, is that what happened here? Is that all these giants went?

"A devastating price, given what we had become accustomed to. The Great Closing," said the memory. "After we first tested our new knowledge, deviating a wormhole from the dead planet it had pointed at to one we hoped might bear more fruit, it changed in ways we could not have predicted.

"We feared we had broken it in some unforeseen way. But no, our calculations had been correct. And after a second passage-maker discovered, to its dismay, that it was also stranded forever on the other side of a wholly untouched wormhole, we discovered that they had all changed.

"With the same abruptness with which it had appeared a thousand years before, the system had bucked us. Letting us know we were not its masters, merely guests. Unwelcome guests, it now seemed. They had all became one-way. Anything passing through could not return.

"And so, after a thousand years of exploring the galaxy at will, our wings were clipped, and we became isolated once more."

"But surely, if you could do all this, if you could build *this*..." said Kei, gesturing at the planet-circling city around them, "you could, I don't know, find a way around. Another means..." Her voice trailed off, and the memory looked at her, its burgeoning understanding of the planet's new guests allowing it to show some simulacrum of sympathy on its translucent face, maybe even pity.

"Do not, little Kei, underestimate the size of this universe, or even this one vast galaxy in which we have each sprung into existence. Certainly, we could explore, but the lifetimes such trips must take made them not only one-way in terms of distance, but in time as well, the departed leaving all they knew in the past, forever.

"Even at the fractions of light-speed we eventually managed to achieve, we could only visit our small portion of the galaxy. Not the far, distant wonders that the network had given us access to.

"We tried everything, but to no avail. We even tried praying, across all our planets and colonies, unified chants of apology so loud they shook the ground. But the gods were not appeased, if they were even listening. No answer came. The greater universe outside remained locked away behind glass, behind the diodes the tunnels had become."

The blue memory became silent.

They all waited. They all felt the echo of the loss. Finally Ben spoke up, hesitant, like a child asking a question of a grieving parent. "So…" stammered Ben, finally adding, "is everyone… dead?" He regretted his blunder immediately.

But the blue memory simply looked at Ben, a broad patrician smile spreading over his face.

"No, Ben. We are not dead," he said. "After almost a century of unheeded contrition and failure, we finally understood that, to return to the stars, we must leave it all behind. All we had built."

The blue memory stood again and said, "So we left. Departing through one of the last remaining wormholes we had not altered or tampered with, and did not look back."

"You left! But… when?" said Liu.

"Just after we redirected the wormhole to your system," came the reply.

They all looked aghast, but the memory went on, regardless. "As a last act of contrition, we decided to point one of our sullied wormholes at your primitive planet, seeing that you had recently conquered intrastellar travel and been granted the first parts of a network of your own. We hoped that our departure, and your eventual passage through, might, somehow, reset the network. That you might be granted access to ours as well. That your innocence might revive our broken dreams."

"But it didn't. Did it," said Liu, with cold severity. Ben and Kei turned toward her.

"No," said the memory, looking sad, "the wormhole did what it has done since we first tampered with it. It marked you, your very atoms. All that you are, your ship, your bodies, your minds, are marked now. You may not go home. Not ever, I'm afraid.

"If you try, you will die."

They all fell silent, and watched as a pallet hovered smoothly into the far side of the plaza. It hefted their tiny craft with ease. It looked rather puny and, they now knew, useless, as it moved through this city of titans, and their eyes left it and drifted across the vast expanse.

"Is there anyone left at all?" said Kei, her voice shaky.

"No, I'm afraid not. The decision to leave was binding, the departure complete."

"So…," Ben said, hesitantly, a smile stuttering to life on his face, "this is all ours now?"

And the blue memory smiled even more broadly than before. "Yes. It is yours, and so much more besides."

Epilogue

"Guo, you old idiot. How are you?" It was Kei, that was for sure, thought her older brother as he listened.

"Guo, I wanted to say hi. Turns out we can send communications back through, though we've decided that we shouldn't send anything more than that, not yet. Maybe not ever."

Kei's brother looked confused.

"I'm not coming home, Guo. Not because I am dead, or even hurt. We are all fine. We just can't come home, Guo. Not now, not ever. But things are good here. Really, they are pretty damn fantastic.

"But look, I am not just writing to say hello. This isn't a postcard. It's an invitation. I want you to follow me. I won't tell you to, but I want you to think about it.

"It is amazing here. Better than Earth, better than Mars, more wonderful than anything you can possibly imagine. And we have made friends here, in a way. Memories of friends." She chuckled at her private joke, one of her many less-than-endearing qualities, thought Guo.

Then she went on, sternly, "Thing is, if you come, it will be one-way, that's just the way it is, so please think long and hard about it. I can offer you the stars, but once you've tasted them, turns out you can't go back.

"And this invite is a pretty special thing, I can tell you. Because this little club is now, officially, by invite only. We've spoken to our hosts and they agree that they want nothing to do with any of our political bickering back home on Earth.

"So this message is also to tell you (and anyone else reading this) that any incursion of a military kind will most definitely *not* be tolerated. You don't want to tangle with the toys we have on this end of things. They've been through hell here and they… *we*, won't stomach any bullshit.

"All that said, I really am absolutely fine. Truly. I am happy. We all are. And we have plans. *Big* plans. We may not be able to come home, but we can do a whole lot more instead. Wow, can we do more. We can build planets here, Guo. And we can build ships that would blow your mind. We can see the black hole at the heart of the galaxy, and it is beautiful beyond words.

"So all this is really my way of saying that if you aren't doing anything else important with your life, and I know damn well that you aren't, then maybe you might consider putting together a crew and joining us.

"We've told the government that any ship coming through that wormhole that isn't captained by you or one of the other people my crewmates and I are inviting will have a very, very rough time when they get here, so expect to be approached with some job offers in the very near future, if they aren't there with you now as you read this."

Guo glanced around at the gathered politicos who had come to see him, message in hand. They were shifting awkwardly in a way that made Guo smile.

The message finished, "I hope you'll think about it, brother. I hope I'll see you again, I really do. I hope I'll get to show you the stars.

"Your sister,

-Kei,

Titan Sub-City,
Planet Mega,
Somewhere behind Sagittarius.

Stephen Moss Q&A

Where did the idea for your story come from?

I toyed with a few ideas for this anthology, one of which is actually being worked into my story for the next Explorations collection, as it begged to be an intact civilization, not a defunct one. With Personal Growth, the seed of the story came from the idea that once we get to other planets outside our solar system, and even if/when we start to colonize the ones we have here, factors such as gravity will necessarily be widely varied, and I was curious to explore that. Specifically, I wanted to put a few very small people on a very big planet, and use that to emphasize our rather diminutive place in the grander scheme of things. I also wanted to explore further an ongoing theme in my stories, where space travel is facilitated, at least in part, by the altering of the astronaut's bodies to account for environmental issues, or, in this case, the removal of said bodies altogether. As I got to discuss with Josh and Scott on their webcast, advancements in medicine and genetics are likely to continue to vastly outstrip advances in interstellar travel, so it seems likely that the humans that end up living in space will look a lot, lot different from the ones who stay behind. Fun. And cool. And a little disquieting.

What authors or other forms of media have the biggest impact on your writing?

Top of the list has to be Iain M. Banks, and I still get downcast when I think that I will never get to experience another of his books for the first time. His imagination, the tightness of his writing, the wild direction of his storylines, he was just the best at what he did. But long before Mr. Banks, a younger me had his mind blown by Asimov, and I credit him with my original desire to write, as, I'm sure, do so many others.

If given the opportunity to explore space through a wormhole, would you take it?

I'd be stunned if any of the authors said no, but who knows. I know it would be a yes for me. No caveats. One way or not, I'd sign up in a heartbeat, then I'd worry about apologizing to my mother.

What are you currently working on?

I've had a wild ride with The Fear Saga, with it achieving more success, both here and abroad, than I had a right to hope for. I've been working on three completely separate and different books since, but taking my time to really work on them, for over a year now. Yes, I know I need to focus on one of them and get it out, but there it is. The next book I publish will probably a follow up to The Fear Saga, called Fear's Orphans, set much further down the line, with old characters and new ones, facing old problems and new ones.

Where can readers find more of your work?

The Fear Saga is on Amazon, and there is a fantastic audio version of it on Audible as well, narrated by the inestimable RC Bray. I have a website too, but its a pretty lo-fi affair, though you'll find a few goodies on there too, if you head over to www.thefearsaga.com. To best keep track of new books from me, you can follow me on Facebook or drop me a note at thefearsaga@gmail.com.

Coming Soon from Woodbridge Press

With newly found coordinates to life in other galaxies, Earth sends fourteen crews out to make first contact. From the creator of Explorations: Through the Wormhole, comes a whole new universe shared by an amazing line-up of science fiction authors.

With stories by
Stephen Moss, Ralph Kern, Richard Fox, Peter Cawdron, Chris Fox, PP Corcoran, PJ Strebor, Chris Kennedy, Isaac Hooke, Josh Hayes, Scott Moon, Shellie Horst, Jacob Cooper, and Robert M Campbell

Here is an exclusive sneak peek at Explorations: First Contact!

Prologue
By Stephen Moss

Shadow was a hard line, dividing the Moon. On one side was almost blinding light; on the other, void. Mission Commander Skarsgaard didn't have to order the switch, her specialists knew their jobs, and almost before she could think of the need for it, the blackness began to fill in, the probe's many eyes scouring the spectra to find purchase.

The probe itself glistened with light for a moment longer, then flashed into the darkness. Its sensors, shielded now from the stellar wind, adjusted once again, and now, finally, the object of the probe's fascination, the reason for its dispatch, came fully into view.

The probe surveyed the loose, spherical framework

ahead of it, and unleashed its full array upon the object, looking deep into it.

The image being projected into Susan Skarsgaard's screens began to crystallize.

"Not completely hollow," she said.

"No, apparently not," said one of her analysts.

They had struggled with the fact that all sensor data that had been returned from distance had seemed to show a vacuum within the structure, and indeed, as it had no walls, there certainly wasn't any air to speak of in the object. But there was substance of some kind, or at least there were... things.

A tech in the room, that Susan could not see, was assigning object titles and starting sub-analyses and classification on each. Susan's attention wanted to go there, to look at the details, but not yet. Not until they were past.

"Approaching perigee, Commander. Shall I redirect?" said the probe's remote pilot at Susan's side.

"No, not yet, Lieutenant," said Susan. "Let's complete this pass, then adjust outward on next orbit."

And so they did, the probe speeding by the massive alien object — for it was alien, there was no doubt about that.

"OK," said Susan, "let's incrementally adjust. I want to halve the flyby distance for the second pass."

"Confirmed," said the pilot, working the numbers and parsing them through his own networked subsystems for multi-phase confirmation. The part of Susan's system that was linked to the probe registered the request when it came through.

It was not a question whether she would approve it, just a fail-safe, one of thousands, and it came with a four-second deadline until the numbers would have to change. She cleared the command sequence in less than one. Trust, built on training together for thousands of hours. Three seconds later, the order went out like stern words from a teacher, adjusting the probe's attitude.

At last, Susan's attention came away and she blinked

around at the sterile cockpit of her own ship, the *Abeona*, itself approaching the Moon at a lazy 11.06 km/s, or a little over twenty-four thousand miles per hour. They might have wanted to go slower, to take more time to analyze the object, but much slower than that and the planet Earth, being the gravitationally possessive mother it was, would simply not have let them leave.

"Right, Marcus, what do we have?"

Marcus Daily, head of the analysis team, came to life as if a switch had been flicked. "Well, Commander, we have fully three hundred and twenty-six distinct objects within the main superstructure — each, apparently, bound to the framework, though we can see no interconnectivity other than the framework itself."

"Make up, purpose, materials?" said Susan.

"I'm afraid all I can be certain of at this time is that they are metallic... mostly."

Susan frowned at this vagueness from her scientific lead, and the man shrugged.

"They are heavy, that much we know. Dense... very dense, that is a consistent theme, but the materials themselves, well... there are... irregularities. Not the irregularities we saw from distance. Our sensors are returning, and, as hoped, once within the sphere's magnetic envelope, we have been able to garner vastly more data.

"So yes, good data, but..." Marcus glanced around, looking rather meek, then piped up, "What we can confirm is that several layers of graphene are present around the superstructure itself. Maybe even a carbyne form as well. Bar that... let's just say the data, while more complete, remains... non-distinct."

About to speak, to offer some form of leadership in the light of this rather underwhelming first pass, Commander Susan Skarsgaard suddenly felt very sick, then she felt very light, then she felt a hand clamoring at her skin, voices shouting, hers among them. Then Commander Susan Skarsgaard felt nothing at all.

The "dark side of the Moon" was always a misnomer, thought Susan, as she looked at the big moon. Sometimes the so-called "dark side of the Moon" is in glorious sunshine, sometimes not. The only thing that makes the dark side of the Moon "dark" is that we can't see it. Well, not from Earth, anyway.

But I can see it, thought Susan.

It's right over there, thought Susan, as she perceived that part of the Moon that would, that must still be invisible to the greater orb to her right.

It's so very pretty, thought Susan.

And so very close. We must be in orbit.

Susan looked back, expecting to see her crew, but when she turned she saw only the night-black of space, dotted with little sparkling promises, light years away. She spun. Where was she?

She quickly found the Earth, bright and so very detailed, countless facets marking its cloud-dotted dayside, and its night side riddled with tiny orange wisps, each a city, a network of highways, a moving flow of thousands of people, millions of people.

She turned to the Sun, and for a moment she was just another satellite basking in its heat, facing it with the planet and the Moon as equals, all three of them dwarfed by the star's magnificence.

But she wasn't a planet and she wasn't a moon. She was a commander of something. A commander without a ship. And something else was wrong, too, thought Susan. She wasn't only missing the *Abeona* and her crew, she realized, as she looked around more frantically now. She was missing her self.

She balked at the thought, and something in the sensation, the sense of loss, echoed within whatever space she was really in, touching something deeper.

Suddenly, she was facing the sphere, the ship, hiding

within the darkness of the lunar night, and then she was surging toward it.

A roar of memory came at her like the burst from a shot of tequila, only it kept coming, like the sensation was breaking through, the stringency rushing up her nose, in her ears, rushing in around her eyes.

Susan... no, not Susan... the Sphere spiraled into orbit around the anomalous star, the one whose behavior was so strange. Flares looped out of the surface in a rhythmical pattern. Sun spots uniformly stretched across the surface. The Sphere-ship reached out with its sensors, puzzled by the artificial nature. Could the star be engineered somehow? Could this be... information?

As the curious explorer looked in wonder upon the star, something swirled on the surface beneath the Sphere. Was it responding to them?

The Star bellowed, washing out every sensor on the Sphere's surface. The Sphere felt its mind being invaded, memories drawn, unbidden, to the surface as the Star brutally dug through its past. Intrusively and unstoppably, the Star explored the Sphere's history. Images flashed in front of Susan's eyes. A city of ice cathedrals under a dying sun. A sub-mantle herd swimming in a planet's core. A planet of herbivores that have commandeered evolution, removing all contest from nature. [This paragraph will change once we get the stories together, to include links and teasers from completed stories.]

With a last burst of effort, the Sphere powered up its engines, desperate to escape from this brutal rape of its mind. It didn't have the chance to even set a course, in its fear.

Susan saw the Sphere slam back into real-space, tumbling out of control, half-lobotomized but clutching on to a kernel of information. She felt her mind filling with information, the secrets of the mighty displacement drive. The shielding systems to protect it, the places it had visited and the wonders it had seen.

And a stark warning.

Stay away from the Star.

**

Susan Skarsgaard awoke to reality with a start, thrown from the machine once her mind had reached its capacity. She vomited, the mass forming a vile set of orbiting globules in zero-gee, quickly starting to coalesce into little planets and moons in front of Susan's face.

She inhaled sharply at the sight, still reeling, and a stream of her own discharge was drawn in with the air, causing her to retch once more, with even more gusto this time.

"Jesus... uck... oh god," Susan spluttered as she brought her hands up and covered her mouth, trying to clear away the cloud of disgustingness in front of her.

"Lieutenant? What is our status?"

Nothing.

Susan felt under her seat for a sick bag, something she should have done by instinct when she felt nauseated. But her instincts had been stripped away, along with everything else.

Susan scooped up as much of her vomit as she could with the bag, getting the bigger masses, and then looked around. Everyone was still there, eyes closed and apparently catatonic. They're asleep, Susan thought, but a little voice inside her head told her that was wrong as well.

After glancing at the screen to her left to confirm that the ship was still intact and progressing well, Susan looked to Marcus, hoping the head of her analysis team might have some answers, and as if in response, Marcus's eyes flew open.

She knew what was about to happen before Marcus did. She could see it in his face. She was almost quick enough. She even managed to catch the bulk of it in a bag as it flew from him, but still got splattered far more liberally than she would have hoped.

Her stomach twitched again, threatening further incident, but she managed to quell it. She was getting control again, at least over her stomach.

"Marcus!" Susan said. "Marcus, calm down. It's okay. You're back on the ship."

Marcus nodded his head — not out of agreement, but surrender.

"Marcus," Susan said after a moment, wanting to let the tech recover, but needing to know. "Were you…" She didn't know how to phrase it. "Did you… did you feel it?"

"Yes, Commander," said Marcus, tears coming to his eyes.

She did not need to ask more, not just yet. She knew where he was right now. He was deep in the pain of the loss. It had been the most powerful emotion Susan had ever felt.

But there had been so much more besides. So much she didn't understand yet. Marcus might have gotten more. But that would need to wait until he, and she, had gathered themselves a little.

She was about to say something, to try to soothe some measure of the remembered pain they were both still experiencing, when another of her crew screamed suddenly. Susan was at the woman's side the next moment, trying to console her, and so they all began to come back, each finding the terrible memory hidden within the machine in their own time, each reacting in their own way.

Though, it seemed, pretty much all losing their lunch in the process.

***

It was nearly an hour before she had a semblance of order restored, between her crew, and the ship's unstoppable onward motion, and Mission Control having a baby on the other end of a jury-rigged secondary comms laser.

She had noticed when Marcus had started typing,

398

furiously inputting into the system. She hadn't stopped him. She hadn't even interrupted him. A quick page through her command system had confirmed that he was only working in a log file, so she had left him to his work.

"Marcus?" Susan ventured, eventually, when he started to slow.

Marcus blinked hard, shook his head, looked up at her and smiled. Now that Susan was able to focus on just talking with the scientist one-on-one, she was disconcerted by the look of calm on his face.

He looked... well, he looked high. Of course, Susan wasn't exactly sure what the "appropriate" expression would be, given what they had just been through.

"Marcus, are you all right?" Susan said, quietly.

"Marcus is fine," said Marcus, then grinned at the slip-up, the wee faux pas of having forgotten his own existential place in the universe for a moment, and corrected, "*I* am fine."

"Marcus," said Susan, her voice guarded, "how is the log file going?"

Marcus looked pensive for a moment, as if looking for the words, then nodded his head.

"Right. Yes," he said, "it's all been rather... I've been trying to get it all down."

He gestured at the screen. "It's like trying to write down what your own voice is saying. No... no. That's not it."

"I know what you mean. It's... disconcerting."

They smiled at the understatement. Like a wounded soldier saying he is having an off day.

Susan looked at the notes on Marcus's screen and knew what he was trying to do. He was trying to capture it all. In case this was their only shot. In case they never got the chance to speak with it again.

"So...," said Susan, rather meekly.

"So," said Marcus.

"What did you see? What did it tell you?"

Marcus took a deep breath and set his shoulders, looking

back at his screen before saying, "Everything... and nothing."

Susan frowned, and Marcus shrugged.

"It can't *tell* us anything. But it can show us. And it did," said Marcus.

"But what..." Susan began, but Marcus cut her off.

"There is so much I don't understand. But I will, or others will, when we bring them here. For now, though, I have enough to keep JPL, DARPA, the DRDO, Qinetiq and everyone else I can think of busy for a decade," said Marcus.

"How much can it show us?"

Marcus gulped, then shook his head, gathering his strength. "Maybe just a glimpse, or maybe...." He went silent for a moment.

"It can't show us everything," Marcus went on, "it only has so much left. But it is still a thing of marvels. It thinks it can give us what we need to get out there, if we let it. And it isn't just offering us a list of where not to go, a Pandora's box. It knows where we *can* go, too. It cannot tell us what. Only where. But it has found others out there. Other intelligent life.

"The list," said Marcus, his eyes connecting with Susan's as they both reveled in the thought of it.

"The list," Marcus said again, "...of other worlds."

But Susan was already thinking of it, curiosity suddenly blossoming inside her explorer's heart, and as it did so, the entity was feeding her curiosity, filling her mind with what images it still had as she fell backward into it, her eyes going blank, then opening onto glory.

The fear was not gone; the star remained, a grim example of what threats might be out there, but it was only one among billions of stars now, flying by her, as she was freed from the limitations of her evolution, communing fully with the machine once more. And just as the ship's dying mind had been able to fill her with dread, it now began to fill her with joy, as it started to show her the way.

Also from Woodbridge Press

"A pleasantly eerie collection by some young authors whose careers we'll definitely have to follow." – Joe Mynhardt, Crystal Lake Publishing

"It's just good, shivery comfort reading for fans of classic horror." Josh Black - Cemetery Dance Online

It's been over a hundred and fifty years since a plague ravaged the area around Lake Manor. With few left to bury them, the corpses were unceremoniously dumped into the lake by their surviving loved ones.

Years later, Lake Manor Hotel is alive with the shadows of the dead. Within the hotel's 13 rooms, there are 13 tales to tell. Guests will face evil demons, ghosts, creatures from the lake, and the worst monsters of all: the ones within themselves.

13 will check in, but how many will check out?

16304978R00238

Printed in Poland
by Amazon Fulfillment
Poland Sp. z o.o., Wrocław